Margaret Atwood is the author of more than thirty books of fiction, poetry, and critical essays. Her novels include *The Handmaid's Tale*, *Cat's Eye* – both shortlisted for the Booker Prize – *The Robber Bride*, and her most recent, *Alias Grace*, which was also shortlisted for the Booker Prize and won the Giller Prize in Canada and the Premio Mondello in Italy. Her work is acclaimed internationally and has been translated into thirty-three languages. She is the recipient of many literary awards and honours from various countries, including Britain, Italy, France, Sweden and Norway, as well as Canada and the United States. Margaret Atwood lives in Toronto, with writer Graeme Gibson. *The Blind Assassin* is her tenth novel and winner of the Booker Prize.

The Blind Assassin

MARGARET ATWOOD

A *Virago* Book

Published by Virago Press 2001
Reprinted 2001

First published in Great Britain by
Bloomsbury Publishing Plc

Copyright © O.W. Toad Ltd 2000

The moral right of the author has been asserted

A CIP catalogue record for this book
is available from the British Library

ISBN 1 86049 879 5

Typeset in Bembo by M Rules
Printed and bound in Great Britain by
Clays Ltd, St Ives plc

Virago Press
A Division of
Little, Brown and Company (UK)
Brettenham House
Lancaster Place
London WC2E 7EN

Imagine the monarch Agha Mohammed Khan, who orders the entire population of the city of Kerman murdered or blinded – no exceptions. His praetorians set energetically to work. They line up the inhabitants, slice off the heads of the adults, gouge out the eyes of the children. . . . Later, processions of blinded children leave the city. Some, wandering around in the countryside, lose their way in the desert and die of thirst. Other groups reach inhabited settlements . . . singing songs about the extermination of the citizens of Kerman. . . .

— RYSZARD KAPUŚCIŃSKI

I swam, the sea was boundless, I saw no shore.
Tanit was merciless, my prayers were answered.
O you who drown in love, remember me.

— INSCRIPTION ON A CARTHAGINIAN FUNERARY URN

The word is a flame burning in a dark glass.

— SHEILA WATSON

CONTENTS

I

The bridge

Ten days after the war ended, my sister Laura drove a car off a bridge. The bridge was being repaired: she went right through the Danger sign. The car fell a hundred feet into the ravine, smashing through the treetops feathery with new leaves, then burst into flames and rolled down into the shallow creek at the bottom. Chunks of the bridge fell on top of it. Nothing much was left of her but charred smithereens.

I was informed of the accident by a policeman: the car was mine, and they'd traced the licence. His tone was respectful: no doubt he recognized Richard's name. He said the tires may have caught on a streetcar track or the brakes may have failed, but he also felt bound to inform me that two witnesses – a retired lawyer and a bank teller, dependable people – had claimed to have seen the whole thing. They'd said Laura had turned the car sharply and deliberately, and had plunged off the bridge with no more fuss than stepping off a curb. They'd noticed her hands on the wheel because of the white gloves she'd been wearing.

It wasn't the brakes, I thought. She had her reasons. Not that they were ever the same as anybody else's reasons. She was completely ruthless in that way.

"I suppose you want someone to identify her," I said. "I'll come down as soon as I can." I could hear the calmness of my own voice, as if from a distance. In reality I could barely get the words out; my mouth was numb, my entire face was rigid with pain. I felt as if I'd been to the dentist. I was furious with Laura for what she'd done, but also with the policeman for implying that she'd done it. A hot wind was blowing around my head, the strands of my hair lifting and swirling in it, like ink spilled in water.

"I'm afraid there will be an inquest, Mrs. Griffen," he said.

"Naturally," I said. "But it was an accident. My sister was never a good driver."

I could picture the smooth oval of Laura's face, her neatly pinned chignon, the dress she would have been wearing: a shirtwaist with a small rounded collar, in a sober colour – navy blue or steel grey or hospital-corridor green. Penitential colours – less like something she'd chosen to put on than like something she'd been locked up in. Her solemn half-smile; the amazed lift of her eyebrows, as if she were admiring the view.

The white gloves: a Pontius Pilate gesture. She was washing her hands of me. Of all of us.

What had she been thinking of as the car sailed off the bridge, then hung suspended in the afternoon sunlight, glinting like a dragonfly for that one instant of held breath before the plummet? Of Alex, of Richard, of bad faith, of our father and his wreckage; of God, perhaps, and her fatal, triangular bargain. Or of the stack of cheap school exercise books that she must have hidden that very morning, in the bureau drawer where I kept my stockings, knowing I would be the one to find them.

When the policeman had gone I went upstairs to change. To visit the morgue I would need gloves, and a hat with a veil. Something to cover the eyes. There might be reporters. I would have to call a taxi. Also I ought to warn Richard, at his office: he would wish to have a statement of grief prepared. I went into my dressing room: I would need black, and a hand-kerchief.

I opened the drawer, I saw the notebooks. I undid the criss-cross of kitchen string that tied them together. I noticed that my teeth were chattering, and that I was cold all over. I must be in shock, I decided.

What I remembered then was Reenie, from when we were little. It was Reenie who'd done the bandaging, of scrapes and cuts and minor injuries: Mother might be resting, or doing good deeds elsewhere, but Reenie was always there. She'd scoop us up and sit us on the white enamel kitchen table, alongside the pie dough she was rolling out or the chicken she was cutting up or the fish she was gutting, and give us a lump of brown sugar to get us to close our mouths. *Tell me where it hurts*, she'd say. *Stop howling. Just calm down and show me where.*

But some people can't tell where it hurts. They can't calm down. They can't ever stop howling.

The Toronto Star, May 26, 1945

QUESTIONS RAISED IN CITY DEATH
SPECIAL TO THE STAR

A coroner's inquest has returned a verdict of accidental death in last week's St. Clair Ave. fatality. Miss Laura Chase, 25, was travelling west on the afternoon of May 18 when her car swerved through the barriers protecting a repair site on the bridge and crashed into the ravine below, catching fire. Miss Chase was killed instantly. Her sister, Mrs. Richard E. Griffen, wife of the prominent manufacturer, gave evidence that Miss Chase suffered from severe headaches affecting her vision. In reply to questioning, she denied any possibility of intoxication as Miss Chase did not drink.

It was the police view that a tire caught in an exposed streetcar track was a contributing factor. Questions were raised as to the adequacy of safety precautions taken by the City, but after expert testimony by City engineer Gordon Perkins these were dismissed.

The accident has occasioned renewed protests over the state of the streetcar tracks on this stretch of roadway. Mr. Herb T. Jolliffe, representing local ratepayers, told *Star* reporters that this was not the first mishap caused by neglected tracks. City Council should take note.

The Blind Assassin. *By Laura Chase.*
Reingold, Jaynes & Moreau, New York, 1947

Prologue: Perennials for the Rock Garden

She has a single photograph of him. She tucked it into a brown envelope on which she'd written *clippings*, and hid the envelope between the pages of *Perennials for the Rock Garden*, where no one else would ever look.

She's preserved this photo carefully, because it's almost all she has left of him. It's black and white, taken by one of those boxy, cumbersome flash cameras from before the war, with their accordion-pleat nozzles and their well-made leather cases that looked like muzzles, with straps and intricate buckles. The photo is of the two of them together, her and this man, on a picnic. *Picnic* is written on the back, in pencil – not his name or hers, just *picnic*. She knows the names, she doesn't need to write them down.

They're sitting under a tree; it might have been an apple tree; she didn't notice the tree much at the time. She's wearing a white blouse with the sleeves rolled to the elbow and a wide skirt tucked around her knees. There must have been a breeze, because of the way the shirt is blowing up against her; or perhaps it wasn't blowing, perhaps it was clinging; perhaps it was hot. It was hot. Holding her hand over the picture, she can still feel the heat coming up from it, like the heat from a sun-warmed stone at midnight.

The man is wearing a light-coloured hat, angled down on his head and partially shading his face. His face appears to be more darkly tanned than hers. She's turned half towards him, and smiling, in a way she can't remember smiling at anyone since. She seems very young in the picture, too young, though she hadn't considered herself too young at the time. He's smiling too – the whiteness of his teeth shows up like a scratched match flaring – but he's holding up his hand, as if to fend her off in play, or else to protect himself from the camera, from the person who must be there, taking the picture; or else to protect himself from those in the future who might be looking at him, who might be looking in at him through this square, lighted window of glazed paper. As if to protect himself from her. As if to protect her. In his outstretched, protecting hand there's the stub end of a cigarette.

She retrieves the brown envelope when she's alone, and slides the photo out from among the newspaper clippings. She lays it flat on the table and stares down into it, as if she's peering into a well or pool – searching beyond her own reflection for something else, something she must have dropped or lost, out of reach but still visible, shimmering like a jewel on sand. She examines every detail. His fingers bleached by the flash or the sun's glare; the folds of their clothing; the leaves of the tree, and the small round shapes hanging there – were they apples, after all? The coarse grass in the foreground. The grass was yellow then because the weather had been dry.

Over to one side – you wouldn't see it at first – there's a hand, cut by the margin, scissored off at the wrist, resting on the grass as if discarded. Left to its own devices.

The trace of blown cloud in the brilliant sky, like ice cream smudged on chrome. His smoke-stained fingers. The distant glint of water. All drowned now.

Drowned, but shining.

II

What will it be, then? he says. Dinner jackets and romance, or shipwrecks on a barren coast? You can have your pick: jungles, tropical islands, mountains. Or another dimension of space – that's what I'm best at.

Another dimension of space? Oh really!

Don't scoff, it's a useful address. Anything you like can happen there. Spaceships and skin-tight uniforms, ray guns, Martians with the bodies of giant squids, that sort of thing.

You choose, she says. You're the professional. How about a desert? I've always wanted to visit one. With an oasis, of course. Some date palms might be nice. She's tearing the crust off her sandwich. She doesn't like the crusts.

Not much scope, with deserts. Not many features, unless you add some tombs. Then you could have a pack of nude women who've been dead for three thousand years, with lithe, curvaceous figures, ruby-red lips, azure hair in a foam of tumbled curls, and eyes like snake-filled pits. But I don't think I could fob those off on you. Lurid isn't your style.

You never know. I might like them.

I doubt it. They're for the huddled masses. Popular on the covers though – they'll writhe all over a fellow, they have to be beaten off with rifle butts.

Could I have another dimension of space, and also the tombs and the dead women, please?

That's a tall order, but I'll see what I can do. I could throw in some sacrificial virgins as well, with metal breastplates and silver ankle chains and diaphanous vestments. And a pack of ravening wolves, extra.

I can see you'll stop at nothing.

You want the dinner jackets instead? Cruise ships, white linen, wrist-kissing and hypocritical slop?

No. All right. Do what you think is best.

Cigarette?

She shakes her head for no. He lights his own, striking the match on his thumbnail.

You'll set fire to yourself, she says.

I never have yet.

She looks at his rolled-up shirt sleeve, white or a pale blue, then his wrist, the browner skin of his hand. He throws out radiance, it must be reflected sun. Why isn't everyone staring? Still, he's too noticeable to be out here – out in the open. There are other people around, sitting on the grass or lying on it, propped on one elbow – other picnickers, in their pale summer clothing. It's all very proper. Nevertheless she feels that the two of them are alone; as if the apple tree they're sitting under is not a tree but a tent; as if there's a line drawn around them with chalk. Inside this line, they're invisible.

Space it is, then, he says. With tombs and virgins and wolves – but on the instalment plan. Agreed?

The instalment plan?

You know, like furniture.

She laughs.

No, I'm serious. You can't skimp, it might take days. We'll have to meet again.

She hesitates. All right, she says. If I can. If I can arrange it.

Good, he says. Now I have to think. He keeps his voice casual. Too much urgency might put her off.

On the Planet of – let's see. Not Saturn, it's too close. On the Planet Zycron, located in another dimension of space, there's a rubble-strewn plain. To the north is the ocean, which is violet in colour. To the west is a range of mountains, said to be roamed after sunset by the voracious undead female inhabitants of the crumbling tombs located there. You see, I've put the tombs in right off the bat.

That's very conscientious of you, she says.

I stick to my bargains. To the south is a burning waste of sand, and to the east are several steep valleys that might once have been rivers.

I suppose there are canals, like Mars?

Oh, canals, and all sorts of things. Abundant traces of an ancient and once highly developed civilization, though this region is now only sparsely inhabited by roaming bands of primitive nomads. In the middle of the plain is a large mound of stones. The land around is arid, with a few scrubby bushes. Not exactly a desert, but close enough. Is there a cheese sandwich left?

She rummages in the paper bag. No, she says, but there's a hard-boiled egg. She's never been this happy before. Everything is fresh again, still to be enacted.

Just what the doctor ordered, he says. A bottle of lemonade, a hard-boiled egg, and Thou. He rolls the egg between his palms, cracking the shell, then peeling it away. She watches his mouth, the jaw, the teeth.

Beside me singing in the public park, she says. Here's the salt for it.

Thanks. You remembered everything.

This arid plain isn't claimed by anyone, he continues. Or rather it's claimed by five different tribes, none strong enough to annihilate the others. All of them wander past this stone heap from time to time, herding their *thulks* – blue sheep-like creatures with vicious tempers – or transporting merchandise of little value on their pack animals, a sort of three-eyed camel.

The pile of stones is called, in their various languages, The Haunt of Flying Snakes, The Heap of Rubble, The Abode of Howling Mothers, The Door of Oblivion, and The Pit of Gnawed Bones. Each tribe tells a similar story about it. Underneath the rocks, they say, a king is buried – a king without a name. Not only the king, but the remains of the magnificent city this king once ruled. The city was destroyed in a battle, and the king was captured and hanged from a date palm as a sign of triumph. At moonrise he was cut down and buried, and the stones were piled up to mark the spot. As for the other inhabitants of the city, they were all killed. Butchered – men, women, children, babies, even the animals. Put to the sword, hacked to pieces. No living thing was spared.

That's horrible.

Stick a shovel into the ground almost anywhere and some horrible thing or other will come to light. Good for the trade, we thrive on bones; without them there'd be no stories. Any more lemonade?

No, she says. We've drunk it all up. Go on.

The real name of the city was erased from memory by the conquerors, and this is why – say the taletellers – the place is now known only by the name of its own destruction. The pile of stones thus marks both an act of deliberate remembrance, and an act of deliberate forgetting. They're fond of paradox in that region. Each of the five tribes claims to have been the victorious attacker. Each recalls the slaughter with relish. Each believes it was ordained by their own god as righteous vengeance, because of the unholy practices carried on in the city. Evil must be cleansed with blood, they say. On that day the blood ran like water, so afterwards it must have been very clean.

Every herdsman or merchant who passes adds a stone to the heap. It's an old custom – you do it in remembrance of the dead, your own dead – but since no one knows who the dead under the pile of stones really were, they all leave their stones on the off chance. They'll get around it by telling you that what happened there must have been the will of their god, and thus by leaving a stone they are honouring this will.

There's also a story that claims the city wasn't really destroyed at all. Instead, through a charm known only to the King, the city and its inhabitants were whisked away and replaced by phantoms of themselves, and it was only these phantoms that were burnt and slaughtered. The real city was shrunk very small and placed in a cave beneath the great heap of stones. Everything that was once there is there still, including the palaces and the gardens filled with trees and flowers; including the people, no bigger than ants, but going about their lives as before – wearing their tiny clothes, giving their tiny banquets, telling their tiny stories, singing their tiny songs.

The King knows what's happened and it gives him nightmares, but the rest of them don't know. They don't know they've become so small. They don't know they're supposed to be dead. They don't even know they've been saved. To them the ceiling of rock looks like a sky: light comes in through a pinhole between the stones, and they think it's the sun.

The leaves of the apple tree rustle. She looks up at the sky, then at her watch. I'm cold, she says. I'm also late. Could you dispose of the evidence? She gathers eggshells, twists up wax paper.

No hurry, surely? It's not cold here.

There's a breeze coming through from the water, she says. The wind must have changed. She leans forward, moving to stand up.

Don't go yet, he says, too quickly.

I have to. They'll be looking for me. If I'm overdue, they'll want to know where I've been.

She smoothes her skirt down, wraps her arms around herself, turns away, the small green apples watching her like eyes.

The Globe and Mail, June 4, 1947

GRIFFEN FOUND IN SAILBOAT
SPECIAL TO THE GLOBE AND MAIL

After an unexplained absence of several days, the body of industrialist Richard E. Griffen, forty-seven, said to have been favoured for the Progressive Conservative candidacy in the Toronto riding of St. David's, was discovered near his summer residence of "Avilion" in Port Ticonderoga, where he was vacationing. Mr. Griffen was found in his sailboat, the *Water Nixie*, which was tied up at his private jetty on the Jogues River. He had apparently suffered a cerebral hemorrhage. Police report that no foul play is suspected.

Mr. Griffen had a distinguished career as the head of a commercial empire that embraced many areas including textiles, garments and light manufacturing, and was commended for his efforts in supplying Allied troops with uniform parts and weapons components during the war. He was a frequent guest at the influential gatherings held at the Pugwash home of industrialist Cyrus Eaton and a leading figure of both the Empire Club and the Granite Club. He was a keen golfer and a well-known figure at the Royal Canadian Yacht Club. The Prime Minister, reached by telephone at his private estate of "Kingsmere," commented, "Mr. Griffen was one of this country's most able men. His loss will be deeply felt."

Mr. Griffen was the brother-in-law of the late Laura Chase, who made her posthumous début as a novelist this spring, and is survived by his sister Mrs. Winifred

(Griffen) Prior, the noted socialite, and by his wife, Mrs. Iris (Chase) Griffen, as well as by his ten-year-old daughter Aimee. The funeral will be held in Toronto at the Church of St. Simon the Apostle on Wednesday.

Why were there people, on Zycron? I mean human beings like us. If it's another dimension of space, shouldn't the inhabitants have been talking lizards or something?

Only in the pulps, he says. That's all made up. In reality it was like this: Earth was colonized by the Zycronites, who developed the ability to travel from one space dimension to another at a period several millennia after the epoch of which we speak. They arrived here eight thousand years ago. They brought a lot of plant seeds with them, which is why we have apples and oranges, not to mention bananas – one look at a banana and you can tell it came from outer space. They also brought animals – horses and dogs and goats and so on. They were the builders of Atlantis. Then they blew themselves up through being too clever. We're descended from the stragglers.

Oh, she says. So that explains it. How very convenient for you.

It'll do in a pinch. As for the other peculiarities of Zycron, it has seven seas, five moons, and three suns, of varying strengths and colours.

What colours? Chocolate, vanilla, and strawberry?

You aren't taking me seriously.

I'm sorry. She tilts her head towards him. Now I'm listening. See?

He says: Before its destruction, the city – let's call it by its former name, Sakiel-Norn, roughly translatable as The Pearl of Destiny – was said to have been the wonder of the world. Even those who claim their ancestors obliterated it take great pleasure in describing its beauty. Natural springs had been made to flow through the carved fountains in the tiled court-yards and gardens of its numerous palaces. Flowers abounded, and the air was filled with singing birds. There were lush plains nearby where herds of fat *gnarr* grazed, and orchards and groves and forests of tall trees that had not yet been cut down by merchants or burned by spiteful enemies. The dry ravines were rivers then; canals leading from them irrigated the fields around the city, and the soil was so rich the heads of grain were said to have measured three inches across.

The aristocrats of Sakiel-Norn were called the Snilfards. They were skilled metalworkers and inventors of ingenious mechanical devices, the secrets of which they carefully guarded. By this period they had invented the clock, the cross-bow, and the hand pump, though they had not yet got so far as the internal combustion engine and still used animals for trans-port.

The male Snilfards wore masks of woven platinum, which moved as the skin of their faces moved, but which served to hide their true emotions. The women veiled their faces in a silk-like cloth made from the cocoon of the *chaz* moth. It was punishable by death to cover your face if you were not a Snilfard, since imperviousness and subterfuge were reserved for the nobility. The Snilfards dressed luxuriously and were connoisseurs of music, and played on various instruments to display their taste and skill. They indulged in court intrigues, held magnificent feasts, and fell elaborately in love with one another's wives. Duels were fought over these affairs, though it was more acceptable in a husband to pretend not to know.

The smallholders, serfs, and slaves were called the Ygnirods. They wore shabby grey tunics with one shoulder bare, and one breast as well for the women, who were – needless to say – fair game for the Snilfard men. The Ygnirods were resentful of their lot in life, but concealed this with a pretense of stupidity. Once in a while they would stage a revolt, which would then be ruthlessly suppressed. The lowest among them were slaves, who could be bought and traded and also killed at will. They were prohibited by law from reading, but had secret codes that they scratched in the dirt with stones. The Snilfards harnessed them to ploughs.

If a Snilfard should become bankrupt, he might be demoted to an Ygnirod. Or he might avoid such a fate by selling his wife or children in order to redeem his debt. It was much rarer for an Ygnirod to achieve the status of Snilfard, since the way up is usually more arduous than the way down: even if he were able to amass the necessary cash and acquire a Snilfard bride for himself or his son, a certain amount of bribery was involved, and it might be some time before he was accepted by Snilfard society.

I suppose this is your Bolshevism coming out, she says. I knew you'd get around to that, sooner or later.

On the contrary. The culture I describe is based on ancient Mesopotamia. It's in the Code of Hammurabi, the laws of the Hittites and so forth. Or some of it is. The part about the veils is, anyway, and selling your wife. I could give you chapter and verse.

Don't give me chapter and verse today, please, she says. I don't have the strength for it, I'm too limp. I'm wilting.

It's August, far too hot. Humidity drifts over them in an invisible mist. Four in the afternoon, the light like melted butter. They're sitting on a park bench, not too close together; a maple tree with exhausted leaves above them, cracked dirt under their feet, sere grass around. A bread crust pecked by sparrows, crumpled papers. Not the best area. A drinking fountain dribbling; three grubby children, a girl in a sunsuit and two boys in shorts, are conspiring beside it.

Her dress is primrose yellow; her arms bare below the elbow, fine pale hairs on them. She's taken off her cotton gloves, wadded them into a ball, her hands nervous. He doesn't mind her nervousness: he likes to think he's already costing her something. She's wearing a straw hat, round like a schoolgirl's; her hair pinned back; a damp strand escaping. People used to cut off strands of hair, save them, wear them in lockets; or if men, next to the heart. He's never understood why, before.

Where are you supposed to be? he says.

Shopping. Look at my shopping bag. I bought some stockings; they're very good – the best silk. They're like wearing nothing. She smiles a little. I've only got fifteen minutes.

She's dropped a glove, it's by her foot. He's keeping an eye on it. If she walks away forgetting it, he'll claim it. Inhale her, in her absence.

When can I see you? he says. The hot breeze stirs the leaves, light falls through, there's pollen all around her, a golden cloud. Dust, really.

You're seeing me now, she says.

Don't be like that, he says. Tell me when. The skin in the V of her dress glistens, a film of sweat.

I don't know yet, she says. She looks over her shoulder, scans the park.

There's nobody around, he says. Nobody you know.

You never know when there will be, she says. You never know who you know.

You should get a dog, he says.

She laughs. A dog? Why?

Then you'd have an excuse. You could take it for walks. Me and the dog.

The dog would be jealous of you, she says. And you'd think I liked the dog better.

But you wouldn't like the dog better, he says. Would you?

She opens her eyes wider. Why wouldn't I?

He says, Dogs can't talk.

The Toronto Star, August 25, 1975

NOVELIST'S NIECE VICTIM OF FALL
SPECIAL TO THE STAR

Aimee Griffen, thirty-eight, daughter of the late Richard E. Griffen, the eminent industrialist, and niece of noted authoress Laura Chase, was found dead in her Church St. basement apartment on Wednesday, having suffered a broken neck as a result of a fall. She had apparently been dead for at least a day. Neighbours Jos and Beatrice Kelley were alerted by Miss Griffen's four-year-old daughter Sabrina, who often came to them for food when her mother could not be located.

Miss Griffen is rumoured to have undergone a lengthy struggle with drug and alcohol addiction, having been hospitalized on several occasions. Her daughter has been placed in the care of Mrs. Winifred Prior, her great-aunt, pending an investigation. Neither Mrs. Prior nor Aimee Griffen's mother, Mrs. Iris Griffen of Port Ticonderoga, was available for comment.

This unfortunate event is yet another example of the laxity of our present social services, and the need for improved legislation to increase protection for children at risk.

The Blind Assassin: The carpets

The line buzzes and crackles. There's thunder, or is it someone listening in? But it's a public phone, they can't trace him.

Where are you? she says. You shouldn't phone here.

He can't hear her breathing, her breath. He wants her to put the receiver against her throat, but he won't ask for that, not yet. I'm around the block, he says. A couple of blocks. I can be in the park, the small one, the one with the sundial.

Oh, I don't think . . .

Just slip out. Say you need some air. He waits.

I'll try.

At the entrance to the park there are two stone gateposts, four-sided, bevelled at the top, Egyptian-looking. No triumphal inscriptions however, no bas-reliefs of chained enemies kneeling. Only No Loitering and Keep Dogs on Leash.

Come in here, he says. Away from the street light.

I can't stay long.

I know. Come in behind here. He takes hold of her arm, guiding her; she's trembling like a wire in a high wind.

There, he says. Nobody can see us. No old ladies out walking their poodles.

No policemen with nightsticks, she says. She laughs briefly. The lamplight filters through the leaves; in it, the whites of her eyes gleam. I shouldn't be here, she says. It's too much of a risk.

There's a stone bench tucked up against some bushes. He puts his jacket around her shoulders. Old tweed, old tobacco, a singed odour. An undertone of salt. His skin's been there, next to the cloth, and now hers is.

There, you'll be warmer. Now we'll defy the law. We'll loiter.

What about Keep Dogs on Leash?

We'll defy that too. He doesn't put his arm around her. He knows she wants him to. She expects it; she feels the touch in advance, as birds feel shadow. He's got his cigarette going. He offers her one; this time she takes it. Brief match-flare inside their cupped hands. Red finger-ends.

She thinks, Any more flame and we'd see the bones. It's like X-rays. We're just a kind of haze, just coloured water. Water does what it likes. It always goes downhill. Her throat fills with smoke.

He says, Now I'll tell you about the children.

The children? What children?

The next instalment. About Zycron, about Sakiel-Norn.

Oh. Yes.

There are children in it.

We didn't say anything about children.

They're slave children. They're required. I can't get along without them.

I don't think I want any children in it, she says.

You can always tell me to stop. Nobody's forcing you. You're free to go, as the police say when you're lucky. He keeps his voice level. She doesn't move away.

He says: Sakiel-Norn is now a heap of stones, but once it was a flourishing centre of trade and exchange. It was at a crossroads where three overland routes came together – one from the east, one from the west, one from the south. To the north it was connected by means of a broad canal to the sea itself, where it possessed a well-fortified harbour. No trace of these diggings and defensive walls remains: after its destruction, the hewn stone blocks were carried off by enemies or strangers for use in their animal pens, their water troughs, and their crude forts, or buried by waves and wind under the drifting sand.

The canal and the harbour were built by slaves, which isn't surprising: slaves were how Sakiel-Norn had achieved its magnificence and power. But it was also renowned for its handi-crafts, especially its weaving. The secrets of the dyes used by its artisans were carefully guarded: its cloth shone like liquid honey, like crushed purple grapes, like a cup of bull's blood poured out in the sun. Its delicate veils were as light as spiderwebs, and its carpets were so soft and fine you would think you were walking on air, an air made to resemble flowers and flowing water.

That's very poetic, she says. I'm surprised.

Think of it as a department store, he says. These were luxury trade goods, when you come right down to it. It's less poetic then.

The carpets were woven by slaves who were invariably chil-dren, because only the fingers of children were small enough for such intricate work. But the incessant close labour demanded of these children caused them to go blind by the age of eight or nine, and their blindness was the measure by which the carpet-sellers valued and extolled their merchandise: *This carpet blinded ten children*, they would say. *This blinded fifteen, this twenty.* Since the price rose accordingly, they always exaggerated. It was the custom for the buyer to scoff at their claims. *Surely only seven, only twelve, only sixteen*, they would say, fingering the carpet. *It's coarse as a dishcloth. It's nothing but a beggar's blanket. It was made by a gnarr.*

Once they were blind, the children would be sold off to brothel-keepers, the girls and the boys alike. The services of children blinded in this way fetched high sums; their touch was so suave and deft, it was said, that under their fingers you could feel the flowers blossoming and the water flowing out of your own skin.

They were also skilled at picking locks. Those of them who escaped took up the profession of cutting throats in the dark, and were greatly in demand as hired assassins. Their sense of hearing was acute; they could walk without sound, and squeeze through the smallest of openings; they could smell the difference between a deep sleeper and one who was restlessly dreaming. They killed as softly as a moth brushing against your neck. They were considered to be without pity. They were much feared.

The stories the children whispered to one another – while they sat weaving their endless carpets, while they could still see – was about this possible future life. It was a saying among them that only the blind are free.

This is too sad, she whispers. Why are you telling me such a sad story?

They're deeper into the shadows now. His arms around her finally. Go easy, he thinks. No sudden moves. He concentrates on his breathing.

I tell you the stories I'm good at, he says. Also the ones you'll believe. You wouldn't believe sweet nothings, would you?

No. I wouldn't believe them.

Besides, it's not a sad story, completely – some of them got away.

But they became throat-cutters.

They didn't have much choice, did they? They couldn't become the carpet-merchants themselves, or the brothel-owners. They didn't have the capital. So they had to take the dirty work. Tough luck for them.

Don't, she says. It's not my fault.

Nor mine either. Let's say we're stuck with the sins of the fathers.

That's unnecessarily cruel, she says coldly.

When is cruelty necessary? he says. And how much of it? Read the newspapers, I didn't invent the world. Anyway, I'm on the side of the throat-cutters. If you had to cut throats or starve, which would you do? Or screw for a living, there's always that.

Now he's gone too far. He's let his anger show. She draws away from him. Here it comes, she says. I need to get back. The leaves around them stir fitfully. She holds out her hand, palm up: there are a few drops of rain. The thunder's nearer now. She slides his jacket off her shoulders. He hasn't kissed her; he won't, not tonight. She senses it as a reprieve.

Stand at your window, he says. Your bedroom window. Leave the light on. Just stand there.

He's startled her. Why? Why on earth?

I want you to. I want to make sure you're safe, he adds, though safety has nothing to do with it.

I'll try, she says. Only for a minute. Where will you be?

Under the tree. The chestnut. You won't see me, but I'll be there.

She thinks, He knows where the window is. He knows what kind of tree. He must have been prowling. Watching her. She shivers a little.

It's raining, she says. It's going to pour. You'll get wet.

It's not cold, he says. I'll be waiting.

The Globe and Mail, February 19, 1998

Prior, Winifred Griffen. At the age of 92, at her Rosedale home, after a protracted illness. In Mrs. Prior, noted philanthropist, the city of Toronto has lost one of its most loyal and long-standing benefactresses. Sister of deceased industrialist Richard Griffen and sister-in law of the eminent novelist Laura Chase, Mrs. Prior served on the board of the Toronto Symphony Orchestra during its formative years, and more recently on the Volunteer Committee of the Art Gallery of Ontario and the Canadian Cancer Society. She was also active in the Granite Club, the Heliconian Club, the Junior League, and the Dominion Drama Festival. She is survived by her great-niece, Sabrina Griffen, currently travelling in India.

The funeral will take place on Tuesday morning at the Church of St. Simon the Apostle, followed by interment at Mount Pleasant Cemetery. Donations to Princess Margaret Hospital in lieu of flowers.

How much time have we got? he says.

A lot, she says. Two or three hours. They're all out somewhere.

Doing what?

I don't know. Making money. Buying things. Good works. Whatever they do. She tucks a strand of hair behind her ear, sits up straighter. She feels on call, whistled for. A cheap feeling. Whose car is this? she says.

A friend's. I'm an important person, I have a friend with a car.

You're making fun of me, she says. He doesn't answer. She pulls at the fingers of a glove. What if anyone sees us?

They'll only see the car. This car is a wreck, it's a poor folks' car. Even if they look right at you they won't see you, because a woman like you isn't supposed to be caught dead in a car like this.

Sometimes you don't like me very much, she says.

I can't think about much else lately, he says. But liking is different. Liking takes time. I don't have the time to *like* you. I can't concentrate on it.

Not there, she says. Look at the sign.

Signs are for other people, he says. Here – down here.

The path is no more than a furrow. Discarded tissues, gum wrappers, used safes like fish bladders. Bottles and pebbles; dried mud, cracked and rutted. She has the wrong shoes for it, the wrong heels. He takes her arm, steadies her. She moves to pull away.

It's practically an open field. Someone will see.

Someone who? We're under the bridge.

The police. Don't. Not yet.

The police don't snoop around in broad daylight, he says. Only at night, with their flashlights, looking for godless perverts.

Tramps then, she says. Maniacs.

Here, he says. In under here. In the shade.

Is there poison ivy?

None at all. I promise. No tramps or maniacs either, except me.

How do you know? About the poison ivy. Have you been here before?

Don't worry so much, he says. Lie down.

Don't. You'll tear it. Wait a minute.

She hears her own voice. It isn't her voice, it's too breathless.

There's a lipstick heart on the cement, surrounding four initials. An L connects them: L for *Loves*. Only those concerned would know whose initials they are – that they've been here, that they've done this. Proclaiming love, withholding the particulars.

Outside the heart, four other letters, like the four points of the compass:

$$\begin{array}{cc} F & U \\ C & K \end{array}$$

The word torn apart, splayed open: the implacable topography of sex.

Smoke taste on his mouth, salt in her own; all around, the smell of crushed weeds and cat, of disregarded corners. Dampness and growth, dirt on the knees, grimy and lush; leggy dandelions stretching towards the light.

Below where they're lying, the ripple of a stream. Above, leafy branches, thin vines with purple flowers; the tall pillars of the bridge lifting up, the iron girders, the wheels going by overhead; the blue sky in splinters. Hard dirt under her back.

He smoothes her forehead, runs a finger along her cheek. You shouldn't worship me, he says. I don't have the only cock in the world. Some day you'll find that out.

It's not a question of that, she says. Anyway I don't worship you. Already he's pushing her away, into the future.

Well, whatever it is, you'll have more of it, once I'm out of your hair.

Meaning what, exactly? You're not in my hair.

That there's life after life, he says. After our life.

Let's talk about something else.

All right, he says. Lie down again. Put your head here. Pushing his damp shirt aside. His arm around her, his other hand fishing in his pocket for the cigarettes, then snapping the match with his thumbnail. Her ear against his shoulder's hollow.

He says, Now where was I?

The carpet-weavers. The blinded children.

Oh yes. I remember.

He says: The wealth of Sakiel-Norn was based on slaves, and especially on the child slaves who wove its famous carpets. But it was bad luck to mention this. The Snilfards claimed that their riches depended not on the slaves, but on their own virtue and right thinking – that is, on the proper sacrifices being made to the gods.

There were lots of gods. Gods always come in handy, they justify almost anything, and the gods of Sakiel-Norn were no exception. All of them were carnivorous; they liked animal sacrifices, but human blood was what they valued most. At the city's founding, so long ago it had passed into legend, nine devout fathers were said to have offered up their own children, to be buried as holy guardians under its nine gates.

Each of the four directions had two of these gates, one for going out and one for coming in: to leave by the same one through which you'd arrived meant an early death. The door of the ninth gate was a horizontal slab of marble on top of a hill in the centre of the city; it opened without moving, and swung between life and death, between the flesh and the spirit. This was the door through which the gods came and went: they didn't need two doors, because unlike mortals they could be on both sides of a door at once. The prophets of Sakiel-Norn had a saying: *What is the real breath of a man – the breathing out or the breathing in?* Such was the nature of the gods.

This ninth gate was also the altar on which the blood of sacrifice was spilled. Boy children were offered to the God of the Three Suns, who was the god of daytime, bright lights, palaces, feasts, furnaces, wars, liquor, entrances, and words; girl children were offered to the Goddess of the Five Moons, patroness of night, mists and shadows, famine, caves, childbirth, exits, and silences. Boy children were brained on the altar with a club and then thrown into the god's mouth, which led to a raging furnace. Girl children had their throats cut and their blood drained out to replenish the five waning moons, so they would not fade and disappear forever.

Nine girls were offered every year, in honour of the nine girls buried at the city gates. Those sacrificed were known as "the Goddess's maidens," and prayers and flowers and incense were offered to them so they would intercede on behalf of the living. The last three months of the year were said to be "faceless months"; they were the months when no crops grew, and the Goddess was said to be fasting. During this time the Sun-god in his mode of war and furnaces held sway, and the mothers of boy children dressed them in girls' clothing for their own protection.

It was the law that the noblest Snilfard families must sacrifice at least one of their daughters. It was an insult to the Goddess to offer any who were blemished or flawed, and as time passed, the Snilfards began to mutilate their girls so they would be spared: they would lop off a finger or an earlobe, or some other small part. Soon the mutilation became symbolic only: an oblong blue tattoo at the V of the collarbone. For a woman to possess one of these caste marks if she wasn't a Snilfard was a capital offence, but the brothel-owners, always eager for trade, would apply them with ink to those of their youngest whores who could put on a show of haughtiness. This appealed to those clients who wished to feel they were violating some blue-blooded Snilfard princess.

At the same time, the Snilfards took to adopting foundlings – the offspring of female slaves and their masters, for the most part – and using these to replace their legitimate daughters. It was cheating, but the noble families were powerful, so it went on with the eye of authority winking.

Then the noble families grew even lazier. They no longer wanted the bother of raising the girls in their own households, so they simply handed them over to the Temple of the Goddess, paying well for their upkeep. As the girl bore the family's name, they'd get credit for the sacrifice. It was like owning a racehorse. This practice was a debased version of the high-minded original, but by that time, in Sakiel-Norn, everything was for sale.

The dedicated girls were shut up inside the temple compound, fed the best of everything to keep them sleek and healthy, and rigorously trained so they would be ready for the great day – able to fulfill their duties with decorum, and without quailing. The ideal sacrifice should be like a dance, was the theory: stately and lyrical, harmonious and graceful. They were not animals, to be crudely butchered; their lives were to be given by them freely. Many believed what they were told: that the welfare of the entire kingdom depended on their selflessness. They spent long hours in prayer, getting into the right frame of mind; they were taught to walk with downcast eyes, and to smile with gentle melancholy, and to sing the songs of the Goddess, which were about absence and silence, about unfulfilled love and unexpressed regret, and wordlessness – songs about the impossibility of singing.

More time went by. Now only a few people still took the gods seriously, and anyone overly pious or observant was considered a crackpot. The citizens continued to perform the ancient rituals because they had always done so, but such things were not the real business of the city.

Despite their isolation, some of the girls came to realize they were being murdered as lip service to an outworn concept. Some tried to run away when they saw the knife. Others took to shrieking when they were taken by the hair and bent backwards over the altar, and yet others cursed the King himself, who served as High Priest on these occasions. One had even bitten him. These intermittent displays of panic and fury were resented by the populace, because the most terrible bad luck would follow. Or it might follow, supposing the Goddess to exist. Anyway, such outbursts could spoil the festivities: everyone enjoyed the sacrifices, even the Ygnirods, even the slaves, because they were allowed to take the day off and get drunk.

Therefore it became the practice to cut out the tongues of the girls three months before they were due to be sacrificed. This was not a mutilation, said the priests, but an improvement –

what could be more fitting for the servants of the Goddess of Silence?

Thus, tongueless, and swollen with words she could never again pronounce, each girl would be led in procession to the sound of solemn music, wrapped in veils and garlanded with flowers, up the winding steps to the city's ninth door. Nowadays you might say she looked like a pampered society bride.

She sits up. That's really uncalled for, she says. You want to get at me. You just love the idea of killing off those poor girls in their bridal veils. I bet they were blondes.

Not at you, he says. Not as such. Anyway I'm not inventing all of this, it has a firm foundation in history. The Hittites . . .

I'm sure, but you're licking your lips over it all the same. You're vengeful – no, you're jealous, though God knows why. I don't care about the Hittites, and history and all of that – it's just an excuse.

Hold on a minute. You agreed to the sacrificial virgins, you put them on the menu. I'm only following orders. What's your objection – the wardrobe? Too much tulle?

Let's not fight, she says. She feels she's about to cry, clenches her hands to stop.

I didn't mean to upset you. Come on now.

She pushes away his arm. You did mean to upset me. You like to know you can.

I thought it amused you. Listening to me perform. Juggling the adjectives. Playing the zany for you.

She tugs her skirt down, tucks in her blouse. Dead girls in bridal veils, why would that amuse me? With their tongues cut out. You must think I'm a brute.

I'll take it back. I'll change it. I'll rewrite history for you. How's that?

You can't, she says. The word has gone forth. You can't cancel half a line of it. I'm leaving. She's on her knees now, ready to stand up.

There's lots of time. Lie down. He takes hold of her wrist.

No. Let go. Look where the sun is. They'll be coming back. I could be in trouble, though I guess for you it's not trouble at all, that kind: it doesn't count. You don't care – all you want is a quick, a quick –

Come on, spit it out.

You know what I mean, she says in a tired voice.

It's not true. I'm sorry. I'm the brute, I got carried away. Anyway it's only a story.

She rests her forehead against her knees. After a minute she says, What am I going to do? After – when you're not here any more?

You'll get over it, he says. You'll live. Here, I'll brush you off.

It doesn't come off, not with just brushing.

Let's do up your buttons, he says. Don't be sad.

The Colonel Henry Parkman High School Home and School and Alumni Association Bulletin, Port Ticonderoga, May 1998

LAURA CHASE MEMORIAL PRIZE TO BE PRESENTED

BY MYRA STURGESS, VICE-PRESIDENT, ALUMNI ASSOCIATION

Colonel Henry Parkman High has been endowed with a valuable new prize by the generous bequest of the late Mrs. Winifred Griffen Prior of Toronto, whose noted brother Richard E. Griffen, will be remembered, as he often vacationed here in Port Ticonderoga and enjoyed sailing on our river. The prize is the Laura Chase Memorial Prize in Creative Writing, of a value of two hundred dollars, to be awarded to a student in the graduating year for the best short story, to be judged by three Alumni Association members, with literary and also moral values considered. Our Principal Mr. Eph Evans, states: "We are grateful to Mrs. Prior for remembering us along with her many other benefactions."

Named in honour of famed local authoress Laura Chase, the first Prize will be presented at Graduation in June. Her sister Mrs. Iris Griffen of the Chase family which contributed so much to our town in earlier days, has graciously consented to present the Prize to the lucky winner, and there's a few weeks left to go, so tell your kids to roll up their creativity sleeves and get cracking!

The Alumni Association will sponsor a Tea in the Gymnasium immediately after the Graduation, tickets available from Myra Sturgess at the Gingerbread House, all proceeds towards new football uniforms which are certainly needed! Donation of baked goods welcome, with nut ingredients clearly marked please.

III

The presentation

This morning I woke with a feeling of dread. I was unable at first to place it, but then I remembered. Today was the day of the ceremony.

The sun was up, the room already too warm. Light filtered in through the net curtains, hanging suspended in the air, sediment in a pond. My head felt like a sack of pulp. Still in my nightgown, damp from some fright I'd pushed aside like foliage, I pulled myself up and out of my tangled bed, then forced myself through the usual dawn rituals – the ceremonies we perform to make ourselves look sane and acceptable to other people. The hair must be smoothed down after whatever apparitions have made it stand on end during the night, the expression of staring disbelief washed from the eyes. The teeth brushed, such as they are. God knows what bones I'd been gnawing in my sleep.

Then I stepped into the shower, holding on to the grip bar Myra's bullied me into, careful not to drop the soap: I'm apprehensive of slipping. Still, the body must be hosed down, to get the smell of nocturnal darkness off the skin. I suspect myself of having an odour I myself can no longer detect – a stink of stale flesh and clouded, aging pee.

Dried, lotioned and powdered, sprayed like mildew, I was in some sense of the word restored. Only there was still the sensation of weightlessness, or rather of being about to step off a cliff. Each time I put a foot out I set it down provisionally, as if the floor might give way underneath me. Nothing but surface tension holding me in place.

Getting my clothes on helped. I am not at my best without scaffolding. (Yet what has become of my real clothes? Surely these shapeless pastels and orthopedic shoes belong on someone else. But they're mine; worse, they suit me now.)

Next came the stairs. I have a horror of tumbling down them – of breaking my neck, lying sprawled with undergarments on display, then melting into a festering puddle before anyone thinks of coming to find me. It would be such an ungainly way to die. I tackled each step at a time, hugging the banister; then along the hall to the kitchen, the fingers of my left hand brushing the wall like a cat's whiskers. (I can still see, mostly. I can still walk. *Be thankful for small mercies*, Reenie would say. *Why should we be?* said Laura. *Why are they so small?*)

I didn't want any breakfast. I drank a glass of water, and passed the time in fidgeting. At half past nine Walter came by to collect me. "Hot enough for you?" he said, his standard opening. In winter it's *cold enough*. *Wet* and *dry* are for spring and fall.

"How are you today, Walter?" I asked him, as I always do.

"Keeping out of mischief," he said, as he always does.

"That's the best that can be expected for any of us," I said. He gave his version of a smile – a thin crack in his face, like mud drying – opened the car door for me, and installed me in the passenger seat. "Big day today, eh?" he said. "Buckle up, or I might get arrested." He said *buckle up* as if it was a joke; he's old enough to remember earlier, more carefree days. He'd have been the kind of youth to drive with one elbow out the window, a hand on his girlfriend's knee. Astounding to reflect that this girlfriend was in fact Myra.

He eased the car delicately away from the curb and we moved off in silence. He's a large man, Walter – square-edged, like a plinth, with a neck that is not so much a neck as an extra shoulder; he exudes a not unpleasant scent of worn leather boots and gasoline. From his checked shirt and baseball cap I

gathered he wasn't planning to attend the graduation ceremony. He doesn't read books, which makes both of us more
comfortable: as far as he's concerned Laura is my sister and it's
a shame she's dead, and that's all.

I should have married someone like Walter. Good with his
hands.

No: I shouldn't have married anyone. That would have
saved a lot of trouble.

Walter stopped the car in front of the high school. It's
postwar modern, fifty years old but still new to me: I can't get
used to the flatness, the blandness. It looks like a packing crate.
Young people and their parents were rippling over the sidewalk
and the lawn and in through the front doors, their clothes in
every summer colour. Myra was waiting for us, yoo-hooing
from the steps, in a white dress covered with huge red roses.
Women with such big bums should not wear large floral prints.
There's something to be said for girdles, not that I'd wish them
back. She'd had her hair done, all tight grey cooked-looking
curls like an English barrister's wig.

"You're late," she said to Walter.

"Nope, I'm not," said Walter. "If I am, everyone else is early,
is all. No reason she should have to sit around cooling her
heels." They're in the habit of speaking of me in the third
person, as if I'm a child or pet.

Walter handed my arm over into Myra's custody and we
went up the front steps together like a three-legged race. I felt
what Myra's hand must have felt: a brittle radius covered slackly
with porridge and string. I should have brought my cane, but
I couldn't see carting it out onto the stage with me. Someone
would be bound to trip over it.

Myra took me backstage and asked me if I'd like to use the
Ladies' – she's good about remembering that – then sat me
down in the dressing room. "You just stay put now," she said.

Then she hurried off, bum lolloping, to make sure all was in order.

The lights around the dressing-room mirror were small round bulbs, as in theatres; they cast a flattering light, but I was not flattered: I looked sick, my skin leached of blood, like meat soaked in water. Was it fear, or true illness? Certainly I did not feel a hundred percent.

I found my comb, made a perfunctory stab at the top of my head. Myra keeps threatening to take me to "her girl," at what she still refers to as the Beauty Parlour – The Hair Port is its official name, with Unisex as an added incentive – but I keep resisting. At least I can still call my hair my own, though it frizzes upwards as if I've been electrocuted. Beneath it there are glimpses of scalp, the greyish pink of mice feet. If I ever get caught in a high wind my hair will all blow off like dandelion fluff, leaving only a tiny pockmarked nubbin of bald head.

Myra had left me one of her special brownies, whipped up for the Alumni Tea – a slab of putty, covered in chocolate sludge – and a plastic screw-top jug of her very own battery-acid coffee. I could neither drink nor eat, but why did God make toilets? I left a few brown crumbs, for authenticity.

Then Myra bustled in and scooped me up and led me forth, and I was having my hand shaken by the principal, and told how good it was of me to have come; then I was passed on to the vice-principal, the president of the Alumni Association, the head of the English department – a woman in a trouser suit – the representative from the Junior Chamber of Commerce, and finally the local member of Parliament, loath as such are to miss a trick. I hadn't seen so many polished teeth on display since Richard's political days.

Myra accompanied me as far as my chair, then whispered, "I'll be right in the wings." The school orchestra struck up with squeaks and flats, and we sang "O Canada!," the words to which I can never remember because they keep changing them. Nowadays they do some of it in French, which once would have been unheard of. We sat down, having affirmed our collective pride in something we can't pronounce.

Then the school chaplain offered a prayer, lecturing God on the many unprecedented challenges that face today's young people. God must have heard this sort of thing before, he's probably as bored with it as the rest of us. The others gave voice in turn: end of the twentieth century, toss out the old, ring in the new, citizens of the future, to you from failing hands and so forth. I allowed my mind to drift; I knew enough to know that the only thing expected of me was that I not disgrace myself. I could have been back again beside the podium, or at some interminable dinner, sitting next to Richard, keeping my mouth shut. If asked, which was seldom, I used to say that my hobby was gardening. A half-truth at best, though tedious enough to pass muster.

Next it was time for the graduates to receive their diplomas. Up they trooped, solemn and radiant, in many sizes, all beautiful as only the young can be beautiful. Even the ugly ones were beautiful, even the surly ones, the fat ones, even the spotty ones. None of them understands this – how beautiful they are. But nevertheless they're irritating, the young. Their posture is appalling as a rule, and judging from their songs they snivel and wallow, *grin and bear it* having gone the way of the foxtrot. They don't understand their own luck.

They barely glanced at me. To them I must have seemed quaint, but I suppose it's everyone's fate to be reduced to quaintness by those younger than themselves. Unless there's blood on the floor, of course. War, pestilence, murder, any kind of ordeal or violence, that's what they respect. Blood means we were serious.

Next came the prizes – Computer Science, Physics, mumble, Business Skills, English Literature, something I didn't catch. Then the Alumni Association man cleared his throat and gave out with a pious spiel about Winifred Griffen Prior, saint on earth. How everyone fibs when it's a question of money! I suppose the old bitch pictured the whole thing when she made her bequest, stingy as it is. She knew my presence would be requested; she wanted me writhing in the town's harsh gaze while her own munificence was lauded. *Spend this in remembrance of me.* I hated to give her the satisfaction, but I couldn't shirk it without seeming frightened or guilty, or else indifferent. Worse: forgetful.

It was Laura's turn next. The politician took it upon himself to do the honours: tact was called for here. Something was said about Laura's local origins, her courage, her "dedication to a chosen goal," whatever that might mean. Nothing about the manner of her death, which everyone in this town believes – despite the verdict at the inquest – was as close to suicide as damn is to swearing. And nothing at all about the book, which most of them surely thought would be best forgotten. Although it isn't, not here: even after fifty years it retains its aura of brimstone and taboo. Hard to fathom, in my opinion: as carnality goes it's old hat, the foul language nothing you can't hear any day on the street corners, the sex as decorous as fan dancers – whimsical almost, like garter belts.

Then of course it was a different story. What people remember isn't the book itself, so much as the furor: ministers in church denounced it as obscene, not only here; the public library was forced to remove it from the shelves, the one bookstore in town refused to stock it. There was word of censoring it. People snuck off to Stratford or London or Toronto even, and obtained their copies on the sly, as was the custom then with condoms. Back at home they drew the curtains and read, with disapproval, with relish, with avidity and glee – even the ones who'd never thought of opening a novel before. There's nothing like a shovelful of dirt to encourage literacy.

(There were doubtless a few kind sentiments expressed. *I couldn't get through it – not enough of a story for me. But the poor thing was so young. Maybe she'd have done better with some other book, if she'd not been taken.* That would have been the best they could say about it.)

What did they want from it? Lechery, smut, confirmation of their worst suspicions. But perhaps some of them wanted, despite themselves, to be seduced. Perhaps they were looking for passion; perhaps they delved into this book as into a mysterious parcel – a gift box at the bottom of which, hidden in layers of rustling tissue paper, lay something they'd always longed for but couldn't ever grasp.

But also they wanted to finger the real people in it – apart from Laura, that is: her actuality was taken for granted. They wanted real bodies, to fit onto the bodies conjured up for them by words. They wanted real lust. Above all they wanted to know: *who was the man?* In bed with the young woman, the lovely, dead young woman; in bed with Laura. Some of them thought they knew, of course. There had been gossip. For those who could put two and two together, it all added up. *Acted like she was pure as the driven. Butter wouldn't melt. Just goes to show you can't tell a book by its cover.*

But Laura had been out of reach by then. I was the one they could get at. The anonymous letters began. Why had I arranged for this piece of filth to be published? And in New York at that – the Great Sodom. Such muck! Had I no shame? I'd allowed my family – so well respected! – to be dishonoured, and along with them the entire town. Laura had never been right in the head, everyone always suspected that, and the book proved it. I should have protected her memory. I should have put a match to the manuscript. Looking at the blur of heads, down there in the audience – the older heads – I could imagine a miasma of old spite, old envy, old condemnation, rising up from them as if from a cooling swamp.

As for the book itself, it remained unmentionable – pushed back out of sight, as if it were some shoddy, disgraceful relative. Such a thin book, so helpless. The uninvited guest at this odd feast, it fluttered at the edges of the stage like an ineffectual moth.

While I was daydreaming my arm was grasped, I was hoisted up, the cheque in its gold-ribboned envelope was thrust into my hand. The winner was announced. I didn't catch her name.

She walked towards me, heels clicking across the stage. She was tall; they're all very tall these days, young girls, it must be something in the food. She had on a black dress, severe among the summer colours; there were silver threads in it, or beading – some sort of glitter. Her hair was long and dark. An oval face, a mouth done in cerise lipstick; a slight frown, focused, intent. Skin with a pale-yellow or brown undertint – could she be Indian, or Arabian, or Chinese? Even in Port Ticonderoga such a thing was possible: everyone is everywhere nowadays.

My heart lurched: yearning ran through me like a cramp. Perhaps my granddaughter – perhaps Sabrina looks like that now, I thought. Perhaps, perhaps not, how would I know? I might not even recognize her. She's been kept away from me so long; she's kept away. What can be done?

"Mrs. Griffen," hissed the politician.

I teetered, regained my balance. Now what had I been intending to say?

"My sister Laura would be so pleased," I gasped into the microphone. My voice was reedy; I thought I might faint. "She liked to help people." This was true, I'd vowed not to say anything untrue. "She was so fond of reading and books." Also true, up to a point. "She would have wished you the very best for your future." True as well.

I managed to hand over the envelope; the girl had to bend down. I whispered into her ear, or meant to whisper – *Bless you. Be careful.* Anyone intending to meddle with words needs such blessing, such warning. Had I actually spoken, or had I simply opened and closed my mouth like a fish?

She smiled, and tiny brilliant sequins flashed and sparkled all over her face and hair. It was a trick of my eyes, and of the stage lights, which were too bright. I should have worn my tinted glasses. I stood there blinking. Then she did something unexpected: she leaned over and kissed me on the cheek. Through her lips I could feel the texture of my own skin: soft as kid-glove leather, crinkled, powdery, ancient.

She in her turn whispered something, but I couldn't quite catch it. Was it a simple thank you, or some other message in – could it be? – a foreign language?

She turned away. The light streaming out from her was so dazzling I had to shut my eyes. I hadn't heard, I couldn't see. Darkness moved closer. Applause battered my ears like beating wings. I staggered and almost fell.

Some alert functionary caught my arm and slotted me back into my chair. Back into obscurity. Back into the long shadow cast by Laura. Out of harm's way.

But the old wound has split open, the invisible blood pours forth. Soon I'll be emptied.

The silver box

The orange tulips are coming out, crumpled and raggedy like the stragglers from some returning army. I greet them with relief, as if waving from a bombed-out building; still, they must make their way as best they can, without much help from me. Sometimes I poke around in the debris of the back garden, clearing away dry stalks and fallen leaves, but that's about as far as I go. I can't kneel very well any more, I can't shove my hands into the dirt.

Yesterday I went to the doctor, to see about these dizzy spells. He told me that I have developed what used to be called *a heart*, as if healthy people didn't have one. It seems I will not after all keep on living forever, merely getting smaller and greyer and dustier, like the Sibyl in her bottle. Having long ago whispered *I want to die*, I now realize that this wish will indeed be fulfilled, and sooner rather than later. No matter that I've changed my mind about it.

I've wrapped myself in a shawl in order to sit outside, sheltered by the overhang of the back porch, at a scarred wooden table I had Walter bring in from the garage. It held the usual things, leftovers from previous owners: a collection of dried-out paint cans, a stack of asphalt shingles, a jar half-filled with rusty nails, a coil of picture wire. Mummified sparrows, mouse nests of mattress stuffing. Walter washed it off with Javex, but it still smells of mice.

Laid out in front of me are a cup of tea, an apple cut into quarters, and a pad of paper with blue lines on it, like men's pyjamas once. I've bought a new pen as well, a cheap one, black plastic with a rolling tip. I remember my first fountain pen, how sleek it felt, how blue the ink made my fingers. It was

Bakelite, with silver trim. The year was 1929. I was thirteen. Laura borrowed this pen – without asking, as she borrowed everything – then broke it, effortlessly. I forgave her, of course. I always did; I had to, because there were only the two of us. The two of us on our thorn-encircled island, waiting for rescue; and, on the mainland, everyone else.

For whom am I writing this? For myself? I think not. I have no picture of myself reading it over at a later time, *later time* having become problematical. For some stranger, in the future, after I'm dead? I have no such ambition, or no such hope.

Perhaps I write for no one. Perhaps for the same person children are writing for, when they scrawl their names in the snow.

I'm not as swift as I was. My fingers are stiff and clumsy, the pen wavers and rambles, it takes me a long time to form the words. And yet I persist, hunched over as if sewing by moonlight.

When I look in the mirror I see an old woman; or not old, because nobody is allowed to be *old* any more. *Older*, then. Sometimes I see an older woman who might look like the grandmother I never knew, or like my own mother, if she'd managed to reach this age. But sometimes I see instead the young girl's face I once spent so much time rearranging and deploring, drowned and floating just beneath my present face, which seems – especially in the afternoons, with the light on a slant – so loose and transparent I could peel it off like a stocking.

The doctor says I need to walk – every day, he says, for my heart. I would rather not. It isn't the idea of the walking that bothers me, it's the going out: I feel too much on show. Do I imagine it, the staring, the whispering? Perhaps, perhaps not.

I am after all a local fixture, like a brick-strewn vacant lot where some important building used to stand.

The temptation is to stay inside; to subside into the kind of recluse whom neighbourhood children regard with derision and a little awe; to let the hedges and weeds grow up, to allow the doors to rust shut, to lie on my bed in some gown-shaped garment and let my hair lengthen and spread out over the pillow and my fingernails to sprout into claws, while candle wax drips onto the carpet. But long ago I made a choice between classicism and romanticism. I prefer to be upright and contained – an urn in daylight.

Perhaps I should not have moved back here to live. But by that time I couldn't think of anywhere else to go. As Reenie used to say, *Better the devil you know.*

Today I made the effort. I went out, I walked. I walked as far as the cemetery: one needs a goal for these otherwise witless excursions. I wore my broad-brimmed straw hat to cut the glare, and my tinted glasses, and took my cane to feel for the curbs. Also a plastic shopping bag.

I went along Erie Street, past a drycleaner's, a portrait photographer's, the few other main-street stores that have managed to survive the drainage caused by the malls on the edge of town. Then Betty's Luncheonette, which is under new ownership again: sooner or later its proprietors get fed up, or die, or move to Florida. Betty's now has a patio garden, where the tourists can sit in the sun and fry to a crisp; it's in the back, that little square of cracked cement where they used to keep the garbage cans. They offer tortellini and cappuccino, boldly proclaimed in the window as if everyone in town just naturally knows what they are. Well, they do by now; they've had a try, if only to acquire sneering rights. *I don't need that fluff on my coffee. Looks like shaving cream. One swallow and you're foaming at the mouth.*

Chicken pot pies were the specialty once, but they're long gone. There are hamburgers, but Myra says to avoid them. She says they use pre-frozen patties made of meat dust. Meat dust, she says, is what is scraped up off the floor after they've cut up frozen cows with an electric saw. She reads a lot of magazines, at the hairdresser's.

The cemetery has a wrought-iron gate, with an intricate scrollwork archway over it, and an inscription: *Though I Walk Through the Valley of the Shadow of Death I Will Fear No Evil, For Thou Art With Me.* Yes, it does feel deceptively safer with two; but *Thou* is a slippery character. Every *Thou* I've known has had a way of going missing. They skip town, or turn perfidious, or else they drop like flies, and then where are you?

Right about here.

The Chase family monument is hard to miss: it's taller than everything else. There are two angels, white marble, Victorian, sentimental but quite well done as such things go, on a large stone cube with scrolled corners. The first angel is standing, her head bowed to the side in an attitude of mourning, one hand placed tenderly on the shoulder of the second one. The second kneels, leaning against the other's thigh, gazing straight ahead, cradling a sheaf of lilies. Their bodies are decorous, the contours shrouded in folds of softly draped, impenetrable mineral, but you can tell they're female. Acid rain is taking its toll of them: their once-keen eyes are blurred now, softened and porous, as if they have cataracts. But perhaps that's my own vision going.

Laura and I used to visit here. We were brought by Reenie, who thought the visiting of family graves was somehow good for children, and later we came by ourselves: it was a pious and therefore acceptable excuse for escape. When she was little, Laura used to say the angels were meant to be us, the two of us.

I told her this couldn't be true, because the angels were put there by our grandmother before we were born. But Laura never paid much attention to that kind of reasoning. She was more interested in forms – in what things were in themselves, not what they weren't. She wanted essences.

Over the years I've made a practice of coming here at least twice a year, to tidy up, if for no other reason. Once I drove, but no longer: my eyes are too bad for that. I bent over painfully and gathered up the withered flowers that had accumulated there, left by Laura's anonymous admirers, and stuffed them into my plastic shopping bag. There are fewer of these tributes than there used to be, though still more than enough. Today some were quite fresh. Once in a while I've found sticks of incense, and candles too, as if Laura were being invoked.

After I'd dealt with the bouquets I walked around the monument, reading through the roll call of defunct Chases engraved on the sides of the cube. *Benjamin Chase and his Beloved Wife Adelia; Norval Chase and his Beloved Wife Liliana. Edgar and Percival, They Shall Not Grow Old As We Who Are Left Grow Old.*

And Laura, as much as she is anywhere. Her essence.

Meat dust.

There was a picture of her in the local paper last week, along with a write-up about the prize – the standard picture, the one from the book jacket, the only one that ever got printed because it's the only one I gave them. It's a studio portrait, the upper body turned away from the photographer, then the head turned back to give a graceful curve to the neck. *A little more, now look up, towards me, that's my girl, now let's see that smile.* Her long hair is blonde, as mine was then – pale, white almost, as if the red undertones had been washed away – the iron, the copper, all the hard metals. A straight nose; a heart-shaped face; large, luminous, guileless eyes; the eyebrows arched, with a perplexed upwards turning at the inner edges. A tinge of stubbornness in the jaw, but you wouldn't see it unless you knew. No makeup to speak of, which gives the face an oddly naked appearance: when you look at the mouth, you're aware you're looking at flesh.

Pretty; beautiful even; touchingly untouched. An advertisement for soap, all natural ingredients. The face looks deaf: it has that vacant, posed imperviousness of all well-brought-up girls of the time. A tabula rasa, not waiting to write, but to be written on.

It's only the book that makes her memorable now.

Laura came back in a small silver-coloured box, like a cigarette box. I knew what the town had to say about that, as much as if I'd been eavesdropping. *Course it's not really her, just the ashes. You wouldn't have thought the Chases would be cremators, they never were before, they wouldn't have stooped to it in their heyday, but it sounds like they might as well just have gone ahead and finished the job off, seeing as she was more or less burnt up already. Still, I guess they felt she should be with family. They'd want her at that big monument thing of theirs with the two angels. Nobody else has two, but that was when the money was burning a hole in their pockets. They liked to show off back then, make a splash; take the lead, you could say. Play the big cheese. They sure did spread it around here once.*

I always hear such things in Reenie's voice. She was our town interpreter, mine and Laura's. Who else did we have to fall back on?

Around behind the monument there's some empty space. I think of it as a reserved seat – permanently reserved, as

Richard used to arrange at the Royal Alexandra Theatre. That's my spot; that's where I'll go to earth.

Poor Aimee is in Toronto, in the Mount Pleasant Cemetery, alongside the Griffens – with Richard and Winifred and their gaudy polished-granite megalith. Winifred saw to that – she staked her claim to Richard and Aimee by barging in right away and ordering their coffins. She who pays the undertaker calls the tune. She'd have barred me from their funerals if she could.

But Laura was the first of them, so Winifred hadn't got her body-snatching routine perfected yet. I said, "She's going home," and that was that. I scattered the ashes over the ground, but kept the silver box. Lucky I didn't bury it: some fan would have pinched it by now. They'll nick anything, those people. A year ago I caught one of them with a jam jar and a trowel, scraping up dirt from the grave.

I wonder about Sabrina – where she'll end up. She's the last of us. I assume she's still on this earth: I haven't heard anything different. It remains to be seen which side of the family she'll choose to be buried with, or whether she'll put herself off in a corner, away from the lot of us. I wouldn't blame her.

The first time she ran away, when she was thirteen, Winifred phoned in a cold rage, accusing me of aiding and abetting, although she didn't go so far as to say *kidnapping*. She demanded to know if Sabrina had come to me.

"I don't believe I'm obliged to tell you," I said, to torment her. Fair is fair: most of the chances for tormenting had so far been hers. She used to send my cards and letters and birthday presents for Sabrina back to me, *Return to Sender* printed on them in her chunky tyrant's handwriting. "Anyway I'm her grandmother. She can always come to me when she wants to. She's always welcome."

"I need hardly remind you that I am her legal guardian."

"If you need hardly remind me, then why are you reminding me?"

Sabrina didn't come to me, though. She never did. It's not hard to guess why. God knows what she'd been told about me. Nothing good.

The Button Factory

The summer heat has come in earnest, settling down over the town like cream soup. Malarial weather, it would have been once; cholera weather. The trees I walk beneath are wilting umbrellas, the paper is damp under my fingers, the words I write feather at the edges like lipstick on an aging mouth. Just climbing the stairs I sprout a thin moustache of sweat.

I shouldn't walk in such heat, it makes my heart beat harder. I notice this with malice. I shouldn't put my heart to such tests, now that I've been informed of its imperfections; yet I take a perverse delight in doing this, as if I am a bully and it is a small whining child whose weaknesses I despise.

In the evenings there's been thunder, a distant bumping and stumbling, like God on a sullen binge. I get up to pee, go back to bed, lie twisting in the damp sheets, listening to the monotonous whirring of the fan. Myra says I should get air conditioning, but I don't want it. Also I can't afford it. "Who would pay for such a thing?" I say to her. She must believe I have a diamond hidden in my forehead, like the toads in fairy tales.

The goal for my walk today was The Button Factory, where I intended to have morning coffee. The doctor has warned me about coffee, but he's only fifty – he goes jogging in shorts, making a spectacle of his hairy legs. He doesn't know every-thing, though that would be news to him. If coffee doesn't kill me, something else will.

Erie Street was languid with tourists, middle-aged for the most part, poking their noses into the souvenir shops, finicking around in the bookstore, at loose ends before driving off after lunch to the nearby summer theatre festival for a few relaxing hours of treachery, sadism, adultery and murder. Some of them were heading in the same direction I was – to The Button Factory, to see what chintzy curios they might acquire in commemoration of their overnight vacation from the twentieth century. Dust-catchers, Reenie would have called such items. She would have applied the same term to the tourists themselves.

I walked along in their pastel company, to where Erie Street turns into Mill Street and runs along the Louveteau River. Port Ticonderoga has two rivers, the Jogues and the Louveteau – the names being relics of the French trading post situated once at their juncture, not that we go in for French around these parts: it's the Jogs and the Lovetow for us. The Louveteau with its swift current was the attraction for the first mills, and then for the electricity plants. The Jogues on the other hand is deep and slow, navigable for thirty miles above Lake Erie. Down it they shipped the limestone that was the town's first industry, thanks to the huge deposits of it left by the retreating inland seas. (Of the Permian, the Jurassic? I used to know.) Most of the houses in town are made from this limestone, mine included.

The abandoned quarries are still there on the outskirts, deep squares and oblongs cut down into the rock as if whole buildings had been lifted out of them, leaving the empty shapes of themselves behind. I sometimes picture the entire town rising out of the shallow prehistoric ocean, unfolding like a sea anemone or the fingers of a rubber glove when you blow into it – sprouting jerkily like those brown, grainy films of flowers opening up that used to be shown in movie theatres – when was that? – before the features. Fossil-hunters poke around out there, looking for extinct fish, ancient fronds, scrolls of coral; and if the teenage kids want to carouse, that's where they do it.

They make bonfires, and drink too much and smoke dope, and grope around in one another's clothing as if they've just invented it, and smash their parents' cars up on the way back to town.

My own back garden adjoins the Louveteau Gorge, where the river narrows and takes a plunge. The drop is steep enough to cause a mist, and a little awe. On summer weekends the tourists stroll along the cliffside path or stand on the very edge, taking pictures; I can see their innocuous, annoying white canvas hats going by. The cliff is crumbling and dangerous, but the town won't spend the money for a fence, it being the opinion here, still, that if you do a damn fool thing you deserve whatever consequences. Cardboard cups from the doughnut shop collect in the eddies below, and once in a while there's a corpse, whether fallen or pushed or jumped is hard to tell, unless of course there's a note.

The Button Factory is on the east bank of the Louveteau, a quarter of a mile upriver from the Gorge. For several decades it stood derelict, its windows broken, its roof leaking, an abode of rats and drunks; then it was rescued from demolition by an energetic citizens' committee, and converted to boutiques. The flower beds have been reconstituted, the exterior sandblasted, the ravages of time and vandalism repaired, though dark wings of soot are still visible around the lower windows, from the fire over sixty years ago.

The building is brownish-red brick, with the large many-paned windows they once used in factories in order to save on lighting. It's quite graceful, as factories go: swag decorations, each with a stone rose in the centre, gabled windows, a mansard roof of green-and-purple slate. Beside it is a tidy parking lot. Welcome Button Factory Visitors, says the sign, in old-style circus type; and, in smaller lettering: Overnight Parking

Prohibited. And under that, in scrawled, enraged black marker: *You are not Fucking God and the Earth is not Your Fucking Driveway*. The authentic local touch.

The front entrance has been widened, a wheelchair ramp installed, the original heavy doors replaced by plate-glass ones: In and Out, Push and Pull, the twentieth century's bossy quadruplets. Inside there's music playing, rural-route fiddles, the one-two-three of some sprightly, heartbroken waltz. There's a skylight, over a central space floored in ersatz cobblestones, with freshly painted green park benches and planters containing a few disgruntled shrubs. The various boutiques are arranged around it: a mall effect.

The bare brick walls are decorated with giant blow-ups of old photos from the town archives. First there's a quote from a newspaper – a Montreal newspaper, not ours – with the date, 1899:

> One must not imagine the dark Satanic mills of Olde England. The factories of Port Ticonderoga are situated amid a profusion of greenery brightened with gay flowers, and are soothed by the sound of the rushing currents; they are clean and well-ventilated, and the workers cheerful and efficient. Standing at sunset on the graceful new Jubilee Bridge which curves like a rainbow of wrought-iron lace over the gushing cascades of the Louveteau River, one views an enchanting faeryland as the lights of the Chase button factory wink on, and are reflected in the sparkling waters.

This wasn't entirely a lie when it was written. At least for a short time, there was prosperity here, and enough to go around.

Next comes my grandfather, in frock coat and top hat and

white whiskers, waiting with a clutch of similarly glossy dignitaries to welcome the Duke of York during his tour across Canada in 1901. Then my father with a wreath, in front of the War Memorial at its dedication – a tall man, solemn-faced, with a moustache and an eye-patch; up close, a collection of black dots. I back away from him to see if he'll come into focus – I try to catch his good eye – but he's not looking at me; he's looking towards the horizon, with his spine straight and his shoulders back, as if he's facing a firing squad. Stalwart, you'd say.

Then a shot of the button factory itself, in 1911, says the caption. Machines with clanking arms like the legs of grasshoppers, and steel cogs and tooth-covered wheels, and stamping pistons going up and down, punching out the shapes; long tables with their rows of workers, bending forward, doing things with their hands. The machines are run by men, in eye-shades and vests, their sleeves rolled up; the workers at the table are women, in upswept hairdos and pinafores. It was the women who counted the buttons and boxed them, or sewed them onto cards with the Chase name printed across them, six or eight or twelve buttons to a card.

Down at the end of the cobblestoned open space is a bar, The Whole Enchilada, with live music on Saturdays, and beer said to be from local micro-breweries. The décor is wooden tabletops placed on barrels, with early-days pine booths along one side. On the menu, displayed in the window – I've never gone inside – are foods I find exotic: patty melts, potato skins, nachos. The fat-drenched staples of the less respectable young, or so I'm told by Myra. She's got a ringside seat right next door, and if there are any tricks happening in The Whole Enchilada, she never misses them. She says a pimp goes there to eat, also a drug pusher, both in broad daylight. She's pointed them out to me, with much thrilled whispering. The pimp was wearing a three-piece suit, and looked like a stockbroker. The drug pusher had a grey moustache and a denim outfit, like an old-time union organizer.

Myra's shop is The Gingerbread House, Gifts and Collectibles. It's got that sweet and spicy scent to it – some kind of cinnamon room spray – and it offers many things: jars of jam with cotton-print fabric tops, heart-shaped pillows stuffed with desiccated herbs that smell like hay, clumsily hinged boxes carved by "traditional craftsmen," quilts purportedly sewn by Mennonites, toilet-cleaning brushes with the heads of smirking ducks. Myra's idea of city folks' idea of country life, the life of their pastoral hicktown ancestors – a little bit of history to take home with you. History, as I recall, was never this winsome, and especially not this clean, but the real thing would never sell: most people prefer a past in which nothing smells.

Myra likes to make presents to me from her stash of treasures. Otherwise put, she dumps items on me that folks won't buy at the shop. I possess a lopsided twig wreath, an incomplete set of wooden napkin rings with pineapples on them, an obese candle scented with what appears to be kerosene. For my birthday she gave me a pair of oven gloves shaped like lobster claws. I'm sure it was kindly meant.

Or perhaps she's softening me up: she's a Baptist, she'd like me to find Jesus, or vice versa, before it's too late. That kind of thing doesn't run in her family: her mother Reenie never went in much for God. There was mutual respect, and if you were in trouble naturally you'd call on him, as with lawyers; but as with lawyers, it would have to be bad trouble. Otherwise it didn't pay to get too mixed up with him. Certainly she didn't want him in her kitchen, as she had enough on her hands as it was.

After some deliberation, I bought a cookie at The Cookie Gremlin – oatmeal and chocolate chip – and a Styrofoam cup of coffee, and sat on one of the park benches, sipping and licking my fingers, resting my feet, listening to the taped music with its lilting, mournful twang.

It was my Grandfather Benjamin who built the button factory, in the early 1870s. There was a demand for buttons, as for clothing and everything connected with it – the population of the continent was expanding at an enormous rate – and buttons could be made cheaply and sold cheaply, and this (said Reenie) was just the ticket for my grandfather, who'd seen the opportunity and used the brains God gave him.

His forbears had come up from Pennsylvania in the 1820s to take advantage of cheap land, and of construction opportunities – the town had been burnt out during the War of 1812, and there was considerable rebuilding to be done. These people were something Germanic and sectarian, crossbred with seventh-generation Puritans – an industrious but fervent mix that produced, in addition to the usual collection of virtuous, lumpen farmers, three circuit riders, two inept land speculators, and one petty embezzler – chancers with a visionary streak and one eye on the horizon. In my grandfather this came out as gambling, although the only thing he ever gambled on was himself.

His father had owned one of the first mills in Port Ticonderoga, a modest grist mill, in the days when everything was run by water. When he'd died, of apoplexy, as it was then called, my grandfather was twenty-six. He inherited the mill, borrowed money, imported the button machinery from the States. The first buttons were made from wood and bone, and the fancier ones from cow horns. These last two materials could be obtained for next to nothing from the several abattoirs in the vicinity, and as for the wood, it lay all round about, clogging up the land, and people were burning it just to get rid of it. With cheap raw materials and cheap labour and an expanding market, how could he have failed to prosper?

The buttons turned out by my grandfather's company were not the kinds of buttons I liked best as a girl. No tiny mother-of-pearl ones, no delicate jet, none in white leather for ladies' gloves. The family buttons were to buttons as rubber overshoes were to footgear – stolid, practical buttons, for overcoats and overalls and work shirts, with something robust and even crude about them. You could picture them on long underwear, holding up the flap at the back, and on the flies of men's trousers. The things they concealed would have been pendulous, vulnerable, shameful, unavoidable – the category of objects the world needs but scorns.

It's hard to see how much glamour would have attached itself to the granddaughters of a man who made such buttons, except for the money. But money or even the rumour of it always casts a dazzling light of sorts, so Laura and I grew up with a certain aura. And in Port Ticonderoga, nobody thought the family buttons were funny or contemptible. Buttons were taken seriously there: too many people's jobs depended on them for it to have been otherwise.

Over the years my grandfather bought up other mills and turned them into factories as well. He had a knitting factory for undershirts and combinations, another one for socks, and another one that made small ceramic objects such as ashtrays. He prided himself on the conditions in his factories: he listened to complaints when anyone was brave enough to make them, he regretted injuries when they'd been brought to his notice. He kept up with mechanical improvements, indeed with improvements of all kinds. He was the first factory owner in town to introduce electric lighting. He thought flower beds were good for the workers' morale – zinnias and snapdragons were his standbys, as they were inexpensive and showy and lasted a long time. He declared that conditions for the females in his employ were as safe as those in their own parlours. (He assumed they had parlours. He assumed these parlours were safe. He liked to think well of everybody.) He refused to tolerate drunkenness on the job, or coarse language, or loose behaviour.

Or this is what is said of him in *The Chase Industries: A History*, a book my grandfather commissioned in 1903 and had privately printed, in green leather covers, with not only the title but his own candid, heavy signature embossed on the front in gold. He used to present copies of this otiose chronicle to his business associates, who must have been surprised, though perhaps not. It must have been considered the done thing, because if it hadn't been, my Grandmother Adelia wouldn't have allowed him to do it.

I sat on the park bench, gnawing away at my cookie. It was huge, the size of a cow pat, the way they make them now – tasteless, crumbly, greasy – and I couldn't seem to make my way through it. It wasn't the right thing for such warm weather. I was feeling a little dizzy too, which could have been the coffee.

I set the cup down beside me and my cane clattered off the bench onto the floor. I leant over sideways, but I couldn't reach it. Then I lost my balance and knocked the coffee over. I could feel it through the cloth of my skirt, lukewarm. There would be a brown patch when I stood up, as if I'd been incontinent. That's what people would think.

Why do we always assume at such moments that everyone in the world is staring at us? Usually nobody is. But Myra was. She must have seen me come in; she must have been keeping an eye on me. She hurried out of her shop. "You're white as a sheet!

You look all in," she said. "Let's just mop that up! Bless your soul, did you walk all the way over here? You can't walk back! I better call Walter – he can run you home."

"I can manage," I told her. "There's nothing wrong with me." But I let her do it.

My bones have been aching again, as they often do in humid weather. They ache like history: things long done with, that still reverberate as pain. When the ache is bad enough it keeps me from sleeping. Every night I yearn for sleep, I strive for it; yet it flutters on ahead of me like a sooty curtain. There are sleeping pills, of course, but the doctor has warned me against them.

Last night, after what seemed hours of damp turmoil, I got up and crept slipperless down the stairs, feeling my way in the faint shine from the street light outside the stairwell window. Once safely arrived at the bottom, I shambled into the kitchen and nosed around in the misty dazzle of the refrigerator. There was nothing much I wanted to eat: the draggled remains of a bunch of celery, a blue-tinged heel of bread, a lemon going soft. An end of cheese, wrapped in greasy paper and hard and translucent as toenails. I've fallen into the habits of the solitary; my meals are snatched and random. Furtive snacks, furtive treats and picnics. I made do with some peanut butter, scooped directly from the jar with a forefinger: why dirty a spoon?

Standing there with the jar in one hand and my finger in my mouth, I had the feeling that someone was about to walk into the room – some other woman, the unseen, valid owner – and ask me what in hell I was doing in her kitchen. I've had it before, the sense that even in the course of my most legitimate and daily actions – peeling a banana, brushing my teeth – I am trespassing.

At night the house was more than ever like a stranger's. I wandered through the front rooms, the dining room, the parlour, hand on the wall for balance. My various possessions were floating in their own pools of shadow, detached from me, denying my ownership of them. I looked them over with a burglar's eye, deciding what might be worth the risk of stealing, what on the other hand I would leave behind. Robbers would take the obvious things – the silver teapot that was my grandmother's, perhaps the hand-painted china. The remaining monogrammed spoons. The television set. Nothing I really want.

All of it will have to be gone through, disposed of by someone or other, when I die. Myra will corner the job, no doubt; she thinks she has inherited me from Reenie. She'll enjoy playing the trusted family retainer. I don't envy her: any life is a rubbish dump even while it's being lived, and more so afterwards. But if a rubbish dump, a surprisingly small one; when you've cleared up after the dead, you know how few green plastic garbage bags you yourself are likely to take up in your turn.

The nutcracker shaped like an alligator, the lone mother-of pearl cuff link, the tortoiseshell comb with missing teeth. The broken silver lighter, the saucerless cup, the cruet stand minus the vinegar. The scattered bones of *home*, the rags, the relics. Shards washed ashore after shipwreck.

Today Myra persuaded me to buy an electric fan – one on a tall stand, better than the creaky little thing I've been relying on. The sort she had in mind was on sale at the new mall across the Jogues River bridge. She would drive me there: she was going anyway, it would be no trouble. It's dispiriting, the way she invents pretexts.

Our route took us past Avilion, or what was once Avilion, now so sadly transformed. Valhalla, it is now. What bureaucratic moron decided this was a suitable name for an old-age home? As I recall, Valhalla was where you went after you were dead, not immediately before. But perhaps some point was intended.

The location is prime – the east bank of the Louveteau River, at the confluence with the Jogues – thus combining a romantic view of the Gorge with a safe mooring for sailboats. The house is large but it looks crowded now, shouldered aside by the flimsy bungalows that went up on the grounds after the war. Three elderly women were sitting on the front porch, one in a wheelchair, furtively smoking, like naughty adolescents in the washroom. One of these days they'll burn the place down for sure.

I haven't been back inside Avilion since they converted it; it reeks no doubt of baby powder and sour urine and day-old boiled potatoes. I'd rather remember it the way it was, even at the time I knew it, when shabbiness was already setting in – the cool, spacious halls, the polished expanse of the kitchen, the Sèvres bowl filled with dried petals on the small round cherry-wood table in the front hall. Upstairs, in Laura's room, there's a chip out of the mantelpiece, from where she dropped a firedog; so typical. I'm the only person who knows this, any more. Considering her appearance – her lucent skin, her look of pliability, her long ballerina's neck – people expected her to be graceful.

Avilion is not the standard-issue limestone. Its planners wanted something more unusual, and so it is constructed of rounded river cobblestones all cemented together. From a distance the effect is warty, like the skin of a dinosaur or the wishing wells in picture books. Ambition's mausoleum, I think of it now.

It isn't a particularly elegant house, but it was once thought imposing in its way – a merchant's palace, with a curved driveway leading to it, a stumpy Gothic turret, and a wide semicircular spooled verandah overlooking the two rivers, where tea was served to ladies in flowered hats during the languid summer afternoons at the century's turn. String quartets were once stationed there for garden parties; my grandmother and her friends used it as a stage, for amateur theatricals, at dusk, with torches set around; Laura and I used to hide under it. It's begun to sag, that verandah; it needs a paint job.

Once there was a gazebo, and a walled kitchen garden, and several plots of ornamentals, and a lily pond with goldfish in it, and a steam-heated glass conservatory, demolished now, that grew ferns and fuschias and the occasional spindly lemon and sour orange. There was a billiards room, and a drawing room and a morning room, and a library with a marble Medusa over the fireplace – the nineteenth-century type of Medusa, with a lovely impervious gaze, the snakes writhing up out of her head like anguished thoughts. The mantelpiece was French: a different one had been ordered, something with Dionysus and vines, but the Medusa came instead, and France was a long way to send it back, and so they used that one.

There was a vast dim dining room with William Morris wallpaper, the Strawberry Thief design, and a chandelier entwined with bronze water-lilies, and three high stained-glass windows, shipped in from England, showing episodes from the story of Tristan and Iseult (the proffering of the love potion, in a ruby-red cup; the lovers, Tristan on one knee, Iseult yearning over him with her yellow hair cascading – hard to render in glass, a little too much like a melting broom; Iseult alone, dejected, in purple draperies, a harp nearby).

The planning and decoration of this house were supervised by my Grandmother Adelia. She died before I was born, but from what I've heard she was as smooth as silk and as cool as a cucumber, but with a will like a bone saw. Also she went in for Culture, which gave her a certain moral authority. It wouldn't now; but people believed, then, that Culture could make you better – a better person. They believed it could uplift you, or the women believed it. They hadn't yet seen Hitler at the opera house.

Adelia's maiden name was Montfort. She was from an established family, or what passed for it in Canada – second-generation Montreal English crossed with Huguenot French. These Montforts had been prosperous once – they'd made a bundle on railroads – but through risky speculations and inertia they were already halfway down the slippery slope. So when time had begun to run out on Adelia with no really acceptable husband in sight, she'd married money – crude money, button money. She was expected to refine this money, like oil.

(She wasn't married, she was married off, said Reenie, rolling out the gingersnaps. The family arranged it. That's what was done in such families, and who's to say it was any worse or better than choosing for yourself? In any case, Adelia Montfort did her duty, and lucky to have the chance, as she was getting long in the tooth by then – she must have been twenty-three, which was counted over the hill in those days.)

I still have a portrait of my grandparents; it's set in a silver frame, with convolvulus blossoms, and was taken soon after their wedding. In the background are a fringed velvet curtain and two ferns on stands. Grandmother Adelia reclines on a chaise, a heavy-lidded, handsome woman, in many draperies and a long double string of pearls and a plunging, lace-bordered neckline, her white forearms boneless as rolled chicken. Grandfather Benjamin sits behind her in formal kit, substantial but embarrassed, as if he's been tarted up for the occasion. They both look corseted.

When I was the age for it – thirteen, fourteen – I used to romanticize Adelia. I would gaze out of my window at night, over the lawns and the moon-silvered beds of ornamentals, and see her trailing wistfully through the grounds in a white lace tea gown. I gave her a languorous, world-weary, faintly mocking smile. Soon I added a lover. She would meet this lover outside the conservatory, which by that time was neglected – my father had no interest in steam-heated orange trees – but I restored it in my mind, and supplied it with hothouse flowers. Orchids, I thought, or camellias. (I didn't know what a camellia was, but I'd read about them.) My grandmother and the lover would disappear inside, and do what? I wasn't sure.

In reality the chances of Adelia having had a lover were nil. The town was too small, its morals were too provincial, she had too far to fall. She wasn't a fool. Also she had no money of her own.

As hostess and household manager, Adelia did well by Benjamin Chase. She prided herself on her taste, and my grandfather deferred to her in this because her taste was one of the things he'd married her for. He was forty by then; he'd worked hard at making his fortune, and now he intended to get his money's worth, which meant being patronized by his new bride about his wardrobe and bullied about his table manners. In his own way he also wanted Culture, or at least the concrete evidence of it. He wanted the right china.

He got that, and the twelve-course dinners that went along with it: celery and salted nuts first, chocolates at the end. Consommé, rissoles, timbales, the fish, the roast, the cheese, the fruit, hothouse grapes draped over the etched-glass epergne. Railway-hotel food, I think of it now; ocean-liner food. Prime ministers came to Port Ticonderoga – by that time the town had several prominent manufacturers, whose support for political parties was valued – and Avilion was where they stayed. There were photographs of Grandfather Benjamin with three prime ministers in turn, framed in gold and hung in the library – Sir John Sparrow Thompson, Sir Mackenzie Bowell, Sir Charles Tupper. They must have preferred the food there to anything else on offer.

Adelia's task would have been to design and order these dinners, then to avoid being seen to devour them. Custom would have dictated that she only pick at her food while in company: chewing and swallowing were such blatantly carnal activities. I expect she had a tray sent up to her room, afterwards. Ate with ten fingers.

Avilion was completed in 1889, and christened by Adelia. She took the name from Tennyson:

> The island-valley of Avilion;
> Where falls not hail, or rain, or any snow,
> Nor ever wind blows loudly; but it lies
> Deep-meadow'd, happy, fair with orchard lawns
> And bowery hollows crown'd with summer sea, . . .

She had this quotation printed on the left-hand inner side of her Christmas cards. (Tennyson was somewhat out of date, by English standards – Oscar Wilde was in the ascendant then, at least among the younger set – but then, everything in Port Ticonderoga was somewhat out of date.)

People – people in town – must have laughed at her for this quotation: even those with social pretensions referred to her as Her Ladyship or the Duchess, though they were wounded if left off her invitation lists. About her Christmas cards they must have said, *Well, she's out of luck about the hail and snow. Maybe she'll have a word with God about that.* Or perhaps, down at the factories: *Seen any of them bowery hollows around here, anywheres but down the front of her dress?* I know their style and I doubt that it's changed a lot.

Adelia was showing off with her Christmas card, but I believe there was more to it. Avilion was where King Arthur went to die. Surely Adelia's choice of name signifies how hopelessly in exile she considered herself to be: she might be able to call into being by sheer force of will some shoddy facsimile of a happy isle, but it would never be the real thing. She wanted a salon; she wanted artistic people, poets and composers and scientific thinkers and the like, as she had seen while visiting her English third cousins, when her family still had money. A golden life, with wide lawns.

But such people were not to be found in Port Ticonderoga, and Benjamin refused to travel. He needed to be near his factories, he said. Most likely he didn't want to be dragged into a crowd that would sneer at him for his button manufacturing, and where there might be unknown pieces of cutlery lying in wait, and where Adelia would feel ashamed because of him.

Adelia declined to travel without him, to Europe or anywhere else. It might have been too tempting – not to come back. To drift away, shedding money gradually like a deflating blimp, a prey to cads and delectable bounders, sinking down into the unmentionable. With a neckline like hers, she would have been susceptible.

Among other things, Adelia went in for sculpture. There were two stone sphinxes flanking the conservatory – Laura and I used to climb up on their backs – and a capering faun leering from behind a stone bench, with pointed ears and a huge grape leaf scrolled across his private parts like a badge of office; and seated beside the lily pond there was a nymph, a modest girl with small adolescent breasts and a rope of marble hair over one shoulder, one foot dipping tentatively into the water. We used to eat apples beside her, and watch the goldfish nibbling at her toes.

(These pieces of statuary were said to be "authentic," but authentic what? And how had Adelia come by them? I suspect a chain of pilfering – some shady European go-between picking them up for a song, forging their provenance, then fobbing them off long-distance on Adelia and pocketing the difference, judging correctly that a rich American – for so he would have tagged her – wouldn't cotton on.)

Adelia designed the family graveyard monument as well, with its two angels. She wanted my grandfather to dig up his forbears and have them relocated there, in order to give the impression of a dynasty, but he never got around to it. As it turned out, she herself was the first to be buried there.

Did Grandfather Benjamin breathe a sigh of relief when Adelia was gone? He may have grown tired of knowing he could never measure up to her exacting standards, though it's clear he admired her to the point of awe. Nothing about Avilion was to be changed, for instance: no picture in it moved, none of its furniture replaced. Perhaps he considered the house itself her true monument.

And so Laura and I were brought up by her. We grew up inside her house; that is to say, inside her conception of herself. And inside her conception of who we ought to be, but weren't. As she was dead by then, we couldn't argue.

My father was the eldest of three sons, each of whom was given Adelia's idea of a high-toned name: Norval and Edgar and Percival, Arthurian revival with a hint of Wagner. I suppose they should have been thankful they weren't called Uther or Sigmund or Ulric. Grandfather Benjamin doted on his sons, and wanted them to learn the button business, but Adelia had loftier aims. She packed them off to Trinity College School in Port Hope, where Benjamin and his machinery couldn't coarsen them. She appreciated the uses of Benjamin's wealth, but preferred to gloss over the sources of it.

The sons came home for the summer holidays. At boarding school and then at university they'd learned a genial contempt for their father, who couldn't read Latin, not even badly, as they did. They would talk about people he didn't know, sing songs he'd never heard of, tell jokes he couldn't understand. They'd go sailing by moonlight in his little yacht, the *Water Nixie*, named by Adelia – another of her wistful Gothicisms. They'd play the mandolin (Edgar) and banjo (Percival), and furtively drink beer, and foul up the tackle, and leave it for him to unscramble. They'd drive around in one of his two new motor cars, even though the roads around town were so bad half the year – snow, then mud, then dust – that there wasn't much of anywhere to drive. There were rumours of loose girls, at least for the two younger boys, and of money changing hands – well, it was only decent to pay these ladies off so they could get themselves fixed up, and who wanted a lot of unauthorized Chase babies crawling around? – but they were not girls from our town, and so it was not held against the sons; rather the reverse, among men at least. People laughed at them a little, but not too much: they were said to be solid enough, and to have the common touch. Edgar and Percival were known as Eddie and Percy, though my father, being shyer and more dignified, was always Norval. They were pleasant-looking boys, a little wild, as boys were expected to be. What did "wild" mean, exactly?

"They were rascals," Reenie told me, "but they were never scoundrels."

"What's the difference?" I asked.

She sighed. "I only hope you'll never find out," she said.

Adelia died in 1913, of cancer – an unnamed and therefore most likely gynecological variety. During the last month of

Adelia's illness, Reenie's mother was brought in as extra help in the kitchen, and Reenie along with her; she was thirteen by then, and the whole thing made a deep impression on her. "The pain was so bad they'd have to give her morphine, every four hours, they had the nurses around the clock. But she wouldn't stay in bed, she'd bite the bullet, she was always up and beautifully dressed as usual, even though you could tell she was half out of her mind. I used to see her walking around the grounds, in her pale colours and a big hat with a veil. She had lovely posture and more backbone than most men, that one. At the end they had to tie her into her bed, for her own good. Your grandfather was heartbroken, you could see it took the starch right out of him." As time went on and I became harder to impress, Reenie added stifled screams and moans and deathbed vows to this story, though I was never sure of her intent. Was she telling me that I too should display such fortitude – such defiance of pain, such bullet-biting – or was she merely revelling in the harrowing details? Both, no doubt.

By the time Adelia died, the three boys were mostly grown up. Did they miss their mother, did they mourn her? Of course they did. How could they fail to be grateful for her dedication to them? Still, she'd kept them on a tight leash, or as tight a one as she could manage. There must have been some loosening of the ties and collars after she'd been properly dug under.

None of the three sons wanted to go into buttons, for which they had inherited their mother's disdain, though they had not also inherited her realism. They knew money didn't grow on trees, but they had few bright ideas about where it did grow instead. Norval – my father – thought he might go into law and then eventually take up politics, as he had plans for improving the country. The other two wanted to travel: once Percy had finished college, they intended to make a prospecting expedition to South America, in search of gold. The open road beckoned.

Who then was to take charge of the Chase industries? Would there be no Chase and Sons? If not, why had Benjamin worked his fingers to the bone? By this time he'd convinced himself he'd done it for some reason apart from his own ambitions, his own desires – some noble end. He'd built up a legacy, he wanted to pass it on, from generation to generation.

This must have been the reproachful undertone of more than one discussion, around the dinner table, over the port. But the boys dug in their heels. You can't force a young man to devote his life to button-making if he doesn't want to. They did not set out to disappoint their father, not on purpose, but neither did they wish to shoulder the lumpy, enervating burden of the mundane.

The trousseau

The new fan has now been purchased. The parts of it came in a large cardboard box, and were assembled by Walter, who carted his toolbox over and screwed it all together. When he'd finished, he said, "That should fix her."

Boats are female for Walter, as are busted car engines and broken lamps and radios – items of any kind that can be fiddled with by men adroit with gadgetry, and restored to a condition as good as new. Why do I find this reassuring? Perhaps I believe, in some childish, faith-filled corner of myself, that Walter might yet take out his pliers and his ratchet set and do the same for me.

The tall fan is installed in the bedroom. I've hauled the old one downstairs to the porch, where it's aimed at the back of my neck. The sensation is pleasant but unnerving, as if a hand of cool air lies gently on my shoulder. Thus aerated, I sit at my wooden table, scratching away with my pen. No, not scratching – pens no longer scratch. The words roll smoothly and soundlessly enough across the page; it's getting them to flow down the arm, it's squeezing them out through the fingers, that is so difficult.

It's almost dusk now. There's no wind; the sound of the rapids washing up through the garden is like one long breath. The blue flowers blend into the air, the red ones are black, the white ones shine, phosphorescent. The tulips have shed their petals, leaving the pistils bare – black, snout-like, sexual. The peonies are almost finished, bedraggled and limp as damp tissue, but the lilies have come out; also the phlox. The last of the mock oranges have dropped their blossoms, leaving the grass strewn with white confetti.

*

In July of 1914, my mother married my father. This called for an explanation, I felt, considering everything.

My best hope was Reenie. When I was at the age to take an interest in such things – ten, eleven, twelve, thirteen – I used to sit at the kitchen table and pick her like a lock.

She'd been less than seventeen when she'd come to Avilion full-time, from a row house on the southeast bank of the Jogues, where the factory workers lived. She said she was Scotch and Irish, not the Catholic Irish, of course, meaning her grandmothers were. She'd started out as a nursemaid for me, but as a result of turnovers and attrition she now our mainstay. How old was she? *None of your beeswax. Old enough to know better. And that's enough of that.* If prodded about her own life, she would clam up. *I keep myself to myself,* she'd say. How prudent that seemed to me once. How miserly, now.

But she knew the family histories, or at least something about them. What she would tell me varied in relation to my age, and also in relation to how distracted she was at the time. Nevertheless, in this way I collected enough fragments of the past to make a reconstruction of it, which must have borne as much relation to the real thing as a mosaic portrait would to the original. I didn't want realism anyway: I wanted things to be highly coloured, simple in outline, without ambiguity, which is what most children want when it comes to the stories of their parents. They want a postcard.

My father had proposed (said Reenie) at a skating party. There was an inlet – an old mill pond – upstream from the falls, where the water moved more slowly. When the winters were cold enough, a sheet of ice would form there that was thick enough to skate on. Here the young peoples' church group would hold its skating parties, which were not called parties but outings.

My mother was a Methodist, but my father was Anglican: thus my mother was below my father's level socially, as such things were accounted then. (If she'd lived, my Grandmother Adelia would never have allowed the marriage, or so I decided later. My mother would have been too far down the ladder for her – also too prudish, too earnest, too provincial. Adelia would have dragged my father off to Montreal – hooked him up to a debutante, at the very least. Someone with better clothes.)

My mother had been young, only eighteen, but she was not a silly, flighty girl, said Reenie. She'd been teaching school; you could be a teacher then when you were under twenty. She didn't *have* to teach: her father was the senior lawyer for Chase Industries, and they were "comfortably off." But, like her own mother, who'd died when she was nine, my mother took her religion seriously. She believed you should help those less fortunate than yourself. She'd taken up teaching the poor as a sort of missionary work, said Reenie admiringly. (Reenie often admired acts of my mother's that she would have thought it stupid to perform herself. As for the poor, she'd grown up among them and considered them feckless. You could teach them till you were blue in the face, but with most you'd just be beating your head against a brick wall, she'd say. *But your mother, bless her good heart, she could never see it.*)

There's a snapshot of my mother at the Normal School, in London, Ontario, taken with two other girls; all three are standing on the front steps of their boarding house, laughing, their arms entwined. The winter snow lies heaped to either side; icicles drip from the roof. My mother is wearing a seal-skin coat; from underneath her hat the ends of her fine hair crackle. She must already have acquired the pince-nez that preceded the owlish glasses I remember – she was near-sighted early – but in this picture she doesn't have them on. One of her feet in its fur-topped boot is visible, the ankle turned coquettishly. She looks courageous, dashing even, like a boyish buccaneer.

After graduating, she'd accepted a position at a one-room school, farther west and north, in what was then the back country. She'd been shocked by the experience – by the poverty, the ignorance, the lice. The children there had been sewn into their underwear in the fall and not unsewn until the spring, a detail that has remained in my mind as particularly squalid. *Of course*, said Reenie, *it was no place for a lady like your mother*.

But my mother felt she was accomplishing something – *doing something* – for at least a few of those unfortunate children, or she hoped she was; and then she'd come home for the Christmas holidays. Her pallor and thinness were commented upon: roses were required in her cheeks. So there she was at the skating party, on the frozen mill pond, in company with my father. He'd laced up her skates for her first, kneeling on one knee.

They'd known each other for some time through their respective fathers. There had been previous, decorous encounters. They'd acted together, in the last of Adelia's garden theatricals – he'd been Ferdinand, she Miranda, in a bowdlerized version of *The Tempest* in which both sex and Caliban had been minimized. In a dress of shell pink, said Reenie, with a wreath of roses; and she spoke the words out perfect, just like an angel. *O brave new world, that has such people in't!* And the unfocused gaze of her dazzled, limpid, myopic eyes. You could see how it all came about.

My father could have looked elsewhere, for a wife with more money, but he must have wanted the tried and true: someone he could depend on. Despite his high spirits – he'd had high spirits once, apparently – he was a serious young man, said Reenie, implying that otherwise my mother would have rejected him. They were both in their own ways earnest; they both wanted to achieve some worthy end or other, change the world for the better. Such alluring, such perilous ideals!

After they had skated around the pond several times, my father asked my mother to marry him. I expect he did it awkwardly, but awkwardness in men was a sign of sincerity then. At this instant, although they must have been touching at shoulder and hip, neither one was looking at the other; they were side by side, right hands joined across the front, left hands joined at the back. (What was she wearing? Reenie knew this too. A blue knitted scarf, a tam and knitted gloves to match. She'd knitted them herself. A winter coat of walking length, hunting green. A handkerchief tucked into her sleeve – an item she never forgot, according to Reenie, unlike some she could name.)

What did my mother do at this crucial moment? She studied the ice. She did not reply at once. This meant yes.

All around them were the snow-covered rocks and the white icicles – everything white. Under their feet was the ice, which was white also, and under that the river water, with its eddies and undertows, dark but unseen. This was how I pictured that time, the time before Laura and I were born – so blank, so innocent, so solid to all appearances, but thin ice all the same. Beneath the surfaces of things was the unsaid, boiling slowly.

Then came the ring, and the announcement in the papers; and then – once Mother had returned from completing the teaching year, which it was her duty to do – there were formal teas. Beautifully set out they were, with rolled asparagus sandwiches and sandwiches with watercress in them, and three kinds of cake – a light, a dark, and a fruit – and the tea itself in silver services, with roses on the table, white or pink or perhaps a pale yellow, but not red. Red was not for engagement teas. Why not? *You'll find out later*, said Reenie.

Then there was the trousseau. Reenie enjoyed reciting the details of this – the nightgowns, the peignoirs, the kinds of lace on them, the pillowcases embroidered with monograms, the sheets and petticoats. She spoke of cupboards and of bureau drawers and linen closets, and of what sorts of things should be kept in them, neatly folded. There was no mention of the bodies over which all these textiles would eventually be draped: weddings, for Reenie, were mostly a question of cloth, at least on the face of it.

Then there was the list of guests to be compiled, the invitations to be written, the flowers to be selected, and so on up to the wedding.

And then, after the wedding, there was the war. Love, then marriage, then catastrophe. In Reenie's version, it seemed inevitable.

The war began in the August of 1914, shortly after my parents' marriage. All three brothers enlisted at once, no question about it. Amazing to consider now, this lack of question. There's a photo of them, a fine trio in their uniforms, with grave, naive foreheads and tender moustaches, their smiles nonchalant, their eyes resolute, posing as the soldiers they had not yet become. Father is the tallest. He always kept this photo on his desk.

They joined the Royal Canadian Regiment, the one you always joined if you were from Port Ticonderoga. Almost immediately they were posted to Bermuda to relieve the British regiment stationed there, and so, for the war's first year, they spent their time going on parade and playing cricket. Also chafing at the bit, or so their letters claimed.

Grandfather Benjamin read these letters avidly. As time wore on without a victory for either side, he became more and more jittery and uncertain. This was not the way things ought to have gone. The irony was that his business was booming. He'd recently expanded into celluloid and rubber, for the buttons that is, which allowed for higher volumes; and due to the political contacts Adelia had helped him to make, his factories received a great many orders to supply the troops. He was as honest as he'd always been, he didn't deliver shoddy goods, he was not a war profiteer in that sense. But it cannot be said that he did not profit.

War is good for the button trade. So many buttons are lost in a war, and have to be replaced – whole boxfuls, whole truckloads of buttons at a time. They're blown to pieces, they sink into the ground, they go up in flames. The same can be said for undergarments. From a financial point of view, the war was a miraculous fire: a huge, alchemical conflagration, the rising smoke of which transformed itself into money. Or it did for my grandfather. But this fact no longer delighted his soul or propped up his sense of his own rectitude, as it might have done in earlier, more self-satisfied years. He wanted his sons back. Not that they'd gone anywhere dangerous yet: they were still in Bermuda, marching around in the sun.

Following their honeymoon (to the Finger Lakes, in New York State), my parents had been staying at Avilion until they could set up their own establishment, and Mother remained there to supervise my grandfather's household. They were short-staffed, because all able hands were needed either for the factories or for the army, but also because it was felt that Avilion should set an example by reducing expenditures. Mother insisted on plain meals – pot roast on Wednesdays, baked beans on a Sunday evening – which suited my grandfather fine. He'd never really been comfortable with Adelia's fancy menus.

In August of 1915, the Royal Canadian Regiment was ordered back to Halifax, to equip for France. It stayed in port for over a week, taking on supplies and new recruits and exchanging tropical uniforms for warmer clothing. The men were issued with Ross rifles, which would later jam in the mud, leaving them helpless.

My mother took the train to Halifax to see my father off. It was crammed with men en route to the Front; she could not get a sleeper, so she travelled sitting up. There were feet in the aisles, and bundles, and spittoons; coughing, snoring – drunken snoring, no doubt. As she looked at the boyish faces around her, the war became real to her, not as an idea but as a physical presence. Her young husband might be killed. His body might perish; it might be torn apart; it might become part of the sacrifice that – it was now clear – would have to be made. Along with this realization came desperation and a shrinking terror, but also – I'm sure – a measure of bleak pride.

I don't know where the two of them stayed in Halifax, or for how long. Was it a respectable hotel or, because rooms were scarce, a cheap dive, a harbourside flophouse? Was it for a few days, a night, a few hours? What passed between them, what was said? The usual sorts of things, I suppose, but what were they? It is no longer possible to know. Then the ship with the regiment in it set sail – it was the SS *Caledonian* – and my mother stood on the dock with the other wives, waving and weeping. Or perhaps not weeping: she would have found it self-indulgent.

Somewhere in France. I cannot describe what is happening here, wrote my father, *and so I will not attempt it. We can only trust that this war is for the best, and that civilization will be preserved and advanced by it. The casualties are* (word scratched out) *numerous. I never knew before what men are capable of. What must be endured is beyond* (word scratched out). *I think of all at home every day, and especially you, my dearest Liliana.*

*

At Avilion, my mother set her will in motion. She believed in public service; she felt she had to roll up her sleeves and do something useful for the war effort. She organized a Comfort Circle, which collected money through rummage sales. This was spent on small boxes containing tobacco and candies, which were sent off to the trenches. She threw open Avilion for these functions, which (said Reenie) was hard on the floors. In addition to the rummage sales, every Tuesday afternoon her group knitted for the troops, in the drawing room – washcloths for the beginners, scarves for the intermediates, balaclavas and gloves for the experts. Soon another battalion of recruits was added, on Thursdays – older, less literate women from south of the Jogues who could knit in their sleep. These made baby garments for the Armenians, said to be starving, and for something called Overseas Refugees. After two hours of knitting, a frugal tea was served in the dining room, with Tristan and Iseult looking wanly down.

When maimed soldiers began to appear, on the streets and in the hospitals of nearby towns – Port Ticonderoga did not yet have a hospital – my mother visited them. She opted for the worst cases – men who were not (said Reenie) likely to win any beauty contests – and from these visits she would return drained and shaken, and might even weep, in the kitchen, drinking the cocoa Reenie would make to prop her up. She did not spare herself, said Reenie. She ruined her health. She went beyond her strength, especially considering her condition.

What virtue was once attached to this notion – of going beyond your strength, of not sparing yourself, of ruining your health! Nobody is born with that kind of selflessness: it can be acquired only by the most relentless discipline, a crushing-out of natural inclination, and by my time the knack or secret of it must have been lost. Or perhaps I didn't try, having suffered from the effects it had on my mother.

As for Laura, she was not selfless, not at all. Instead she was skinless, which is a different thing.

I was born in early June of 1916. Shortly afterwards, Percy was killed in heavy shelling at the Ypres Salient, and in July Eddie died at the Somme. Or it was assumed he had died: where he'd been last seen there was a large crater. These were hard events for my mother, but much harder for my grandfather. In August he had a devastating stroke, which affected his speech and his memory.

Unofficially, my mother took over the running of the factories. She interposed herself between my grandfather – said to be convalescing – and everyone else, and met daily with the male secretary and with the various factory foremen. As she was the only one who could understand what my grandfather was saying, or who claimed she could, she became his interpreter; and as the only one allowed to hold his hand, she guided his signature; and who's to say she didn't use her own judgment sometimes?

Not that there were no problems. When the war began, a sixth of the workers had been women. By the end of it this number was two-thirds. The remaining men were old, or partially crippled, or in some other way unfit for war. These resented the ascendancy of the women, and grumbled about them or made vulgar jokes, and in their turn the women considered them weaklings or slackers and held them in ill-disguised contempt. The natural order of things – what my mother felt to be the natural order – was turning turtle. Still, the pay was good, and money greases the wheels, and on the whole my mother was able to keep things running smoothly enough.

I imagine my grandfather, sitting in his library at night, in his green leather-covered chair studded with brass nails, at his desk, which was mahogany. His fingers are tented together, those of his feeling hand and those of his hand without feeling. He's listening for someone. The door is half-open; he sees a shadow outside it. He says, "Come in" – he intends to say it – but nobody enters, or answers.

The brusque nurse arrives. She asks him what he can be thinking of, sitting alone in the dark like that. He hears a sound, but it isn't words, it's more like ravens; he doesn't answer. She takes him by the arm, lifts him easily out of his chair, shuffles him off to bed. Her white skirts rustle. He hears a dry wind, blowing through weedy autumn fields. He hears the whisper of snow.

Did he know his two sons were dead? Was he wishing them alive again, safe home? Would it have been a sadder ending for him, to have had his wish come true? It might have been – it often is – but such thoughts are not consoling.

The gramophone

Last night I watched the weather channel, as is my habit.
Elsewhere in the world there are floods: roiling brown water,
bloated cows floating by, survivors huddled on rooftops.
Thousands have drowned. Global warming is held accountable: people must stop burning things up, it is said. Gasoline,
oil, whole forests. But they won't stop. Greed and hunger lash
them on, as usual.

Where was I? I turn back the page: the war is still raging. *Raging*
is what they used to say, for wars; still do, for all I know. But on
this page, a fresh, clean page, I will cause the war to end – I alone,
with a stroke of my black plastic pen. All I have to do is write:
1918. November 11. Armistice Day.

There. It's over. The guns are silent. The men who are left
alive look up at the sky, their faces grimed, their clothing
sodden; they climb out of their foxholes and filthy burrows.
Both sides feel they have lost. In the towns, in the countryside, here and across the ocean, the church bells all begin to
ring. (I can remember that, the bells ringing. It's one of my
first memories. It was so strange – the air was so full of sound,
and at the same time so empty. Reenie took me outside to
hear. There were tears running down her face. *Thank God*, she
said. The day was chilly, there was frost on the fallen leaves, a
skim of ice on the lily pond. I broke it with a stick. Where was
Mother?)

Father had been wounded at the Somme, but he'd recovered
from that and had been made a second lieutenant. He was
wounded again at Vimy Ridge, though not severely, and was
made a captain. He was wounded again at Bourlon Wood, this

time worse. It was while he was recovering in England that the war ended.

He missed the jubilant welcome for the returning troops at Halifax, the victory parades and so forth, but there was a special reception in Port Ticonderoga just for him. The train stopped. Cheering broke out. Hands reached up to help him down, then hesitated. He emerged. He had one good eye and one good leg. His face was gaunt, seamed, fanatical.

Farewells can be shattering, but returns are surely worse. Solid flesh can never live up to the bright shadow cast by its absence. Time and distance blur the edges; then suddenly the beloved has arrived, and it's noon with its merciless light, and every spot and pore and wrinkle and bristle stands clear.

Thus my mother and my father. How could either of them atone to the other for having changed so much? For failing to be what was expected. How could there not be grudges? Grudges held silently and unjustly, because there was nobody to blame, or nobody you could put your finger on. The war was not a person. Why blame a hurricane?

There they stand, on the railway platform. The town band plays, brass mostly. He's in his uniform; his medals are like holes shot in the cloth, through which the dull gleam of his real, metal body can be seen. Beside him, invisible, are his brothers – the two lost boys, the ones he feels he has lost. My mother is there in her best dress, a belted affair with lapels, and a hat with a crisp ribbon. She smiles tremulously. Neither knows quite what to do. The newspaper camera catches them in its flash; they stare, as if surprised in crime. My father is wearing a black patch over his right eye. His left eye glares balefully. Underneath the patch, not yet revealed, is a web of scarred flesh, his missing eye the spider.

"Chase Heir Hero Returns," the paper will trumpet. That's another thing: my father is now the heir, which is to say he's fatherless as well as brotherless. The kingdom is in his hands. It feels like mud.

Did my mother cry? It's possible. They must have kissed awkwardly, as if at a box social, one for which he'd bought the wrong ticket. This wasn't what he'd remembered, this efficient, careworn woman, with a pince-nez like some maiden aunt's glinting on a silver chain around her neck. They were now strangers, and — it must have occurred to them — they always had been. How harsh the light was. How much older they'd become. There was no trace of the young man who'd once knelt so deferentially on the ice to lace up her skates, or of the young woman who'd sweetly accepted this homage.

Something else materialized like a sword between them. Of course he'd had other women, the kind who hung around battlefields, taking advantage. Whores, not to mince a word my mother would never have pronounced. She must have been able to tell, the first time he laid a hand on her: the timidity, the reverence, would have been gone. Probably he'd held out against temptation through Bermuda, then through England, up to the time when Eddie and Percy were killed and he himself was wounded. After that he'd clutched at life, at whatever handfuls of it might come within his reach. How could she fail to understand his need for it, under the circumstances?

She did understand, or at least she understood that she was supposed to understand. She understood, and said nothing about it, and prayed for the power to forgive, and did forgive. But he can't have found living with her forgiveness all that easy. Breakfast in a haze of forgiveness: coffee with forgiveness, porridge with forgiveness, forgiveness on the buttered toast. He would have been helpless against it, for how can you repudiate something that is never spoken? She resented, too, the nurse, or the many nurses, who had tended my father in the various hospitals. She wished him to owe his recovery to her alone – to her care, to her tireless devotion. That is the other side of selflessness: its tyranny.

However, my father wasn't so healthy as all that. In fact he was a shattered wreck, as witness the shouts in the dark, the nightmares, the sudden fits of rage, the bowl or glass thrown against the wall or floor, though never at her. He was broken, and needed mending: therefore she could still be useful. She would create around him an atmosphere of calm, she would indulge him, she would coddle him, she would put flowers on his breakfast table and arrange his favourite dinners. At least he hadn't caught some evil disease.

However, a much worse thing had happened: my father was now an atheist. Over the trenches God had burst like a balloon, and there was nothing left of him but grubby little scraps of hypocrisy. Religion was just a stick to beat the soldiers with, and anyone who declared otherwise was full of pious drivel. What had been served by the gallantry of Percy and Eddie – by their bravery, their hideous deaths? What had been accomplished? They'd been killed by the blunderings of a pack of incompetent and criminal old men who might just as well have cut their throats and heaved them over the side of the SS *Caledonian*. All the talk of fighting for God and Civilization made him vomit.

My mother was appalled. Was he saying that Percy and Eddie had died for no higher purpose? That all those poor men had died for nothing? As for God, who else had seen them through this time of trial and suffering? She begged him at the very least to keep his atheism to himself. Then she was deeply ashamed for having asked this – as if what mattered most to her was the opinion of the neighbours, and not the relationship in which my father's living soul stood to God.

He did respect her wish, though. He saw the necessity of it. Anyway, he only said such things when he'd been drinking. He'd never used to drink before the war, not in any regular, determined way, but he did now. He drank and paced the floor, his bad foot dragging. After a while he would begin to shake. My mother would attempt to soothe him, but he didn't want to be soothed. He would climb up into the stumpy turret of Avilion, saying he wished to smoke. Really it was an excuse to be alone. Up there he would talk to himself and slam against the walls, and end by drinking himself numb. He left my mother's presence to do this because he was still a gentleman in his own view, or he held on to the shreds of the costume. He didn't want to frighten her. Also he felt badly, I suppose, that her well-meant ministrations grated on him so much.

Light step, heavy step, light step, heavy step, like an animal with one foot in a trap. Groaning and muffled shouts. Broken glass. These sounds would wake me up: the floor of the turret was above my room.

Then there would be footsteps descending; then silence, a black outline looming outside the closed oblong of my bedroom door. I couldn't see him there, but I could feel him, a shambling monster with one eye, so sad. I'd become used to the sounds, I didn't think he would ever hurt me, but I treated him gingerly all the same.

I don't wish to give the impression that he did this every night. Also these sessions – seizures, perhaps – became fewer and farther apart, in time. But you could see one coming on by the tightening of my mother's mouth. She had a kind of radar, she could detect the waves of his building rage.

Do I mean to say he didn't love her? Not at all. He loved her; in some ways he was devoted to her. But he couldn't reach her, and it was the same on her side. It was as if they'd drunk some fatal potion that would keep them forever apart, even though they lived in the same house, ate at the same table, slept in the same bed.

What would that be like – to long, to yearn for one who is right there before your eyes, day in and day out? I'll never know.

After some months my father began his disreputable rambles. Not in our town though, or not at first. He'd take the train in to Toronto, "on business," and go drinking, and also tomcatting, as it was then called. Word got around, surprisingly quickly, as a scandal is likely to do. Oddly enough, both my mother and my father were more respected in town because of it. Who could blame him, considering? As for her, despite what she had to put up with, not one word of complaint was ever heard to cross her lips. Which was entirely as it should be.

(How do I know all these things? I don't know them, not in the usual sense of knowing. But in households like ours there's often more in silences than in what is actually said – in the lips pressed together, the head turned away, the quick sideways glance. The shoulders drawn up as if carrying a heavy weight. No wonder we took to listening at doors, Laura and I.)

My father had an array of walking sticks, with special handles – ivory, silver, ebony. He made a point of dressing neatly. He'd never expected to end up running the family business, but now that he'd taken it on he intended to do it well. He could have sold out, but as it happened there were no buyers, not then, or not at his price. Also he felt he had an obligation, if not to the memory of his father, then to those of his dead brothers. He had the letterhead changed to Chase and Sons, even though there was only one son left. He wanted to have sons of his own, two of them preferably, to replace the lost ones. He wanted to persevere.

The men in his factories at first revered him. It wasn't just the medals. As soon as the war was over, the women had stepped aside or else been pushed, and their jobs had been filled by the returning men – whatever men were still capable of holding a job, that is. But there weren't enough jobs to go around: the wartime demand had ended. All over the country there were shutdowns and layoffs, but not in my father's factories. He hired, he overhired. He hired veterans. He said the country's lack of gratitude was despicable, and that its businessmen should now pay back something of what was owed. Very few of them did, though. They turned a blind eye, but my father, who had a real blind eye, could not turn it. Thus began his reputation for being a renegade, and a bit of a fool.

To all appearances I was my father's child. I looked more like him; I'd inherited his scowl, his dogged skepticism. (As well as, eventually, his medals. He left them to me.) Reenie would say – when I was being recalcitrant – that I had a hard nature and she knew where I got it from. Laura on the other hand was my mother's child. She had the piousness, in some ways; she had the high, pure forehead.

But appearances are deceptive. I could never have driven off a bridge. My father could have. My mother couldn't.

Here we are in the autumn of 1919, the three of us together – my father, my mother, myself – making an effort. It's November; it's almost bedtime. We're sitting in the morning room at Avilion. It has a fireplace in it, with a fire, as the weather has turned cool. My mother is recovering from a recent, mysterious illness, said to have something to do with her nerves. She's mending clothes. She doesn't need to do this – she could hire someone – but she wants to do it; she likes to have something to occupy her hands. She's sewing on a button, torn from one of my dresses: I am said to be hard on my clothes. On the round table at her elbow is her sweetgrass-bordered sewing basket, woven by Indians, with her scissors and her spools of thread and her wooden darning egg; also her new round glasses, keeping watch. She doesn't need them for close work.

Her dress is sky blue, with a broad white collar and white cuffs edged in piquet. Her hair has begun to go white prematurely. She would no more think of dyeing it than she would of cutting off her hand, and thus she has a young woman's face in a nest of thistledown. It's parted in the middle, this hair, and flows back in wide, springy waves to an intricate knot of twists and coils at the back of her head. (By the time of her death five years later, it would be bobbed, more fashionable, less compelling.) Her eyelids are lowered, her cheeks rounded, as is her stomach; her half-smile is tender. The electric lamp with its yellow-pink shade casts a soft glow over her face.

Across from her is my father, on a settee. He leans back against the cushions, but he's restless. He has his hand on the knee of his bad leg; the leg jiggles up and down. (*The good leg, the bad leg* – these terms are of interest to me. What has the bad leg done, to be called bad? Is its hidden, mutilated state a punishment?)

I sit beside him, though not too close. His arm lies along the sofa back behind me, but does not touch. I have my alphabet book; I'm reading to him from it, to show that I can read. I can't though, I've only memorized the shapes of the letters, and the words that go with the pictures. On an end table there's a gramophone, with a speaker rising up out of it like a huge metal flower. My own voice sounds to me like the voice that sometimes comes out of it: small and thin and faraway; something you could turn off with a finger.

A is for Apple Pie,
Baked fresh and hot:
Some have a little,
And others a lot.

I glance up at my father to see if he's paying any attention. Sometimes when you speak to him he doesn't hear. He catches me looking, smiles faintly down at me.

B is for Baby,
So pink and so sweet,
With two tiny hands
And two tiny feet.

My father has gone back to gazing out the window. (Did he place himself outside this window, looking in? An orphan, forever excluded – a night wanderer? This is what he was supposed to have been fighting for – this fireside idyll, this comfortable scene out of a Shredded Wheat advertisement: the rounded, rosy-cheeked wife, so kind and good, the obedient, worshipful child. This flatness, this boredom. Could it be he was feeling a certain nostalgia for the war, despite its stench and meaningless carnage? For that questionless life of instinct?)

F is for Fire,
Good servant, bad master.
When left to itself
It burns faster and faster.

The picture in the book is of a leaping man covered in flames – wings of fire coming from his heels and shoulders, little fiery horns sprouting from his head. He's looking over his shoulder with a mischievous, enticing smile, and he has no clothes on. The fire can't hurt him, nothing can hurt him. I am in love with him for this reason. I've added extra flames with my crayons.

My mother jabs her needle through the button, cuts the thread. I read on in a voice of increasing anxiety, through suave M and N, through quirky Q and hard R and the sibilant menaces of S. My father stares into the flames, watching the fields and woods and houses and towns and men and brothers go up in smoke, his bad leg moving by itself like a dog's running in dreams. This is his home, this besieged castle; he is its werewolf. The chilly lemon-coloured sunset outside the window fades to grey. I don't know it yet, but Laura is about to be born.

Bread day

Not enough rain, say the farmers. The cicadas pierce the air with their searing one-note calls; dust eddies across the roads; from the weedy patches at the verges, grasshoppers whir. The leaves of the maples hang from their branches like limp gloves; on the sidewalk my shadow crackles.

I walk early, before the full blare of the sun. The doctor eggs me on: I'm making progress, he tells me; but towards what? I think of my heart as my companion on an endless forced march, the two of us roped together, unwilling conspirators in some plot or tactic we've got no handle on. Where are we going? Towards the next day. It hasn't escaped me that the object that keeps me alive is the same one that will kill me. In this way it's like love, or a certain kind of it.

Today I went again to the cemetery. Someone had left a bunch of orange and red zinnias on Laura's grave; hot-coloured flowers, far from soothing. They were withering by the time I got to them, though they still gave off their peppery smell. I suspect they'd been stolen from the flower beds in front of The Button Factory, by a cheapskate devotee or else a mildly crazy one; but then, it's the sort of thing Laura herself would have done. She had only the haziest notions of ownership.

On my way back I stopped in at the doughnut shop: it was heating up outside, and I wanted some shade. The place is far from new; indeed it's almost seedy, despite its jaunty modernity – the pale-yellow tiles, the white plastic tables bolted to the floor, their moulded chairs attached. It reminds me of some institution or other; a kindergarten in a poorer neighbourhood perhaps, or a drop-in centre for the mentally challenged. Not too many things you could throw around or use for stabbing:

even the cutlery is plastic. The odour is of deep-fat-frying oil blended with pine-scented disinfectant, with a wash of tepid coffee over all.

I purchased a small iced tea and an Old-fashioned Glazed, which squeaked between my teeth like Styrofoam. After I'd consumed half of it, which was all I could get down, I picked my way across the slippery floor to the women's washroom. In the course of my walks I've been compiling a map in my head of all the easily accessible washrooms in Port Ticonderoga – so useful if you're caught short – and the one in the doughnut shop is my current favourite. Not that it's cleaner than the rest, or more likely to have toilet paper, but it offers inscriptions. They all do, but in most locales these are painted over frequently, whereas in the doughnut shop they remain on view much longer. Thus you have not only the text, but the commentary on it as well.

The best sequence at the moment is the one in the middle cubicle. The first sentence is in pencil, in rounded lettering like those on Roman tombs, engraved deeply in the paint: *Don't Eat Anything You Aren't Prepared to Kill.*

Then, in green marker: *Don't Kill Anything You Aren't Prepared to Eat.*

Under that, in ballpoint, *Don't Kill.*

Under that, in purple marker: *Don't Eat.*

And under that, the last word to date, in bold black lettering: *Fuck Vegetarians – "All Gods Are Carnivorous" – Laura Chase.*

Thus Laura lives on.

It took Laura a long time to get herself born into this world, said Reenie. *It was like she couldn't decide whether or not it was really such a smart idea. Then she was sickly at first, and we almost lost her – I guess she was still making up her mind. But in the end she decided to give it a try, and so she took ahold of life, and got some better.*

Reenie believed that people decided when it was their time to die; similarly, they had a voice in whether or not they would be born. Once I'd reached the talking-back age, I used to say, *I never asked to be born*, as if that were a clinching argument; and Reenie would retort, *Of course you did. Just like everyone else.* Once alive you were on the hook for it, as far as Reenie was concerned.

After Laura's birth my mother was more tired than usual. She lost altitude; she lost resilience. Her will faltered; her days took on a quality of trudging. She had to rest more, said the doctor. She was not a well woman, said Reenie to Mrs. Hillcoate, who came in to help with the laundry. It was as if my former mother had been stolen away by the elves, and this other mother – this older and greyer and saggier and more discouraged one – had been left behind in her place. I was only four then, and was frightened by the change in her, and wanted to be held and reassured; but my mother no longer had the energy for this. (Why do I say *no longer*? Her comportment as a mother had always been instructive rather than cherishing. At heart she remained a schoolteacher.)

I soon found that if I could keep quiet, without clamouring for attention, and above all if I could be helpful – especially with the baby, with Laura, watching beside her and rocking her cradle so she would sleep, not a thing she did easily or for long – I would be permitted to remain in the same room with my mother. If not, I would be sent away. So that was the accommodation I made: silence, helpfulness.

I should have screamed. I should have thrown tantrums. It's the squeaky wheel that gets the grease, as Reenie used to say.

(There I sat on Mother's night table, in a silver frame, in a dark dress with a white lace collar, visible hand clutching the baby's crocheted white blanket in an awkward, ferocious grip, eyes accusing the camera or whoever was wielding it. Laura herself is almost out of sight, in this picture. Nothing can be seen of her but the top of her downy head, and one tiny hand, fingers curled around my thumb. Was I angry because I'd been told to hold the baby, or was I in fact defending it? Shielding it – reluctant to let it go?)

Laura was an uneasy baby, though more anxious than fractious. She was an uneasy small child as well. Closet doors worried her, and bureau drawers. It was as if she were always listening, to something in the distance or under the floor – something that was coming closer soundlessly, like a train made of wind. She had unaccountable crises – a dead crow would start her weeping, a cat smashed by a car, a dark cloud in a clear sky. On the other hand, she had an uncanny resistance to physical pain: if she burnt her mouth or cut herself, as a rule she didn't cry. It was ill will, the ill will of the universe, that distressed her.

She was particularly alarmed by the maimed veterans on the street corners – the loungers, the pencil-sellers, the panhandlers, too shattered to work at anything. One glaring red-faced man with no legs who pushed himself around on a flat cart would always set her off. Perhaps it was the fury in his eyes.

As most small children do, Laura believed words meant what they said, but she carried it to extremes. You couldn't say *Get lost* or *Go jump in the lake* and expect no consequences. *What did you say to Laura? Don't you ever learn?* Reenie would scold. But even Reenie herself didn't learn altogether. She once told Laura to bite her tongue because that would keep the questions from coming out, and after that Laura couldn't chew for days.

★

Now I am coming to my mother's death. It would be trite to say that this event changed everything, but it would also be true, and so I will write it down:

This event changed everything.

It happened on a Tuesday. A bread day. All of our bread – enough in a batch for the entire week – was made in the kitchen at Avilion. Although there was a small bakery in Port Ticonderoga by then, Reenie said store bread was for the lazy, and the baker added chalk to it to stretch out the flour and also extra yeast to swell the loaves up with air so you'd think you were getting more. And so she made the bread herself.

The kitchen of Avilion wasn't dark, like the sooty Victorian cavern it must once have been, thirty years before. Instead it was white – white walls, white enamelled table, white wood-burning range, black-and-white tiled floor – with daffodil-yellow curtains at the new, enlarged windows. (It had been redone after the war as one of my father's sheepish, propitia-tory gifts to my mother.) Reenie considered this kitchen the latest thing, and as a result of my mother's having taught her about germs and their nasty ways and their hiding places, she kept it faultlessly clean.

On bread days Reenie would give us scraps of dough for bread men, with raisins for the eyes and buttons. Then she would bake them for us. I would eat mine, but Laura would save hers up. Once Reenie found a whole row of them in Laura's top drawer, hard as rock, wrapped up in her handker-chiefs like tiny bun-faced mummies. Reenie said they would attract mice and would have to go straight into the garbage, but Laura held out for a mass burial in the kitchen garden, behind the rhubarb bush. She said there had to be prayers. If not, she would never eat her dinner any more. She was always a hard bargainer, once she got down to it.

Reenie dug the hole. It was the gardener's day off; she used his spade, which was off-limits to anyone else, but this was an emergency. "God pity her husband," said Reenie, as Laura laid her bread men out in a neat row. "She's stubborn as a pig."

"I'm not going to have a husband anyway," said Laura. "I'm going to live by myself in the garage."

"I'm not going to have one either," I said, not to be outdone.

"Fat chance of that," said Reenie. "You like your nice soft bed. You'd have to sleep on the cement and get all covered in grease and oil."

"I'm going to live in the conservatory," I said.

"It's not heated any more," said Reenie. "You'd freeze to death in the winters."

"I'll sleep in one of the motor cars," said Laura.

On that horrible Tuesday we'd had breakfast in the kitchen, with Reenie. It was oatmeal porridge and toast with marmalade. Sometimes we had it with Mother, but that day she was too tired. Mother was stricter, and made us sit up straight and eat the crusts. "Remember the starving Armenians," she would say.

Perhaps the Armenians were no longer starving by then. The war was long over, order had been restored. But their plight must have remained in Mother's mind as a kind of slogan. A slogan, an invocation, a prayer, a charm. Toast crusts must be eaten in memory of these Armenians, whoever they may have been; not to eat them was a sacrilege. Laura and I must have understood the weight of this charm, because it never failed to work.

Mother didn't eat her crusts that day. I remember that. Laura went on at her about it – *What about the crusts, what about the starving Armenians?* – until finally Mother admitted that she didn't feel well. When she said that, I felt an electric chill run through me, because I knew it. I'd known it all along.

Reenie said God made people the way she herself made bread, and that was why the mothers' tummies got fat when they were going to have a baby: it was the dough rising. She said her dimples were God's thumbprints. She said she had three dimples and some people had none, because God didn't make everyone the same, otherwise he would just get bored of it all, and so he dished things out unevenly. It didn't seem fair, but it would come out fair at the end.

Laura was six, by the time I'm remembering. I was nine. I knew that babies weren't made out of bread dough – that was a story for little kids like Laura. Still, no detailed explanation had been offered.

In the afternoons Mother had been sitting in the gazebo, knitting. She was knitting a tiny sweater, like the ones she still knitted for the Overseas Refugees. Was this one for a refugee too? I wanted to know. *Perhaps*, she'd say, and smile. After a while she would doze off, her eyes sliding heavily shut, her round glasses slipping down. She told us she had eyes in the back of her head, and that was how she knew when we'd done something wrong. I pictured these eyes as flat and shiny and without colour, like the glasses.

It wasn't like her to sleep so much in the afternoons. There were a lot of things that weren't like her. Laura wasn't worried, but I was. I was putting two and two together, out of what I'd been told and what I'd overheard. What I'd been told: "Your mother needs her rest, so you'll have to keep Laura out of her hair." What I'd overheard (Reenie to Mrs. Hillcoate): "The doctor's not pleased. It might be nip and tuck. Of course she'd never say a word, but she's not a well woman. Some men can never leave well enough alone." So I knew my mother was in danger of some kind, something to do with her health and something to do with Father, though I was unsure what this danger might be.

I've said Laura wasn't worried, but she was clinging to Mother more than usual. She sat cross-legged in the cool space beneath the gazebo when Mother was resting, or behind her chair when she was writing letters. When Mother was in the kitchen, Laura liked to be under the kitchen table. She'd drag a cushion in there, and her alphabet book, the one that used to be mine. She had a lot of things that used to be mine.

Laura could read by now, or at least she could read the alphabet book. Her favourite letter was *L*, because it was her own letter, the one that began her name, *L is for Laura*. I never had a favourite letter that began my name – *I is for Iris* – because *I* was everybody's letter.

L is for Lily,
So pure and so white;
It opens by day,
And it closes at night.

The picture in the book was of two children in old-fashioned straw bonnets, next to a water lily with a fairy sitting on it – bare-naked, with shimmering, gauzy wings. Reenie used to say that if she came across a thing like that she'd go after it with the fly swatter. She'd say it to me, for a joke, but she didn't say it to Laura because Laura might take it seriously and get upset.

Laura was *different*. *Different* meant *strange*, I knew that, but I would pester Reenie. "What do you mean, different?"

"Not the same as other people," Reenie would say.

But perhaps Laura wasn't very different from other people

after all. Perhaps she was the same – the same as some odd, skewed element in them that most people keep hidden but that Laura did not, and this was why she frightened them. Because she did frighten them – or if not frighten, then alarm them in some way; though more, of course, as she got older.

Tuesday morning, then, in the kitchen. Reenie and Mother were making the bread. No: Reenie was making the bread, and Mother was having a cup of tea. Reenie had said to Mother that she wouldn't be surprised if there was thunder later in the day, the air was so heavy, and shouldn't Mother be out in the shade, or lying down; but Mother had said she hated doing nothing. She said it made her feel useless; she said she'd like to keep Reenie company.

Mother could walk on water as far as Reenie was concerned, and in any case she had no power to order her around. So Mother sat drinking her tea while Reenie stood at the table, turning the mound of bread dough, pushing down into it with both hands, folding, turning, pushing down. Her hands were covered with flour; she looked as if she had white floury gloves on. There was flour on the bib of her apron too. She had half-circles of sweat under her arms, darkening the yellow daisies on her house dress. Some of the loaves were already shaped and in the pans, with a clean, damp dishtowel over each one. The humid mushroom smell filled the kitchen.

The kitchen was hot, because the oven needed a good bed of coals, and also because there was a heat wave. The window was open, the wave of heat rolled in through it. The flour for the bread came out of the big barrel in the pantry. You should never climb into that barrel because the flour could get into your nose and mouth and smother you. Reenie had known a baby who was stuck into the flour barrel upside down by its brothers and sisters and almost choked to death.

Laura and I were under the kitchen table. I was reading an illustrated book for children called *Great Men of History*. Napoleon was in exile on the island of St. Helena, standing on a cliff with his hand inside his coat. I thought he must have a stomachache. Laura was restless. She crawled out from under the table to get a drink of water. "You want some dough to make a bread man?" said Reenie.

"No," said Laura.

"No, *thank* you," said Mother.

Laura crawled back under the table. We could see the two pairs of feet, Mother's narrow ones and Reenie's wider ones in their sturdy shoes, and Mother's skinny legs and Reenie's plump ones in their pinky-brown stockings. We could hear the muffled turning and thumping of the bread dough. Then all of a sudden the teacup shattered and Mother was down on the floor, and Reenie was kneeling beside her. "Oh dear God," she was saying. "Iris, go get your father."

I ran to the library. The telephone was ringing, but Father wasn't there. I climbed up the stairs to his turret, usually a forbidden place. The door was unlocked: nothing was in the room but a chair and several ashtrays. He wasn't in the front parlour, he wasn't in the morning room, he wasn't in the garage. He must be at the factory, I thought, but I wasn't sure of the way, and also it was too far. I didn't know where else to look.

I went back into the kitchen and crept under the table, where Laura sat hugging her knees. She wasn't crying. There was something on the floor that looked like blood, a trail of it, dark-red spots on the white tiles. I put a finger down, licked it – it was blood. I got a cloth and wiped it up. "Don't look," I told Laura.

After a while Reenie came down the back stairs and cranked the telephone and rang up the doctor – not that he was in, he was gadding about somewhere as usual. Then she phoned the factory and demanded Father. He could not be located. "Find him if you can. Tell him it's an emergency," she said. Then she hurried upstairs again. She'd forgotten all about the bread, which rose too high, and fell back in on itself, and was ruined.

"She shouldn't have been in that hot kitchen," said Reenie to Mrs. Hillcoate, "not in this weather with a thunderstorm coming, but she won't spare herself, you can't tell her anything."

"Did she have a lot of pain?" asked Mrs. Hillcoate, in a pitying, interested voice.

"I've seen worse," said Reenie. "Thank God for small mercies. It slipped out just like a kitten, but I have to say she bled buckets. We'll need to burn the mattress, I don't know how we'd ever get it clean."

"Oh dear, well, she can always have another," said Mrs. Hillcoate. "It must have been meant. There must have been something wrong with it."

"Not from what I heard, she can't," said Reenie. "Doctor says that better be the end of that, because another one would kill her and this one almost did."

"Some women shouldn't marry," said Mrs. Hillcoate. "They're not suited to it. You have to be strong. My own mother had ten, and never blinked an eye. Not that they all lived."

"Mine had eleven," said Reenie. "It wore her right down to the ground."

I knew from past experience that this was the prelude to a contest about the hardness of their mothers' lives, and that soon they would be onto the subject of laundry. I took Laura by the hand and we tiptoed up the back stairs. We were worried, but very curious as well: we wanted to find out what had happened to Mother, but also we wanted to see the kitten. There it was, beside a pile of blood-soaked sheets on the hall floor outside Mother's room, in an enamel basin. But it wasn't a kitten. It was grey, like an old cooked potato, with a head that was too big; it was all curled up. Its eyes were squinched shut, as if the light was hurting it.

"What is it?" Laura whispered. "It's not a kitten." She squatted down, peering.

"Let's go downstairs," I said. The doctor was still in the room, we could hear his footsteps. I didn't want him to catch us, because I knew this creature was forbidden to us; I knew we shouldn't have seen it. Especially not Laura – it was the kind of sight, like a squashed animal, that as a rule would make her scream, and then I would get blamed.

"It's a baby," said Laura. "It's not finished." She was surprisingly calm. "The poor thing. It didn't want to get itself born."

In the late afternoon Reenie took us in to see Mother. She was lying in bed with her head propped up on two pillows; her thin arms were outside the sheet; her whitening hair was transparent. Her wedding ring glinted on her left hand, her fists bunched the sheet at her sides. Her mouth was pulled tight as if she was considering something; it was the look she had when she was making lists. Her eyes were closed. With the curved eyelids rolled down over them, her eyes looked even bigger than they did when they were open. Her glasses were sitting on the night table beside the water jug, each round eye of them shining and empty.

"She's asleep," Reenie whispered. "Don't touch her."

Mother's eyes slid open. Her mouth flickered; the fingers of her near hand unfolded. "You can give her a hug," said Reenie, "but not too hard." I did as I was told. Laura burrowed her head fiercely against Mother's side, underneath her arm. There was the starchy pale-blue lavender smell of the sheets, the soap smell of Mother, and underneath that a hot smell of rust, mixed with the sweetly acid scent of damp but smouldering leaves.

Mother died five days later. She died of a fever; also of being weak, because she could not manage to get her strength back, said Reenie. During this time the doctor came and went, and a succession of crisp, brittle nurses occupied the easy chair in the bedroom. Reenie hurried up and down the stairs with basins, with towels, with cups of broth. Father shuttled restlessly back and forth to the factory, and appeared at the dinner table haggard as a beggar. Where had he been, that afternoon when he could not be found? Nobody said.

Laura crouched in the upstairs hallway. I was told to play with her in order to keep her out of harm's way, but she didn't want that. She sat with her arms wrapped around her knees and her chin on them, and a thoughtful, secret expression, as if she were sucking on a candy. We weren't allowed to have candies. But when I made her show me, it was only a round white stone.

During this last week I was allowed to see Mother every morning, but only for a few minutes. I wasn't allowed to talk to her, because (said Reenie) she was rambling. That meant she thought she was somewhere else. Each day there was less of her. Her cheekbones were prominent; she smelled of milk, and of something raw, something rancid, like the brown paper meat came wrapped in.

I was sulky during these visits. I could see how ill she was, and I resented her for it. I felt she was in some way betraying me – that she was shirking her duties, that she'd abdicated. It didn't occur to me that she might die. I'd been afraid of this possibility earlier, but now I was so terrified that I'd put it out of my mind.

On the last morning, which I did not know would be the

last, Mother seemed more like herself. She was frailer, but at the same time more packed together – more dense. She looked at me as if she saw me. "It's so bright in here," she whispered. "Could you just pull the curtains?" I did as I was told, then went back to stand by her bedside, twisting the handkerchief Reenie had given me in case I cried. My mother took hold of my hand; her own was hot and dry, the fingers like soft wire.

"Be a good girl," she said. "I hope you'll be a good sister to Laura. I know you try to be."

I nodded. I didn't know what to say. I felt I was the victim of an injustice: why was it always me who was supposed to be a good sister to Laura, instead of the other way around? Surely my mother loved Laura more than she loved me.

Perhaps she didn't; perhaps she loved us both equally. Or perhaps she no longer had the energy to love anyone: she'd moved beyond that, out into the ice-cold stratosphere, far beyond the warm, dense magnetic field of love. But I couldn't imagine such a thing. Her love for us was a given – solid and tangible, like a cake. The only question was which of us was going to get the bigger slice.

(What fabrications they are, mothers. Scarecrows, wax dolls for us to stick pins into, crude diagrams. We deny them an existence of their own, we make them up to suit ourselves – our own hungers, our own wishes, our own deficiencies. Now that I've been one myself, I know.)

My mother held me steady in her sky-blue gaze. What an effort it must have been for her to keep her eyes open. How far away I must have seemed – a distant, wavering pink blob. How hard it must have been for her to concentrate on me! Yet I saw none of her stoicism, if that's what it was.

I wanted to say that she was mistaken in me, in my intentions. I didn't always try to be a good sister: quite the reverse. Sometimes I called Laura a pest and told her not to bother me, and only last week I'd found her licking an envelope – one of my own special envelopes, for thank-you notes – and had told her that the glue on them was made from boiled horses, which had caused her to retch and sniffle. Sometimes I hid from her, inside a hollow lilac bush beside the conservatory, where I would read books with my fingers stuck into my ears while she wandered around looking for me, fruitlessly calling my name. So often I got away with the minimum required.

But I had no words to express this, my disagreement with my mother's version of things. I didn't know I was about to be left with her idea of me; with her idea of my goodness pinned onto me like a badge, and no chance to throw it back at her (as would have been the normal course of affairs with a mother and a daughter – if she'd lived, as I'd grown older).

Black ribbons

Tonight there's a lurid sunset, taking its time to fade. In the east, lightning flickering over the underslung sky, then sudden thunder, an abrupt door slammed shut. The house is like an oven, despite my new fan. I've brought a lamp outside; sometimes I see better in the dimness.

I've written nothing for the past week. I lost the heart for it. Why set down such melancholy events? But I've begun again, I notice. I've taken up my black scrawl; it unwinds in a long dark thread of ink across the page, tangled but legible. Do I have some notion of leaving a signature, after all? After all I've done to avoid it, *Iris, her mark*, however truncated: initials chalked on the sidewalk, or a pirate's X on the map, revealing the beach where the treasure was buried.

Why is it we want so badly to memorialize ourselves? Even while we're still alive. We wish to assert our existence, like dogs peeing on fire hydrants. We put on display our framed photographs, our parchment diplomas, our silver-plated cups; we monogram our linen, we carve our names on trees, we scrawl them on washroom walls. It's all the same impulse. What do we hope from it? Applause, envy, respect? Or simply attention, of any kind we can get?

At the very least we want a witness. We can't stand the idea of our own voices falling silent finally, like a radio running down.

The day after Mother's funeral I was sent with Laura out into the garden. Reenie sent us out; she said she needed to put her feet up because she'd been run off them all day. "I'm at the end of my tether," she said. She had purply smudges under her eyes, and I guessed she'd been crying, in secret so as not to disturb anyone, and that she would do it some more once we were out of the way.

"We'll be quiet," I said. I didn't want to go outside – it looked too bright, too glaring, and my eyelids felt swollen and pink – but Reenie said we had to, and anyway the fresh air would do us good. We weren't told to go out and play, because that would have been disrespectful so soon after Mother's death. We were just told to go out.

The funeral reception had been held at Avilion. It was not called a wake – wakes were held on the other side of the Jogues River, and were rowdy and disreputable, with liquor. No: ours was a reception. The funeral had been packed – the factory workmen had come, their wives, their children, and of course the town notables – the bankers, the clergymen, the lawyers, the doctors – but the reception was not for all, although it might as well have been. Reenie said to Mrs. Hillcoate, who'd been hired to help out, that Jesus might have multiplied the loaves and fishes, but Captain Chase was not Jesus and should not be expected to feed the multitudes, although as usual he hadn't known where to draw the line and she only hoped nobody would be stampeded to death.

Those invited had crammed themselves into the house, deferential, lugubrious, avid with curiosity. Reenie had counted the spoons both before and after, and said we should have used the second-best ones and that some folks would make off with anything that wasn't nailed down just to have a souvenir, and considering the way they ate, she might as well have laid out shovels instead of spoons anyway.

Despite this, there was some food left over – half a ham, a small heap of cookies, various ravaged cakes – and Laura and I had been sneaking into the pantry on the sly. Reenie knew we were doing it, but she didn't have the energy right then to stop us – to say, "You'll spoil your supper" or "Stop nibbling in my pantry or you'll turn into mice" or "Eat one more smidgen and you'll burst" – or to utter any of the other warnings or predictions in which I'd always taken a secret comfort.

This one time we'd been allowed to stuff ourselves unchecked. I'd eaten too many cookies, too many slivers of ham; I'd eaten a whole slice of fruitcake. We were still in our black dresses, which were too hot. Reenie had braided our hair tightly and pulled it back, with one stiff black grosgrain ribbon at the top of each braid and one at the bottom: four severe black butterflies for each of us.

Outside, the sunlight made me squint. I resented the intense greenness of the leaves, the intense yellowness and redness of the flowers: their assurance, the flickering display they were making, as if they had the right. I thought of beheading them, of laying waste. I felt desolate, and also grouchy and bloated. Sugar buzzed in my head.

Laura wanted us to climb up on the sphinxes beside the conservatory, but I said no. Then she wanted to go and sit beside the stone nymph and watch the goldfish. I couldn't see much harm in that. Laura skipped ahead of me on the lawn. She was annoyingly light-hearted, as if she didn't have a care in the world; she'd been that way all through Mother's funeral. She seemed puzzled by the grief of those around her. What rankled even more was that people seemed to feel sorrier for her because of this than they did for me.

"Poor lamb," they said. "She's too young, she doesn't realize."

"Mother is with God," Laura said. True, this was the official version, the import of all the prayers that had been offered up; but Laura had a way of believing such things, not in the double way everyone else believed them, but with a tranquil single-mindedness that made me want to shake her.

We sat on the ledge around the lily pond; each lily pad shone in the sun like wet green rubber. I'd had to boost Laura up. She leaned against the stone nymph, swinging her legs, dabbling her fingers in the water, humming to herself.

"You shouldn't sing," I told her. "Mother's dead."

"No she's not," Laura said complacently. "She's not really dead. She's in Heaven with the little baby."

I pushed her off the ledge. Not into the pond though — I did have some sense. I pushed her onto the grass. It wasn't a long drop and the ground was soft; she couldn't have been hurt much. She sprawled on her back, then rolled over and looked up at me wide-eyed, as if she couldn't believe what I'd just done. Her mouth opened into a perfect rosebud O, like a child blowing out birthday candles in a picture book. Then she began to cry.

(I have to admit I was gratified by this. I'd wanted her to suffer too — as much as me. I was tired of her getting away with being so young.)

Laura picked herself up off the grass and ran along the back driveway towards the kitchen, wailing as if she'd been knifed. I ran after her: it would be better to be on the spot when she reached someone in charge, in case she accused me. She had an awkward run: her arms stuck out oddly, her spindly little legs flung themselves out sideways, the stiff bows flopped around at the ends of her braids, her black skirt jounced. She fell once on the way, and this time she really hurt herself — skinned her hand. When I saw this, I was relieved: a little blood would cover up for my malice.

The soda

Sometime in the month after Mother died — I can't remember when, exactly — Father said he was going to take me into town. He'd never paid much attention to me, or to Laura either — he'd left us to Mother, and then to Reenie — so I was startled by this proposal.

He didn't take Laura. He didn't even suggest it.

He announced the upcoming excursion at the breakfast table. He'd begun insisting that Laura and I have breakfast with him, instead of in the kitchen with Reenie, as before. We sat at one end of the long table, he sat at the other. He rarely spoke to us: he read the paper instead, and we were too in awe of him to interrupt. (We worshipped him, of course. It was either that or hate him. He did not invite the more moderate emotions.)

The sun coming through the stained-glass windows threw coloured lights all over him, as if he'd been dipped in drawing ink. I can still remember the cobalt of his cheek, the lurid cranberry of his fingers. Laura and I had such colours at our disposal as well. We'd shift our porridge dishes a little to the left, a little to the right, so that even our dull grey oatmeal was transformed to green or blue or red or violet: magic food, either charmed or poisoned depending on my whim or Laura's mood. Then we'd make faces at each other while eating, but silently, silently. The goal was to get away with such behaviour without alerting him. Well, we had to do something to amuse ourselves.

On that unusual day, Father came back from the factories early and we walked into town. It wasn't that far; at that time, nothing in the town was very far from anything else. Father preferred walking to driving, or to having himself driven. I suppose it was because of his bad leg: he wanted to show he could. He liked to stride around town, and he did stride, despite his limp. I scuttled along beside him, trying to match his ragged pace.

"We'll go to Betty's," said my father. "I'll buy you a soda." Neither of these things had ever happened before. Betty's Luncheonette was for the townspeople, not for Laura and me, said Reenie. It wouldn't do to lower our standards. Also, sodas were a ruinous indulgence and would rot your teeth. That two such forbidden things should be offered at once, and so casually, made me feel almost panicky.

On the main street of Port Ticonderoga there were five churches and four banks, all made of stone, all chunky. Sometimes you had to read the names on them to tell the difference, although the banks lacked steeples. Betty's Luncheonette was beside one of the banks. It had an awning of green-and-white stripes, and a picture of a chicken pot pie in the window that looked like an infant's hat made of pastry dough, with a frill around the edge. Inside, the light was a dim yellow, and the air smelled of vanilla and coffee and melted cheese. The ceiling was made of stamped tin; fans hung down out of it with blades on them like airplane propellers. Several women wearing hats were sitting at small ornate white tables; my father nodded to them, they nodded back.

There were booths of dark wood along one side. My father sat down in one of them, and I slid in across from him. He asked me what kind of soda I would like, but I wasn't used to being alone with him in a public place and it made me shy. Also I didn't know what kinds there were. So he ordered a strawberry soda for me and a cup of coffee for himself.

The waitress had a black dress and a white cap and eyebrows plucked to thin curves, and a red mouth shiny as jam. She called my father Captain Chase and he called her Agnes. By this, and by the way he leaned his elbows on the table, I realized he must already be familiar with this place.

Agnes said was this his little girl, and how sweet; she threw me a glance of dislike. She brought him his coffee almost immediately, wobbling a little on her high heels, and when she set it down she touched his hand briefly. (I took note of this touch, though I could not yet interpret it.) Then she brought the soda for me, in a cone-shaped glass like a dunce cap upside down; it came with two straws. The bubbles went up my nose and made my eyes water.

My father put a sugar cube into his coffee and stirred it, and tapped the spoon on the side of the cup. I studied him over the rim of my soda glass. All of a sudden he looked different; he looked like someone I had never seen before – more tenuous, less solid somehow, but more detailed. I rarely saw him this close up. His hair was combed straight back and cut short at the sides, and was receding from his temples; his good eye was a flat blue, like blue paper. His wrecked, still-handsome face had the same abstracted air it often had in the mornings, at the breakfast table, as if he were listening to a song, or a distant explosion. His moustache was greyer than I'd noticed before, and it seemed odd, now that I considered it, that men had such bristles growing on their faces and women did not. Even his ordinary clothes had turned mysterious in the dim vanilla-scented light, as if they belonged to someone else and he had only borrowed them. They were too big for him, that was it. He had shrunk. But at the same time he was taller.

He smiled at me, and asked if I was enjoying my soda. After that he was silent and thoughtful. Then he took a cigarette out of the silver case he always carried, and lit it, and blew out smoke. "If anything happens," he said finally, "you must promise to look after Laura."

I nodded solemnly. What was *anything*? What could happen? I dreaded some piece of bad news, though I couldn't have put a name to it. Maybe he might be going away – going overseas. Stories of the war had not been lost on me. However he did not explain further.

"Shake hands on it?" he said. We reached our hands across the table; his was hard and dry, like a leather suitcase handle. His one blue eye assessed me, as if speculating about whether I could be depended on. I lifted my chin, straightened my shoulders. I wanted desperately to deserve his good opinion.

"What can you buy for a nickel?" he said then. I was caught off-guard by this question, tongue-tied: I didn't know. Laura and I were not given any money of our own to spend, because Reenie said we needed to learn the value of a dollar.

From the inside pocket of his dark suit he took out his memorandum book in its pigskin cover and tore out a sheet of paper. Then he began talking about buttons. It was never too early, he said, for me to learn the simple principles of economics, which I would need to know in order to act responsibly, when I was older.

"Suppose you begin with two buttons," he said. He said your expenses would be what it cost you to make the buttons, and your gross revenues would be how much you could sell the buttons for, and your net profit would be that figure minus your expenses, over a given time. You could then keep some of the net profit for yourself and use the rest of it to make four buttons, and then you would sell those and be able to make eight. He drew a little chart with his silver pencil: two buttons, then four buttons, then eight buttons. Buttons multiplied bewilderingly on the page; in the column next to them, the money piled up. It was like shelling peas – peas in this bowl, pods in that. He asked me if I understood.

I scanned his face to see if he was serious. I'd heard him

denounce the button factory often enough as a trap, a quick-sand, a jinx, an albatross, but that was when he'd been drinking. Right now he was sober enough. He didn't look as if he was explaining, he looked as if he was apologizing. He wanted something from me, apart from an answer to his question. It was as if he wanted me to forgive him, to absolve him from some crime; but what had he done to me? Nothing I could think of.

I felt confused, and also inadequate: whatever it was he was asking or demanding, it was beyond me. This was the first time a man would expect more from me than I was capable of giving, but it would not be the last.

"Yes," I said.

In the week before she died – one of those dreadful mornings – my mother said a strange thing, though I didn't consider it strange at the time. She said, "Underneath it all, your father loves you."

She wasn't in the habit of speaking to us about feelings, and especially not about love – her own love or anyone else's, except God's. But parents were supposed to love their children, so I must have taken this thing she said as a reassurance: despite appearances, my father was as other fathers were, or were considered to be.

Now I think it was more complicated than that. It may have been a warning. It may also have been a burden. Even if love was *underneath it all*, there was a great deal piled on top, and what would you find when you dug down? Not a simple gift, pure gold and shining; instead, something ancient and possibly baneful, like an iron charm rusting among old bones. A talisman of sorts, this love, but a heavy one; a heavy thing for me to carry around with me, slung on its iron chain around my neck.

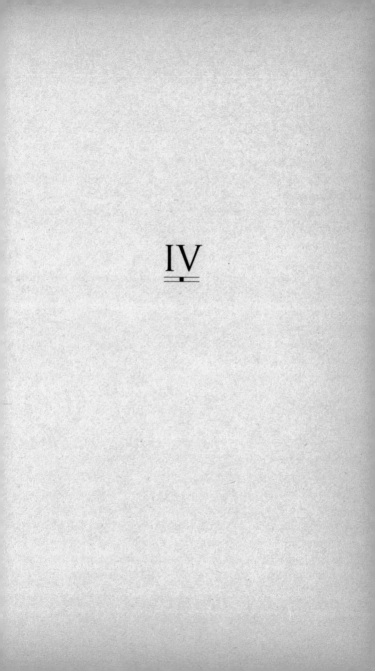

IV

The rain is light, but steady since noon. Mist rises from the trees, from the roadways. She comes past the front window with its painted coffee cup, white with a green stripe around it and three steam trails coming up out of it in wavering lines, as if three clutching fingers have slid down the wet glass. The door is marked CAFE in peeling gold letters; she opens it and steps inside, shaking her umbrella. It's cream-coloured, as is her poplin raincoat. She throws back the hood.

He's in the last booth, beside the swing door to the kitchen, as he said he'd be. The walls are yellowed by smoke, the heavy booths are painted a dull brown, each with a metal hen's-claw hook for coats. Men sit in the booths, only men, in baggy jackets like worn blankets, no ties, jagged haircuts, their legs apart and feet in boots planted flat to the floorboards. Hands like stumps: those hands could rescue you or beat you to a pulp and they would look the same while doing either thing. Blunt instruments, and their eyes as well. There's a smell in the room, of rotting planks and spilled vinegar and sour wool trousers and old meat and one shower a week, of scrimping and cheating and resentment. She knows it's important to act as if she doesn't notice the smell.

He lifts a hand, and the other men look at her with suspicion and contempt as she hurries towards him, her heels clacking on the wood. She sits down across from him, smiles with relief: he's here. He's still here.

Judas Priest, he says, you might as well have worn mink.

What did I do? What's wrong?

Your coat.

It's just a coat. An ordinary raincoat, she says, faltering. What's wrong with it?

Christ, he says, look at yourself. Look around you. It's too clean.

I can't get it right for you, can I? she says. I won't ever get it right.

You do, he says. You know what you get right. But you don't think anything through.

You didn't tell me. I've never been down here before – to a place like this. And I can hardly rush out the door looking like a cleaning woman – have you thought of that?

If you just had a scarf or something. To cover your hair.

My hair, she says despairingly. What next? What's wrong with my hair?

It's too blonde. It stands out. Blondes are like white mice, you only find them in cages. They wouldn't last long in nature. They're too conspicuous.

You're not being kind.

I detest kindness, he says. I detest people who pride themselves on being kind. Snot-nosed nickel-and-dime do-gooders, doling out the kindness. They're contemptible.

I'm kind, she says, trying to smile. I'm kind to you, at any rate.

If I thought that's all it was – lukewarm milk-and-water kindness – I'd be gone. Midnight train, bat out of hell. I'd take my chances. I'm no charity case, I'm not looking for nooky handouts.

He's in a savage mood. She wonders why. She hasn't seen him for a week. Or it might be the rain.

Perhaps it isn't kindness then, she says. Perhaps it's selfishness. Perhaps I'm ruthlessly selfish.

I'd like that better, he says. I prefer you greedy. He stubs out his cigarette, reaches for another, thinks better of it. He's still smoking ready-mades, a luxury for him. He must be rationing them. She wonders if he's got enough money, but she can't ask.

I don't want you sitting across from me like this, you're too far away.

I know, she says. But there's nowhere else. It's too wet.

I'll find us a place. Somewhere out of the snow.

It isn't snowing.

But it will, he says. The north wind will blow.

And we shall have snow. And what will the robbers do then, poor things? At least she's made him grin, though it's more like a wince. Where have you been sleeping? she says.

Never mind. You don't need to know. That way, if they ever get hold of you and ask you any questions, you won't have to lie.

I'm not such a bad liar, she says, trying to smile.

Maybe not for an amateur, he says. But the professionals, they'd find you out, all right. They'd open you up like a package.

They're still looking for you? Haven't they given up?

Not yet. That's what I hear.

It's awful, isn't it, she says. It's all so awful. Still, we're lucky, aren't we?

Why are we lucky? He's back to his gloomy mood.

At least we're both here, at least we have . . .

The waiter is standing beside the booth. He has his shirt sleeves rolled up, a full-length apron soft with old dirt, strands of hair arranged across his scalp like oily ribbon. His fingers are like toes.

Coffee?

Yes please, she says. Black. No sugar.

She waits until the waiter leaves. Is it safe?

The coffee? You mean does it have germs? It shouldn't, it's been boiled for hours. He's sneering at her but she chooses not to understand him.

No, I mean, is it safe here.

He's a friend of a friend. Anyway I'm keeping an eye on the door – I could make it out the back way. There's an alley.

You didn't do it, did you, she says.

I've told you. I could have though, I was there. Anyway it doesn't matter, because I fill their bill just fine. They'd love to see me nailed to the wall. Me and my bad ideas.

You've got to get away, she says hopelessly. She thinks of the word *clasp*, how outworn it is. Yet this is what she wants – to clasp him in her arms.

Not yet, he says. I shouldn't go yet. I shouldn't take trains, I shouldn't cross borders. Word has it that's where they're watching.

I worry about you, she says. I dream about it. I worry all the time.

Don't worry, darling, he says. You'll get thin, and then your lovely tits and ass will waste away to nothing. You'll be no good to anybody then.

She puts her hand up to her cheek as if he's slapped her. I wish you wouldn't talk like that.

I know you do, he says. Girls with coats like yours do have those wishes.

The Port Ticonderoga Herald and Banner, March 16, 1933

CHASE SUPPORTS RELIEF EFFORT
BY ELWOOD R. MURRAY, EDITOR-IN-CHIEF

In a public-spirited gesture such as this town has come to expect, Captain Norval Chase, President of Chase Industries Ltd., announced yesterday that Chase Industries will donate three boxcars of factory "seconds" to the relief efforts on behalf of those parts of the country most hard-hit by the Depression. Included will be baby blankets, children's pullovers, and an assortment of practical undergarments for both men and women.

Captain Chase expressed to the *Herald and Banner* that in this time of national crisis, all must pitch in as was done in the War, especially those in Ontario which has been more fortunate than some. Attacked by his competitors most notably Mr. Richard Griffen of Royal Classic Knitwear in Toronto, who have accused him of dumping his overruns on the market as free giveaways and thus depriving the working man of wages, Captain Chase stated that as recipients of these items cannot afford to purchase them he is not doing anyone out of sales.

He added that all portions of the country have suffered their setbacks and Chase Industries currently faces a scale down of its operations due to reduced demand. He said he would make every attempt to keep factories running but may soon be under the necessity, of either layoffs or part hours and wages.

We can only applaud Captain Chase's efforts, a man who holds to his word, unlike the strikebreaking and lockout tactics in centres such as Winnipeg and Montreal, which has kept Port Ticonderoga a law-abiding town and clear of the scenes of Union riots, brutal violence and Communist-inspired bloodshed which have marred other cities with considerable destruction of property and injury as well as loss of life.

Is this where you're living? she says. She twists the gloves in her hands, as if they're wet and she's wringing them out.

This is where I'm staying, he says. It's a different thing.

The house is one of a row, all red brick darkened by grime, narrow and tall, with steeply angled roofs. There's an oblong of dusty grass in front, a few parched weeds growing beside the walk. A brown paper bag torn open.

Four steps up to the porch. Lace curtains dangle in the front window. He takes out his key.

She glances back over her shoulder as she steps inside. Don't worry, he says, nobody's watching. This is my friend's place anyway. I'm here today and gone tomorrow.

You have a lot of friends, she says.

Not a lot, he says. You don't need many if there's no rotten apples.

There's a vestibule with a row of brass hooks for coats, a worn linoleum floor in a pattern of brown-and-yellow squares, an inner door with a frosted glass panel bearing a design of herons or cranes. Birds with long legs bending their graceful snake-necks among the reeds and lilies, left over from an earlier age: gaslight. He opens the door with a second key and they step into the dim inner hallway; he flicks on the light switch. Overhead, a fixture with three pink glass blossoms, two of the bulbs missing.

Don't look so dismayed, darling, he says. None of it will rub off on you. Just don't touch anything.

Oh, it might, she says with a small breathless laugh. I have to touch you. You'll rub off.

He pulls the glass door shut behind them. Another door on

the left, varnished and dark: she imagines a censorious ear pressed against it from the inside, a creaking, as if of weight shifting from foot to foot. Some malevolent grey-haired crone – wouldn't that match the lace curtains? A long battered flight of stairs goes up, with carpeting treads nailed on and a gap-toothed banister. The wallpaper is a trellis design, with grapevines and roses entwined, pink once, now the light brown of milky tea. He puts his arms carefully around her, brushes his lips over the side of her neck, her throat; not the mouth. She shivers.

I'm easy to get rid of afterwards, he says, whispering. You can just go home and take a shower.

Don't say that, she says, whispering also. You're making fun. You never believe I mean it.

You mean it enough for this, he says. She slides her arm around his waist and they go up the stairs a little clumsily, a little heavily; their bodies slow them down. Halfway up there's a round window of coloured glass: through the cobalt blue of the sky, the grapes in dime-store purple, the headache red of the flowers, light falls, staining their faces. On the second-floor landing he kisses her again, this time harder, sliding her skirt up her silky legs as far as the tops of her stockings, fingering the little hard rubber nipples there, pressing her up against the wall. She always wears a girdle: getting her out of it is like peeling the skin off a seal.

Her hat tumbles off, her arms are around his neck, her head and body arched backwards as if someone's pulling down on her hair. Her hair itself has come unpinned, uncoiled; he smoothes his hand down it, the pale tapering swath of it, and thinks of flame, the single shimmering flame of a white candle, turned upside down. But a flame can't burn downwards.

The room is on the third floor, the servants' quarters they must once have been. Once they're inside he puts on the chain.

The room is small and close and dim, with one window, open a few inches, the blind pulled most of the way down, white net curtains looped to either side. The afternoon sun is hitting the blind, turning it golden. The air smells of dry rot, but also of soap: there's a tiny triangular sink in one corner, a foxed mirror hanging above it; crammed underneath it, the square-edged black box of his typewriter. His toothbrush in an enamelled tin cup; not a new toothbrush. It's too intimate. She turns her eyes away. There's a darkly varnished bureau scarred with cigarette burns and the marks from wet glasses, but most of the space is taken up by the bed. It's the brass kind, outmoded and maid-enish and painted white except for the knobs. It will probably creak. Thinking of this, she flushes.

She can tell he's taken pains with the bed – changed the sheets or at least the pillowcase, smoothed out the faded Nile-green chenille spread. She almost wishes he hadn't, because seeing this causes her a pang of something like pity, as if a starving peasant has offered her his last piece of bread. Pity isn't what she wants to feel. She doesn't want to feel he is in any way vulnerable. Only she is allowed to be that. She sets her purse and gloves down on top of the bureau. She's conscious suddenly of this as a social situation. As a social situation it's absurd.

Sorry there's no butler, he says. Want a drink? Cheap scotch.

Yes please, she says. He keeps the bottle in the top bureau drawer; he takes it out, and two glasses, and pours. Say when.

When, please.

No ice, he says, but you can have water.

That's all right. She gulps the whisky, coughs a little, smiles at him, standing with her back against the bureau.

Short and hard and straight up, he says, the way you love it. He sits down on the bed with his drink. Here's to loving it. He raises his glass. He's not smiling back.

You're unusually mean today.

Self-defence, he says.

I don't love *it*, I love you, she says. I do know the difference.

Up to a point, he says. Or so you think. It saves face.

Give me one good reason why I shouldn't just walk out of here.

He grins. Come over here then.

Although he knows she wants him to, he won't say he loves her. Perhaps it would leave him armourless, like an admission of guilt.

I'll take my stockings off first. They run as soon as you look at them.

Like you, he says. Leave them on. Come over here now.

The sun has moved across; there's just a wedge of light remaining, on the left side of the drawn blind. Outside, a streetcar rumbles past, bell clanging. Streetcars must have been going past all this time. Why then has the effect been silence? Silence and his breath, their breaths, labouring, withheld, trying not to make any noise. Or not too much noise. Why should pleasure sound so much like distress? Like someone wounded. He'd put his hand over her mouth.

The room is darker now, yet she sees more. The bedspread heaped onto the floor, the sheet twisted around and over them like a thick cloth vine; the single bulb, unshaded, the cream-coloured wallpaper with its blue violets, tiny and silly, stained beige where the roof must have leaked; the chain protecting the door. The chain protecting the door: it's flimsy enough. One good shove, one kick with a boot. If that were to happen, what would she do? She feels the walls thinning, turning to ice. They're fish in a bowl.

He lights two cigarettes, hands her one. They both sigh in. He runs his free hand down her, then again, taking her in through his fingers. He wonders how much time she has; he doesn't ask. Instead he takes hold of her wrist. She's wearing a small gold watch. He covers its face.

So, he says. Bedtime story?

Yes, please, she says.

Where were we?

You'd just cut out the tongues of those poor girls in their bridal veils.

Oh yes. And you protested. If you don't like this story I could tell you a different one, but I can't promise it would be any more civilized. It might be worse. It might be modern. Instead of a few dead Zycronians, we could have acres of stinking mud and hundreds of thousands of . . .

I'll keep this one, she says quickly. Anyway it's the one you want to tell me.

She stubs out her cigarette in the brown glass ashtray, then settles herself against him, ear to his chest. She likes to hear his voice this way, as if it begins not in his throat but in his body, like a hum or a growl, or like a voice speaking from deep underground. Like the blood moving through her own heart: a word, a word, a word.

The Mail and Empire, December 5, 1934

PLAUDITS FOR BENNETT
SPECIAL TO THE MAIL AND EMPIRE

In a speech to the Empire Club last evening, Mr. Richard E. Griffen, Toronto financier and outspoken President of Royal Classic Knitwear, had moderate praise for Prime Minister R.B. Bennett and brickbats for his critics.

Referring to Sunday's boisterous Maple Leaf Gardens rally in Toronto, when 15,000 Communists staged a hysterical welcome for their leader Tim Buck, jailed for seditious conspiracy but paroled Saturday from Kingston's Portsmouth Penitentiary, Mr. Griffen expressed himself alarmed by the Government's "caving in to pressure" in the form of a petition signed by 200,000 "deluded bleeding hearts." Mr. Bennett's policy of "the iron heel of ruthlessness" had been correct, he said, as imprisonment of those plotting to topple elected governments and confiscate private property was the only way to deal with subversion.

As for the tens of thousands of immigrants deported under Section 98, including those sent back to countries such as Germany and Italy where they face internment, these had advocated tyrannical rule and now would get a first-hand taste of it, Mr. Griffen stated.

Turning to the economy, he said that although unemployment remained high, with consequent unrest and Communists and their sympathizers continuing to profit from it, there were hopeful signs and he was confident that the Depression would be over by spring. Meanwhile the only sane policy was to stay the course and allow the system to correct itself. Any inclination towards the soft socialism of Mr. Roosevelt should be resisted, as such efforts could only further sicken the ailing economy. Although the plight of the unemployed was to be deplored, many were idle from inclination, and force should be used promptly and effectively against illegal strikers and outside agitators.

Mr. Griffen's remarks were roundly applauded.

Now then. Let's say it's dark. The suns, all three of them, have set. A couple of moons have risen. In the foothills the wolves are abroad. The chosen girl is waiting her turn to be sacrificed. She's been fed her last, elaborate meal, she's been scented and anointed, songs have been sung in her praise, prayers have been offered. Now she's lying on a bed of red and gold brocade, shut up in the Temple's innermost chamber, which smells of the mixture of petals and incense and crushed aromatic spices customarily strewn on the biers of the dead. The bed itself is called the Bed of One Night, because no girl ever spends two nights in it. Among the girls themselves, when they still have their tongues, it's called the Bed of Voiceless Tears.

At midnight she will be visited by the Lord of the Underworld, who is said to be dressed in rusty armour. The Underworld is the place of tearing apart and of disintegration: all souls must pass through it on their way to the land of the Gods, and some – the most sinful ones – must remain there. Every dedicated Temple maiden must undergo a visitation from the rusty Lord the night before her sacrifice, for if not, her soul will be unsatisfied, and instead of travelling to the land of the Gods she will be forced to join the band of beautiful nude dead women with azure hair, curvaceous figures, ruby-red lips and eyes like snake-filled pits, who hang around the ancient ruined tombs in the desolate mountains to the West. You see, I didn't forget them.

I appreciate your thoughtfulness.

Nothing's too good for you. Any other little thing you want added, just let me know. Anyway. Like many peoples, ancient and modern, the Zycronians are afraid of virgins, dead ones especially. Women betrayed in love who have died unmarried are driven to seek in death what they've so unfortunately missed out on in life. They sleep in the ruined tombs by day, and by night they prey upon unwary travellers, in particular any young men foolhardy enough to go there. They leap onto these young men and suck out their essence, and turn them into obedient zombies, bound to satisfy the nude dead women's unnatural cravings on demand.

What bad luck for the young men, she says. Is there no defence against these vicious creatures?

You can stick spears into them, or mash them to a pulp with rocks. But there are so many of them – it's like fighting off an octopus, they're all over a fellow before he knows it. Anyway, they hypnotize you – they ruin your willpower. It's the first thing they do. As soon as you catch sight of one, you're rooted to the spot.

I can imagine. More scotch?

I think I could stand it. Thanks. The girl – what do you think her name should be?

I don't know. You choose. You know the territory.

I'll think about it. Anyway, there she lies on the Bed of One Night, a prey to anticipation. She doesn't know which will be worse, having her throat cut or the next few hours. It's one of the open secrets of the Temple that the Lord of the Underworld isn't real, but merely one of the courtiers in disguise. Like everything else in Sakiel-Norn this position is for sale, and large amounts are said to change hands for the privilege – under the table, of course. The recipient of the payoffs is the High Priestess, who is as venal as they come, and known to be partial to sapphires. She excuses herself by vowing to use the money for charitable purposes, and she does use some of it for that, when she remembers. The girls can hardly complain about this part of their ordeal, being without tongues or even writing materials, and anyway they're all dead the next day. *Pennies from heaven*, says the High Priestess to herself as she totes up the cash.

Meanwhile, off in the distance a large, ragged horde of barbarians is on the march, intent on capturing the far-famed city of Sakiel-Norn, then looting it and burning it to the ground. They've already done this very same thing to several other cities farther west. No one – no one among the civilized nations, that is – can account for their success. They are neither well clothed nor well armed, they can't read, and they possess no ingenious metal contraptions.

Not only that, they have no king, only a leader. This leader has no name as such; he gave up his name when he became the leader, and was given a title instead. His title is the Servant of Rejoicing. His followers refer to him also as the Scourge of the All-Powerful, the Right Fist of the Invincible, the Purger of Iniquities, and the Defender of Virtue and Justice. The barbarians' original homeland is unknown, but it is agreed that they come from the northwest, where the ill winds also originate. By their enemies they're called the People of Desolation, but they term themselves the People of Joy.

Their current leader bears the marks of divine favour: he was born with a caul, is wounded in the foot, and has a star-shaped mark on his forehead. He falls into trances and communes with the other world whenever he is at a loss as to what to do next. He's on his way to destroy Sakiel-Norn because of an order brought to him by a messenger of the Gods.

This messenger appeared to him in the guise of a flame, with numerous eyes and wings of fire shooting out. Such messengers are known to speak in torturous parables and to take many forms: burning *thulks* or stones that can speak, or walking flowers, or bird-headed creatures with human bodies. Or else they might look like anyone at all. Travellers in ones or twos, men rumoured to be thieves or magicians, foreigners who speak several languages, and beggars by the side of the road are the most likely to be such messengers, say the People of Desolation: therefore all of these need to be handled with great circumspection, at least until their true nature can be discovered.

If they turn out to be divine emissaries, it's best to give them food and wine and the use of a woman if required, to listen respectfully to their messages, and then to let them go on their way. Otherwise, they should be stoned to death and their possessions confiscated. You may be sure that all travellers, magicians, strangers or beggars who find themselves in the vicinity of the People of Desolation take care to provide themselves with a stash of obscure parables – *cloud words*, they're called, or *knotted silk* – enigmatic enough to be useful on various occasions, as circumstances may dictate. To travel among the People of Joy without a riddle or a puzzling rhyme would be to court certain death.

According to the words of the flame with eyes, the city of Sakiel-Norn has been marked out for destruction on account of its luxury, its worship of false gods, and in especial its abhorrent child sacrifices. Because of this practice, all the people in the city, including the slaves and the children and maidens destined for sacrifice, are to be put to the sword. To kill even those whose proposed deaths are the reason for this killing may not seem just, but for the People of Joy it isn't guilt or innocence that determines such things, it's whether or not you've been tainted, and as far as the People of Joy are concerned everyone in a tainted city is as tainted as everyone else.

The horde rolls forward, raising a dark dust cloud as it moves; this cloud flies over it like a flag. It is not however close enough to have been spotted by the sentries posted on the walls of Sakiel-Norn. Others who might give warning – outlying herdsmen, merchants in transit, and so forth – are relentlessly run down and hacked to pieces, with the exception of any who might possibly be divine messengers.

The Servant of Rejoicing rides ahead, his heart pure, his brow furrowed, his eyes burning. Over his shoulders is a rough leather cloak, on his head is his badge of office, a red conical hat. Behind him are his followers, eyeteeth bared. Herbivores flee before them, scavengers follow, wolves lope alongside.

Meanwhile, in the unsuspecting city, there's a plot underway to topple the King. This has been set in motion (as is customary) by several highly trusted courtiers. They've employed the most skilful of the blind assassins, a youth who was once a weaver of rugs and then a child prostitute, but who since his escape has become renowned for his soundlessness, his stealth, and his pitiless hand with a knife. His name is X.

Why X?

Men like that are always called X. Names are no use to them, names only pin them down. Anyway, X is for X-ray – if you're X, you can pass through solid walls and see through women's clothing.

But X is blind, she says.

All the better. He sees through women's clothing with the inner eye that is the bliss of solitude.

Poor Wordsworth! Don't be blasphemous! she says, delighted.

I can't help it, I was blasphemous from a child.

X is to make his way into the compound of the Temple of the Five Moons, find the door to the chamber where the next day's maiden sacrifice is being kept, and slit the throat of the sentry. He must then kill the girl herself, hide the body beneath the fabled Bed of One Night, and dress himself in the girl's ceremonial veils. He's supposed to wait until the courtier playing the Lord of the Underworld – who is, in fact, none other than the leader of the impending palace coup – has come, taken what he has paid for, and gone away again. The courtier has paid good coin and wants his money's worth, which doesn't mean a dead girl, however freshly killed. He wants the heart still beating.

But there's been a foul-up in the arrangements. The timing has been misunderstood: as things stand, the blind assassin will be first past the post.

This is too gruesome, she says. You have a twisted mind.

He runs his finger along her bare arm. You want me to continue? As a rule I do this for money. You're getting it for nothing, you should be grateful. Anyway, you don't know what's going to happen. I'm only just thickening the plot.

I'd say it was pretty thick already.

Thick plots are my specialty. If you want a thinner kind, look elsewhere.

All right then. Go on.

Disguised in the murdered girl's clothing, the assassin is to wait until morning and then allow himself to be led up the steps to the altar, where, at the moment of sacrifice, he will stab the King. The King will thus appear to have been struck down by the Goddess herself, and his death will be the signal for a carefully orchestrated uprising.

Certain of the rougher elements, having been bribed, will stage a riot. After this, events will follow the time-honoured pattern. The Temple priestesses will be taken into custody, for their own safety it will be said, but in reality to force them to uphold the plotters' claim to spiritual authority. The nobles loyal to the King will be speared where they stand; their male offspring will also be killed, to avoid revenge later; their daughters will be married off to the victors to legitimize the seizure of their families' wealth, and their pampered and no doubt adulterous wives will be tossed to the mob. Once the mighty have fallen, it's a distinct pleasure to be able to wipe your feet on them.

The blind assassin plans to escape in the ensuing confusion, returning later to claim the other half of his generous fee. In reality the plotters intend to cut him down at once, as it would never do if he were caught, and – in the event of the plot's failure – forced to talk. His corpse will be well hidden, because everyone knows that the blind assassins work only for hire, and sooner or later people might begin to ask who had hired him. Arranging a king's death is one thing, but being found out is quite another.

The girl who is thus far nameless lies on her bed of red brocade, awaiting the ersatz Lord of the Underworld and saying a word-less farewell to this life. The blind assassin creeps down the cor-ridor, dressed in the grey robes of a Temple servant. He reaches the door. The sentry is a woman, since no men are allowed to serve inside the compound. Through his grey veil the assassin whispers to her that he carries a message from the High Priestess, for her ear alone. The woman leans down, the knife moves once, the lightning of the Gods is merciful. His sightless hands dart towards the jangle of keys.

The key turns in the lock. Inside the room, the girl hears it. She sits up.

His voice stops. He's listening to something outside in the street.

She raises herself on an elbow. What is it? she says. It's just a car door.

Do me a favour, he says. Put on your slip like a good girl and take a peek out the window.

What if someone sees me? she says. It's broad daylight.

It's all right. They won't know you. They'll just see a woman in a slip, it's not an uncommon sight around here; they'll just think you're a . . .

A woman of easy virtue? she says lightly. Is that what you think too?

A ruined maiden. Not the same thing.

That's very gallant of you.

Sometimes I'm my own worst enemy.

If it weren't for you I'd be a whole lot more ruined, she says. She's at the window now, she raises the blind. Her slip is the chill green of shore ice, broken ice. He won't be able to hold on to her, not for long. She'll melt, she'll drift away, she'll slide out of his hands.

Anything out there? he says.

Nothing out of the ordinary.

Come back to bed.

But she's looked in the mirror over the sink, she's seen herself. Her nude face, her rummaged hair. She checks her gold watch. God, what a wreck, she says. I've got to go.

The Mail and Empire, December 15, 1934

ARMY QUELLS STRIKE VIOLENCE
PORT TICONDEROGA, ONT.

Fresh violence broke out yesterday in Port Ticonderoga, a continuation of the week's turmoil in connection with the closure, strike and lockout at Chase and Sons Industries Ltd. Police forces proving outnumbered and reinforcements having been requested by the provincial legislature, the Prime Minister authorized intervention in the interests of public safety by a detachment of the Royal Canadian Regiment, which arrived at two o'clock in the afternoon. The situation has now been declared stable.

Prior to order being restored, a meeting of strikers ran out of control. Shop windows were broken all along the town's main street, with extensive looting. Several shop owners attempting to defend their property are in hospital recovering from contusions. One policeman is said to be in grave danger from concussion, having been struck on the head by a brick. A fire that broke out in Factory One during the early hours, but which was subdued by the town's firefighters, is being investigated, and arson is suspected. The night watchman, Mr. Al Davidson, was dragged to safety out of the path of the flames, but was found to have died due to a blow on the head and smoke inhalation. The perpetrators of this outrage are being sought, with several suspects already identified.

The editor of the Port Ticonderoga newspaper, Mr. Elwood R. Murray, stated that the trouble had been caused by liquor introduced into the crowd by several outside agitators. He claimed that the local workmen were law-abiding and would not have rioted unless provoked.

Mr. Norval Chase, President of Chase and Sons Industries, was unavailable for comment.

A different house this week, a different room. At least there's space to turn around between door and bed. The curtains are Mexican, striped in yellow and blue and red; the bed has a bird's-eye maple headboard; there's a Hudson's Bay blanket, crimson and scratchy, that's been tossed onto the floor. A Spanish bullfight poster on the wall. An armchair, maroon leather; a desk, fumed oak; a jar with pencils, all neatly sharpened; a rack of pipes. Tobacco particulate thickens the air.

A shelf of books: Auden, Veblen, Spengler, Steinbeck, Dos Passos. *Tropic of Cancer*, out in plain view, it must have been smuggled. *Salammbô*, *Strange Fugitive*, *Twilight of the Idols*, *A Farewell to Arms*. Barbusse, Montherlant. *Hammurabis Gesetz: Juristische Erläuterung.* This new friend has intellectual interests, she thinks. Also more money. Therefore less trustworthy. He has three different hats topping his bentwood coat stand, as well as a plaid dressing gown, pure cashmere.

Have you read any of these books? she'd asked, after they'd come in and he'd locked the door. While she was taking off her hat and gloves.

Some, he said. He didn't elaborate. Turn your head. He untangled a leaf from her hair.

Already they're falling.

She wonders if the friend knows. Not just that there's a woman – they'll have something worked out between them so the friend won't barge in, men do that – but who she is. Her name and so on. She hopes not. She can tell by the books, and especially by the bullfight poster, that this friend would be hostile to her on principle.

Today he'd been less impetuous, more pensive. He'd wanted to linger, to hold back. To scrutinize.

Why are you looking at me like that?

I'm memorizing you.

Why? she said, putting her hand over his eyes. She didn't like being examined like that. Fingered.

To have you later, he said. Once I've gone.

Don't. Don't spoil today.

Make hay while the sun shines, he said. That your motto?

More like waste not, want not, she said. He'd laughed then.

Now she's wound herself in the sheet, tucked it across her breasts; she lies against him, legs hidden in a long sinuous fishtail of white cotton. He has his hands behind his head; he's gazing up at the ceiling. She feeds him sips of her drink, rye and water this time. Cheaper than scotch. She's been meaning to bring something decent of her own – something drinkable – but so far she's forgotten.

Go on, she says.

I have to be inspired, he says.

What can I do to inspire you? I don't have to be back till five.

I'll take a rain check on the real inspiration, he says. I have to build up my strength. Give me half an hour.

O lente, lente currite noctis equi!

What?

Run slowly, slowly, horses of the night. It's from Ovid, she says. In Latin the line goes at a slow gallop. That was clumsy, he'll think she's showing off. She can never tell what he may or may not recognize. Sometimes he pretends not to know a thing, and then after she's explained it he reveals that he does know it, he knew it all along. He draws her out, then chokes her off.

★

You're an odd duck, he says. Why are they the horses of the night?

They pull Time's chariot. He's with his mistress. It means he wants the night to stretch out, so he can spend more time with her.

What for? he says lazily. Five minutes not enough for him? Nothing better to do?

She sits up. Are you tired? Am I boring you? Should I leave?

Lie down again. You ain't goin' nowheres.

She wishes he wouldn't do that – talk like a movie cowboy. He does it to put her at a disadvantage. Nevertheless, she stretches out, slides her arm across him.

Put your hand here, ma'am. That'll do fine. He closes his eyes. Mistress, he says. What a quaint term. Mid-Victorian. I should be kissing your dainty shoe, or plying you with chocolates.

Maybe I am quaint. Maybe I'm mid-Victorian. *Lover*, then. Or *piece of tail*. Is that more forward-looking? More even-steven for you?

Sure. But I think I prefer *mistress*. Because things ain't even-steven, are they?

No, she says. They're not. Anyway, go on.

He says: As night falls, the People of Joy have encamped a day's march from the city. Female slaves, captives from previous conquests, pour out the scarlet *hrang* from the skin bottles in which it is fermented, and cringe and stoop and serve, carrying bowls of gristly, undercooked stew made from rustled *thulks*. The official wives sit in the shadows, eyes bright in the dark ovals of their head-scarves, watching for impertinences. They know they'll sleep alone tonight, but they can whip the captured girls later for clumsiness or disrespect, and they will.

The men crouch around their small fires, wrapped in their leather cloaks, eating their suppers, muttering among themselves.

Their mood is not jovial. Tomorrow, or the day after that – depending on their speed and on the watchfulness of the enemy – they will have to fight, and this time they may not win. True, the fiery-eyed messenger who spoke to the Fist of the Invincible One promised they will be given victory if they continue to be pious and obedient and brave and cunning, but there are always so many ifs in these matters.

If they lose, they'll be killed, and their women and children as well. They're not expecting mercy. If they win, they themselves must do the killing, which isn't always so enjoyable as is sometimes believed. They must kill everyone in the city: these are the instructions. No boy child is to be left alive, to grow up lusting to revenge his slaughtered father; no girl child, to corrupt the People of Joy with her depraved ways. From cities conquered earlier they've kept back the young girls and doled them out among the soldiers, one or two or three each according to prowess and merit, but the divine messenger has now said that enough is enough.

All this killing will be tiring, and also noisy. Killing on such a grand scale is very strenuous, also polluting, and must be done thoroughly or else the People of Joy will be in bad trouble. The All-Powerful One has a way of insisting on the letter of the law.

Their horses are tethered apart. They are few in number, and ridden only by the chief men – slender, skittish horses, with hardened mouths and long woebegone faces and tender, cowardly eyes. None of this is their fault: they were dragged into it.

If you own a horse you are permitted to kick and beat it, but not to kill it and eat it, because long ago a messenger of the All-Powerful One appeared in the form of the first horse. The horses remember this, it is said, and are proud of it. It is why they allow only the leaders to ride them. Or that is the reason given.

Mayfair, May 1935

TORONTO HIGH NOON GOSSIP
BY YORK

Spring made a frolicsome entrance this April, heralded by a veritable cavalcade of chauffeured limousines as eminent guests flocked to one of the most interesting receptions of the season, the charming April 6th affair given at her imposing Tudor-beamed Rosedale residence by Mrs. Winifred Griffen Prior, in honour of Miss Iris Chase of Port Ticonderoga, Ontario. Miss Chase is the daughter of Captain Norval Chase, and the grand-daughter of the late Mrs. Benjamin Montfort Chase, of Montreal. She is to wed Mrs. Griffen Prior's brother, Mr. Richard Griffen, long considered one of the most eligible bachelors of this province, at a brilliant May wedding which promises to be among the not-to-be-missed events on the bridal calendar.

Last season's "Debs" and their mothers were eager to cast eyes on the youthful bride-to-be, who was fetching in a demure Schiaparelli creation of blistered bisque crêpe, with slim-cut skirt and peplum, trimmed with accents of black velvet and jet. Against a setting of white narcissi, white trellis-work bowers, and lighted tapers in silver sconces festooned with bunches of faux black Muscadine grapes bedecked with spiralling silver ribbon, Mrs. Prior received in a gracious Chanel gown of ashes-of-roses with a draped skirt, its bodice ornamented with discreet seed pearls. Miss Chase's sister and bridesmaid, Miss Laura Chase, in leaf-green velveteen with watermelon satin accents, was also in attendance.

Among the distinguished crowd were the Lieutenant-

Governor and his wife, Mrs. Herbert A. Bruce, Col. and Mrs. R.Y. Eaton and their daughter Miss Margaret Eaton, the Hon. W.D. and Mrs. Ross and their daughters Miss Susan Ross and Miss Isobel Ross, Mrs. A.L. Ellsworth and her two daughters, Mrs. Beverley Balmer and Miss Elaine Ellsworth, Miss Jocelyn Boone and Miss Daphne Boone, and Mr. and Mrs. Grant Pepler.

The Blind Assassin: The bronze bell

It's midnight. In the city of Sakiel-Norn, a single bronze bell tolls to mark the moment when the Broken God, nightly avatar of the God of Three Suns, reaches the lowermost point of his descent into the darkness and after a ferocious combat is torn apart by the Lord of the Underworld and his band of dead warriors who live down there. He will be gathered together by the Goddess, brought back to life, and nursed to renewed health and vigour, and will emerge at dawn as usual, regenerated, filled with light.

Although the Broken God is a popular figure, nobody in the city really believes this tale about him any more. Still, the women in each household make his image out of clay and the men smash him to pieces on the darkest night of the year, and then the women make a new image of him the next day. For the children, there are small gods of sweetened bread for them to eat; for the children with their greedy little mouths represent the future, which like time itself will devour all now alive.

The King sits alone in the highest tower of his lavish palace, from which he is observing the stars and interpreting the omens and auguries for the next week. He has laid aside his woven platinum face mask, as there is no one present from whom he needs to conceal his emotions: he may smile and frown at will, just like any common Ygnirod. It's such a relief.

Right now he's smiling, a pensive smile: he's considering his latest amour, with the plump wife of a minor civil servant. She's stupid as a *thulk*, but she has a soft dense mouth like a waterlogged velvet cushion and tapered fingers deft as fish, and sly narrow eyes, and an educated knack. However, she's becoming too demanding, and also indiscreet. She's been nagging at him to compose a poem to the nape of her neck, or to some other part of her anatomy, as is the practice among the more foppish of the court lovers, but his talents do not lie in that direction. Why are women such trophy-hunters, why do they want mementoes? Or does she wish him to make a fool of himself, as a demonstration of her power?

A shame, but he'll have to get rid of her. He'll ruin her husband financially – do him the honour of dining at his house, with all of his most trusted courtiers, until the poor idiot's resources are exhausted. Then the woman will be sold into slavery to pay the debt. It might even do her good – firm up her muscles. It's a definite pleasure to imagine her minus her veil, her face bared to every passing stare, toting her new mistress's footstool or pet blue-billed *wibular* and scowling all the way. He could always have her assassinated, but that seems a little harsh: all she's really guilty of is a lust for bad poetry. He's not a tyrant.

A disembowelled *oorm* lies before him. Idly he pokes at the feathers. He doesn't care about the stars – he no longer believes all that gibberish – but he will have to squint at them for a while anyway and come up with some pronouncement. The multiplying of wealth and a bountiful harvest should do the trick in the short run, and people always forget about prophecies unless they come true.

He wonders whether there's any validity to the information he's received, from a reliable private source – his barber – that there is yet another plot being hatched against him. Will he have to make arrests again, resort to torture and executions? No doubt. Perceived softness is as bad for public order as actual softness. A tight grip on the reins is desirable. If heads must roll, his will not be among them. He will be forced to act, to protect himself; yet he feels a strange inertia. Running a kingdom is a constant strain: if he relaxes his guard, even for a moment, they'll be on him, whoever they are.

Off to the north he thinks he sees a flickering, as if something is on fire there, but then it's gone. Lightning, perhaps. He passes his hand over his eyes.

I feel sorry for him. I think he's only doing the best he can.

I think we need another drink. How about it?

I bet you're going to kill him off. You have that glint.

In all justice he'd deserve it. I think he's a bastard, myself. But kings have to be, don't they? Survival of the fittest and so forth. Weak to the wall.

You don't really believe that.

Is there another? Squeeze the bottle, will you? Because really I'm very thirsty.

I'll see. She gets up, trailing the sheet. The bottle is on the desk. No need to wrap up, he says. I enjoy the view.

She looks back at him over her shoulder. She says: It adds mystery. Toss over your glass. I wish you'd stop buying this rotgut.

It's all I can afford. Anyway I've got no taste. It's because I'm an orphan. The Presbyterians ruined me, in the orphanage. It's why I'm so gloomy and dismal.

Don't play that grubby old orphan card. My heart does not bleed.

It does, though, he says. I count on it. Apart from your legs and your very fine ass, that's what I admire most about you – the bloodiness of your heart.

It's not my heart that's bloody, it's my mind. I'm bloody-minded. Or so I've been told.

He laughs. Here's to your bloody mind then. Down the hatch.

She drinks, makes a face.

Comes out the same as it goes in, he says cheerfully. Speaking of which, I have to see a man about a dog. He gets up, goes to the window, raises the sash a little.

You can't do that!

It's a side driveway. I won't hit anyone.

At least keep behind the curtain! What about me?

What about you? You've seen a naked man before. You don't always close your eyes.

I don't mean that, I mean I can't pee out a window. I'll burst.

My pal's dressing gown, he says. See it? That plaid thing on the stand. Just check to make sure the hall's clear. The landlady's a nosy old bitch, but as long as you're wearing plaid she won't see you. You'll blend in – this dump is plaid to the core.

Well then, he says. Where was I?

It's midnight, she says. A single bronze bell tolls.

Oh yes. It's midnight. A single bronze bell tolls. As the sound dies away, the blind assassin turns the key in the door. His heart is beating hard, as it always does at such moments: moments of considerable danger to himself. If he is caught, the death that will be prepared for him will be prolonged and painful.

He feels nothing about the death he is about to inflict, nor does he care to know the reasons for it. Who is to be assassinated and why is the business of the rich and powerful, and he hates them all equally. They are the ones who took away his eyesight and forced themselves into his body by the dozens when he was too young to do anything about it, and he would welcome the chance to butcher every single one of them – them, and anyone involved in their doings, as this girl is. It means nothing to him that she's little more than a decorated and bejewelled prisoner. It means nothing to him that the same people who have made him blind have made her mute. He'll do his job and take his pay and that will be the end of it.

In any case she'll be killed tomorrow if he doesn't kill her himself tonight, and he'll be quicker and not nearly so clumsy. He's doing her a favour. There have been too many blundered sacrifices. None of these kings is any good with a knife.

He hopes she won't make too much fuss. He's been told she can't scream: about the loudest sound she can make, with her tongueless, wounded mouth, is a high, stifled mewing, like a cat in a sack. That's fine. Nevertheless he'll take precautions.

He drags the corpse of the sentry inside the room so no one will stumble across it in the corridor. Then he moves inside as well, soundless in his bare feet, and locks the door.

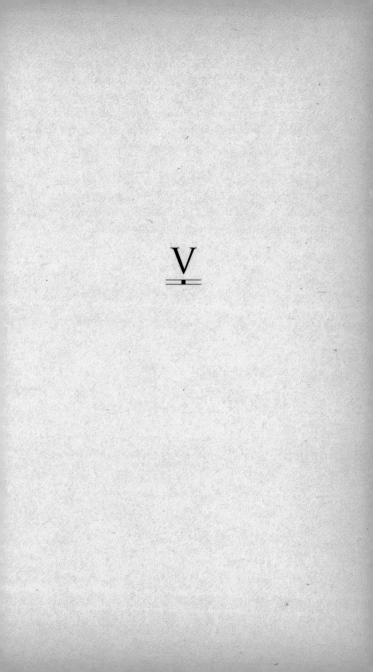

V

The fur coat

This morning the tornado warnings were out, on the weather channel, and by mid-afternoon the sky had turned a baleful shade of green and the branches of the trees had begun to thrash around as if some huge, enraged animal was fighting its way through. The storm passed directly overhead: flicked snakes' tongues of white light, stacks of tin pie plates tumbling. *Count a thousand and one*, Reenie used to tell us. *If you can say that, it's a mile away.* She said never to use the telephone during a thunderstorm or the lightning would come right through into your ear and then you'd be deaf. She said never to take a bath then either, because the lightning could run out of the tap like water. She said if the hair stood up on the back of your neck you should jump into the air, because that was the only thing that could save you.

The storm was gone by nightfall, but it was still dank as a drain. I rolled around in the muddle of my bed, listening to my heart limping against the bedsprings, trying to get comfortable. Finally I gave up on sleep and pulled a long sweater on over my nightgown, and negotiated the stairs. Then I put on my plastic raincoat with the hood and slipped my feet into my rubber boots, and went outside. The damp wood of the porch steps was treacherous. The paint's worn off them, they may be rotting.

In the faint light all was monochrome. The air was moist and still. The chrysanthemums on the front lawn sparkled with shining drops; a battalion of slugs was no doubt munching away at the few remaining leaves of the lupins. Slugs are said to like beer; I keep thinking I should put some out for them. Better them than me: it was never the form of alcohol I preferred. I wanted nervelessness quicker.

I tapped and crept my way along the damp sidewalk. There was a full moon, ringed with a pale haze; under the street lights my foreshortened shadow slid before me like a goblin. I felt I was doing a daring thing: an older woman, solitary, walking by night. A stranger might have considered me defenceless. And indeed I was a little frightened, or at least apprehensive enough to make my heart beat harder. As Myra keeps telling me so kindly, old ladies are prime targets for muggers. They are said to come in from Toronto, these muggers, as all ills do. Probably they come in on the bus, their mugging tools disguised as umbrellas, or as golf clubs. There are no lengths to which they will not go, says Myra darkly.

I went three blocks to the main route through town, then stopped to gaze across the satiny wet tarmac towards Walter's garage. Walter was sitting in the lighthouse of the glass booth, in the middle of the inky, empty pool of flat asphalt. Leaning forward in his red cap, he looked like an aging jockey on an invisible horse, or like the captain of his fate, piloting an eerie ship through outer space. In point of fact he was watching The Sports Network on his miniature TV, as I happen to know from Myra. I did not go over to speak to him: he would have been alarmed by the sight of me, looming out of the darkness in my rubber boots and nightgown like some crazed octogenarian stalker. Still, it was comforting to know that there was at least one other human being awake at that time of night.

On the way back I heard footsteps behind me. Now you've done it, I told myself, here comes the mugger. But it was only a young woman in a black raincoat, carrying a bag or small suitcase. She passed me at a fast clip, head craned forward.

Sabrina, I thought. She's come back after all. How forgiven I felt, for that instant – how blessed, how filled with grace, as if time had rolled backwards and my dry old wooden cane had burst operatically into flower. But on second glance – no, on third – it was not Sabrina at all; only some stranger. Who am I anyway, to deserve such a miraculous outcome? How can I expect it?

I do expect it though. Against all reason.

But enough of that. I take up the burden of my tale, as they used to say in poems. Back to Avilion.

Mother was dead. *Things would never be the same.* I was told to keep a stiff upper lip. Who told me that? Reenie certainly, Father perhaps. Funny, they never say anything about the lower lip. That's the one you're supposed to bite, to substitute one kind of pain for another.

At first Laura used to spend a lot of time inside Mother's fur coat. It was made of sealskin, and still had Mother's handkerchief in the pocket. Laura would get inside it and try to do up the buttons, until she hit on a way of doing them up first and then crawling in underneath. I think she must have been praying in there, or conjuring: conjuring Mother back. Whatever it was, it didn't work. And then the coat was given away to charity.

Soon Laura began to ask where the baby had gone, the one that did not look like a kitten. *To Heaven* no longer satisfied her – after it was in the basin, was what she meant. Reenie said the doctor took it away. But why wasn't there a funeral? Because it was born too little, said Reenie. How could anything so little kill Mother? Reenie said, *Never mind*. She said, *You'll know when you're older.* She said, *What you don't know won't hurt you.* A dubious maxim: sometimes what you don't know can hurt you very much.

In the nighttimes Laura would creep into my room and shake me awake, then climb into bed with me. She couldn't sleep: it was because of God. Up until the funeral, she and God had been on good terms. *God loves you*, said the Sunday-school teacher at the Methodist church, where Mother had sent us, and where Reenie continued to send us on general principles, and Laura had believed it. But now she was no longer so sure.

She began to fret about God's exact location. It was the Sunday-school teacher's fault: *God is everywhere*, she'd said, and Laura wanted to know: was God in the sun, was God in the moon, was God in the kitchen, the bathroom, was he under the bed? ("I'd like to wring that woman's neck," said Reenie.) Laura didn't want God popping out at her unexpectedly, not hard to understand considering his recent behaviour. *Open your mouth and close your eyes and I'll give you a big surprise*, Reenie used to say, holding a cookie behind her back, but Laura would no longer do it. She wanted her eyes open. It wasn't that she distrusted Reenie, only that she feared surprises.

Probably God was in the broom closet. It seemed the most likely place. He was lurking in there like some eccentric and possibly dangerous uncle, but she couldn't be certain whether he was there at any given moment because she was afraid to open the door. "God is in your heart," said the Sunday-school teacher, and that was even worse. If in the broom closet, something might have been possible, such as locking the door.

God never slept, it said in the hymn – *No careless slumber shall His eyelids close*. Instead he roamed around the house at night, spying on people – seeing if they'd been good enough, or sending plagues to finish them off, or indulging in some other whim. Sooner or later he was bound to do something unpleasant, as he'd often done in the Bible. "Listen, that's him," Laura would say. The light footstep, the heavy footstep.

"That's not God. It's only Father. He's in the turret."

"What's he doing?"

"Smoking." I didn't want to say *drinking*. It seemed disloyal.

★

I felt most tenderly towards Laura when she was asleep – her mouth a little open, her eyelashes still wet – but she was a restless sleeper; she groaned and kicked, and snored sometimes, and kept me from getting to sleep myself. I would climb down out of the bed and tiptoe across the floor, and hoist myself up to look out the bedroom window. When there was a moon the flower gardens would be silvery grey, as if all the colours had been sucked out of them. I could see the stone nymph, foreshortened; the moon was reflected in her lily pond, and she was dipping her toes into its cold light. Shivering, I would get back into bed, and lie watching the moving shadows of the curtains and listening to the gurglings and crackings of the house as it shifted itself. Wondering what I'd done wrong.

Children believe that everything bad that happens is somehow their fault, and in this I was no exception; but they also believe in happy endings, despite all evidence to the contrary, and I was no exception in that either. I only wished the happy ending would hurry up, because – especially at night, when Laura was asleep and I did not have to cheer her up – I felt so desolate.

In the mornings I would help Laura to dress – that had been my task even when Mother was alive – and make sure she brushed her teeth and washed her face. At lunchtime Reenie would sometimes let us have a picnic. We'd have buttered white bread spread with grape jelly translucent as cellophane, and raw carrots, and cut-up apples. We'd have corned beef turned out of the tin, the shape of it like an Aztec temple. We'd have hard-boiled eggs. We'd put these things on plates, and take them outside, and eat them here and there – by the pool, in the conservatory. If it was raining we'd eat them inside.

"Remember the starving Armenians," Laura would say, hands clasped, eyes closed, bowing over the crusts of her jelly sandwich. I knew she was saying it because Mother used to, and it made me want to cry. "There are no starving Armenians, they're just made up," I told her once, but she wouldn't have it.

We were left on our own a lot at that time. We learned Avilion inside out: its crevices, its caves, its tunnels. We peered into the hiding place under the back stairs, which contained a jumble of discarded overshoes and single mittens, and an umbrella with broken ribs. We explored the various branches of the cellar – the coal cellar for the coal; the root cellar for the cabbages and squashes laid out on a board, and the beets and carrots growing whiskery in their box of sand, and the potatoes with their blind albino tentacles, like the legs of crabs; the cold cellar for the apples in their barrels, and for the shelves of preserves – dusty jams and jellies glinting like uncut gems, chutneys and pickles and strawberries and peeled tomatoes and applesauce, all in Crown sealing jars. There was a wine cellar too, but it was kept locked; only Father had the key.

We found the damp dirt-floored grotto beneath the veran-dah, reached by crawling between the hollyhocks, where only spidery dandelions tried to grow, and creeping Charlie, its crushed-mint smell mingling with cat spray and (once) the hot, sick stink of an alarmed garter snake. We found the attic, with boxes of old books and stored quilts and three empty trunks, and a broken harmonium, and Grandmother Adelia's headless dress form, a pallid, musty torso.

Holding our breaths, we would make our way stealthily through our labyrinths of shadow. We took solace in this – in our secrecy, our knowledge of hidden pathways, our belief that we could not be seen.

Listen to the clock ticking, I said. It was a pendulum clock – an antique, white and gold china; it had been Grandfather's; it stood on the mantelpiece in the library. Laura thought I'd said *licking*. And it was true, the brass pendulum swinging back and forth did look like a tongue, licking the lips of an invisible mouth. Eating up the time.

It became autumn. Laura and I picked milkweed pods and opened them, to feel the scale-shaped seeds overlapping like the skin of a dragon. We pulled the seeds out and scattered them on their flossy parachutes, leaving the leathery brownish-yellow tongue, soft as the inside of an elbow. Then we went to the Jubilee Bridge and threw the pods into the river to see how long they'd sail, before they capsized or were swept away. Did we think about them as holding people, or a person? I'm not sure. But there was a certain satisfaction in watching them go under.

It became winter. The sky was a hazy grey, the sun low in the sky, a wan pinkish colour, like fish blood. Icicles, heavy and opaque and thick as a wrist, hung dripping from the roof and windowsills as if suspended in the act of falling. We broke them off and sucked the ends. Reenie told us that if we did that our tongues would turn black and drop off, but I knew this was false, having done it before.

Avilion had a boathouse then, and an icehouse, down by the jetty. In the boathouse was Grandfather's elderly sailboat, now Father's – the *Water Nixie*, high and dry and put to bed for the winter. In the icehouse was the ice, cut from the Jogues River and hauled up in blocks by horses, and stored there covered in sawdust, waiting for the summer when it would be rare.

Laura and I went out onto the slippery jetty, which we were forbidden to do. Reenie said that if we fell off and went through, we wouldn't last an instant, because the water was cold as death. Our boots would fill, we'd sink like stones. We threw some real stones out to see what would happen to them; they skittered across the ice, rested there, remained in view. Our breath made a white smoke; we blew it out in puffs, like trains, and shifted from one cold foot to the other. Under our boot-soles the snow creaked. We held hands and our mittens froze stuck together, so that when we took them off there were two woollen hands holding on to each other, empty and blue.

At the bottom of the Louveteau's rapids, jagged chunks of ice had piled up against one another. The ice was white at noon, light green in the twilight; the smaller pieces made a tinkling sound, like bells. In the centre of the river the water ran open and black. Children called from the hill on the other side, hidden by trees, their voices high and thin and happy in the cold air. They were tobogganing, which we were not allowed to do. I thought of walking out onto the jagged shore ice, to see how solid it was.

It became spring. The willow branches turned yellow, the dogwoods red. The Louveteau River was in spate; bushes and trees torn up by their roots eddied and snagged. A woman jumped off the Jubilee Bridge above the rapids and the body wasn't found for two days. It was fished out downstream, and was far from a pretty sight because going down those rapids was like being run through a meat grinder. Not the best way to depart this earth, said Reenie – not if you were interested in your looks, though most likely you wouldn't be at such a time.

Mrs. Hillcoate knew of half a dozen such jumpers, over the years. You'd read about them in the paper. One was a girl she'd gone to school with who'd married a railroad worker. He was away a lot, she said, so what did he expect? "Up the spout," she said. "And no excuse." Reenie nodded, as if this explained everything.

"No matter how stupid the man may be, most of them can count," she said, "at least on their fingers. I expect there was knuckle sandwiches. But no sense in shutting the barn door with the horse gone."

"What horse?" said Laura.

"She must have been in some other kind of trouble too," said Mrs. Hillcoate. "If you've got trouble, you've most likely got more than the one kind."

"What is the spout?" Laura whispered to me. "What spout?" But I didn't know.

As well as jumping, said Reenie, women like that might walk into the river upstream and then be sucked under the surface by the weight of their wet clothing, so they couldn't swim to safety even if they'd wanted to. A man would be more deliberate. They would hang themselves from the crossbeams of their barns, or blow their heads off with their shotguns; or if intending to drown, they would attach rocks, or other heavy objects – axe-heads, bags of nails. They didn't like to take any chances on a serious thing like that. But it was a woman's way just to walk in and resign herself, and let the water take her. It was hard to tell from Reenie's tone whether she approved of these differences or not.

I turned ten in June. Reenie made a cake, though she said maybe we shouldn't be having one, it was too soon after Mother's death, but then, life had to go on, so maybe the cake wouldn't hurt. *Hurt what*? said Laura. *Mother's feelings*, I said. Was Mother watching us, then, from Heaven? But I became obstinate and smug, and wouldn't tell. Laura wouldn't eat any of the cake, not after she'd heard that about Mother's feelings, so I ate both our pieces.

It was an effort for me now to recall the details of my grief – the exact forms it had taken – although at will I could summon up an echo of it, like a small whining dog locked in the cellar. What had I done on the day Mother died? I could hardly remember that, or what she'd really looked like: now she looked only like her photographs. I did remember the wrongness of her bed when she was suddenly no longer in it: how empty it had seemed. The way the afternoon light came slantwise in through the window and fell so silently across the hardwood floor, the dust motes floating in it like mist. The smell of beeswax furniture polish, and of wilted chrysanthemums, and the lingering aroma of bedpan and disinfectant. I could remember her absence, now, much better than her presence.

Reenie said to Mrs. Hillcoate that although nobody could ever take the place of Mrs. Chase, who'd been a saint on earth if there could be such a thing, she herself had done what she could, and she'd kept up a cheerful front for our sakes because least said, soonest mended, and luckily we did seem to be getting over it, though still waters ran deep and I was too quiet for my own good. I was the brooding type, she said; it was bound to come out somehow. As for Laura, who could tell, because she'd always been an odd child anyway.

Reenie said we were together too much. She said Laura was learning ways that were too old for her, and I was being kept back. We should each of us be with children our own age, but the few children in town who might have been suitable for us had already been sent away to school – to private schools like the ones we should be sent off to by rights, but Captain Chase could never seem to get around to arranging it, and anyway it would be too many changes all at once, and although I was cool as a cucumber and would certainly be able to manage it, Laura was young for her age, and, come to that, too young altogether. Also she was too nervous. She was the type to panic and thrash around and drown in six inches of water, through not keeping her head.

Laura and I sat on the back stairs with the door open a crack, hands over our mouths to keep from laughing. We enjoyed the delights of espionage. But it did neither of us much good to overhear such things about ourselves.

The Weary Soldier

Today I walked to the bank – early, to avoid the worst heat, but also to be there when it opened. That way I could be sure of getting someone's attention, a thing I needed since they'd made yet another mistake on my statement. I can still add and subtract, I tell them, unlike those machines of yours, and they smile at me like waiters, the kind who spit in your soup in the kitchen. I always ask to see the manager, the manager is always "in a meeting," I always get shifted off to some smirking, patronizing elf just out of short pants who sees himself as a future plutocrat.

I feel despised there, for having so little money; also for once having had so much. I never actually had it, of course. Father had it, and then Richard. But money was imputed to me, the same way crimes are imputed to those who've simply been present at them.

The bank has Roman pillars, to remind us to render unto Caesar the things that are Caesar's, such as those ridiculous service charges. For two cents I'd keep my money in a sock under the mattress just to spite them. But word would get around, I suppose – word that I'd become a loony old eccentric of the kind found dead in a hovel crammed with hundreds of empty cat food tins and a couple of million bucks stashed in five-dollar bills between the pages of yellowing newspapers. I have no desire to become an object of attention to the local hopheads and amateur second-storey men, with their bloodshot eyes and twitchy fingers.

On the way back from the bank I walked around by the Town Hall, with its Italianate bell tower and its Florentine two-tone brickwork, its flagpole that needs painting, its field gun present at the Somme. Also its two bronze statues, both commissioned by the Chase family. The right-hand one, commissioned by my Grandmother Adelia, is of Colonel Parkman, a veteran of the last decisive battle fought in the American Revolution, that of Fort Ticonderoga, now in New York State. Once in a while we'll get some confused Germans or Englishmen or even Americans wandering through town, looking for the Fort Ticonderoga battlefield. *Wrong town*, they're told. *Come to think of it, wrong country. You want the next one over.*

It was Colonel Parkman who upped stakes, crossed the border, and named our town, thus perversely commemorating a battle in which he'd lost. (Though perhaps that's not so unusual: many people take a curatorial interest in their own scars.) He's shown astride his horse, waving a sword and about to gallop into the nearby petunia bed: a craggy man with seasoned eyes and a pointed beard, every sculptor's idea of every cavalry leader. No one knows what Colonel Parkman really looked like, since he left no pictorial evidence of himself and the statue wasn't erected until 1885, but he looks like this now. Such is the tyranny of Art.

On the left-hand side of the lawn, also with a petunia bed, is an equally mythic figure: the Weary Soldier, his three top shirt buttons undone, his neck bowed as if for the headman's axe, his uniform rumpled, his helmet askew, leaning on his malfunctioning Ross rifle. Forever young, forever exhausted, he tops the War Memorial, his skin burning green in the sun, pigeon droppings running down his face like tears.

The Weary Soldier was a project of my father's. The sculptress was Callista Fitzsimmons, who'd come highly recommended by Frances Loring, convenor of the War Memorial Committee of the Ontario Society of Artists. There was some local objection to Miss Fitzsimmons — a woman wasn't considered appropriate for the subject – but Father steamrollered the meeting of potential sponsors: wasn't Miss Loring herself a woman, he asked? Thus inspiring several irreverent comments, *How can you tell* being the cleanest of them. In private, he said that he who pays the piper calls the tune, and since the rest of them were such cheapskates they'd better either dig deep or knuckle under.

Miss Callista Fitzsimmons was not only a woman, she was also twenty-eight years old and a redhead. She began coming to Avilion frequently, to confer with Father on the proposed design. These sessions would take place in the library, with the door open at first and then not. She was put up in one of the guest rooms, the second-best one at first and then the best. Soon she was there almost every weekend, and her room became known as "her" room.

Father seemed happier; certainly he was drinking less. He had the grounds tidied up, at least enough to be presentable; he had the drive regravelled; he had the *Water Nixie* scraped and painted and refitted. Sometimes there were informal weekend house parties, the guests being artistic friends of Callista's from Toronto. These artists, among whom there were no names that might currently be recognized, did not wear dinner jackets or even suits to dinner, but V-necked sweaters; they ate scratch meals on the lawn, and discussed the finer points of Art, and smoked and drank and argued. The girl artists used too many towels in the bathrooms, no doubt because they'd never seen the inside of a proper bathtub before, was Reenie's theory. Also they had grubby fingernails, which they bit.

When there were no house parties Father and Callista would go off on picnics, in one of the cars – the roadster, not the sedan – with a basket packed grudgingly by Reenie. Or they'd go sailing, Callista in slacks with her hands in the pockets, like Coco Chanel, and one of Father's old crewneck jerseys.

Sometimes they would drive all the way to Windsor, and stop at roadhouses that featured cocktails and ferocious piano-playing and raffish dancing – roadhouses frequented by gangsters involved in the rum-running, who would come up from Chicago and Detroit to make their deals with the law-abiding distillers on the Canadian side. (It was Prohibition in the United States then; liquor flowed across the border like very expensive water; dead bodies with the ends of their fingers cut off and nothing in their pockets were tossed into the Detroit River and ended up on the beaches of Lake Erie, causing debate as to who was to incur the expense of burying them.) On these trips Father and Callista would stay away all night, and sometimes for several nights. Once they went to Niagara Falls, which made Reenie envious, and once to Buffalo; but they went to Buffalo on a train.

We got these details from Callista, who was not stingy with details. She told us that Father needed "pepping up," and that this pepping-up was good for him. She said he needed to kick up his heels, to mingle more in life. She said she and Father were "great pals." She took to calling us "the kids;" she said we could call her "Callie."

(Laura wanted to know if Father danced too, at the road-houses: it was hard to imagine, because of his ruined leg. Callista said no, but that it was fun for him to watch. I have come to doubt that. It is never much fun to watch other people dance when you can't do it yourself.)

I was in awe of Callista because she was an artist, and was consulted like a man, and strode around and shook hands like one as well, and smoked cigarettes in a short black holder, and knew about Coco Chanel. She had pierced ears, and her red ʰ ⸌done with henna, I now realize) was wound around with She wore flowing robe-like garments in bold swirling ⸌ia, heliotrope, and saffron were the names of the colours. She told me these designs were from Paris, and were inspired by White Russian émigrés. She explained what those were. She was full of explanations.

"One of his floozies," said Reenie to Mrs. Hillcoate. "Just one more of them on the string, which Lord knows was as long as your arm already, but you'd think he'd have the decency not to bring her in under the same roof, with her not cold in the grave he might as well have dug his very own self."

"What's a floozie?" said Laura.

"Mind your own beeswax," said Reenie. It was a sign of her anger that she kept on talking even though Laura and I were in the kitchen. (Later I told Laura what a floozie was: it was a girl who chewed gum. But Callie Fitzsimmons didn't do that.)

"Little pitchers have big ears," said Mrs. Hillcoate warningly, but Reenie went on.

"As for those outlandish get-ups she wears, she might as well go to church in her scanties. Against the light you can see the sun, the moon and the stars, and everything in between. Not that she's got much to show, she's one of those flappers, she's flat as a boy."

"I'd never have the nerve," said Mrs. Hillcoate.

"You can't call it nerve," said Reenie. "She don't give a rat's ass." (When Reenie got worked up her grammar slipped.) "There's something missing, if you ask me; she's two bricks short of a load. She went skinny-dipping in the lily pond, with all the frogs and goldfish – I met her coming back across the lawn, with only a towel and what God gave Eve. She just nodded and smiled, she didn't bat an eye."

"I did hear about that," said Mrs. Hillcoate. "I thought it was only gossip. It sounded far-fetched."

"She's a gold-digger," said Reenie. "She only wants to get her hooks into him, then clean him out."

"What's a gold-digger? What are hooks?" said Laura.

Flapper made me think of limp, wet washing on the line, in the wind. Callista Fitzsimmons was nothing like that.

There was a squabble over the War Memorial, and not only because of the rumours about Father and Callista Fitzsimmons. Some people in town thought the Weary Soldier statue was too dejected-looking, and also too slovenly: they objected to the unbuttoned shirt. They wanted something more triumphant, like the Goddess of Victory on the memorial two towns over, which had angel's wings and wind-swept robes and was holding a three-pronged implement that looked like a toasting fork. They also wanted "For Those Who Willingly Made the Supreme Sacrifice" to be written on the front.

Father refused to back down on the sculpture, saying they could consider themselves lucky the Weary Soldier had two arms and two legs, not to mention a head, and that if they didn't watch out he'd go in for bare-naked realism all the way and the statue would be made of rotting body fragments, of which he had stepped on a good many in his day. As for the inscription, there was nothing willing about the sacrifice, as it had not been the intention of the dead to get themselves blown to Kingdom come. He himself favoured "Lest We Forget," which put the onus where it should be: on our own forgetfulness. He said a damn sight too many people had been a damn sight too forgetful. He rarely swore in public, so it made an impression. He got his way, of course, since he was paying.

The Chamber of Commerce stumped up for the four bronze plaques, with the honour rolls of the fallen and the names of the battles. They wanted their own name printed at the bottom, but Father shamed them out of it. The War Memorial was for the dead, he told them – not for those who'd remained alive, much less reaped the benefits. This kind of talk got him resented by some.

The memorial was unveiled in the November of 1928, on Remembrance Day. There was a large crowd, despite the chill drizzle. The Weary Soldier had been mounted on a four-sided pyramid of rounded river stones, like the stones of Avilion, and the bronze plaques were bordered with lilies and poppies, intertwined with maple leaves. There had been some argument about this too. Callie Fitzsimmons said the design was old-fashioned and banal, with all those droopy flowers and leaves – *Victorian*, the artists' worst insult in those days. She wanted something starker, more modern. But the people in town liked it, and Father said you had to compromise sometimes.

At the ceremony, bagpipes were played. ("Better outdoors than in," said Reenie.) Then there was the main sermon, by the Presbyterian minister, who talked about *those who had willingly made the Supreme Sacrifice* – the town's dig at Father, to show he couldn't hog the proceedings and money couldn't buy everything, and they'd got that phrase in despite him. Then more speeches were made, and prayers were said – many speeches and many prayers, because the ministers of every kind of church in town had to be represented. Though there were no Catholics on the organizing committee, even the Catholic priest was allowed to say a piece. My father pushed for this, on the grounds that a dead Catholic soldier was just as dead as a dead Protestant one.

Reenie said that was one way of looking at it.

"What is the other way?" said Laura.

My father laid the first wreath. Laura and I watched, hand in hand; Reenie cried. The Royal Canadian Regiment had sent a delegation, all the way from Wolseley Barracks in London, and Major M. K. Greene laid a wreath. Wreaths were then laid by just about everyone you could think of – the Legion, followed by the Lions, the Kinsmen, the Rotary Club, the

Oddfellows, the Orange Order, the Knights of Columbus, the Chamber of Commerce, and the I.O.D.E. among others – with the last one being Mrs. Wilmer Sullivan for Mothers of the Fallen, who had lost three sons. "Abide with Me" was sung, then "Last Post" was played, a little shakily, by a bugler from the Scouts band, followed by two minutes of silence and a rifle volley fired by the Militia. Then we had "Reveille."

Father stood with head bowed, but he was visibly shaking, whether from grief or rage it is hard to say. He wore his uniform under a greatcoat, and leaned with his two leather-gloved hands on his cane.

Callie Fitzsimmons was there, but she kept in the back-ground. It was not the sort of occasion on which the artist should step forward and make a bow, she'd told us. She wore a decorous black coat and a regular skirt instead of a robe, and a hat that concealed most of her face, but was whispered about all the same.

Afterwards Reenie made cocoa, for Laura and me, in the kitchen, to warm us up because we'd got chilled in the drizzle. A cup was offered as well to Mrs. Hillcoate, who said she wouldn't say no to it.

"Why is it called a memorial?" said Laura.

"It's for us to remember the dead," said Reenie.

"Why?" said Laura. "What for? Do they like it?"

"It's not for them, it's more for us," said Reenie. "You'll understand when you're older." Laura was always being told this, and discounted it. She wanted to understand now. She upended her cocoa.

"Can I have more? What is the Supreme Sacrifice?"

"The soldiers gave their lives for the rest of us. I certainly hope your eyes aren't bigger than your stomach, because if I make this I'll expect you to finish it."

"Why did they give their lives? Did they want to?"

"No, but they did it anyway. That's why it's a sacrifice," said Reenie. "Now that's enough of that. Here's your cocoa."

"They gave their lives to God, because that's what God wants. It's like Jesus, who died for all of our sins," said Mrs. Hillcoate, who was a Baptist, and considered herself the ultimate authority.

A week later Laura and I were walking along the path beside the Louveteau, below the Gorge. There was mist that day, rising from the river, swirling like skim milk in the air, dripping from the bare twigs of the bushes. The stones of the path were slippery.

All of a sudden Laura was in the river. Luckily we weren't right beside the main current, so she wasn't swept away. I screamed and ran downstream and got hold of her by the coat; her clothes weren't waterlogged yet, but still she was very heavy, and I almost fell in myself. I managed to pull her along to where there was a flat ledge; then I hauled her out. She was sopping like a wet sheep, and I was pretty wet myself. Then I shook her. By that time she was shivering and crying.

"You did it on purpose!" I said. "I saw you! You could've drowned!" Laura gulped and sobbed. I hugged her. "Why did you?"

"So God would let Mother be alive again," she wailed.

"God doesn't want you to be dead," I said. "That would make him very mad! If he wanted Mother to be alive, he could do it anyway, without you drowning yourself." This was the only way to talk to Laura when she got into such moods: you had to pretend you knew something about God that she didn't.

She wiped her nose with the back of her hand. "How do *you* know?"

"Because look – he let me save you! See? If he wanted you to be dead, then I'd have fallen in too. We'd both be dead! Now come on, you have to get dry. I won't tell Reenie. I'll say it was an accident, I'll say you slipped. But don't do anything like that again. Okay?"

Laura said nothing, but she allowed me to lead her home. There was a lot of frightened clucking and dithering and scolding, and a cup of beef broth and a warm bath and a hot-water bottle for Laura, whose mishap was put down to her well-known clumsiness; she was told to watch where she was going. Father said *Well done* to me; I wondered what he would have said if I'd lost her. Reenie said it was a good thing we had at least half a wit between the two of us, but what had we been doing down there in the first place? And in the mist, at that. She said I should have known better.

I lay awake for hours that night, arms wrapped around myself, hugging myself tight. My feet were stone cold, my teeth were chattering. I couldn't get out of my mind the image of Laura, in the icy black water of the Louveteau – how her hair had spread out like smoke in a swirling wind, how her wet face had gleamed silvery, how she had glared at me when I'd grabbed her by the coat. How hard it had been to hold on to her. How close I had come to letting go.

Miss Violence

Instead of school, Laura and I were provided with a succession of tutors, men and women both. We didn't think they were necessary, and did our best to discourage them. We would fix them with our light-blue stares, or pretend to be deaf or stupid; we'd never look them in the eye, only in the forehead. It often took longer than you'd think to get rid of them: as a rule they'd put up with quite a lot from us, because they were browbeaten by life and needed the pay. We had nothing against them as individuals; we simply didn't want to be burdened with them.

When we weren't with these tutors we were supposed to stay at Avilion, either inside the house or on the grounds. But who was there to police us? The tutors were easy to elude, they didn't know our secret pathways, and Reenie couldn't keep track of us every minute, as she herself often pointed out. Whenever we could, we would steal away from Avilion and roam the town, despite Reenie's belief that the world was full of criminals and anarchists and sinister Orientals with opium pipes, thin moustaches like twisted rope and long pointed fingernails, and dope fiends and white slavers, waiting to snatch us away and hold us to ransom for Father's money.

One of Reenie's many brothers had something to do with cheap magazines, the pulpy, trashy kind you could buy in drugstores, and the worse ones you could get only under the counter. What was his job? *Distribution*, Reenie called it. Smuggling them into the country, I now believe. In any case he would sometimes give the leftovers to Reenie, and despite her efforts to conceal them from us we would get our hands on them sooner or later. Some of them were about romance, and although Reenie devoured these we had little use for them. We preferred – or I preferred, and Laura tagged along – those with stories about other lands or even other planets. Spaceships from the future, where women would wear very short skirts made of shiny fabric and everything would gleam; asteroids where the plants could talk, roamed by monsters with enormous eyes and fangs; long-ago countries inhabited by lithe girls with topaz eyes and opaline skin, dressed in cheesecloth trousers and little metal brassieres like two funnels joined by a chain. Heroes in harsh costumes, their winged helmets bristling with spikes.

Silly, Reenie called these. *Like nothing on earth.* But that's what I liked about them.

The criminals and white slavers were in the detective magazines, with their pistol-strewn, blood-drenched covers. In these, the wide-eyed heiresses to great fortunes were always being conked out with ether and tied up with clothesline – much more than was needed – and locked into yacht cabins or abandoned church crypts, or the dank cellars of castles. Laura and I believed in the existence of such men, but we weren't too afraid of them, because we knew what to expect. They would have large, dark motor cars, and would be wearing overcoats and thick gloves and black fedoras, and we would be able to spot them immediately and run away.

But we never saw any. The only hostile forces we encountered were the factory workers' children, the younger ones, who didn't yet know that we were supposed to be untouchable. They would follow us in twos and threes, silent and curious or calling names; once in a while they'd throw stones, although they never hit us. We were most vulnerable to them when poking along the narrow path down beside the Louveteau, with the cliff overhead – things could be dropped on us there – or in back alleyways, which we learned to avoid.

We would go along Erie Street, examining the store windows: the five and dime was our favourite. Or we would peer in through the chain-link fence at the primary school, which was for ordinary children – workers' children – with its cinder playground and its high carved doorways marked Boys and Girls. At recess there was a lot of screaming, and the children were not clean, especially after they'd been fighting or had been pushed down onto the cinders. We were thankful that we didn't have to attend this school. (Were we indeed thankful? Or, on the other hand, did we feel excluded? Perhaps both.)

We wore hats for these excursions. We had the idea that they were a protection; that they made us, in a way, invisible. A lady never went out without her hat, said Reenie. She also said *gloves*, but we didn't always bother with those. Straw hats are what I remember, from that time: not pale straw, a burnt colour. And the damp heat of June, the air drowsy with pollen. The blue glare of the sky. The indolence, the loitering.

How I would like to have them back, those pointless afternoons – the boredom, the aimlessness, the unformed possibilities. And I do have them back, in a way; except now there won't be much of whatever happens next.

The tutor we had by this time had lasted longer than most. She was a forty-year-old woman with a wardrobe of faded cashmere cardigans that hinted at an earlier, more prosperous existence, and a roll of mouse-hair pinned to the back of her head. Her name was Miss Goreham – Miss Violet Goreham. I nicknamed her Miss Violence behind her back, because I thought it was such an unlikely combination, and after that I could scarcely look at her without giggling. The name stuck, though; I taught it to Laura, and then of course Reenie found out about it. She told us we were naughty to make fun of Miss Goreham in this way; the poor thing had come down in the world and deserved our pity, because she was an old maid. What was that? A woman with no husband. Miss Goreham had been doomed to a life of single blessedness, said Reenie with a trace of contempt.

"But you don't have a husband either," said Laura.

"That's different," said Reenie. "I never yet saw a man I'd stoop to blow my nose on, but I've turned away my share. I've had my offers."

"Maybe Miss Violence has too," I said, just to be contradictory. I was approaching that age.

"No," said Reenie, "she hasn't."

"How do you know?" said Laura.

"You can tell by the look of her," said Reenie. "Anyway if she'd had any offer at all, even if the man had three heads and a tail, she'd of grabbed him quick as a snake."

We got along with Miss Violence because she let us do what we liked. She realized early on that she lacked the forcefulness to control us, and had wisely decided not to bother trying. We took our lessons in the mornings, in the library, which had once been Grandfather Benjamin's and was now Father's, and Miss Violence simply gave us the run of it. The shelves were full of heavy leather-backed books with the titles stamped in dim gold, and I doubt that Grandfather Benjamin ever read them: they were only Grandmother Adelia's idea of what he ought to have read.

I'd pick out books that interested me: *A Tale of Two Cities*, by Charles Dickens; Macaulay's histories; *The Conquest of Mexico* and *The Conquest of Peru*, illustrated. I read poetry, as well, and Miss Violence occasionally made a half-hearted attempt at teaching by having me read it out loud. *In Xanadu did Kubla Khan, A stately pleasure-dome decree. In Flanders fields the poppies blow, Between the crosses, row on row.*

"Don't jog along," said Miss Violence. "The lines should *flow*, dear. Pretend you're a fountain." Although she herself was lumpy and inelegant, she had high standards of delicacy and a long list of things she wanted us to pretend to be: flowering trees, butterflies, the gentle breezes. Anything but little girls with dirty knees and their fingers up their noses: about matters of personal hygiene she was fastidious.

"Don't chew your coloured pencils, dear," said Miss Violence to Laura. "You aren't a rodent. Look, your mouth is all green. It's bad for your teeth."

I read *Evangeline*, by Henry Wadsworth Longfellow; I read Elizabeth Barrett Browning's *Sonnets from the Portuguese*. *How do I love thee? Let me count the ways*. "Beautiful," sighed Miss Violence. She was gushy, or as gushy as her dejected nature would allow, on the subject of Elizabeth Barrett Browning; also E. Pauline Johnson, the Mohawk Princess.

And oh, the river runs swifter now;
The eddies circle about my bow.
Swirl, swirl!
How the ripples curl
In many a dangerous pool awhirl!

"Stirring, dear," said Miss Violence.

Or I read Alfred, Lord Tennyson, a man whose majesty was second only to God's, in the opinion of Miss Violence.

With blackest moss the flower-plots
        Were thickly crusted, one and all:
The rusted nails fell from the knots
        That held the pear to the gable-wall. . . .
                She only said, "My life is dreary,
                        He cometh not," she said;
                She said, "I am aweary, aweary,
                        I would that I were dead!"

"Why did she wish that?" said Laura, who did not usually show much interest in my recitations.

"It was love, dear," said Miss Violence. "It was boundless love. But it was unrequited."

"Why?"

Miss Violence sighed. "It's a poem, dear," she said. "Lord Tennyson wrote it and I suppose he knew best. A poem does not reason why. 'Beauty is truth, truth beauty – that is all ye know on earth, and all ye need to know.'"

Laura looked at her with scorn, and went back to her colouring. I turned the page: I'd already skimmed the whole poem, and found that nothing else happened in it.

> Break, break, break,
> On thy cold gray stones, O Sea!
> And I would that my tongue could utter
> The thoughts that arise in me.

"Lovely, dear," said Miss Violence. She was fond of boundless love, but she was equally fond of hopeless melancholy.

There was a thin book bound in snuff-coloured leather, which had belonged to Grandmother Adelia: *The Rubáiyát of Omar Khayyám*, by Edward Fitzgerald. (Edward Fitzgerald hadn't really written it, and yet he was said to be the author. How to account for it? I didn't try to.) Miss Violence would sometimes read from this book, to show me how poetry ought to be pronounced:

> A Book of Verses underneath the Bough,
> A Jug of Wine, a Loaf of Bread – and Thou
>   Beside me singing in the Wilderness –
> Oh, Wilderness were Paradise enow!

She gasped out the Oh as if someone had kicked her in the chest; similarly the Thou. I thought it was a lot of fuss to make about a picnic, and wondered what they'd had on the bread. "Of course it wasn't real wine, dear," said Miss Violence. "It refers to the Communion Service."

> Would but some wingèd Angel ere too late
> Arrest the yet unfolded Roll of Fate,
>   And make the stern Recorder otherwise
> Enregister, or quite obliterate!

> Ah, Love! Could you and I with Him conspire
> To grasp this sorry Scheme of Things entire,
>   Would we not shatter it to bits — and then
> Remould it nearer to the heart's Desire!

"So true," said Miss Violence, with a sigh. But she sighed about everything. She fit into Avilion very well — into its obsolete Victorian splendours, its air of aesthetic decay, of departed grace, of wan regret. Her attitudes and even her faded cashmeres went with the wallpaper.

Laura didn't read much. Instead she would copy pictures, or else she'd colour in the black-and-white illustrations in thick, erudite books of travel and history with her coloured pencils. (Miss Violence let her do this, on the assumption that no one else would notice.) Laura had strange but very definite ideas about which colours were required: she'd make a tree blue or red, she'd make the sky pink or green. If there was a picture of someone she disapproved she'd do the face purple or dark grey to obliterate the features.

She liked to draw the pyramids, from a book on Egypt; she liked to colour in the Egyptian idols. Also Assyrian statues with the bodies of winged lions and the heads of eagles or men. That was from a book by Sir Henry Layard, who'd discovered the statues in the ruins of Nineveh and had them shipped to England; they were said to be illustrations of the angels described in the Book of Ezekiel. Miss Violence did not consider these pictures very nice – the statues looked pagan, and also bloodthirsty – but Laura was not to be deterred. In the face of criticism she would just crouch farther over the page and colour away as if her life depended on it.

"Back straight, dear," Miss Violence would say. "Pretend your spine is a tree, growing up towards the sun." But Laura was not interested in this kind of pretending.

"I don't want to be a tree," she would say.

"Better a tree than a hunchback, dear," Miss Violence would sigh, "and if you don't pay attention to your posture, that's what you'll turn into."

Much of the time Miss Violence sat by the window and read romantic novels from the lending library. She also liked to leaf through my Grandmother Adelia's tooled-leather scrapbooks, with their dainty embossed invitations carefully glued in, their menus printed up at the newspaper office, and the subsequent newspaper clippings – the charity teas, the improving lectures illustrated by lantern slides – the hardy, amiable travellers to Paris and Greece and even India, the Swedenborgians, the Fabians, the Vegetarians, all the various promoters of self-improvement, with once in a while something truly outré – a missionary to Africa, or the Sahara, or New Guinea, describing how the natives practised witchcraft or hid their women behind elaborate wooden masks or decorated the skulls of their ancestors with red paint and cowrie shells. All the yellowing paper evidence of that luxurious, ambitious, relentless vanished life, which Miss Violence pored over inch by inch, as if remembering it, smiling with gentle vicarious pleasure.

She had a packet of tinsel stars, gold and silver, which she would stick onto things we'd done. Sometimes she took us out to collect wildflowers, which we pressed between two sheets of blotting paper, with a heavy book on top. We grew fond of her, although we didn't cry when she left. She cried, however – wetly, inelegantly, the way she did everything.

I became thirteen. I'd been growing, in ways that were not my fault, although they seemed to annoy Father as much as if they had been. He began to take an interest in my posture, in my speech, in my deportment generally. My clothing should be simple and plain, with white blouses and dark pleated skirts, and dark velvet dresses for church. Clothes that looked like uniforms – that looked like sailor suits, but were not. My shoulders should be straight, with no slouching. I should not sprawl, chew gum, fidget, or chatter. The values he required were those of the army: neatness, obedience, silence, and no evident sexuality. Sexuality, although it was never spoken of, was to be nipped in the bud. He had let me run wild for too long. It was time for me to be taken in hand.

Laura came in for some of this hectoring too, although she had not yet reached the age for it. (What was the age for it? The pubescent age, it's clear to me now. But then I was merely confused. What crime had I committed? Why was I being treated like the inmate of some curious reform school?)

"You're being too hard on the kiddies," said Callista. "They're not boys."

"Unfortunately," said Father.

It was Callista I went to on the day I found I had developed a horrible disease, because blood was seeping out from between my legs: surely I was dying! Callista laughed. Then she explained. "It's just a nuisance," she said. She said I should refer to it as "my friend," or else "a visitor." Reenie had more Presbyterian ideas. "It's the curse," she said. She stopped short of saying that it was yet one more peculiar arrangement of God's, devised to make life disagreeable: it was just the way things were, she said. As for the blood, you tore up rags. (She did not say *blood*, she said *mess*.) She made me a cup of chamomile tea, which tasted the way spoiled lettuce smelled; also a hot-water bottle, for the cramps. Neither one helped.

Laura found a splotch of blood on my bedsheets and began to weep. She concluded that I was dying. I would die like Mother, she sobbed, without telling her first. I would have a little grey baby like a kitten and then I would die.

I told her not to be an idiot. I said this blood had nothing to do with babies. (Callista hadn't gone into that part, having no doubt decided that too much of this kind of information at once might warp my psyche.)

"It'll happen to you one day too," I said to Laura. "When you're my age. It's a thing that happens to girls."

Laura was indignant. She refused to believe it. As with so much else, she was convinced that an exception would be made in her case.

There's a studio portrait of Laura and me, taken at this time. I'm wearing the regulation dark velvet dress, a style too young for me: I have, noticeably, what used to be called *bosoms*. Laura sits beside me, in an identical dress. We both have white knee socks, patent-leather Mary Janes; our legs are crossed decorously at the ankle, right over left, as instructed. I have my arm around Laura, but tentatively, as if ordered to place it there. Laura on her part has her hands folded in her lap. Each of us has her light hair parted in the middle and pulled back tightly from her face. Both of us are smiling, in that apprehensive way children have when told they must be good and smile, as if the two things are the same: it's a smile imposed by the threat of disapproval. The threat and the disapproval would have been Father's. We were afraid of them, but did not know how to avoid them.

Ovid's Metamorphoses

Father had decided, correctly enough, that our education had been neglected. He wanted us taught French, but also Mathematics and Latin – brisk mental exercises that would act as a corrective for our excessive dreaminess. Geography too would be bracing. Although he'd barely noticed her during her tenure, he decreed that Miss Violence and her lax, musty, rose-tinted ways must be scrubbed away. He wanted the lacy, frilly, somewhat murky edges trimmed off us as if we were lettuces, leaving a plain, sound core. He didn't understand why we liked what we liked. He wanted us turned into the semblances of boys, one way or another. Well, what do you expect? He'd never had sisters.

In the place of Miss Violence, he engaged a man called Mr. Erskine, who'd once taught at a boys' school in England but had been packed off to Canada, suddenly, for his health. He did not seem at all unhealthy to us: he never coughed, for instance. He was stocky, tweed-covered, thirty or thirty-five perhaps, with reddish hair and a plump wet red mouth, and a tiny goatee and a cutting irony and a nasty temper, and a smell like the bottom of a damp laundry hamper.

It was soon clear that inattentiveness and staring at Mr. Erskine's forehead would not rid us of him. First of all he gave us tests, to determine what we knew. Not much, it appeared, though more than we saw fit to divulge. He then told Father that we had the brains of insects or marmots. We were nothing short of deplorable, and it was a wonder we were not cretins. We had developed slothful mental habits – we had been *allowed* to develop them, he added reprovingly. Happily, it was not too late. My father said that in that case Mr. Erskine should work us up into shape.

To us, Mr. Erskine said that our laziness, our arrogance, our tendency to lollygag and daydream, and our sloppy sentimentality had all but ruined us for the serious business of life. No one expected us to be geniuses, and it would be conferring no favours if we were, but there was surely a minimum, even for girls: we would be nothing but encumbrances to any man foolish enough to marry us unless we were made to pull up our socks.

He ordered a large stack of school exercise books, the cheap kind with ruled lines and flimsy cardboard covers. He ordered a supply of plain lead pencils, with erasers. These were the magic wands, he said, by means of which we were about to transform ourselves, with his assistance.

He said *assistance* with a smirk.

He threw out Miss Goreham's tinsel stars.

The library was too distracting for us, he said. He asked for and received two school desks, which he installed in one of the extra bedrooms; he had the bed removed, along with all the other furniture, so there was just the bare room left. The door locked with a key, and he had the key. Now we would be able to roll up our sleeves and get down to it.

Mr. Erskine's methods were direct. He was a hair-puller, an ear-twister. He would whack the desks beside our fingers with his ruler, and the actual fingers too, or cuff us across the back of the head when exasperated, or, as a last resort, hurl books at us or hit us across the backs of our legs. His sarcasm was withering, at least to me: Laura frequently thought he meant exactly what he said, which angered him further. He was not moved by tears; in fact I believe he enjoyed them.

He was not like this every day. Things would go along on an even keel for a week at a time. He might display patience, even a sort of clumsy kindness. Then there would be an outburst, and he would go on the rampage. Never knowing what he might do, or when he might do it, was the worst.

We could not complain to Father, because wasn't Mr. Erskine acting under his orders? He said he was. But we complained to Reenie, of course. She was outraged. I was too old to be treated like that, she said, and Laura was too nervous, and both of us were – well, who did he think he was? Raised in a gutter and putting on airs, like all the English who ended up over here, thinking they could lord it, and if he took a bath once a month she'd eat her own shirt. When Laura came to Reenie with welts on the palms of her hands, Reenie confronted Mr. Erskine, but was told to mind her own business. She was the one who'd spoiled us, said Mr. Erskine. She'd spoiled us with overindulgence and babying – that much was obvious – and now it was up to him to repair the damage she had done.

Laura said that unless Mr. Erskine went away, she would go away herself. She would run away. She would jump out the window.

"Don't do that, my pet," said Reenie. "We'll put on our thinking caps. We'll fix his wagon!"

"He hasn't got a wagon," sobbed Laura.

Callista Fitzsimmons might have been some help, but she could see which way the wind was blowing: we weren't her children, we were Father's. He had chosen his course of action, and it would have been a tactical mistake for her to meddle. It was a case of *sauve qui peut*, an expression which, due to Mr. Erskine's diligence, I could now translate.

Mr. Erskine's idea of Mathematics was simple enough: we needed to know how to balance household accounts, which meant adding and subtracting and double-entry book-keeping.

His idea of French was verb forms and *Phaedra*, with a reliance on pithy maxims from noted authors. *Si jeunesse savait, si vieillesse pouvait* – Estienne; *C'est de quoi j'ai le plus de peur que la peur* – Montaigne; *Le cœur a ses raisons que la raison ne connaît point* – Pascal; *L'histoire, cette vieille dame exaltée et menteuse* – de Maupassant. *Il ne faut pas toucher aux idoles: la dorure en reste aux mains* – Flaubert. *Dieu s'est fait homme; soit. Le diable s'est fait femme* – Victor Hugo. And so forth.

His idea of Geography was the capital cities of Europe. His idea of Latin was Caesar subduing the Gauls and crossing the Rubicon, *alea iacta est*; and, after that, selections from Virgil's *Aeneid* – he was fond of the suicide of Dido – or from Ovid's *Metamorphoses*, the parts where unpleasant things were done by the gods to various young women. The rape of Europa by a large white bull, of Leda by a swan, of Danae by a shower of gold – these would at least hold our attention, he said, with his ironic smile. He was right about that. For a change, he would have us translate Latin love poems of a cynical kind. *Odi et amo* – that sort of thing. He got a kick out of watching us struggle with the poets' bad opinions of the kinds of girls we were apparently destined to be.

"*Rapio, rapere, rapui, raptum*," said Mr. Erskine. "'To seize and carry off.' The English word *rapture* comes from the same root. Decline." *Smack* went the ruler.

We learned. We did learn, in a spirit of vengefulness: we would give Mr. Erskine no excuses. There was nothing he wanted more than to get a foot on each of our necks – well, he would be denied the pleasure, if possible. What we really learned from him was how to cheat. It was difficult to fake the mathematics, but we spent many hours in the late afternoons cribbing up our translations of Ovid from a couple of books in Grandfather's library – old translations by eminent Victorians, with small print and complicated vocabularies. We would get the sense of the passage from these books, then substitute other, simpler words, and add a few mistakes, to make it look as if we'd done it ourselves. Whatever we did, though, Mr. Erskine would slash up our translations with his red pencil and write savage comments in the margins. We didn't learn very much Latin, but we learned a great deal about forgery. We also learned how to make our faces blank and stiff, as if they'd been starched. It was best not to react to Mr. Erskine in any visible way, especially not by flinching.

For a while Laura became alert to Mr. Erskine, but physical pain – her own pain, that is – did not have much of a hold over her. Her attention would wander away, even when he was shouting. He had such a limited range. She would gaze at the wallpaper – a design of rosebuds and ribbons – or out the window. She developed the ability to subtract herself in the blink of an eye – one minute she'd be focused on you, the next she'd be elsewhere. Or rather you would be elsewhere: she'd dismiss you, as if she'd waved an invisible wand; as if it was you yourself who'd been made to vanish.

Mr. Erskine could not stand being negated in this fashion. He took to shaking her – to snap her out of it, he said. *You're not the Sleeping Beauty*, he would yell. Sometimes he threw her against the wall, or shook her with his hands around her neck. When he shook her she'd close her eyes and go limp, which incensed him further. At first I tried to intervene, but it did no good. I would simply be pushed aside with one swipe of his tweedy, malodorous arm.

"Don't annoy him," I said to Laura.

"It doesn't matter whether I annoy him or not," said Laura. "Anyway, he's not annoyed. He only wants to put his hand up my blouse."

"I've never seen him do that," I said. "Why would he?"

"He does it when you're not looking," said Laura. "Or under my skirt. What he likes is panties." She said it so calmly I thought she must have made it up, or misunderstood. Misunderstood Mr. Erskine's hands, their intentions. What she'd described was so implausible. It didn't seem to me like the sort of thing a grown-up man would do, or be interested in doing at all, because wasn't Laura only a little girl?

"Shouldn't we tell Reenie?" I asked tentatively.

"She might not believe me," said Laura. "You don't."

But Reenie did believe her, or she elected to believe her, and that was the end of Mr. Erskine. She knew better than to take him on in single combat: he would just accuse Laura of telling dirty lies, and then things would be worse than ever. Four days later she marched into Father's office at the button factory with a handful of contraband photographs. They weren't the sort of thing that would raise more than an eyebrow today, but they were scandalous then – women in black stockings with pudding-shaped breasts spilling out over their gigantic brassières, the same women with nothing on at all, in contorted, splay-legged positions. She said she'd found them under Mr. Erskine's bed when she'd been sweeping out his room, and was this the sort of man who ought to be trusted with Captain Chase's young daughters?

There was an interested audience, which included a group of factory workers and Father's lawyer and, incidentally, Reenie's future husband, Ron Hincks. The sight of Reenie, her dimpled cheeks flushed, her eyes blazing like an avenging Fury's, the black snail of her hair coming unpinned, brandishing a clutch of huge-boobed, bushy-tailed, bare-naked women, was too much for him. Mentally he fell on his knees before her, and from that day on he began his pursuit of her, which was in the end successful. But that is another story.

If there was one thing Port Ticonderoga would not stand for, said Father's lawyer in an advisory tone, it was this kind of smut in the hands of the teachers of innocent youth.

Father realized he could not keep Mr. Erskine in the house after that without being considered an ogre.

(I have long suspected Reenie of having got hold of the photographs herself, from the brother who was in the magazine distribution business, and who could easily have managed it. I suspect Mr. Erskine was guiltless in respect of these photographs. If anything, his tastes ran to children, not to large brassières. But by that time he could not expect fair play from Reenie.)

Mr. Erskine departed, protesting his innocence – indignant, but also shaken. Laura said that her prayers had been answered. She said she'd prayed to have Mr. Erskine expelled from our house, and that God had heard her. Reenie, she said, had been doing His will, filthy pictures and all. I wondered what God thought of that, supposing He existed – a thing I increasingly doubted.

Laura, on the other hand, had taken to religion in a serious way during Mr. Erskine's tenure: she was still frightened of God, but forced to choose between one irascible, unpredictable tyrant and another, she'd chosen the one that was bigger, and also farther away.

Once the choice had been made she took it to extremes, as she took everything. "I'm going to become a nun," she announced placidly, while we were eating our lunchtime sandwiches at the kitchen table.

"You can't," said Reenie. "They wouldn't have you. You're not a Catholic."

"I could become one," said Laura. "I could join up."

"Well," said Reenie, "you'll have to cut off your hair. Underneath those veils of theirs, a nun is bald as an egg."

This was a shrewd move of Reenie's. Laura hadn't known about that. If she had one vanity, it was her hair. "Why do they?" she said.

"They think God wants them to. They think God wants them to offer up their hair to him, which just goes to show how ignorant they are. What would he want with it?" said Reenie. "The idea! All that hair!"

"What do they do with the hair?" said Laura. "Once it's been cut off."

Reenie was snapping beans: snap, snap, snap. "It gets turned into wigs, for rich women," she said. She didn't miss a beat, but I knew this was a fib, like her earlier stories about babies being made from dough. "Snooty-nosed rich women. You wouldn't want to see your lovely hair walking around on someone else's big fat mucky-muck head."

Laura gave up the idea of being a nun, or so it seemed; but who could tell what she might fall for next? She had a heightened capacity for belief. She left herself open, she entrusted herself, she gave herself over, she put herself at the mercy. A little incredulity would have been a first line of defence.

Several years had now gone by – wasted, as it were, on Mr. Erskine. Though I shouldn't say *wasted*: I'd learned many things from him, although not always the things he'd set out to teach. In addition to lying and cheating, I'd learned half-concealed insolence and silent resistance. I'd learned that revenge is a dish best eaten cold. I'd learned not to get caught.

Meanwhile the Depression had set in. Father didn't lose much in the Crash, but he lost some. He also lost his margin of error. He ought to have shut down the factories in response to lessened demand; he ought to have banked his money – hoarded it, as others in his position were doing. That would have been the sensible thing. But he didn't do that. He couldn't bear to. He couldn't bear to throw his men out of work. He owed them allegiance, these men of his. Never mind that some of them were women.

A meagreness settled over Avilion. Our bedrooms became cold in winter, our sheets threadbare. Reenie cut them down the worn-out middles, then sewed the sides together. A number of the rooms were shut off; most of the servants were let go. There was no longer a gardener, and the weeds crept stealthily in. Father said he would need our cooperation to keep things going – to get through this bad patch. We could help Reenie in the house, he said, since we were so averse to Latin and mathematics. We could learn how to stretch a dollar. That meant, in practice, beans or salt cod or rabbits for dinner, and darning our own stockings.

Laura refused to eat the rabbits. They looked like skinned babies, she said. You'd have to be a cannibal to eat them.

Reenie said Father was too good for his own good. She also said he was too prideful. A man should admit when he was beat. She didn't know what things were coming to, but rack and ruin was the likeliest outcome.

I was now sixteen. My formal education, such as it was, had come to an end. I was hanging around, but for what? What would become of me next?

Reenie had her preferences. She'd taken to reading *Mayfair* magazine, with its descriptions of society festivities, and the social pages in the newspapers – the weddings, the charity balls, the luxury vacations. She memorized lists of names – names of the prominent, of cruise ships, of good hotels. I ought to be given a début, she said, with all the proper trimmings – teas to meet the important society mothers, receptions and fashionable outings, a formal dance with eligible young men invited. Avilion would be filled with well-dressed people again, as in the old days; there would be string quartets, and torches on the lawn. Our family was at least as good as the families whose daughters were provided for in this way – as good, or better.

Father ought to have kept some money in the bank just for that. If only my mother had remained alive, Reenie said, everything would have been done up right.

I doubted that. From what I'd heard about Mother, she might have insisted I be sent to school – the Alma Ladies' College, or some such worthy, dreary institution – to learn something functional but equally dreary, like shorthand; but as for a début, that would have been vanity. She'd never had one herself.

Grandmother Adelia was different, and far enough removed in time so that I could idealize her. She would have taken pains with me; she'd have spared no scheme or expense. I mooned around in the library, studying the pictures of her that still hung on the walls: the portrait in oils, done in 1900, in which she wore a sphinx-like smile and a dress the colour of dried red roses, with a plunging neckline from which her bare throat emerged abruptly, like an arm from behind a magician's curtain; the gilt-framed black-and-white photographs, showing her in picture hats, or with ostrich feathers, or in evening gowns with tiaras and white kid gloves, alone or with various now-forgotten dignitaries. She would have sat me down and given me the necessary advice: how to dress, what to say, how to behave on all occasions. How to avoid making myself ridiculous, for which I could already see there was ample scope. Despite her ferretings in the society pages, Reenie didn't know enough for that.

The button factory picnic

The Labour Day weekend has come and gone, leaving a detritus of plastic cups and floating bottles and gently withering balloons in the backwash of the river's eddies. Now September is asserting itself. Though at noon the sun is no less hot, morning by morning it rises later, trailing mist, and in the cooler evenings the crickets rasp and creak. Wild asters cluster in the garden, having rooted themselves there some time ago – tiny white ones, others bushier and sky-coloured, others with rusty stems, a deeper purple. Once, in my days of desultory gardening, I would have branded them weeds and pulled them out. Now I no longer make such distinctions.

It's better weather for walking now, not so much glare and shimmer. The tourists are thinning out, and those remaining are at least decently covered: no more giant shorts and bulging sun-dresses, no more poached red legs.

Today I set out for the Camp Grounds. I set out, but when I was halfway there Myra came by in her car and offered me a lift, and I'm ashamed to say I accepted it: I was out of breath, I'd already realized it was too far. Myra wanted to know where I was going, and why – she must have inherited the sheep-herding instinct, from Reenie. I told her where; as for the why, I said I just wanted to see the place again, for old times' sake. Too dangerous, she said: you never knew what might be crawling through the undergrowth out there. She made me promise to sit down on a park bench, out in plain view, and wait for her. She said she'd come back in an hour to collect me.

More and more I feel like a letter – deposited here, collected there. But a letter addressed to no one.

The Camp Grounds isn't much to look at. It's a stretch of

land between the road and the Jogues River – an acre or two –
with trees and scrubby brushwood on it, and mosquitoes in
spring, from the swampy patch in the middle. Herons hunt
there; you can sometimes hear their hoarse cries, like a stick
scraped on rough tin. Now and then a few bird-watchers poke
about in the woebegone way they have, as if looking for something they've lost.

In the shadows there are glints of silver, from cigarette packs,
and the pallid, deflated tubers of tossed condoms, and discarded
squares of Kleenex lacy with rain. Dogs and cats stake their
claims, avid couples sneak in among the trees, though less than
they used to – there are so many other options now. Drunks
sleep under the denser bushes in summer, and teenaged kids
sometimes go there to smoke and sniff whatever they smoke
and sniff. Candle stubs have been found, and burned spoons,
and the odd throwaway needle. I hear all this from Myra, who
thinks it's a disgrace. She knows what the candle stubs and
spoons are for: they are *drug paraphernalia*. Vice is everywhere,
it seems. *Et in Arcadia ego*.

A decade or two ago there was an attempt to clean this area
up. A sign was erected – The Colonel Parkman Park, which
sounded inane – and three rustic picnic tables and a plastic
waste bin and a couple of portable toilet cubicles were placed
there, for the convenience of out-of-town visitors it was said,
though these preferred to guzzle their beer and strew their trash
somewhere with a clearer view of the river. Then a few
trigger-happy lads used the sign for shotgun practice, and the
tables and toilets were removed by the provincial government
– something to do with budgets – and the waste bin never got
emptied, although it was frequently pillaged by raccoons; so
they took that away as well, and now the place is reverting.

It's called the Camp Grounds because that was where the
religious camp meetings used to be held, with big tents like a

circus and fervent, imported preachers. In those days the space was better tended, or else more trampled down. Small travelling fairs pitched their booths and rides and tethered their ponies and donkeys, parades wound themselves up there, and dispersed into picnics. It was a place for gatherings of any outdoor kind.

This was where the Chase and Sons Labour Day Celebration used to be held. That was the formal name, though people just called it the button factory picnic. It was always the Saturday before the official Monday Labour Day, with its earnest rhetoric and marching bands and homemade banners. There were balloons and a merry-go-round, and harmless, foolish games – sack races, egg-and-spoon, relay races in which the baton was a carrot. Barbershop quartets would sing, not too badly; the Scouts bugle corps would honk its way through a number or two; squads of children performed Highland flings and Irish step-dances on a raised wooden platform like a boxing ring, the music provided by a wind-up gramophone. There was a Best-Dressed Pet contest, and also one for babies. The food was corn on the cob, potato salad, hot dogs. Ladies' Auxiliaries put on bake sales in aid of this or that, offering pies and cookies and cakes, and jars of jam and chutney and pickles, each with a first-name label: Rhoda's Chow-chow, Pearl's Plum Compote.

There was horsing around – hijinks. Nothing stronger than lemonade was served over the counter, but the men brought flasks and mickeys, and as dusk came on there might be scuffles, or shouting and raucous laughter through the trees, followed by splashes along the shore as some man or youth was thrown in fully dressed, or else minus his pants. The Jogues was shallow enough along there so almost nobody drowned. After dark there were fireworks. In the heyday of this picnic, or what I recall as its heyday, there was also square dancing, with fiddles.

But by the year I'm remembering now, which is 1934, that sort of excess gaiety had been curtailed.

About three in the afternoon Father would make a speech, from the step-dancing platform. It was always a short speech, but it was listened to attentively by the older men; also by the women, since they either worked for the company themselves or were married to someone who did. As times got harder, even the younger men began to listen to the speech; even the girls, in their summer dresses and semi-bared arms. The speech never said much, but you could read between the lines. "Reason to be pleased" was good; "grounds for optimism" was bad.

That year the weather was hot and dry, as it had been for too long. There hadn't been as many balloons as usual; there was no merry-go-round. The corn on the cob was too old, the kernels wrinkled like knuckles; the lemonade was watery, the hot dogs ran out early. Still, there had been no layoffs at Chase Industries, not yet. Slowdowns, but no layoffs.

Father said "grounds for optimism" four times, but "reason to be pleased" not once. There were anxious looks.

When Laura and I were younger we'd enjoyed this picnic; now we didn't, but our presence was a duty. We had to show the flag. That had been drummed into us from an early age: Mother had always made a point of going, no matter how unwell she might have been feeling.

After Mother had died and Reenie had taken over the running of us, she'd paid scrupulous attention to our outfits for this day: not too casual, because this would be contemptuous, as if we didn't care what the townspeople thought of us; but not too dressed-up either, because that would be lording it over. By now we were old enough to pick out our own clothes – I'd just turned eighteen, Laura was fourteen and a half – though we no longer had as many options to choose from. The overblown display of luxury had always been discouraged in our household, though we'd had what Reenie called *good things*, but recently the definition of luxury had narrowed down so it had come to mean anything new. For the picnic we both wore our blue dirndl skirts and white blouses from the summer before. Laura had my hat from three seasons ago; I myself had last year's hat, with the ribbon changed.

Laura didn't seem to mind. I did though. I said so, and Laura said I was worldly.

We listened to the speech. (Or I listened. Laura had the attitude of listening – eyes wide, head cocked attentively to one side – but you could never tell what she was listening to.) Father had always managed to carry off this speech, no matter what he might have been drinking, but this time he stumbled over the text. He moved the typed page closer to his good eye, then farther away, with a perplexed stare, as if it was a bill for something he hadn't ordered. His clothes used to be elegant, then they'd become elegant but well worn, but by that day they verged on the seedy. His hair was ragged around the ears, in need of a trim; he seemed harried – ferocious even, like a highwayman cornered.

After the speech, for which there was no more than dutiful applause, some of the men gathered in close groups, talking among themselves in lowered voices. Others sat under the trees, on outspread jackets or blankets, or lay down with handkerchiefs over their faces and dozed off. Only men did this; the women remained awake, watchful. Mothers herded their young children down to the river, to paddle at the gritty little beach there. Off to the side a dusty baseball game had started up; an eddy of spectators watched it groggily.

I went to help Reenie at her bake sale. What was it in aid of? I can't recall. But I did this helping every year now – it was expected. I told Laura she ought to come too, but she acted as though she hadn't heard me and strolled off, dangling her hat by its floppy brim.

I let her go. I was supposed to keep an eye on her: Reenie didn't waste any sleep on my account, but Laura in her opinion was altogether too confiding, too cozy with strangers. The white slavers were always on the prowl, and Laura was their natural target. She'd get into a strange car, open an unfamiliar door, cross the wrong street, and that would be that, because she didn't draw lines, or not where other people drew them, and you couldn't warn her because she didn't understand such warnings. It wasn't that she flouted rules: she simply forgot about them.

I was tired of keeping an eye on Laura, who didn't appreciate it. I was tired of being held accountable for her lapses, her failures to comply. I was tired of being held accountable, period. I wanted to go to Europe, or to New York, or even to Montreal – to nightclubs, to soirées, to all the exciting places mentioned in Reenie's social magazines – but I was needed at home. *Needed at home, needed at home* – it sounded like a life sentence. Worse, like a dirge. I was stuck in Port Ticonderoga, proud bastion of the common-and-garden-variety button and of lower-priced long johns for budget-minded shoppers. I would stagnate here, nothing would ever happen to me, I would end up an old maid like Miss Violence, pitied and derided. This at bottom was my fear. I wanted to be elsewhere, but I saw no way to get there. Once in a while I found myself hoping that I would be abducted by white slavers, even though I didn't believe in them. At least it would be a change.

The bake-sale table had an awning over it, and tea towels or pieces of waxed paper shielding the goods from flies. Reenie had contributed pies, not a form of baking she ever truly mastered. Her pies had gluey, underdone fillings, and crusts that were tough but flexible, like beige kelp or huge leathery mushrooms. In better times they sold well enough – it was understood that they were ceremonial objects, not food as such – but they weren't moving briskly today. Money was in short supply, and in exchange for it people wanted something they could actually eat.

As I stood behind the table, Reenie in an undertone retailed the latest news. Four men had been thrown into the river already, with the sky still blazing white, and not altogether in fun. There had been arguments, having to do with politics, said Reenie; voices had been raised. Apart from the usual river shenanigans, there had been scuffles. Elwood Murray had been knocked down. He was the editor of the weekly paper, having inherited it from two generations of newspaper Murrays: he wrote most of it, and took the pictures for it as well. Luckily he hadn't been ducked, as that would have damaged his camera, which had cost a good deal of money even second-hand, as Reenie happened to know. He had a nosebleed, and was sitting under a tree with a glass of lemonade and two women fussing around him with dampened handkerchiefs; I could see him from where I was standing.

Was it political, this knocking-down? Reenie didn't know, but people didn't like him listening in on what they were saying. In prosperous times Elwood Murray was considered a fool, and maybe what Reenie called a pansy – well, he wasn't married, and at his age that had to mean something – but he was tolerated and even appreciated, within decent limits, as long as he put in all the names for social events and got them spelled right. But these were not prosperous times, and Elwood Murray was too nosy for his own good. You don't want every little thing about you written up, said Reenie. Nobody in their right mind would want that.

I caught sight of Father, walking among the picnicking workers with his lopsided gait. He was nodding in his abrupt way at this man and that, a nod in which his head appeared to move back on his neck rather than forward. His black eye-patch turned from side to side; from a distance it looked like a hole in his head. His moustache curved like a single dark side-ways tusk above his mouth, which clenched now and then into something he must have intended for a smile. His hands were hidden in his pockets.

Beside him was a younger man, a little taller than Father, though unlike Father he had no rumples, no angles. *Sleek* was the word you thought of. He was wearing a natty Panama and a linen suit that appeared to emit light, it was so fresh and clean. He was very obviously from out of town.

"Who's that with Father?" I said to Reenie.

Reenie looked without appearing to look, then gave a short laugh. "That's Mr. Royal Classic, in the flesh. He certainly has the nerve."

"I thought it must be him," I said.

Mr. Royal Classic was Richard Griffen, of Royal Classic Knitwear in Toronto. Our workers — Father's workers — referred to it derisively as Royal Classic Shitwear, because Mr. Griffen was not only Father's chief competitor, he was also an adversary of sorts. He'd attacked Father in the press for being too soft on the unemployed, on Relief, and on pinkos gener-ally. Also on unions, which was gratuitous because Port Ticonderoga did not have any unions in it and Father's dim views on them were no secret. But now for some reason, Father had invited Richard Griffen to dinner at Avilion, fol-lowing the picnic, and on very short notice as well. Only four days.

Reenie felt Mr. Griffen had been sprung on her. As every-one knew, you had to put on a better show for your enemies than for your friends, and four days was not long enough for her to prepare for such an event, especially considering that there hadn't been any of what you'd call fine dining at Avilion since the days of Grandmother Adelia. True, Callie Fitzsimmons sometimes brought friends for the weekend, but that was different, because they were only artists and should be grateful for whatever they were given. They would sometimes be found in the kitchen at night, raiding the pantry, making their own sandwiches out of leftovers. *The bottomless pits*, Reenie called them.

"He's new money, anyhow," said Reenie scornfully, surveying Richard Griffen. "Look at the fancy pants." She was unforgiving of anyone who criticized Father (anyone, that is, except herself), and scornful of those who rose in the world and then acted above their level, or what she considered their level; and it was a known fact that the Griffens were common as dirt, or at least their grandfather was. He'd got hold of his business through cheating the Jews, said Reenie in an ambiguous tone – was this something of a feat, in her books? – but exactly how he had done it she couldn't say. (In fairness, Reenie may have invented these slurs on the Griffens. She sometimes attributed to people the histories she felt they ought to have had.)

Behind Father and Mr. Griffen, walking with Callie Fitzsimmons, was a woman I assumed was Richard Griffen's wife – youngish, thin, stylish, trailing diaphanous orange-tinted muslin like the steam from a watery tomato soup. Her picture hat was green, as were her high-heeled slingbacks and a wispy scarf affair she'd draped around her neck. She was overdressed for the picnic. As I watched, she stopped and lifted one foot and peered back over her shoulder to see if there was something stuck on her heel. I hoped there was. Still, I thought how nice it would be to have such lovely clothes, such wicked new-money clothes, instead of the virtuous, dowdy, down-at-heels garments that were our mode of necessity these days.

"Where's Laura?" said Reenie in sudden alarm.

"I have no idea," I said. I had gotten into the habit of snapping at Reenie, especially when she bossed me around. *You're not my mother* had become my most withering riposte.

"You should know better than to let her out of your sight," said Reenie. "*Anybody* could be here." *Anybody* was one of her bugbears. You never knew what intrusions, what thefts and gaffes *anybody* might commit.

I found Laura sitting on the grass under a tree, talking with a young man – a man, not a boy – a darkish man, with a light-coloured hat. His style was indeterminate – not a factory worker, but not anything else either, or nothing definite. No tie, but then it was a picnic. A blue shirt, a little frayed around the edges. An impromptu, a proletarian mode. A lot of young men were affecting it then – a lot of university students. In the winters they wore knitted vests, with horizontal stripes.

"Hello," said Laura. "Where did you go off to? This is my sister Iris, this is Alex."

"Mister . . .?" I said. How had Laura got on a first-name basis so quickly?

"Alex Thomas," said the young man. He was polite but cautious. He scrambled to his feet and reached out his hand, and I took it. Then I found myself sitting down beside them. It seemed the best thing to do, in order to protect Laura.

"You're from out of town, Mr. Thomas?"

"Yes. I'm visiting people here." He sounded like what Reenie would call a *nice* young man, meaning *not poor*. But not rich either.

"He's a friend of Callie's," said Laura. "She was just here, she introduced us. He came on the same train with her." She was explaining a little too much.

"Did you meet Richard Griffen?" I said to Laura. "He was with Father. The one who's coming to dinner?"

"Richard Griffen, the sweatshop tycoon?" said the young man.

"Alex – Mr. Thomas knows about ancient Egypt," said Laura. "He was telling me about hieroglyphs." She looked at him. I'd never seen her look at anyone else in quite the same way. Startled, dazzled? Hard to put a name to such a look.

"That sounds interesting," I said. I could hear my voice pronouncing *interesting* in that sneering way people have. I needed some way of telling this Alex Thomas that Laura was only fourteen, but I couldn't think of anything that wouldn't make her angry.

Alex Thomas produced a packet of cigarettes from his shirt pocket – Craven A's, as I recall. He tapped one out for himself. I was a little surprised that he smoked ready-mades – it didn't go with his shirt. Packaged cigarettes were a luxury: the factory workers rolled their own, some with one hand.

"Thank you, I will," I said. I'd only smoked a few cigarettes before, and those on the sly, filched from the silver box of them kept on top of the piano. He looked hard at me, which I suppose was what I'd wanted, then offered the package. He lit a match with his thumb, held it for me.

"You shouldn't do that," said Laura. "You could set yourself on fire."

Elwood Murray appeared before us, upright and jaunty again. The front of his shirt was still damp and splashed with pink, from where the women with the wet handkerchiefs had tried to get out the blood; the insides of his nostrils were ringed in dark red.

"Hello, Mr. Murray," said Laura. "Are you all right?"

"Some of the boys got a little carried away," said Elwood Murray, as if shyly revealing that he'd won some sort of a prize. "It was all in good fun. May I?" Then he took our picture with his flash camera. He always said *May I* before taking a picture for the paper but he never waited for the answer. Alex Thomas raised his hand as if to fend him off.

"I know these two lovely ladies, of course," Elwood Murray said to him, "but your name is?"

Reenie was suddenly there. Her hat was askew, and she was red in the face and breathless. "Your father's been looking all over for you," she said.

I knew this to be untrue. Nevertheless Laura and I had to get up from the shade of the tree and brush our skirts down and go with her, like ducklings being herded.

Alex Thomas waved us goodbye. It was a sardonic wave, or so I thought.

"Don't you know any better?" Reenie said. "Sprawled on the grass with Lord knows who. And for heaven's sakes, Iris, throw away that cigarette, you're not a tramp. What if your father sees you?"

"Father smokes like a furnace," I said, in what I hoped was an insolent tone.

"That's different," said Reenie.

"Mr. Thomas," said Laura. "Mr. Alex Thomas. He is a student of divinity. Or he was until recently," she added scrupulously. "He lost his faith. His conscience would not let him continue."

Alex Thomas's conscience had evidently made a big impression on Laura, but it cut no ice with Reenie. "What's he working at now, then?" she said. "Something fishy, or I'm a Chinaman. He has a slippery look."

"What's wrong with him?" I said to Reenie. I hadn't liked him, but surely he was now being judged without a hearing.

"What's right with him, is more like it," said Reenie. "Rolling around on the lawn in full view of everyone." She was talking more to me than to Laura. "At least you had your skirt tucked in." Reenie said a girl alone with a man should be able to hold a dime between her knees. She was always afraid that people – men – would see our legs, the part above the knee. Of women who allowed this to happen, she would say: *Curtain's up, where's the show?* Or, *Might as well hang out a sign.* Or, more balefully, *She's asking for it, she'll get what's coming to her,* or, in the worst cases, *She's an accident waiting to happen.*

"We weren't rolling," Laura said. "There was no hill."

"Rolling or not, you know what I mean," said Reenie.

"We weren't doing anything," I said. "We were talking."

"That's beside the point," said Reenie. "People could see you."

"Next time we're not doing anything we'll hide in the bushes," I said.

"Who is he anyway?" said Reenie, who usually ignored my head-on challenges, since by now there was nothing she could do about them. *Who is he* meant *Who are his parents.*

"He's an orphan," said Laura. "He was adopted, from an orphanage. A Presbyterian minister and his wife adopted him." She seemed to have winkled this information out of Alex Thomas in a very short time, but this was one of her skills, if it can be called that – she'd just keep on asking questions, of the personal kind we'd been taught were rude, until the other person, in shame or outrage, would be forced to stop answering.

"An orphan!" said Reenie. "He could be anybody!"

"What's wrong with orphans?" I said. I knew what was wrong with them in Reenie's books: they didn't know who their fathers were, and that made them unreliable, if not down-right degenerate. *Born in a ditch* was how Reenie would put it. *Born in a ditch, left on a doorstep.*

"They can't be trusted," said Reenie. "They worm their way in. They don't know where to draw the line."

"Well anyway," said Laura, "I've invited him to dinner."

"Now that takes the gold-plated gingerbread," said Reenie.

Loaf givers

There's a wild plum tree at the back of the garden, on the other side of the fence. It's ancient, gnarled, the branches knuckled with black knot. Walter says it should come down, but I've pointed out that, technically speaking, it isn't mine. In any case, I have a fondness for it. It blossoms every spring, unasked, untended; in the late summer it drops plums into my garden, small blue oval ones with a bloom on them like dust. Such generosity. I picked up the last windfalls this morning – those few the squirrels and raccoons and drunken yellow-jackets had left me – and ate them greedily, the juice of their bruised flesh bloodying my chin. I didn't notice it until Myra dropped by with another of her tuna casseroles. *My goodness*, she said, with her breathless avian laugh. *Who've you been fighting?*

I remember that Labour Day dinner in every detail, because it was the only time all of us were ever in the same room together.

The revels were still going on out at the Camp Grounds, but not in any form you'd want to witness close up, as the surreptitious consumption of cheap liquor was now in full swing. Laura and I had left early, to help Reenie with the dinner preparations.

These had been going on for some days. As soon as Reenie had been informed about the party, she'd dug out her one cookbook, *The Boston Cooking-School Cookbook*, by Fannie Merritt Farmer. It wasn't hers really: it had belonged to Grandmother Adelia, who'd consulted it – along with her various cooks, of course – when planning her twelve-course dinners. Reenie had inherited it, although she didn't use it for her daily cooking – all of that was in her head, according to her. But this was a question of the fancy stuff.

I had read this cookbook, or looked into it at least, in the days in which I'd been romanticizing my grandmother. (I'd given that up by now. I knew I would have been thwarted by her, just as I was thwarted by Reenie and my father, and would have been thwarted by my mother, if she hadn't died. It was the purpose in life of all older people to thwart me. They were devoted to nothing else.)

The cookbook had a plain cover, a no-nonsense mustard colour, and inside it there were plain doings as well. Fannie Merritt Farmer was relentlessly pragmatic – cut and dried, in a terse New England way. She assumed you knew nothing, and started from there: "A beverage is any drink. Water is the beverage provided for man by Nature. All beverages contain a large percentage of water, and therefore their uses should be considered: I. To quench thirst. II. To introduce water into the circulatory system. III. To regulate body temperature. IV. To assist in carrying off water. V. To nourish. VI. To stimulate the nervous system and various organs. VII. For medicinal purposes," and so forth.

Taste and pleasure did not form part of her lists, but at the front of the book there was a curious epigraph by John Ruskin:

> Cookery means the knowledge of Medea and of Circe and of Helen and of the Queen of Sheba. It means the knowledge of all herbs and fruits and balms and spices, and all that is healing and sweet in the fields and groves and savory in meats. It means carefulness and inventiveness and willingness and readiness of appliances. It means the economy of your grandmothers and the science of the modern chemist; it means testing and no wasting; it means English thoroughness and French and Arabian

hospitality; and, in fine, it means that you are to be perfectly and always ladies – loaf givers.

I found it difficult to picture Helen of Troy in an apron, with her sleeves rolled up to the elbow and her cheek dabbled with flour; and from what I knew about Circe and Medea, the only things they'd ever cooked up were magic potions, for poisoning heirs apparent or changing men into pigs. As for the Queen of Sheba, I doubt she ever made so much as a piece of toast. I wondered where Mr. Ruskin got his peculiar ideas, about ladies and cookery both. Still, it was an image that must have appealed to a great many middle-class women of my grandmother's time. They were to be sedate in bearing, unapproachable, regal even, but possessed of arcane and potentially lethal recipes, and capable of inspiring the most incendiary passions in men. And on top of that, perfectly and always ladies – loaf givers. The distributors of gracious largesse.

Had anyone ever taken this sort of thing seriously? My grandmother had. All you needed to do was to look at her portraits – at that cat-ate-the-canary smile, those droopy eyelids. Who did she think she was, the Queen of Sheba? Without a doubt.

When we got back from the picnic, Reenie was rushing around in the kitchen. She didn't look much like Helen of Troy: despite all the work she'd done in advance, she was flustered, and in a foul temper; she was sweating, and her hair was coming down. She said we would just have to take things as they came, because what else could we expect, since she could not do miracles and that included making silk purses out of sows' ears. And an extra place too, at zero hour, for this Alex person, whatever he called himself. Smart Alex, by the look of him.

"He calls himself by his name," said Laura. "The same as anyone."

"He's not the same as anyone," said Reenie. "You can tell

that at a glance. He's most likely some half-breed Indian, or else a gypsy. He's certainly not from the same pea patch as the rest of us."

Laura said nothing. She was not given to compunction as a rule, but this time she did seem to feel a little contrite for having invited Alex Thomas on the spur of the moment. She couldn't uninvite him however, as she pointed out – that would have been miles beyond mere rudeness. Invited was invited, no matter who it might be.

Father knew that too, although he was far from pleased: Laura had jumped the gun and usurped his own position as host, and next thing he knew she'd be inviting every orphan and bum and hard-luck case to his dinner table as if he was Good King Wenceslas. These saintly impulses of hers had to be curbed, he said; he wasn't running an almshouse.

Callie Fitzsimmons had attempted to mollify him: Alex was not a hard-luck case, she'd assured him. True, the young man had no visible job, but he did seem to have a source of revenue, or at any rate he'd never been known to put the twist on anyone. What might that source of income be? said Father. Darned if Callie knew: Alex was close-mouthed on the subject. Maybe he robbed banks, said Father with heavy sarcasm. Not at all, said Callie; anyway, Alex was known to some of her friends. Father said the one thing did not preclude the other. He was turning sour on the artists by then. One too many of them had taken up Marxism and the workers, and accused him of grinding the peasants.

"Alex is all right. He's just a youngster," Callie said. "He just came along for the ride. He's just a pal." She didn't want Father to get the wrong idea – that Alex Thomas might be a boyfriend of hers, in any competitive way.

"What can I do to help?" said Laura, in the kitchen.

"The last thing I need," said Reenie, "is another fly in the ointment. All I ask is that you keep yourself out of the way and don't knock anything over. Iris can help. At least she's not all thumbs." Reenie had the notion that helping her was a sign of favour: she was still annoyed with Laura, and was cutting her out. But this form of punishment was lost on Laura. She took her sun hat, and went out to wander around on the lawn.

Part of the job assigned me was to do the flowers for the table, and the seating arrangement as well. For the flowers I'd cut some zinnias from the borders – just about all there was at that time of year. For the seating arrangement I'd put Alex Thomas beside myself, with Callie on the other side and Laura at the far end. That way, I'd felt, he'd be insulated, or at least Laura would.

Laura and I did not have proper dinner dresses. We had dresses, however. They were the usual dark-blue velvet, left over from when we were younger, with the hems let down and a black ribbon sewn over the top of the worn hemline to conceal it. They'd once had white lace collars, and Laura's still did; I'd taken the lace off mine, which gave it a lower neckline. These dresses were too tight, or mine was; Laura's as well, come to think of it. Laura was not old enough by common standards to be attending a dinner party like this, but Callie said it would have been cruel to make her sit all alone in her room, especially since she, personally, had invited one of our guests. Father said he supposed that was right. Then he said that in any case, now that she'd shot up like a weed she looked as old as I did. It was hard to tell what age he thought that was. He could never keep track of our birthdays.

At the appointed time the guests foregathered in the drawing room for sherry, which was served by an unmarried cousin of Reenie's impressed for this event. Laura and I were not allowed to have any sherry, or any wine at dinner. Laura did not seem to resent this exclusion, but I did. Reenie sided with Father on this, but then she was a teetotaller anyway. "Lips that touch liquor will never touch mine," she'd say, emptying the dregs of the wine glasses down the sink. (She was wrong about that, however – less than a year after this dinner party, she married Ron Hincks, a notable tippler in his day. Myra, take note if you're reading this: in the days before he was hewn into a pillar of the community by Reenie, your father was a notable souse.)

Reenie's cousin was older than Reenie, and dowdy to the point of pain. She wore a black dress and a white apron, as was proper, but her stockings were brown cotton and sagging, and her hands could have been cleaner. In the daytimes she worked at the grocer's, where one of her jobs was bagging potatoes; it's hard to scrub off that kind of grime.

Reenie had made canapés featuring sliced olives, hard-boiled eggs, and tiny pickles; also some baked cheese pastry balls, which had not come out as expected. These were set on one of Grandmother Adelia's best platters, hand-painted china from Germany, in a design of dark-red peonies with gold leaves and stems. On top of the platter was a doily, in the centre was a dish of salted nuts, with the canapés arranged like the petals of a flower, all bristling with toothpicks. The cousin thrust them at our guests abruptly, menacingly even, as if enacting a stick-up.

"This stuff looks pretty septic," said Father in the ironic tone I'd come to recognize as his voice of disguised anger. "Better beg off or you'll suffer later." Callie laughed, but Winifred Griffen Prior graciously lifted a cheese ball and inserted it into her mouth in that way women have when they don't want their lipstick to come off – lips pushed outward, into a sort of funnel – and said it was *interesting*. The cousin had forgotten the cocktail napkins, so Winifred was left with greasy fingers. I watched her curiously to see whether she would lick them or wipe them on her dress, or perhaps on our sofa, but I moved my eyes away at the wrong time, and so I missed it. My hunch was the sofa.

Winifred was not (as I'd thought) Richard Griffen's wife, but his sister. (Was she married, widowed, or divorced? It wasn't entirely clear. She used her given name after the Mrs., which would indicate some sort of damage to the erstwhile Mr. Prior, if indeed he was erstwhile. He was seldom mentioned and never seen, and was said to have a lot of money, and to be "travelling." Later, when Winifred and I were no longer on speaking terms, I used to concoct stories for myself about this Mr. Prior: Winifred had got him stuffed and kept him in moth-balls in a cardboard box, or she and the chauffeur had walled him up in the cellar in order to indulge in lascivious orgies. The orgies may not have been that far from the mark, although I have to say that whatever Winifred did in that direction was always done discreetly. She covered her tracks – a virtue of sorts, I suppose.)

That evening Winifred wore a black dress, simply cut but voraciously elegant, set off by a triple string of pearls. Her earrings were minute bunches of grapes, pearl also but with gold stems and leaves. Callie Fitzsimmons, by contrast, was pointedly underdressed. For a couple of years now she'd set aside her fuchsia and saffron draperies, her bold Russian-émigré designs, even her cigarette holder. Now she went in for slacks in the daytime, and V-neck sweaters, and rolled-up shirt sleeves; she'd cut her hair too, and shortened her name to Cal.

She'd given up the monuments to dead soldiers: there was no longer much of a demand for them. Now she did bas-reliefs of workers and farmers, and fishermen in oilskins, and Indian trappers, and aproned mothers toting babies on their hips and shielding their eyes while looking at the sun. The only patrons who could afford to commission these were insurance companies and banks, who would surely want to apply them to the outsides of their buildings in order to show they were in tune with the times. It was discouraging to be employed by such blatant capitalists, said Callie, but the main thing was the message, and at least anyone going past the banks and so forth on the street would be able to see these bas-reliefs, free of charge. It was art for the people, she said.

She'd had some idea that Father might help her out – get her some more bank jobs. But Father had said dryly that he and the banks were no longer what you'd call hand in glove.

For this evening she wore a jersey dress the colour of a duster – taupe was the name of this colour, she'd told us; it was French for *mole*. On anyone else it would have looked like a droopy bag with sleeves and a belt, but Callie managed to make it seem the height, not of fashion or chic exactly – this dress implied that such things were beneath notice – but rather of something easy to overlook but sharp, like a common kitchen implement – an ice pick, say – just before the murder. As a dress, it was a raised fist, but in a silent crowd.

Father wore his dinner jacket, which was in need of pressing. Richard Griffen wore his, which wasn't. Alex Thomas wore a brown jacket and grey flannels, too heavy for the weather; also a tie, red spots on a blue ground. His shirt was white, the collar too roomy. His clothes looked as if he'd borrowed them. Well, he hadn't expected to be invited to dinner.

"What a charming house," said Winifred Griffen Prior with an arranged smile, as we walked into the dining room. "It's so – so well preserved! What amazing stained-glass windows – how *fin de siècle*! It must be like living in a museum!"

What she meant was *outmoded*. I felt humiliated: I'd always thought those windows were quite fine. But I could see that Winifred's judgment was the judgment of the outside world – the world that knew such things and passed sentence accordingly, that world I'd been so desperately longing to join. I could see now how unfit I was for it. How countrified, how raw.

"They are particularly fine examples," said Richard, "of a certain period. The panelling is also of high quality." Despite his pedantry and his condescending tone, I felt grateful to him: it didn't occur to me that he was taking inventory. He knew a tottering regime when he saw one: he knew we were up for auction, or soon would be.

"By *museum*, do you mean dusty?" said Alex Thomas. "Or perhaps you meant *obsolete*."

Father scowled. Winifred, to do her justice, blushed.

"You shouldn't pick on those weaker than yourself," said Callie in a pleased undertone.

"Why not?" said Alex. "Everyone else does."

Reenie had gone the whole hog on the menu, or as much of that hog as we could by that time afford. But she'd bitten off more than she could chew. Mock Bisque, Perch à la Provençale, Chicken à la Providence – on it came, one course after another, unrolling in an inevitable procession, like a tidal wave, or doom. There was a tinny taste to the bisque, a floury taste to the chicken, which had been treated too roughly and had shrunk and toughened. It was not quite decent to see so many people in one room together, chewing with such thoughtfulness and vigour. Mastication was the right name for it – not eating.

Winifred Prior was pushing things around on her plate as if playing dominoes. I felt a rage against her: I was determined to eat up everything, even the bones. I would not let Reenie down. In the old days, I thought, she'd never have been stuck like this – caught short, exposed, and thereby exposing us. In the old days they'd have brought in experts.

Beside me, Alex Thomas too was doing his duty. He was sawing away as if life depended on it; the chicken squeaked under his knife. (Not that Reenie was grateful to him for his dedication. She kept tabs on who had eaten what, you may be sure. *That Alex What's-his-name certainly had an appetite on him*, was her comment. *You'd think he'd been starved in a cellar.*)

Under the circumstances, conversation was sporadic. There was a lull after the cheese course, however – the cheddar too young and bouncy, the cream too old, the *bleu* too high – during which we could pause and take stock, and look around us.

Father turned his one blue eye on Alex Thomas. "So, young man," he said, in what he may have thought was a friendly tone, "what brings you to our fair city?" He sounded like a pater-familias in a stodgy Victorian play. I looked down at the table.

"I'm visiting friends, sir," Alex said, politely enough. (We would hear Reenie, later, on the subject of his politeness. Orphans were well mannered because good manners had been beaten into them, in the orphanages. Only an orphan could be so self-assured, but this aplomb of theirs concealed a vengeful nature – underneath, they were jeering at everyone. Well, of course they'd be vengeful, considering how they'd been fobbed off. Most anarchists and kidnappers were orphans.)

"My daughter tells me you are preparing for the ministry," said Father. (Neither Laura nor I had said anything about this – it must have been Reenie, and predictably, or perhaps mali-ciously, she'd got it a little wrong.)

"I was, sir," said Alex. "But I had to give it up. We came to a parting of the ways."

"And now?" said Father, who was used to getting concrete answers.

"Now I live by my wits," said Alex. He smiled, to show self-deprecation.

"Must be hard for you," Richard murmured and Winifred laughed. I was surprised: I hadn't credited him with that kind of wit.

"He must mean he's a newspaper reporter," she said. "A spy in our midst!"

Alex smiled again, and said nothing. Father scowled. As far as he was concerned, newspaper reporters were vermin. Not only did they lie, they preyed on the misery of others – *corpse flies* was his term for them. He did make an exception for Elwood Murray, because he'd known the family. *Drivelmonger* was the worst he would say about Elwood.

After that the conversation turned to the general state of affairs – politics, economics – as it was likely to in those days. Worse and worse, was Father's opinion; about to turn the corner, was Richard's. It was hard to know what to think, said Winifred, but she certainly hoped they'd be able to keep the lid on.

"The lid on what?" said Laura, who hadn't said anything so far. It was as if a chair had spoken.

"On the possibility of social turmoil," said Father, in his reprimanding tone that meant she was not to say any more.

Alex said he doubted it. He'd just come back from the camps, he said.

"The camps?" said Father, puzzled. "What camps?"

"The relief camps, sir," said Alex. "Bennett's labour camps, for the unemployed. Ten hours a day and slim pickings. The boys aren't too keen on it – I'd say they're getting restless."

"Beggars can't be choosers," said Richard. "It's better than riding the rails. They get three square meals, which is more than a workman with a family to support may get, and I'm told the food's not bad. You'd think they'd be grateful, but that sort never are."

"They're not any particular sort," said Alex.

"My God, an armchair pinko," said Richard. Alex looked down at his plate.

"If he's one, so am I," said Callie. "But I don't think you have to be a pinko in order to realize . . ."

"What were you doing out there?" said Father, cutting her off. (He and Callie had been arguing quite a lot lately. Callie wanted him to embrace the union movement. He said Callie wanted two and two to make five.)

Just then the *bombe glacée* made an entrance. We had an electric refrigerator by then – we'd got it just before the Crash – and Reenie, although suspicious of its freezing compartment, had made good use of it for this evening. The *bombe* was shaped like a football, and was bright green and hard as flint, and took all our attention for a while.

While the coffee was being served the fireworks display began, down at the Camp Grounds. We all went out on the dock to watch. It was a lovely view, as you could see not only the fireworks themselves but their reflections in the Jogues River. Fountains of red and yellow and blue were cascading into the air – exploding stars, chrysanthemums, willow trees made of light.

"The Chinese invented gunpowder," said Alex, "but they never used it for guns. Only fireworks. I can't say I really enjoy them, though. They're too much like heavy artillery."

"Are you a pacifist?" I said. It seemed like the sort of thing he might be. If he said yes, I intended to disagree with him, because I wanted his attention. He was talking mostly to Laura.

"Not a pacifist," said Alex. "But my parents were both killed in the war. Or I assume they must have been killed."

Now we'll get the orphan story, I thought. After all the fuss Reenie's been making, I hope it's a good one.

"You don't know for sure?" said Laura.

"No," said Alex. "I'm told that I was found sitting on a mound of charred rubble, in a burned-out house. Everyone else there was dead. Apparently I'd been hiding under a washtub or a cooking pot – a metal container of some kind."

"Where was this? Who found you?" Laura whispered.

"It's not clear," said Alex. "They don't really know. It wasn't France or Germany. East of that – one of those little countries. I must have been passed from hand to hand; then the Red Cross got hold of me one way or another."

"Do you remember it?" I said.

"Not really. A few details were misplaced along the way – my name and so forth – and then I ended up with the missionaries, who felt that forgetfulness would be the best thing for me, all things considered. They were Presbyterians, a tidy bunch. We all had our heads shaved, for the lice. I can recall the feeling of suddenly having no hair – how cool it was. That's when my memories really begin."

Although I was beginning to like him better, I'm ashamed to admit that I was more than a little skeptical about this story. There was too much melodrama in it – too much luck, both bad and good. I was still too young to be a believer in coincidence. And if he'd been trying to make an impression on Laura – was he trying? – he couldn't have chosen a better way.

"It must be terrible," I said, "not to know who you really are."

"I used to think that," said Alex. "But then it came to me that *who I really am* is a person who doesn't need to know who he really is, in the usual sense. What does it mean, anyway – family background and so forth? People use it mostly as an excuse for their own snobbery, or else their failings. I'm free of the temptation, that's all. I'm free of the strings. Nothing ties me down." He said something else, but there was an explosion in the sky and I couldn't hear. Laura heard though; she nodded gravely.

(What was it he said? I found out later. He said, *At least you're never homesick.*)

A dandelion of light burst above us. We all looked up. It's hard not to, at such times. It's hard not to stand there with your mouth open.

Was that the beginning, that evening – on the dock at Avilion, with the fireworks dazzling the sky? It's hard to know. Beginnings are sudden, but also insidious. They creep up on you sideways, they keep to the shadows, they lurk unrecognized. Then, later, they spring.

Hand-tinting

Wild geese fly south, creaking like anguished hinges; along the riverbank the candles of the sumacs burn dull red. It's the first week of October. Season of woollen garments taken out of mothballs; of nocturnal mists and dew and slippery front steps, and late-blooming slugs; of snapdragons having one last fling; of those frilly ornamental pink-and-purple cabbages that never used to exist, but are all over everywhere now.

Season of chrysanthemums, the funeral flower; white ones, that is. The dead must get so tired of them.

The morning was brisk and fair. I picked a small bunch of yellow and pink snapdragons from the front garden and took them to the cemetery, to place them at the family tomb for the two pensive angels on their white cube: it would be something different for them, I thought. Once there I performed my small ritual – the circumlocution of the monument, the reading of the names. I think I do it silently, but once in a while I catch the sound of my own voice, muttering away like some Jesuit saying a breviary.

To pronounce the name of the dead is to make them live again, said the ancient Egyptians: not always what one might wish.

When I'd been all the way around the monument, I found a girl – a young woman – kneeling before the tomb, or before Laura's place on it. Her head was bowed. She was wearing black: black jeans, black T-shirt and jacket, a small black knapsack of the kind they carry now instead of purses. She had long dark hair – like Sabrina's, I thought with a sudden lurching of the heart: Sabrina has come back, from India or wherever she's been. She's come back without warning. She's changed her mind about me. She was intending to surprise me, and now I've spoiled it.

But when I peered more closely, I saw this girl was a stranger: some overwrought graduate student, no doubt. At first I'd thought she was praying, but no, she was placing a flower: a single white carnation, the stem wrapped in tinfoil. As she stood up, I saw that she was crying.

Laura touches people. I do not.

After the button factory picnic, there was the usual sort of account of it in the *Herald and Banner* – which baby had won the Most Beautiful Baby contest, who'd got Best Dog. Also what Father had said in his speech, much abbreviated: Elwood Murray put an optimistic gloss on everything, so it sounded like business as usual. There were also some photos – the winning dog, a dark mop-shaped silhouette; the winning baby, fat as a pincushion, in a frilled bonnet; the step-dancers holding up a giant cardboard shamrock; Father at the podium. It wasn't a good picture of him: he had his mouth half-open, and looked as if he were yawning.

One of the pictures was of Alex Thomas, with the two of us – me to the left of him, Laura to the right, like bookends. Both of us were looking at him and smiling; he was smiling too, but he'd thrust his hand up in front of him, as gangland criminals did to shield themselves from the flashbulbs when they were being arrested. He'd only managed to blot out half of his face, however. The caption was, "Miss Chase and Miss Laura Chase Entertain an Out-of-Town Visitor."

Elwood Murray hadn't managed to track us down that afternoon, in order to find out Alex's name, and when he'd called at the house he'd got Reenie, who'd said our names should not be bandied about with God knows who, and had refused to tell him. He'd printed the picture anyway, and Reenie was affronted, as much by us as by Elwood Murray. She thought this photo verged in the immodest, even though our legs weren't showing. She thought we both had silly leers on our faces, like lovelorn geese; with our mouths gaping open like that we might as well have been drooling. We'd made a sorry spectacle of ourselves: everyone in town would laugh at us behind our backs, for mooning over some young thug who looked like an Indian – or, worse, a Jew – and with his sleeves rolled up like that, a Communist into the bargain.

"That Elwood Murray ought to be spanked," she said. "Thinks he's so all-fired cute." She tore the paper up and stuffed it into the kindling box, so Father wouldn't see it. He must have seen it anyway, down at the factory, but if so he made no comment.

Laura paid a call on Elwood Murray. She did not reproach him or repeat any of what Reenie had said about him. Instead she told him she wanted to become a photographer, like him. No: she wouldn't have told such a lie. That was only what he inferred. What she really said was that she wanted to learn how to make photographic prints from negatives. This was the literal truth.

Elwood Murray was flattered by this mark of favour from the heights of Avilion – although mischievous, he was a fearful snob – and agreed to let her help him in the darkroom three afternoons a week. She could watch him print the portraits he did on the side, of weddings and children's graduations and so forth. Although the type was set and the newspaper run off by a couple of men in the back room, Elwood did almost everything else around the weekly paper, including his own developing.

Perhaps he might teach her how to do hand-tinting, as well, he said: it was the coming thing. People would bring in their old black-and-white prints to have them rendered more vivid by the addition of living colour. This was done by bleaching out the darkest areas with a brush, then treating the print with sepia toner to give a pink underglow. After that came the tinting. The colours came in little tubes and bottles, and had to be very carefully applied with tiny brushes, the excess fastidiously blotted off. You needed taste and the ability to blend, so the cheeks wouldn't look like circles of rouge or the flesh like beige cloth. You needed good eyesight and a steady hand. It was an art, said Elwood — one he was quite proud to have mastered, if he did say so himself. He kept a revolving selection of these hand-tinted photos in one corner of the newspaper-office window, as a sort of advertisement. Enhance Your Memories, said the hand-lettered sign he'd placed beside them.

Young men in the now-outdated uniforms of the Great War were the most frequent subjects; also brides and grooms. Then there were graduation portraits, First Communions, solemn family groups, infants in christening gear, girls in formal gowns, children in party outfits, cats and dogs. There was the occasional eccentric pet — a tortoise, a macaw — and, infrequently, a baby in a coffin, waxen-faced, surrounded by ruffles.

The colours never came out clear, the way they would on a piece of white paper: there was a misty look to them, as if they were seen through cheesecloth. They didn't make the people seem more real; rather they became ultra-real: citizens of an odd half-country, lurid yet muted, where realism was beside the point.

Laura told me what she was doing vis-a-vis Elwood Murray; she also told Reenie. I expected a protest, an uproar; I expected Reenie to say that Laura was lowering herself, or acting in a tawdry, compromising fashion. Who could tell what might go on in a darkroom, with a young girl and a man and the lights off? But Reenie took the view that it wasn't as if Elwood was paying Laura to work for him: rather he was teaching her, and that was quite different. It put him on a level with the hired help. As for Laura being in a darkroom with him, no one would think any harm of it, because Elwood was such a pansy. I suspect Reenie was secretly relieved to have Laura showing an interest in something other than God.

Laura certainly showed an interest, but as usual she went overboard. She nicked some of Elwood's hand-tinting materials and brought them home with her. I found this out by accident: I was in the library, dipping into the books at random, when I noticed the framed photographs of Grandfather Benjamin, each with a different prime minister. Sir John Sparrow Thompson's face was now a delicate mauve, Sir Mackenzie Bowell's a bilious green, Sir Charles Tupper's a pale orange. Grandfather Benjamin's beard and whiskers had been done in light crimson.

That evening I caught her in the act. There on her dressing table were the little tubes, the tiny brushes. Also the formal portrait of Laura and me in our velvet dresses and Mary Janes. Laura had removed the print from its frame, and was tinting me a light blue. "Laura," I said, "what in heaven's name are you up to? Why did you colour those pictures? The ones in the library. Father will be livid."

"I was just practising," said Laura. "Anyway, those men needed some enhancing. I think they look better."

"They look bizarre," I said. "Or very ill. Nobody's face is green! Or mauve."

Laura was unperturbed. "It's the colours of their souls," she said. "It's the colours they *ought* to have been."

"You'll get in big trouble! They'll know who did it."

"Nobody ever *looks* at those," she said. "Nobody *cares*."

"Well, you'd better not lay a finger on Grandmother Adelia," I said. "Nor the dead uncles! Father would have your hide!"

"I wanted to do them in gold, to show they're in glory," she said. "But there isn't any gold. The uncles, not Grandmother. I'd do her a steel grey."

"Don't you dare! Father doesn't believe in glory. And you'd better take those paints back before you're accused of theft."

"I haven't used much," said Laura. "Anyway, I brought Elwood a jar of jam. It's a fair trade."

"Reenie's jam, I suppose. "Out of the cold cellar – did you ask her? She counts that jam, you know." I picked up the photograph of the two of us. "Why am I blue?"

"Because you're asleep," said Laura.

The tinting materials weren't the only things she nicked. One of Laura's jobs was filing. Elwood liked his office kept very neatly, and his darkroom as well. His negatives were placed in glassine envelopes, filed according to the date on which they'd been taken, so it was easy for Laura to locate the negative of the picnic shot. She made two black-and-white prints of it, one day when Elwood had gone out and she had the run of the place to herself. She didn't tell anybody about this, not even me – not until later. After she'd made the prints, she slipped the negative into her handbag and took it home with her. She did not consider it stealing: Elwood had stolen the picture in the first place by not asking permission of us, and she was only taking away from him something that had never really belonged to him anyway.

After she'd accomplished what she'd set out to do, Laura stopped going to Elwood Murray's office. She gave him no reason, and no warning. I felt this was clumsy of her, and indeed it was, because Elwood felt slighted. He tried to find out from Reenie if Laura was ill, but all Reenie would say was that Laura must have changed her mind about photography. She was full of ideas, that girl; she always had some bee in her bonnet, and now she must have a different one.

This aroused Elwood's curiosity. He began to keep an eye on Laura, above and beyond his usual nosiness. I wouldn't call it spying exactly – it wasn't as if he lurked behind bushes. He just noticed her more. (He hadn't found out about the purloined negative yet, however. It didn't occur to him that Laura might have had an ulterior motive in seeking him out. Laura had such a direct gaze, such blankly open eyes, such a pure, rounded forehead, that few ever suspected her of duplicity.)

At first Elwood found nothing much to notice. Laura was to be observed walking along the main street, making her way to church on Sunday mornings, where she taught Sunday school to the five-year-olds. On three other mornings of the week, she helped out at the United Church soup kitchen, which had been set up beside the train station. Its mission was to dish out bowls of cabbagy soup to the hungry, dirty men and boys who were riding the rails: a worthy effort, but one that was not viewed with approval by everyone in town. Some felt these men were seditious conspirators, or worse, Communists; others, that there should be no free meals, because they them-selves had to work for every mouthful. Shouts of "Get a job!" were heard. (The insults were by no means one way, though the ones from the itinerant men were more muted. Of course they resented Laura and all the churchy do-gooders like her. Of course they had ways of letting their feelings be known. A joke, a sneer, a jostle, a sullen leer. There is nothing more onerous than enforced gratitude.)

The local police stood by to make sure that these men did not get any smart ideas into their heads, such as remaining in Port Ticonderoga. They were to be shuffled along, moved else-where. But they weren't allowed to hop the boxcars right in the train station, because the railway company wouldn't put up with that. There were scuffles and fist fights, and – as Elwood Murray put it, in print – nightsticks were freely employed.

So these men would trudge along the railway tracks and try to hop farther down the line, but that was more difficult because by then the trains would have gathered speed. There were several accidents, and one death – a boy who couldn't have been more than sixteen fell under the wheels and was virtually cut in two. (Laura locked herself in her room for three days after that, and would eat nothing: she'd served a bowl of soup to this boy.) Elwood Murray wrote an editorial in which he said that the mishap was regrettable but not the fault of the railway, and certainly not that of the town: if you took foolhardy risks, what could you expect?

Laura begged bones from Reenie, for the church soup pot. Reenie said she was not made of bones; bones did not grow on trees. She needed most of the bones for herself – for Avilion, for us. She said a penny saved was a penny earned, and didn't Laura see that during these hard times Father needed all the pennies he could get? But she couldn't ever resist Laura for long, and a bone or two or three would be forthcoming. Laura didn't want to touch the bones, or even see them – she was squeamish that way – so Reenie would wrap them up for her. "There you are. Those bums will eat us out of house and home," she would sigh. "I've put in an onion." She didn't think Laura should be working at the soup kitchen – it was too rough for a young girl like her.

"It's wrong to call them bums," said Laura. "Everyone turns them away. They only want work. All they want is a job."

"I daresay," said Reenie in a skeptical, maddening voice. To me, privately, she would say, "She's the spitting image of her mother."

I didn't go to the soup kitchen with Laura. She didn't ask me to, and in any case I wouldn't have had the time: Father had now taken it into his head that I must learn the ins and outs of the button business, as was my duty. *Faute de mieux*, I was to be the son in Chase and Sons, and if I was ever going to run the show I needed to get my hands dirty.

I knew I had no business abilities, but I was too cowed to object. I accompanied Father to the factory every morning, to see (he said) how things worked in the real world. If I'd been a boy he would have started me working at the assembly line, on the military analogy that an officer should not expect his men to perform any job he could not perform himself. As it was, he set me to taking inventory and balancing shipping accounts — raw materials in, finished product out.

I was bad at it, more or less intentionally. I was bored, and also intimidated. When I arrived at the factory every morning in my convent-like skirts and blouses, walking at Father's heels like a dog, I would have to pass the lines of workers. I felt scorned by the women and stared at by the men. I knew they were making jokes about me behind my back — jokes that had to do with my deportment (the women) and my body (the men), and that this was their way of getting even. In some ways I didn't blame them — in their place I would have done the same — but I felt affronted by them nonetheless.

La-di-da. Thinks she's the Queen of Sheba.

A good shagging would take her down a peg.

Father noticed none of this. Or he chose not to notice.

One afternoon Elwood Murray arrived at Reenie's back door with the inflated chest and self-important manner of the bearer of unpleasant news. I was helping Reenie with the canning: it was late September, and we were doing up the last of the tomatoes from the kitchen garden. Reenie had always been frugal, but in these times waste was a sin. She must have realized how thin the thread was becoming — the thread of excess dollars that attached her to her job.

There was something we should know, said Elwood Murray,

for our own good. Reenie took a look at him, him and his puffed-up stance, evaluating the gravity of his news, and judged it serious enough to invite him in. She even offered him a cup of tea. Then she asked him to wait until she'd lifted the last jars out of the boiling water with the tongs and had the tops screwed on. Then she sat down.

Here was the news. Miss Laura Chase had been seen around town – said Elwood – in the company of a young man, the very same young man she'd been photographed with at the button factory picnic. They'd first been spotted down by the soup kitchen; then, later, sitting on a park bench – on more than one park bench – and smoking cigarettes. Or the man had been smoking; as to Laura, he couldn't swear to it, he said, pursing his mouth. They'd been seen beside the War Memorial by the Town Hall, and leaning on the railings of the Jubilee Bridge, looking down at the rapids – a traditional spot for courtship. They may even have been glimpsed out by the Camp Grounds, which was an almost certain sign of dubious behaviour, or the prelude to it – though he couldn't vouch for this, as he hadn't witnessed it himself.

Anyway, he thought we should know. The man was a grown man, and wasn't Miss Laura only fourteen? Such a shame, him taking advantage of her like that. He sat back in his chair, shaking his head in sorrow, smug as a woodchuck, his eyes glittering with malicious pleasure.

Reenie was furious. She hated anyone getting the jump on her in the gossip department. "We certainly thank you for informing us," she said with stiff politeness. "A stitch in time saves nine." This was her way of defending Laura's honour: nothing had happened, yet, that couldn't be forestalled.

"What did I tell you," said Reenie, after Elwood Murray had gone. "He's got no shame." She did not mean Elwood, of course, but Alex Thomas.

When confronted, Laura denied nothing, except the Camp Grounds sighting. The park benches and so forth – yes, she had sat on them, though not for very long. Nor could she understand why Reenie was making all this fuss. Alex Thomas wasn't a two-bit sweetheart (the expression Reenie had used). Nor was he a lounge lizard (the other expression). She denied ever having smoked a cigarette in her life. As for "spooning" – also from Reenie – she thought that was disgusting. What had she done to inspire such low suspicions? She evidently didn't know.

Being Laura, I thought, was like being tone deaf: the music played and you heard something, but it wasn't what everyone else heard.

According to Laura, on all of these occasions – and there had been only three of them – she and Alex Thomas had been engaged in serious discussion. What about? About God. Alex Thomas had lost his faith, and Laura was trying to help him regain it. It was hard work because he was very cynical, or maybe *skeptical* was what she meant. He thought that the modern age would be an age of this world rather than the next – of man, for mankind – and he was all for it. He claimed not to have a soul, and said he didn't give a hang what might happen to him after he was dead. Still, she meant to keep on with her efforts, however difficult the task might appear.

I coughed into my hand. I didn't dare laugh. I'd seen Laura use that virtuous expression on Mr. Erskine often enough, and I thought that was what she was doing now: pulling the wool over. Reenie, hands on hips, legs apart, mouth open, looked like a hen at bay.

"Why's he still in town, is what I'd like to know," said Reenie, baffled, shifting her ground. "I thought he was just visiting."

"Oh, he has some business here," said Laura mildly. "But he can be where he wants to be. It's not a slave state. Except for the wage slaves, of course." I guessed that the attempt at conversion hadn't been all one way: Alex Thomas had been getting his own oar in. If things went on in this fashion we'd have a little Bolshevik on our hands.

"Isn't he too old?" I said.

Laura gave me a fierce look – *too old for what?* – daring me to butt in. "The soul has no age," she said.

"People are talking," said Reenie: always her clinching argument.

"That is their own concern," said Laura. Her tone was one of lofty irritation: other people were her cross to bear.

Reenie and I were both at a loss. What could be done? We could have told Father, who might then have forbidden Laura to see Alex Thomas. But she wouldn't have obeyed, not with a soul at stake. Telling Father would have caused more trouble than it would be worth, we decided; and after all, what had actually taken place? Nothing you could put your finger on. (Reenie and I were confidants by then, on this matter; we'd put our heads together.)

As the days passed I came to feel that Laura was making a fool of me, though I couldn't specify how, exactly. I didn't think she was lying as such, but neither was she telling the entire truth. Once I saw her with Alex Thomas, deep in conversation, ambling along past the War Memorial; once at the Jubilee Bridge, once idling outside Betty's Luncheonette, oblivious to turning heads, mine included. It was sheer defiance.

"You have to talk sense to her," Reenie said to me. But I couldn't talk sense to Laura. Increasingly, I couldn't talk to her at all; or I could talk, but did she listen? It was like talking to a sheet of white blotting paper: the words went out of my mouth and disappeared behind her face as if into a wall of falling snow.

When I wasn't spending time at the button factory – an

exercise that was daily appearing more futile, even to Father – I began to wander around by myself. I would march along by the riverbank, trying to pretend I had a destination, or stand on the Jubilee Bridge as if waiting for someone, gazing down at the black water and remembering the stories of women who had thrown themselves into it. They'd done it for love, because that was the effect love had on you. It snuck up on you, it grabbed hold of you before you knew it, and then there was nothing you could do. Once you were in it – in love – you would be swept away, regardless. Or so the books had it.

Or I would walk along the main street, giving serious attention to what was in the shop windows – the pairs of socks and shoes, the hats and gloves, the screwdrivers and wrenches. I would study the posters of movie stars in the glass cases outside the Bijou Theatre and compare them with how I myself looked, or might look if I combed my hair down over one eye and had the proper clothes. I wasn't allowed to go inside; I didn't enter a movie theatre until after I was married, because Reenie said the Bijou was cheapening, for young girls by themselves at any rate. Men went there on the prowl, dirty-minded men. They would take the seat next to you and stick their hands onto you like flypaper, and before you knew it they'd be climbing all over you.

In Reenie's descriptions the girl or woman would always be inert, but with many handholds on her, like a jungle gym. She would be magically deprived of the ability to scream or move. She would be transfixed, she would be paralysed – with shock, or outrage, or shame. She would have no recourse.

The cold cellar

A nip in the air; the clouds high and windblown. Sheaves of dried Indian corn have appeared on the choicer front doors; on the porches the jack-o'-lanterns have taken up their grinning vigils. A week from now the candy-minded children will take to the streets, dressed as ballerinas and zombies and space aliens and skeletons and gypsy fortune-tellers and dead rock stars, and as usual I will turn out the lights and pretend not to be home. It's not dislike of them as such, but self-defence – should any of the wee ones disappear, I don't want to be accused of having lured them in and eaten them.

I told this to Myra, who is doing a brisk trade in squat orange candles and black ceramic cats and sateen bats, and in decorative stuffed-cloth witches, their heads made of dried-out apples. She laughed. She thought I was making a joke.

I had a sluggish day yesterday – my heart was pinching me, I could barely move off the sofa – but this morning, after taking my pill, I felt oddly energetic. I walked quite briskly as far as the doughnut shop. There I inspected the washroom wall, on which the latest entry is: *If you can't say anything nice don't say anything at all*, followed by: *If you can't suck anything nice don't suck anything at all*. It's good to know that freedom of speech is still in full swing in this country.

Then I bought a coffee and a chocolate-glazed doughnut, and took them outside to one of the benches provided by the management, placed handily right beside the garbage bin. There I sat, in the still-warm sunlight, basking like a turtle. People strolled by – two overfed women with a baby carriage, a younger, thinner woman in a black leather coat with silver studs in it like nail-heads and another one in her nose, three old geezers in windbreakers. I got the feeling they were staring at me. Am I still that notorious, or that paranoid? Or perhaps I'd merely been talking to myself out loud. It's hard to know. Does my voice simply flow out of me like air when I'm not paying attention? A shrivelled whispering, winter vines rustling, the sibilance of autumn wind in dry grass.

Who cares what people think, I told myself. If they want to listen in, they're welcome.

Who cares, who cares. The perennial adolescent riposte. I cared, of course. I cared what people thought. I always did care. Unlike Laura, I have never had the courage of my convictions.

A dog came over; I gave it half of the doughnut. "Be my guest," I said to it. That's what Reenie would say when she caught you eavesdropping.

All through October – the October of 1934 – there had been talk of what was going on at the button factory. Outside agitators were hanging around, it was said; they were stirring things up, especially among the young hotheads. There was talk of collective bargaining, of workers' rights, of unions. Unions were surely illegal, or closed-shop unions were – weren't they? No one seemed quite to know. In any case they had a whiff of brimstone about them.

The people doing the stirring up were ruffians and hired criminals (according to Mrs. Hillcoate). Not only were they outside agitators, they were foreign outside agitators, which was somehow more frightening. Small dark men with moustaches, who'd signed their names in blood and sworn to be loyal unto death, and who would start riots and stop at nothing, and set bombs and creep in at night and slit our throats while we slept (according to Reenie). These were their methods, these ruthless Bolsheviks and union organizers, who were all the same at heart (according to Elwood Murray). They wanted

Free Love, and the destruction of the family, and the deaths by firing squad of anyone who had money – any money at all – or a watch, or a wedding ring. This was what had been done in Russia. So it was said.

It was also said that Father's factories were in trouble.

Both rumours – the outside agitators, the trouble – were publicly denied. Both were believed.

Father had laid off some of his workers in September – some of the younger ones, better able to fend for themselves, according to his theories – and had asked the remainder to accept shorter hours. There just wasn't enough business, he'd explained, to keep all the factories going at full production capacity. The customers weren't buying buttons, or not the kind of buttons made by Chase and Sons, which depended on high volumes to be profitable. Nor were they buying cheap, serviceable undergarments: they were mending instead, they were making do. Not everyone in the country was out of work, of course, but those with jobs did not feel very secure about holding on to them. Naturally they were saving their money up, rather than spending it. You couldn't blame them. You'd do the same in their place.

Arithmetic had entered the picture, with its many legs, its many spines and heads, its pitiless eyes made of zeroes. Two and two made four, was its message. But what if you didn't have two and two? Then things wouldn't add up. And they didn't add up, I couldn't get them to; I couldn't get the red numbers in the inventory books to turn black. This worried me horribly; it was as if it were my own personal fault. When I closed my eyes at night I could see the numbers on the page before me, laid out in rows on my square oak desk at the button factory – those rows of red numbers like so many mechanical caterpillars, munching away at what was left of the money. When what you could manage to sell a thing for was less than what it paid you to make it – which was what had been going on at Chase and Sons for some time – this was how the numbers behaved. It was bad behaviour – without love, without justice, without mercy – but what could you expect? The numbers were only numbers. They had no choice in the matter.

In the first week of December, Father announced a shutdown. It was temporary, he said. He hoped it would be very temporary. He talked about retreating and retrenching in order to regroup. He asked for understanding and patience, and was greeted with a watchful silence by the assembled workers. After the announcement he went back to Avilion and shut himself up in his turret and drank himself blind. Things were broken up there – glass objects. Bottles, no doubt. Laura and I sat in my room, on my bed, holding hands tightly and listening to the fury and grief rampaging around up there, right above our heads, like an interior thunderstorm. Father hadn't done anything on that grand a scale for some time.

He must have felt he'd let his men down. That he'd failed. That nothing he could do had been enough.

"I will pray for him," said Laura.

"Does God care?" I said. "I don't think he gives a tinker's damn, actually. If there is a God."

"You can't know that," said Laura, "until after."

After what? I knew well enough, we'd had this conversation before. *After we're dead.*

Several days after Father's announcement, the union revealed its power. There was already a core group of members, and now they wanted everyone in. A meeting was held outside the locked button factory and a call issued to all the workers to join up, because when Father reopened the factories, it was said, he would cut to the bone and they'd all be expected to take starvation wages. He was just like all the rest of them, he'd stuff his money into a bank in hard times like these, then sit on his hands until people were beaten down and driven right into the ground; then he'd seize the opportunity to grow fat off the backs of the workers. Him and his big house and fancy daughters – those frivolous parasites who lived off the sweat of the masses.

You could tell these so-called organizers were from out of town, said Reenie, who was telling us about all this as we sat at the kitchen table. (We'd stopped having meals in the dining room, because Father had stopped eating there. He was barricaded in his turret; Reenie took a tray up.) Those roughnecks had no sense of what was decent, bringing the two of us into it like that, when everyone knew we had nothing to do with anything. She told us to pay no attention, which was easier said than done.

There were still some who were loyal to Father. At the meeting, we heard, there had been disagreements, then voices raised, then scuffling. Tempers were set loose. One man was kicked in the head, and carted off to the hospital with concussion. It was one of the strikers – they were calling themselves *the strikers*, now – but this injury was blamed on the strikers themselves, because once you started that sort of disruption, who could tell where it would end?

Better not to start. Better to keep your mouth shut. Much better.

Callie Fitzsimmons came to see Father. She was very worried about him, she said. She was worried that he was going down the drain. *Morally*, is what she meant. How could he treat his workers in this cavalier and also cheapskate fashion? Father told her to face reality. He called her a Job's comforter. He also said, *Who put you up to this, one of your pinko pals?* She said she had come on her own hook, out of love, because although a capitalist he'd always been a decent man, but now she found he'd turned into a heartless plutocrat. He said you couldn't be a plutocrat if you were broke. She said he could liquidate his assets. He said his assets weren't worth much more than her ass, which as far as he could tell she'd been giving away for nothing to anybody who'd asked. She said he hadn't scorned the free handouts. He said yes, but the hidden costs had been too high – first all the food in his house for her artistic pals, then his blood and now his soul. She called him a bourgeois reactionary. He called her a corpse fly. By that time they were shouting at each other. Then there was a slamming of doors, and a car skidded away down the gravel, and that was the end of that.

Was Reenie glad or sorry? Sorry. She hadn't liked Callie, but she'd got used to her, and Callie had been good for Father once upon a time. Who would replace her? Some other floozie, and better the devil you know.

The next week there was a call for a general strike, to show solidarity with the Chase and Sons workers. All stores and businesses must close, was the edict. All public services must be shut down. The telephones, the mail delivery. No milk, no bread, no ice. (Who was issuing these edicts? No one thought they were really coming from the man who actually spoke the words of them. This man claimed to be local, right from our own town, and was once thought to be – he was a Morton, a Morgan, something like that – but surely it had become clear that he was not local, not underneath it. He couldn't have been, to behave like that. Who was his grandfather, anyway?)

So it was not this man. He was not the brains behind it, said Reenie, because he did not have any brains to begin with. Dark forces were at work.

Laura was worried about Alex Thomas. He was mixed up in it somehow, she said. She knew he was. He was bound to be, according to his lights.

In the early afternoon of that same day, Richard Griffen arrived at Avilion in a car, with two other cars accompanying him. They were large cars, sleek and low-slung. There were five other men altogether, four of them quite big, in dark over-coats and grey fedoras. Richard Griffen and one of the men went into Father's study, along with Father. Two of the others posted themselves at the house doors, front and back, and two went off somewhere in one of the expensive cars. Laura and I watched the comings and goings of the cars from Laura's bedroom window. We'd been told to keep out of the way, which meant out of earshot as well. When we asked Reenie what was going on, she looked worried, and said our guess was as good as hers, but she was keeping her ear to the track.

Richard Griffen did not stay to dinner. When he left, two of the cars went with him. The third one stayed behind, and three of the big men stayed with it. They took up unobtrusive resi-dence in the former chauffeur's quarters, over the garage.

They were detectives, said Reenie. They must be. That was why they always had their overcoats on: it hid the guns, which they kept in their armpits. The guns were revolvers. She knew this from her various magazines. She said they were there to protect us, and if we saw anyone out of the ordinary creeping around the garden at night – besides these three men, of course – we were to scream.

The next day there was rioting, along the main streets of the town. Many men present at it had never been seen before, or if they had been seen, they hadn't been remembered. Who'd remember a tramp? But some of them hadn't been tramps, they'd been international agitators in disguise. They'd been spying, all along. How had they got here so quickly? On the tops of trains, it was said. That was how men like them travelled around.

The rioting started at a rally outside the town hall. First there were speeches in which goons and company thugs were mentioned; then Father, rendered in cardboard and wearing a top hat and smoking a cigar – not things he ever did – was burned in effigy, to loud cheering. Two rag dolls in frilly pink dresses were soaked in kerosene and tossed onto the flames as well. They were supposed to be us – Laura and me, said Reenie. Jokes had been made about them being hot little dollies. (Laura's strolls around town with Alex had not gone unremarked.) It was Ron Hincks who'd told her this, said Reenie, thinking she should know. He said the two of us shouldn't go downtown right now because feelings were running high and you never knew. He said we should stay at Avilion, where we would be safe. He said it was a crying shame about the dolls, and he'd like to get his hands on whoever had cooked that one up.

Those main-street stores and businesses that had refused to close down had their windows broken. Then the ones that had closed also had their windows broken. After that, looting took place, and matters got severely out of hand. The newspaper was invaded and the offices wrecked; Elwood Murray was roughed up, and the machines in the printing shop at the back were smashed. His darkroom escaped, but his camera did not. It was a mournful time for him, which we heard all about, many times, afterwards.

That night the button factory caught on fire. Flames shot out the windows on the lower floor: I couldn't see them from my room, but the fire truck clanged past, going to the rescue. I was dismayed and frightened, of course, but I have to admit there was something exciting about this as well. As I was listening to the clanging, and to the distant shouts from the same direction, I heard someone coming up the back stairs. I thought it might be Reenie, but it wasn't. It was Laura; she had her outdoor coat on.

"Where have you been?" I asked her. "We're supposed to stay put. Father has enough worries without you wandering off."

"I was only in the conservatory," she said. "I was praying. I needed a quiet place."

They did manage to put out the fire, but a lot of damage had been done to the building. That was the first report. Then Mrs. Hillcoate arrived, out of breath and bearing clean laundry, and was allowed in past the guards. Arson, she said: they'd found the cans of gasoline. The night watchman was lying dead on the floor. He had a bump on his head.

Two men had been seen running away. Had they been recognized? Not conclusively, but it was being rumoured that one of them was Miss Laura's young man. Reenie said he wasn't her young man, Laura didn't have a young man, he was only an acquaintance. Well, whatever he was, said Mrs. Hillcoate, he'd most likely burnt down the button factory and conked poor Al Davidson on the head and killed him dead as a rat, and he'd better make himself scarce around this town if he knew what was good for him.

At dinner Laura said she wasn't hungry. She said she couldn't eat right then: she would make up a tray for herself, to have later. I watched her carrying it up the back stairs to her room. It had double helpings of everything – rabbit, squash, boiled potatoes. Usually she treated eating as a kind of fidgeting – something to do with your hands at the dinner table, while other people were talking – or else as a chore she had to get through, like polishing the silver. A sort of tedious maintenance routine. I wondered when she had suddenly developed such optimism about food.

The next day, troops from the Royal Canadian Regiment arrived to restore order. This was Father's old regiment, from the war. He took it very hard, to see these soldiers turned against their own people – his own people, or the people he'd thought were his. That they no longer shared his view of them did not require any great genius to figure out, but he took that hard as well. Had they loved him, then, only for his money? It appeared so.

After the Royal Canadian Regiment had got things under control, the Mounties arrived. Three of them appeared outside our front door. They knocked politely, then stood in the hall, their shiny boots creaking against the waxed parquet, their stiff brown hats in their hands. They wanted to talk to Laura.

"Come with me, please, Iris," Laura whispered when summoned. "I can't see them alone." She looked very young, very white.

The two of us sat together on the settee in the morning room, beside the old gramophone. The Mounties sat in chairs. They did not look like my idea of a Mountie, being too old, too thick around the waist. One of them was younger, but he was not in charge. The middle one did the talking. He said that they apologized for disturbing us at what must be a difficult time, but the matter was of some urgency. What they wanted to talk about was Mr. Alex Thomas. Was Laura aware that this man was a known subversive and radical, and had been in the relief camps, causing agitation and stirring up trouble?

Laura said that as far as she knew he had just been teaching the men how to read.

That was one way of looking at it, said the Mountie. And if he was innocent, then he naturally had nothing to hide, and would come forward if required, didn't she agree? Where might he be keeping himself these days?

Laura said she couldn't say.

The question was repeated in a different way. This man was under suspicion: didn't Laura want to help locate the criminal who might well have set fire to her father's factory and may have been the cause of death of a loyal employee? If eyewitnesses were to be trusted, that is.

I said that eyewitnesses were not to be trusted, because whoever was seen running away had been viewed only from the back, and besides it had been dark.

"Miss Laura?" said the Mountie, ignoring me.

Laura said that even if she could say, she wouldn't. She said you were innocent until proven guilty. Also it was against her Christian principles to throw a man to the lions. She said she was sorry about the dead watchman, but it was not Alex Thomas's fault, because Alex Thomas would never have done such a thing. But she could not say anything more.

She was holding on to my arm, down near the wrist; I could feel the tremors coming from her, like a train track vibrating.

The chief Mountie said something about obstructing justice.

At this point I said that Laura was only just fifteen, and could not be held responsible in the way an adult would be. I said that what she had told them was of course confidential, and if it went any farther than this room – to the newspapers, for instance – then Father would know who to thank.

The Mounties smiled, and stood up, and took their leave; they were decorous and reassuring. They may have seen the impropriety of pursuing this line of investigation. Although on the ropes, Father still had friends.

"All right," I said to Laura, once they were gone. "I know you've got him in this house. You'd better tell me where."

"I put him in the cold cellar," said Laura, her bottom lip trembling.

"The cold cellar!" I said. "What a stupid place! Why there?"

"So he would have enough to eat, in an emergency," said Laura, and burst into tears. I wrapped my arms around her, and she snuffled against my shoulder.

"Enough to eat?" I said. "Enough jam and jelly and pickles? Really Laura, you take the cake." Then we both began to laugh, and after we had laughed and Laura had wiped her eyes, I said, "We've got to get him out of there. What if Reenie goes down for a jar of jam or something and comes across him by mistake? She'd have a heart attack."

We laughed some more. We were very on edge. Then I said the attic would be better, because nobody ever went up there. I would arrange it all, I said. She'd better go up to bed: it was obvious that the strain was telling on her and she was all worn out. She sighed a little, like a tired child, then did as I'd suggested. She'd been living on her nerves, carrying around this immense weight of knowledge like some evil packsack, and now she'd handed it over to me she was free to sleep.

Was it my belief that I was doing this only to spare her – to help her, to take care of her, as I had always done?

Yes. That is what I did believe.

I waited until Reenie had cleared up in the kitchen and turned in for the night. Then I went down the cellar stairs, into the chill, the dimness, the smell of spidery dampness. I went past the door to the coal cellar, the locked wine cellar door. The door to the cold cellar closed with a latch. I knocked, lifted it, went in. There was a scuttling noise. It was dark, of course; just the light from the corridor. The top of the apple barrel held the remains of Laura's dinner – the rabbit bones. It looked like some primitive altar.

I didn't see him at first; he was behind the apple barrel. Then I could make him out. A knee, a foot. "It's all right," I whispered. "It's only me."

"Ah," he said in his normal voice. "The devoted sister."

"Shh," I said. The light switch was a chain hanging from the bulb. I pulled it, the light went on. Alex Thomas was unwinding himself, scrambling out from behind the barrel. He crouched, blinking, sheepish, like a man caught with his pants undone.

"You should be ashamed of yourself," I said.

"You've come to kick me out, or turn me over to the proper authorities, I assume," he said with a smile.

"Don't be silly," I said. "I certainly wouldn't want you to be discovered here. Father couldn't stand the scandal."

"Capitalist's Daughter Aids Bolshevik Murderer?" he said. "Love Nest Among the Jelly Jars Revealed? That sort of scandal?"

I frowned at him. This was not a joking matter.

"Rest easy. Laura and I aren't up to anything," he said. "She's a great kid, but she's a saint in training, and I'm not a baby snatcher." He'd stood up by now and was dusting himself off.

"Then why is she hiding you?" I asked.

"Matter of principle. Once I asked, she had to accept. I fall into the right category for her."

"What category?"

"'The least of these,' I guess," he said. "To quote Jesus." I found that quite cynical. Then he said that bumping into Laura had been a sort of accident. He'd run into her in the conservatory. What had he been doing there? Hiding, obviously. He'd hoped also, he said, to be able to talk to me.

"Me?" I said. "Why on earth, me?"

"I thought you'd know what to do. You seem like the practical type. Your sister is less . . ."

"Laura seems to have managed well enough," I said shortly. I didn't like it when other people criticized Laura – her vagueness, her simplicity, her fecklessness. Criticism of Laura was reserved for me. "How did she get you past those men at the doors?" I said. "Into the house? The ones in overcoats."

"Even men in overcoats have to take a leak sometimes," he said.

I was taken aback by this vulgarity – it was at odds with his dinner-party politeness – but perhaps it was a sample of the orphanish jeering Reenie had predicted. I decided to ignore it. "You didn't set the fire, I take it," I said. I meant to sound sarcastic, but it wasn't received that way.

"I'm not that stupid," he said. "I wouldn't set a fire for no reason."

"Everyone thinks it was you."

"It wasn't, though," he said. "But it would be very convenient for certain people to take that view."

"What certain people? Why?" I wasn't pushing him this time; I was baffled.

"Use your head," he said. But he wouldn't say any more.

The attic

I got a candle from the stash of them in the kitchen, on hand
for power blackouts, and lit it, and led Alex Thomas out of the
cellar and through the kitchen and up the back stairs, then up
the narrower stairs to the attic, where I installed him behind the
three empty trunks. There were some old quilts stored in a
cedar chest up there, and I hauled them out for bedding.

"No one will come," I said. "If they do, get underneath the
quilts. Don't walk around, they might hear the footsteps. Don't
turn on the light." (There was a single bulb with a pull chain in
the attic, just as in the cold cellar.) "We'll bring you something
to eat in the morning," I added, not knowing how I would
make good on this promise.

I went downstairs, then came back up again with a chamber
pot, which I set down without a word. It was a detail that had
always worried me, in Reenie's stories about kidnappers –
what about the facilities? It would be one thing to be locked
into a crypt, quite another to be reduced to squatting in a
corner with your skirt hauled up.

Alex Thomas nodded, and said, "Good girl. You're a pal. I
knew you were practical."

In the morning Laura and I held a whispered conference in
her bedroom. The subjects discussed were the procuring of
food and drink, the need for watchfulness, and the emptying of
the chamber pot. One of us – pretending to be reading – would
stand guard in my room, with the door open: we could see the
door to the attic stairs from there. The other would fetch and
carry. We agreed to take these tasks in rotation. The big hurdle
would be Reenie, who was sure to smell a rat if we acted too
furtive.

We hadn't worked out any plan for what we would do if we were found out. We never did work out such a plan. It was all improvisation.

Alex Thomas's first breakfast was our toast crusts. As a rule, we did not eat our crusts until nagged – it was still Reenie's habit to say *Remember the starving Armenians* – but this time, when Reenie looked, the crusts were gone. They were actually in Laura's navy-blue skirt pocket.

"Alex Thomas must be the starving Armenians," I whispered, as we hurried up the stairs. But Laura didn't think this was funny. She thought it was accurate.

Mornings and evenings were the times of our visits. We raided the pantry, salvaged the leftovers. We smuggled up raw carrots, bacon rinds, half-eaten boiled eggs, pieces of bread folded over, with butter and jam inside. Once a leg of fricasseed chicken – a daring coup. Also glasses of water, cups of milk, cold coffee. We carted away the empty dishes, stashed them under our beds until the coast was clear, then washed them in our bathroom sink before replacing them in the kitchen cupboard. (I did this: Laura was too clumsy.) We didn't use the good china. What if something got broken? Even an everyday plate might have been noticed: Reenie kept track. So we were very cautious with the tableware.

Was Reenie suspicious of us? I expect so. She could usually tell when we were up to something. But she could also tell when it was more politic not to know exactly what that something might be. I expect she was preparing herself to say she'd had no idea, in case we were caught. She did tell us, once, not to go filching the raisins; she said we were acting like bottomless pits, and where did we get such hollow legs all of a sudden? And she was annoyed about the quarter of a pumpkin pie that went missing. Laura said she'd eaten it; she'd had a sudden fit of hunger, she said.

"Crust and all?" said Reenie sharply. Laura never ate the pie crusts from Reenie's pies. Nobody did. Nor did Alex Thomas.

"I fed it to the birds," said Laura. True enough: that's what she had done, afterwards.

Alex Thomas was at first appreciative of our efforts. He said we were good pals, and that without us his goose would have been cooked. Then he wanted cigarettes – he was dying for a smoke. We brought him some from the silver box on the piano, but warned him to limit himself to one a day – the fumes might be detected. (He ignored this stricture.)

Then he said the worst thing about the attic was not being able to keep clean. He said his mouth felt like a drain. We stole the old toothbrush Reenie used for cleaning the silver, and scrubbed it off for him as best we could; he said it was better than nothing. One day we brought him a wash basin and a towel, and a jug with warm water. Afterwards he waited till nobody was underneath and threw the dirty water out the attic window. It had been raining, so the ground was wet anyway and the splash was not noticed. A little later, when the coast seemed clear, we allowed him down the attic stairs and shut him up in the bathroom the two of us shared, so he could have a proper wash. (We'd told Reenie we'd help out by taking over the cleaning of this bathroom, on which her comment was: *Wonders never cease.*)

While Alex Thomas's washing-up was going forward Laura sat in her bedroom, I sat in mine, each guarding a bathroom door. I tried not to think about what was going on in there. The image of him with all his clothes off was painful to me, in some way that did not bear contemplating.

Alex Thomas was featured in newspaper editorials, not only in our own paper. He was an arsonist and murderer, it was said, and of the worst kind – one who killed from cold-blooded fanaticism. He had come to Port Ticonderoga to infiltrate the working force, and to sow seeds of dissension, in which he had succeeded, as witness the general strike and the rioting. He was an example of the evils of a university education – a smart boy, too smart for his own good, whose wits had been turned through bad company and worse books. His adoptive father, a Presbyterian minister, was quoted as saying that he prayed every night for Alex's soul, but that this was a generation of vipers. His rescue of Alex as a child from the horrors of war was not passed over: Alex was a brand snatched from the burning, he said, but it was always a risk to take a stranger into your home. The implication was that such brands were better left unsnatched.

In addition to all of that, the police had printed a Wanted poster of Alex, and had stuck it up in the post office, and in other public places as well. Luckily it wasn't a very clear picture: Alex had his hand in front of him, which partly obscured his face. It was the photo from the newspaper, the one Elwood Murray had taken of the three of us, at the button factory picnic. (Laura and I were cut off at the sides, naturally.) Elwood Murray had let it be known that he could have printed a better picture from the negative, but when he went to look, the negative was gone. Well, that was no surprise: a number of things had been destroyed when the newspaper office was wrecked.

We brought Alex the newspaper clippings, and one of the Wanted posters too – Laura had purloined it from a telephone pole. He read about himself with rueful dismay. "They want my head on a platter," was what he said.

After a few days, he asked if we could bring him some paper – writing paper. There was a stack of school exercise books left over from Mr. Erskine: we brought him those, and a pencil as well.

"What do you think he's writing?" Laura asked. We couldn't decide. A prisoner's journal, a vindication of himself? Perhaps a letter, to someone who might rescue him. But he didn't ask us to mail anything, so it couldn't have been a letter.

Tending Alex Thomas brought Laura and me closer together than we had been for a while. He was our guilty secret, and also our virtuous project – one we could finally share. We were two good little Samaritans, lifting out of the ditch the man fallen among thieves. We were Mary and Martha, ministering to – well, not Jesus, even Laura did not go that far, but it was obvious which of us she had cast in these roles. I was to be Martha, keeping busy with household chores in the background; she was to be Mary, laying pure devotion at Alex's feet. (Which does a man prefer? Bacon and eggs, or worship? Sometimes one, sometimes the other, depending how hungry he is.)

Laura carried the food scraps up the attic stairs as if they were a temple offering. She carried the chamber pot down as if it were a reliquary, or a precious candle on the verge of flickering out.

At night, after Alex Thomas had been fed and watered, we would talk him over – how he'd looked that day, whether he was too thin, whether he'd coughed – we didn't want him to get sick. What he might need, what we should try to steal for him the next day. Then we would climb into our respective beds. I don't know about Laura, but I would picture him up there in the attic, directly above me. He too would be trying to sleep, tossing and turning in his bed of musty quilts. Then he would be sleeping. Then he would be dreaming, long dreams of war and fire, and of disintegrating villages, their fragments strewn about.

I don't know at what point these dreams of his changed to dreams of pursuit and escape; I don't know at what point I joined him in these dreams, fleeing with him hand in hand, at dusk, away from a burning building, across the furrowed December fields, the stubbled earth in which the frost was now beginning to set in, towards the dark line of the distant woods.

But it wasn't his dream really, I did know that. It was my own. It was Avilion that was burning, its broken pieces that were scattered over the ground – the good china, the Sèvres bowl with rose petals, the silver cigarette box from the top of the piano. The piano itself, the stained-glass windows from the dining room – the blood-red cup, Iseult's cracked harp – everything I'd been longing to get away from, true, but not through destruction. I'd wanted to leave home, but have it stay in place, waiting for me, unchanged, so I could step back into it at will.

One day, when Laura was out – it was no longer dangerous for her, the men in overcoats had gone away and the Mounties as well, the streets were orderly again – I decided to make a solo trip to the attic. I had an offering to make – a pocketful of currants and dried figs, snatched from the makings for the Christmas pudding. I scouted – Reenie was safely occupied with Mrs. Hillcoate, in the kitchen – then went to the attic door and knocked. We had a special knock by then, one knock followed by three more in quick succession. Then I tiptoed up the narrow attic stairs.

Alex Thomas was crouched beside the small oval window, trying to take advantage of what daylight there was. Evidently he hadn't heard my knock: his back was turned towards me, and he had one of the quilts around his shoulders. He seemed to be writing. I could smell cigarette smoke – yes, he was smoking, there was his hand with the cigarette in it. I didn't think he should be doing this so near a quilt.

I did not quite know how to announce my presence. "I'm here," I said.

He jumped, and dropped the cigarette. It fell onto the quilt.

I gasped, and dropped to my knees to put it out – I had the now-familiar vision of Avilion going up in flames. "It's all right," he said. He was kneeling too, both of us searching for any remaining sparks. Then the next thing I knew we were on the floor, and he had hold of me and was kissing me on the mouth.

I hadn't expected this.

Had I expected this? Was it so sudden, or were there preliminaries: a touch, a gaze? Did I do anything to provoke him? Nothing I can recall, but is what I remember the same thing as what actually happened?

It is now: I am the only survivor.

In any case, it was just as Reenie had said, about the men in movie theatres, except that what I felt was not outrage. But the rest of it was true enough: I was transfixed, I could not move, I had no recourse. My bones had turned to melting wax. He got almost all of my buttons undone before I was able to rouse myself, to pull myself away, to flee.

I did this wordlessly. As I scrambled down the attic stairs, pushing back my hair, tucking in my blouse, I had the impression that – behind my back – he was laughing at me.

I didn't know exactly what might occur if I let such a thing happen again, but whatever it was would be dangerous, at least for me. I would be asking for it, I would get what was coming to me, I would be an accident waiting to happen. I couldn't afford to be alone in the attic with Alex Thomas again, nor could I confide in Laura the reason why. It would be too hurtful to her: she would never be able to understand it. (There was another possibility – he might have been doing a similar kind of thing with Laura. But no, I couldn't believe that. She never would have allowed it. Would she?)

"We have to get him out of town," I said to Laura. "We can't keep this up. They're sure to notice."

"Not yet," said Laura. "They're still watching the train tracks." She was in a position to know this, as she was still doing her work with the church soup kitchen.

"Well, somewhere else in town then," I said.

"Where? There isn't anywhere else. And this is the best place – this is the one place they'd never think to look."

Alex Thomas said he didn't want to get snowed in. He said a winter in the attic would drive him buggy. He said he was going stir-crazy. He said he would walk a couple of miles down the tracks, and hop a freight – there was a high bank there that made it easier. He said that if only he could get as far as Toronto, he could hide out – he had friends there, and they had friends. Then he'd get across to the States, one way or another, where he'd be safer. From what he'd read in the papers, the authorities suspected he might be there already. They certainly weren't still looking for him in Port Ticonderoga.

By the first week in January, we decided it was safe enough for him to leave. We filched an old coat of Father's from the back corner of the cloak room for him, and packed him a lunch – bread and cheese, an apple – and sent him away on his travels. (Father later missed the coat and Laura said she'd given it to a tramp, which was a partial truth. As this act was entirely in character for her it wasn't questioned, only grumbled about.)

On the night of his departure we let Alex out the back door. He said he owed a lot to us; he said he wouldn't forget it. He gave each of us a hug, a brotherly hug of equal duration for each. It was obvious he wanted to be quit of us. Apart from the fact that it was night, it was oddly as if he were going off to school. Afterwards we cried, like mothers. It was also the relief – that he'd gone away, that he was off our hands – but that is like mothers too.

★

He left behind one of the cheap exercise books we'd given him. Of course we opened it immediately to see if he'd written anything in it. What were we hoping for? A farewell note, expressing undying gratitude? Kind sentiments about ourselves? Something of that sort.

This is what we found:

anchoryne	nacrod
berel	onyxor
carchineal	porphyrial
diamite	quartzephyr
ebonort	rhint
fulgor	sapphyrion
glutz	tristok
hortz	ulinth
iridis	vorver
jocynth	wotanite
kalkil	xenor
lazaris	yorula
malachont	zycron

"Precious stones?" said Laura.

"No. They don't sound right," I said.

"Is it a foreign language?"

I didn't know. I thought this list looked suspiciously like a code. Perhaps Alex Thomas was (after all) what other people accused him of being: a spy of some kind.

"I think we should get rid of this," I said.

"I will," said Laura quickly. "I'll burn it in my fireplace." She folded it up, and slid it into her pocket.

A week after Alex Thomas's departure, Laura came to my room. "I think you should have this," she said. It was a print of the photograph of the three of us, the one Elwood Murray had taken at the picnic. But she'd cut herself out of it – only her hand remained. She couldn't have got rid of this hand without making a wobbly margin. She hadn't coloured this picture at all, except for her own cut-off hand. This had been tinted a very pale yellow.

"For goodness' sake, Laura!" I said. "Where did you get this?"

"I made some prints," she said. "When I was working at Elwood Murray's. I've got the negative too."

I didn't know whether to be angry or alarmed. Cutting up the picture like that was a very strange thing to have done. The sight of Laura's light-yellow hand, creeping towards Alex across the grass like an incandescent crab, gave me a chill down the back of my spine. "Why on earth did you do that?"

"Because that's what you want to remember," she said. This was so audacious that I gasped. She gave me a direct look, which in anyone else would have been a challenge. But this was Laura: her tone was neither sulky nor jealous. As far as she was concerned she was simply stating a fact.

"It's all right," she said. "I have another one, for me."

"And I'm not in yours?"

"No," she said. "You're not. None of you but your hand." This was the closest she ever came, in my hearing, to a confession of love for Alex Thomas. Except for the day before her death, that is. Not that she used the word *love*, even then.

I ought to have thrown this mutilated picture away, but I didn't.

Things settled back into their accustomed, monotonous order. By unspoken consent, Laura and I did not mention Alex Thomas between us any more. There was too much that could

not be said, on either side. At first I used to go up to the attic –
a faint odour of smoke was still detectable there – but I stopped
doing that after a while, as it served no good purpose.

We busied ourselves with daily life again, insofar as that was
possible. There was a little more money now, because Father
would get the insurance after all, for the burned factory building. It wasn't enough, but we had been given – he said – a
breathing space.

The Imperial Room

The season is turning on its hinges, the earth swings farther from the light; under the roadside bushes the paper trash of summer drifts like an omen of snow. The air is drying out, preparing us for the coming Sahara of centrally heated winter. Already the ends of my thumbs are fissuring, my face withering further. If I could see my skin in the mirror – if I could only get close enough, or far enough away – it would be crisscrossed by tiny lines, in between the main wrinkles, like scrimshaw.

Last night I dreamt that my legs were covered with hair. Not a little hair but a great deal of it – dark hair sprouting in tufts and tendrils as I watched, spreading up over my thighs like the pelt of an animal. The winter was coming, I dreamed, and so I would hibernate. First I would grow fur, then crawl into a cave, then go to sleep. It all seemed normal, as if I'd done it before. Then I remembered, even in the dream, that I'd never been a hairy woman in that way and was now bald as a newt, or at least my legs were; so although they appeared to be attached to my body, these hairy legs couldn't possibly be mine. Also they had no feeling in them. They were the legs of something else, or someone. All I had to do was follow the legs, run my hand along them, to find out who or what it was.

The alarm of this woke me, or so I believed. I dreamt that Richard was back. I could hear him breathing in the bed beside me. Yet there was nobody there.

I woke up then in reality. My legs were asleep: I'd been lying twisted. I fumbled for the bedside lamp, decoded my watch: it was two in the morning. My heart was hammering painfully, as if I'd been running. It's true, what they used to say, I thought. A nightmare can kill you.

I hasten on, making my way crabwise across the paper. It's a slow race now, between me and my heart, but I intend to get there first. Where is there? The end, or *The End*. One or the other. Both are destinations, of a sort.

The January and February of 1935. High winter. Snow fell, breath hardened; furnaces burned, smoke arose, radiators clanked. Cars ran off roads into ditches; their drivers, despairing of help, kept their engines running and were asphyxiated. Dead tramps were found on park benches and in abandoned warehouses, rigid as mannequins, as if posing for a store-window advertisement of poverty. Corpses that could not be buried because their graves could not be dug in the steel-hard ground waited their turn in the outbuildings of nervous undertakers. Rats did well. Mothers with children, unable to find work or pay their rent, were bundled out into the snow, bag and baggage. Children skated on the frozen millpond of the Louveteau River, and two went through the ice, and one drowned. Pipes froze and burst.

Laura and I were less and less together. Indeed she was scarcely to be seen: she was helping with the United Church relief drive, or so she said. Reenie said that come next month she'd only be working for us three days a week; she said her feet were bothering her, which was her way of covering up the fact that we could no longer afford her full-time. I knew it anyway, it was plain as the nose on your face. As the nose on Father's face, which looked like the morning after a train wreck. He'd been spending a lot of time up in his turret lately.

The button factory was empty, its interior charred and shattered. There was not the money to repair it: the insurance company was balking, citing the mysterious circumstances surrounding the arson. It was whispered about that all was not as it appeared: some even hinted that Father had set the fire himself, a slanderous allegation. The two other factories were still closed; Father was racking his brains for some way to reopen them. He was going to Toronto more and more often, on business. Sometimes he'd take me with him, and we would stay at the Royal York Hotel, considered to be the top hotel then. It was where all the company presidents and doctors and lawyers who were so inclined kept their mistresses and conducted their week-long binges, but I didn't know that at the time.

Who paid for these jaunts of ours? I have a suspicion it was Richard, who was present on these occasions. He was the one Father was doing the business with: the last one left, of a narrowed field. The business concerned the sale of the factories, and was complicated. Father had tried to sell before, but in these times nobody was buying, not with the conditions he set. He wanted to sell only a minority interest. He wanted to keep control. He wanted a capital injection. He wanted the factories opened again, so that his men would have jobs. He called them "his men," as if they were still in the army and he was still their captain. He did not want to cut his losses and desert them, for as everyone knows, or once knew, a captain should go down with the ship. They wouldn't bother, now. Now they'd cash in and bail out, and move to Florida.

Father said he needed me along "to take notes," but I never took any. I believed I was there just so he could have someone with him – for moral support. He certainly needed it. He was thin as a stick, and his hands shook constantly. It cost him an effort to write his own name.

Laura did not come on these excursions. Her presence was not required. She stayed behind, doling out the three-day-old bread, the watery soup. She'd taken to skimping on meals herself, as if she didn't feel entitled to eat.

"Jesus ate," said Reenie. "He ate all kinds of things. He didn't stint."

"Yes," said Laura, "but I'm not Jesus."

"Well, thank the Lord she's got the sense to know that much at least," Reenie grumbled to me. She scraped the remaining two-thirds of Laura's dinner into the stock pot, because it would be a sin and a shame to have it go to waste. It was a point of pride with Reenie during those years that she never threw anything out.

Father no longer kept a chauffeur, and no longer trusted himself to drive. He and I would go in to Toronto by train, arriving at Union Station, crossing the street to the hotel. I was supposed to amuse myself somehow in the afternoons, while the business was being done. Mostly however I sat in my room, because I was afraid of the city and ashamed of my dowdy clothes, which make me look years younger than I was. I would read magazines: *Ladies' Home Journal*, *Collier's*, *Mayfair*. Mostly I read the short stories, which had to do with romance. I had no interest in casseroles or crochet patterns, although the beauty tips held my attention. Also I read the advertisements. A Latex foundation garment with two-way stretch would help me play better bridge. Although I might smoke like a chimney, who cared, because my mouth would taste clean as a whistle if I stuck to Spuds. Something called Larvex would end my moth worries. At the Bigwin Inn, on the beautiful Lake of Bays where every moment was exhilarating, I could do musical slenderizing exercises on the beach.

After the day's business was done, all three of us – Father, Richard, and myself – would have dinner at a restaurant. On these occasions I would say nothing, because what was there for me to say? The subjects were economics and politics, the

Depression, the situation in Europe, the worrisome advances being made by World Communism. Richard was of the opinion that Hitler had certainly pulled Germany together from a financial point of view. He was less approving of Mussolini, who was a dabbler and a dilettante. Richard had been approached to make an investment in a new fabric the Italians were developing – very hush-hush – made out of heated milk protein. But if this stuff got wet, said Richard, it smelled horribly of cheese, and the ladies in North America would therefore never accept it. He'd stick with rayon, though it wrinkled when damp, and he'd keep his ear to the tracks and pick up anything promising. There was bound to be something coming along, some artificial fabric that would put silk right out of business, and cotton to a large extent as well. What the ladies wanted was a product that wouldn't need to be ironed – that could be hung on the line, that would dry wrinkle-free. They also wanted stockings that were durable as well as sheer, so they could show off their legs. Wasn't that right? he asked me, with a smile. He had a habit of appealing to me on matters concerning the ladies.

I nodded. I always nodded. I never listened very closely, not only because these conversations bored me but also because they pained me. It hurt me to see my father agreeing with sentiments I felt he didn't share.

Richard said he would have had us to dinner at his own home, but since he was a bachelor it would have been a slap-dash affair. He lived in a cheerless flat, he said; he said he was practically a monk. "What is life without a wife?" he said, smiling. It sounded like a quotation. I think it was one.

Richard proposed to me in the Imperial Room of the Royal York Hotel. He'd invited me to lunch, along with Father; but then at the last minute, as we were walking through the hotel corridors on our way to the lift, Father said he couldn't attend. I'd have to go by myself, he said.

Of course it was a put-up job between the two of them.

"Richard will be asking you something," said Father to me. His tone was apologetic.

"Oh?" I said. Probably something about ironing, but I didn't much care. As far as I was concerned Richard was a grown-up man. He was thirty-five, I was eighteen. He was well on the other side of being interesting.

"I think he may be asking you to marry him," he said.

We were in the lobby by then. I sat down. "Oh," I said. I could suddenly see what should have been obvious for some time. I wanted to laugh, as if at a trick. Also I felt as if my stomach had vanished. Yet my voice remained calm. "What should I do?"

"I've already given my consent," said Father. "So it's up to you." Then he added: "A certain amount depends on it."

"A certain amount?"

"I have to consider your futures. In case anything should happen to me, that is. Laura's future, in particular." What he was saying was that unless I married Richard, we wouldn't have any money. What he was also saying was that the two of us – me, and especially Laura – would never be able to fend for ourselves. "I have to consider the factories as well," he said. "I have to consider the business. It might still be saved, but the bankers are after me. They're hot on the trail. They won't wait much longer." He was leaning on his cane, gazing down at the carpet, and I saw how ashamed he was. How beaten down. "I don't want it all to have been for nothing. Your grandfather, and then . . . Fifty, sixty years of hard work, down the drain."

"Oh. I see." I was cornered. It wasn't as if I had any alternatives to propose.

"They'd take Avilion, as well. They'd sell it."

"They would?"

"It's mortgaged up to the hilt."

"Oh."

"A certain amount of resolve might be required. A certain amount of courage. Biting the bullet and so forth."

I said nothing.

"But naturally," he said, "whatever decision you make will be your own concern."

I said nothing.

"I wouldn't want you doing anything you were dead set against," he said, looking past me with his good eye, frowning a little, as if an object of great significance had just come into view. There was nothing behind me but a wall.

I said nothing.

"Good. That's that, then." He seemed relieved. "He has a lot of common sense, Griffen. I believe he's sound, underneath it all."

"I guess so," I said. "I'm sure he's very sound."

"You'd be in good hands. And Laura too, of course."

"Of course," I said faintly. "Laura too."

"Chin up, then."

Do I blame him? No. Not any more. Hindsight is twenty-twenty, but he was only doing what would have been considered – was considered, then – the responsible thing. He was doing the best he knew how.

Richard joined us as if on cue, and the two men shook hands. My own hand was taken, squeezed briefly. Then my elbow. That was how men steered women around in those days – by the elbow – and so I was steered by the elbow into the Imperial Room. Richard said he'd wanted the Venetian Café, which was lighter and more festive in atmosphere, but unfortunately it had been fully booked.

It's odd to remember this now, but the Royal York Hotel was the tallest building in Toronto then, and the Imperial Room was the biggest dining room. Richard was fond of big. The room itself had rows of large square pillars, a tessellated ceiling, a line of chandeliers, each with a tassel at the bottom end: a congealed opulence. It felt leathery, ponderous, paunchy – veined somehow. *Porphyry* is the word that comes to mind, though there may not have been any.

It was noon, one of those unsettling winter days that are brighter than they ought to be. The white sunlight was falling in shafts through the gaps in the heavy drapes, which must have been maroon, I think, and were certainly velvet. Underneath the usual hotel dining-room smells of steam-table vegetables and lukewarm fish there was an odour of hot metal and smouldering cloth. The table Richard had reserved was in a dim corner, away from the abrasive daylight. There was a red rosebud in a bud vase; I stared over it at Richard, curious as to how he would go about things. Would he take my hand, press it, hesitate, stutter? I didn't think so.

I didn't dislike him unduly. I didn't like him. I had few opinions about him because I'd never thought much about him, although I had – from time to time – noticed the suavity of his clothes. He was pompous at times, but at least he wasn't what you'd call ugly, not at all. I supposed he was very eligible. I felt a little dizzy. I still didn't know what I would do.

The waiter came. Richard ordered. Then he looked at his watch. Then he talked. I heard little of what he said. He smiled. He produced a small black velvet-covered box, opened it. Inside was a glittering shard of light.

I spent that night lying huddled and shivering in the vast bed of the hotel. My feet were icy, my knees drawn up, my head sideways on the pillow; in front of me the arctic waste of starched white bedsheet stretched out to infinity. I knew I could never traverse it, regain the track, get back to where it was warm; I knew I was directionless; I knew I was lost. I would be discovered here years later by some intrepid team – fallen in my tracks, one arm outflung as if grasping at straws, my features desiccated, my fingers gnawed by wolves.

What I was experiencing was dread, but it was not dread of Richard as such. It was as if the illuminated dome of the Royal York Hotel had been wrenched off and I was being stared at by a malign presence located somewhere above the black spangled empty surface of the sky. It was God, looking down with his blank, ironic searchlight of an eye. He was observing me; he was observing my predicament; he was observing my failure to believe in him. There was no floor to my room: I was suspended in the air, about to plummet. My fall would be endless – endlessly down.

Such dismal feelings however do not often persist in the clear light of morning, when you are young.

The Arcadian Court

Outside the window, in the darkened yard, there's snow. That kissing sound against the glass. It will melt off because it's only November, but still it's a foretaste. I don't know why I find it so exciting. I know what's coming: slush, darkness, flu, black ice, wind, salt stains on boots. But still there's a sense of anticipation: you tense for the combat. Winter is something you can go out into, confront, then foil by retreating back indoors. Still, I wish this house had a fireplace.

The house I lived in with Richard had a fireplace. It had four fireplaces. There was one in our bedroom, as I recall. Flames licking on flesh.

I unroll the sleeves of my sweater, pull the cuffs down over my hands. Like those fingerless gloves they used to wear – green-grocers, people like that – for working in the cold. It's been a warm autumn so far, but I can't let myself be lulled into carelessness. I should get the furnace serviced. Dig out the flannel nightgown. Lay in some tinned baked beans, some candles, some matches. An ice storm like last winter's could shut down everything, and then you're left with no electricity and an unworkable toilet, and no drinking water except what you can melt.

The garden has nothing in it but dead leaves and brittle stalks and a few diehard chrysanthemums. The sun is losing altitude; it's dark early now. I write at the kitchen table, indoors. I miss the sound of the rapids. Sometimes there's wind, blowing through the leafless branches, which is much the same although less dependable.

The week after the engagement had taken place I was packed off to have lunch with Richard's sister, Winifred Griffen Prior.

The invitation had come from her, but it was Richard who had packed me off really, I felt. I may have been wrong about that, because Winifred pulled a lot of strings, and may have pulled Richard's on this occasion. Most likely it was the two of them together.

The lunch was to take place in the Arcadian Court. This was where the ladies lunched, up at the top of Simpsons department store, on Queen Street – a high, wide space, said to be "Byzantine" in design (which meant it had archways and potted palms), done in lilac and silver, with streamlined contours for the lighting fixtures and the chairs. A balcony ran around it halfway up, with wrought-iron railings; that was for men only, for businessmen. They could sit up there and look down on the ladies, feathered and twittering, as if in an aviary.

I'd worn my best daytime outfit, the only possible outfit I had for such an occasion: a navy-blue suit with a pleated skirt, a white blouse with a bow at the neck, a navy-blue hat like a boater. This ensemble made me look like a schoolgirl, or a Salvation Army canvasser. I won't even mention my shoes; even now the thought of them is too discouraging. I kept my pristine engagement ring folded into my cotton-gloved fist, aware that, worn with clothes like mine, it must look like a rhinestone, or else like something I'd stolen.

The maître d' glanced at me as if surely I was in the wrong place, or at least the wrong entrance – was I wanting a job? I did look down-at-heels, and too young to be having a ladies' lunch. But then I gave Winifred's name and it was all right, because Winifred absolutely lived at the Arcadian Court. (*Absolutely lived* was her own expression.)

At least I didn't have to wait, drinking a glass of ice water by myself with the well-dressed women staring at me and wondering how I'd got in, because there was Winifred already, sitting at one of the pale tables. She was taller than I'd remembered – *slender*, or perhaps *willowy*, you'd say, though some of that was foundation garment. She had on a green ensemble – not a pastel green but a vibrant green, almost flagrant. (When chlorophyll chewing gum came into fashion two decades later, it was that colour.) She had green alligator shoes to match. They were glossy, rubbery, slightly wet-looking, like lily pads, and I thought I had never seen such exquisite, unusual shoes. Her hat was the same shade – a round swirl of green fabric, balanced on her head like a poisonous cake.

Right at that moment she was doing something I had been taught never to do because it was cheap: she was looking at her face in the mirror of her compact, in public. Worse, she was powdering her nose. While I hesitated, not wishing to let her know I'd caught her in this vulgar act, she snapped the compact shut and slipped it into her shiny green alligator purse as if there was nothing to it. Then she stretched her neck and slowly turned her powdered face and looked around her with a white glare, like a headlight. Then she saw me, and smiled, and held out a languid, welcoming hand. She had a silver bangle, which I coveted instantly.

"Call me Freddie," she said after I'd sat down. "All my chums do, and I want us to be great chums." It was the fashion then for women like Winifred to favour diminutives that made them sound like youths: Billie, Bobbie, Willie, Charlie. I had no such nickname, so could not offer one in return.

"Oh, is that the ring?" she said. "It is a beauty, isn't it? I helped Richard pick it out – he likes me to go shopping for him. It does give men such migraines, doesn't it, shopping? He thought perhaps an emerald, but there's really nothing like a diamond, is there?"

While saying this, she examined me with interest and a certain chilly amusement, to see how I would take it – this reduction of my engagement ring to a minor errand. Her eyes were intelligent and oddly large, with green eyeshadow on the lids. Her pencilled eyebrows were plucked into a smoothly arched line, giving her that expression of boredom and, at the same time, incredulous astonishment, which was cultivated by the film stars of that era, though I doubt that Winifred was ever much astonished. Her lipstick was a dark pinkish orange, a shade that had just come in – *shrimp* was the proper name for it, as I'd learned from my afternoon magazines. Her mouth had the same cinematic quality as the eyebrows, the two halves of the upper lip drawn into Cupid's-bow points. Her voice was what was called a whisky voice – low, deep almost, with a rough, scraped overlay to it like a cat's tongue – like velvet made of leather.

(She was a card player, I discovered later. Bridge, not poker – she would have been good at poker, good at bluffing, but it was too risky, too much a gamble; she liked to bid on known quantities. She played golf as well, but mostly for the social contacts; she wasn't as good at it as she made out. Tennis was too strenuous for her; she would not have wanted to be caught sweating. She "sailed," which meant, for her, sitting on a cushion on a boat, in a hat, with a drink.)

Winifred asked me what I would like to eat. I said anything at all. She called me "dear," and said that the Waldorf salad was marvellous. I said that would be fine.

I didn't see how I could ever work up to calling her *Freddie*: it seemed too familiar, disrespectful even. She was after all an adult – thirty, or twenty-nine at least. She was six or seven years younger than Richard, but they were pals: "Richard and I are such great pals," she said to me confidingly, for the first time but not for the last. It was a threat, of course, as was much of what she would say to me in this easy and confiding tone. It meant not only that she had claims that predated mine, and loyalties I could not hope to understand, but also that if I ever crossed Richard there would be the two of them to reckon with.

It was she who arranged things for Richard, she told me – social events, cocktail parties and dinners and so forth – because he was a bachelor, and, as she said (and would continue to say, year after year), "Us gals run that end of things." Then she said that she was just delighted that Richard had finally decided to settle down, and with a nice young girl like me. There'd been a couple of close things – some previous entanglements. (This was how Winifred always spoke of women in relation to Richard – *entanglements*, like nets, or webs, or snares, or merely like pieces of gummy string left lying around on the ground, that you might get caught on your shoe by mistake.)

Luckily Richard had escaped from these entanglements, not that women did not chase after him. They chased after him in *droves*, said Winifred, lowering her whisky voice, and I had an image of Richard, his clothing torn, his carefully arranged hair dishevelled, fleeing in panic while a pack of baying females coursed after him. But I could not believe in such an image. I couldn't imagine Richard running, or hurrying, or even being afraid. I couldn't imagine him in peril.

I nodded and smiled, unsure of where I myself was assumed to stand. Was I one of the sticky entanglers? Perhaps. On the surface of things however I was being led to understand that Richard had a high intrinsic value, and that I'd better mind my p's and q's if I was to live up to it. "But I'm sure you'll manage," said Winifred, smiling a little. "You're so *young*." If anything, this youthfulness of mine should have made managing less likely, which was what Winifred was counting on. She had no intention of giving up any managing, herself.

Our Waldorf salads came. Winifred watched me pick up my knife and fork – at least I didn't eat with my hands, her expression said – and gave a little sigh. I was hard slogging for her, I now realize. No doubt she thought I was sullen, or unforthcoming: I had no small talk, I was so ignorant, so *rural*. Or perhaps her sigh was a sigh of anticipation – of anticipated work, because I was a lump of unmoulded clay, and now she would have to roll up her sleeves and get down to moulding me.

No time like the present. She dug right in. Her method was one of hint, of suggestion. (She had another method – the bludgeon – but I didn't encounter it at this lunch.) She said she'd known my grandmother, or at least she'd known *of* her. The Montfort women of Montreal had been celebrated for their style, she said, but of course Adelia Montfort had died before I was born. This was her way of saying that despite my pedigree we were in effect starting from scratch.

My clothes were the least of it, she implied. Clothes could always be purchased, naturally, but I would have to learn to wear them to effect. "As if they're your skin, dear," she said. My hair was out of the question – long, unwaved, combed straight back, held with a clip. It was a clear case for a pair of scissors and a cold wave. Then there was the question of my fingernails. Nothing too brash, mind you; I was too young for brashness. "You could be charming," said Winifred. "Absolutely. With a little effort."

I listened humbly, resentfully. I knew I did not have charm. Neither Laura nor I had it. We were too secretive for charm, or else too blunt. We'd never learned it, because Reenie had spoiled us. She felt that *who we were* ought to be enough for anybody. We shouldn't have to lay ourselves out for people, court them with coaxings and wheedlings and eye-batting displays. I expect Father could see a point to charm in some quarters, but he hadn't instilled any of it in us. He'd wanted us to be more like boys, and now we were. You don't teach boys to be charming. It makes people think they are devious.

Winifred watched me eat, a quizzical smile on her lips. Already I was becoming a string of adjectives in her head – a string of funny anecdotes she would retail to her chums, the Billies and Bobbies and Charlies. *Dressed like a charity case. Ate as if they'd never fed her. And the shoes!*

"Well," she said, once she'd poked at her salad – Winifred never finished a meal – "now we'll have to put our heads together."

I didn't know what she meant. She gave another little sigh. "Plan the wedding," she said. "We don't have very much time. I thought, St. Simon the Apostle, and then the Royal York ballroom, the centre one, for the reception."

I must have assumed I would simply be handed over to Richard, like a parcel; but no, there would have to be ceremonies – more than one of them. Cocktail parties, teas, bridal showers, portraits taken, for the papers. It would be like my own mother's wedding, in the stories told by Reenie, but backwards somehow and with pieces missing. Where was the romantic prelude, with the young man kneeling at my feet? I felt a wave of dismay travel up from my knees until it reached my face. Winifred saw it, but did nothing to reassure me. She didn't want me reassured.

"Don't worry, my dear," she said, in a tone that indicated scant hope. She patted my arm. "I'll take you in hand." I could feel my will seeping out of me – any power I still might have left, over my own actions. (Really! I think now. Really she was a sort of madame. Really she was a pimp.)

"My goodness, look at the time," she said. She had a watch that was silver and fluid, like a ribbon of poured metal; it had dots on it instead of numbers. "I have to dash. They'll bring you some tea, and a flan or something if you like. Young girls have such sweet tooths. Or is that sweet teeth?" She laughed, and stood up, and gave me a shrimp-coloured kiss, not on the cheek but on the forehead. That served to keep me in my place, which was – it seemed clear – to be that of a child.

I watched her move through the rippling pastel space of the Arcadian Court as if gliding, with little nods and tiny calibrated waves of the hand. The air parted before her like long grass; her legs did not appear to be attached to her hips, but directly to her waist; nothing joggled. I could feel parts of my own body bulging out, over the sides of straps and the tops of stockings. I longed to be able to duplicate that walk, so smooth and fleshless and invulnerable.

I was not married from Avilion, but from Winifred's half-timbered fake-Tudor barn in Rosedale. It was felt to be more convenient, as most of the guests would be from Toronto. It would also be less embarrassing for my father, who could no longer afford the kind of wedding Winifred felt was her due.

He could not even afford the clothes: Winifred took care of those. Stowed away in my luggage – in one of my several brand-new trunks – were a tennis skirt although I didn't play, a bathing suit although I couldn't swim, and several dancing frocks, although I didn't know how to dance. Where could I have studied such accomplishments? Not at Avilion; not even the swimming, because Reenie wouldn't let us go in. But Winifred had insisted on these outfits. She said I'd need to dress the part, no matter what my deficiencies, which should never be admitted by me. "Say you have a headache," she told me. "It's always an acceptable excuse."

She told me many other things as well. "It's all right to show boredom," she said. "Just never show fear. They'll smell it on you, like sharks, and come in for the kill. You can look at the edge of the table – it lowers your eyelids – but never look at the floor, it makes your neck look weak. Don't stand up straight, you're not a soldier. Never *cringe*. If someone makes a remark that's insulting to you, say *Excuse me?* as if you haven't heard; nine times out of ten they won't have the face to repeat it. Never raise your voice to a waiter, it's vulgar. Make them bend down, it's what they're for. Don't fidget with your gloves or your hair. Always look as if you have something better to do, but never show impatience. When in doubt, go to the powder room, but go slowly. Grace comes from indifference." Such were her sermons. I have to admit, despite my loathing of her, that they have proved to be of considerable value in my life.

The night before the wedding I spent in one of Winifred's best bedrooms. "Make yourself beautiful," said Winifred gaily, implying that I wasn't. She'd given me some cold cream and some cotton gloves – I was to put the cream on, then the gloves over it. This treatment was supposed to make your hands all white and soft – the texture of uncooked bacon fat. I stood in the ensuite bathroom, listening to the clatter of the water as it fell against the porcelain of the tub and probing at my face in the mirror. I seemed to myself erased, featureless, like an oval of used soap, or the moon on the wane.

Laura came in from her own bedroom through the connecting door and sat down on the closed toilet. She'd never made a habit of knocking, where I was concerned. She was wearing a plain white cotton nightgown, formerly mine, and had tied her hair back; the wheat-coloured coil of it hung over one shoulder. Her feet were bare.

"Where are your slippers?" I said. Her expression was doleful. With that, and the white gown and the bare feet, she looked like a penitent – like a heretic in an old painting, on her way to execution. She held her hands clasped in front of her, the fingers surrounding an O of space left open, as if she ought to be holding a lighted candle.

"I forgot them." When dressed up, she looked older than she was because of her height, but now she looked younger; she looked about twelve, and smelled like a baby. It was the shampoo she was using – she used baby shampoo because it was cheaper. She went in for small, futile economies. She gazed around the bathroom, then down at the tiled floor. "I don't want you to get married," she said.

"You've made that clear enough," I said. She'd been sullen throughout the proceedings – the receptions, the fittings, the rehearsals – barely civil towards Richard, towards Winifred blankly obedient, like a servant girl under indenture. Towards me, angry, as if this wedding was a malicious whim at best, at worst a rejection of her. At first I'd thought she might be envious of me, but it wasn't exactly that. "Why shouldn't I get married?"

"You're too young," she said.

"Mother was eighteen. Anyway I'm almost nineteen."

"But that was who she loved. She wanted to."

"How do you know I don't?" I said, exasperated.

That stopped her for a moment. "You can't *want* to," she said, looking up at me. Her eyes were damp and pink: she'd been crying. This annoyed me: what right had she to be doing the crying? It ought to have been me, if anyone.

"What I want isn't the point," I said harshly. "It's the only sensible thing. We don't have any money, or haven't you noticed? Would you like us to be thrown out on the street?"

"We could get jobs," she said. My cologne was on the window ledge beside her; she sprayed herself with it, absent-mindedly. It was Liù, by Guerlain, a present from Richard. (Chosen, as she'd let me know, by Winifred. *Men get so confused at perfume counters, don't they? Scent goes right to their heads.*)

"Don't be stupid," I said. "What would we do? Break that and your name is mud."

"Oh, we could do lots of things," she said vaguely, setting the cologne down. "We could be waitresses."

"We couldn't live on that. Waitresses make next to nothing. They have to grovel for tips. They all get flat feet. You don't know what anything costs," I said. It was like trying to explain arithmetic to a bird. "The factories are closed, Avilion is falling to pieces, they're going to sell it; the banks are out for blood. Haven't you looked at Father? Haven't you *seen* him? He's like an old man."

"It's for him, then," she said. "What you're doing. I guess that explains something. I guess it's brave."

"I'm doing what I think is right," I said. I felt so virtuous, and at the same time so hard done by, I almost wept. But that would have been game over.

"It's not right," she said. "It's not right at all. You could break it off, it's not too late. You could run away tonight and leave a note. I'd come with you."

"Stop pestering, Laura. I'm old enough to know what I'm doing."

"But you'll have to let him *touch* you, you know. It's not just kissing. You'll have to let him . . ."

"Don't worry about me," I said. "Leave me alone. I've got my eyes open."

"Like a sleepwalker," she said. She picked up a container of my dusting powder, opened it, sniffed it, and managed to spill a handful of it onto the floor. "Well, you'll have nice clothes, anyway," she said.

I could have hit her. It was, of course, my secret consolation.

After she'd gone, leaving a trail of dusty white footprints, I sat on the edge of the bed, staring at my open steamer trunk. It was a very fashionable one, a pale yellow on the outside but dark blue on the inside, steel-bound, the nail-heads twinkling like hard metallic stars. It was tidily packed, with everything complete for the honeymoon voyage, but it seemed to me full of darkness – of emptiness, empty space.

That's my trousseau, I thought. All at once it was a threatening word – so foreign, so final. It sounded like *trussed* – what was done to raw turkeys with skewers and pieces of string.

Toothbrush, I thought. I will need that. My body sat there, inert.

Trousseau came from the French word for *trunk. Trousseau.* That's all it meant: things you put into a trunk. So there was no use in getting upset about it, because it just meant baggage. It meant all the things I was taking with me, packed away.

The tango

Here's the wedding picture:

A young woman in a white satin dress cut on the bias, the fabric sleek, with a train fanned around the feet like spilled molasses. There's something gangly about the stance, the placement of the hips, the feet, as if her spine is wrong for this dress – too straight. You'd need to have a shrug for such a dress, a slouch, a sinuous curve, a sort of tubercular hunch.

A veil falling straight down on either side of the head, a width of it over the brow, casting too dark a shadow across the eyes. No teeth shown in the smile. A chaplet of small white roses; a cascade of larger roses, pink and white ones mingled with stephanotis, in her white-gloved arms – arms with the elbows a little too far out. *Chaplet, cascade* – these were the terms used in the newspapers. An evocation of nuns, and of fresh, perilous water. "A Beautiful Bride," was the caption. They said such things then. In her case beauty was mandatory, with so much money involved.

(I say "her," because I don't recall having been present, not in any meaningful sense of the word. I and the girl in the picture have ceased to be the same person. I am her outcome, the result of the life she once lived headlong; whereas she, if she can be said to exist at all, is composed only of what I remember. I have the better view – I can see her clearly, most of the time. But even if she knew enough to look, she can't see me at all.)

Richard stands beside me, admirable in the terms of that time and place, by which I mean young enough, not ugly, and well-to-do. He looks substantial, but at the same time quizzical: one eyebrow cocked, lower lip thrust a little out, mouth on the verge of a smile, as if at some secret, dubious joke.

Carnation in the buttonhole, hair combed back like a shiny rubber bathing cap, stuck to his head with the goo they used to put on back then. But a handsome man despite it. I have to admit that. Debonaire. Man about town.

There are some posed group portraits, too – a background scrum of groomsmen in their formal attire, much the same for weddings as for funerals and headwaiters; a foreground of clean, gleaming bridesmaids, their bouquets foaming with blossom. Laura managed to ruin each of these pictures. In one she's resolutely scowling, in another she must have moved her head so that her face is a blur, like a pigeon smashing into glass. In a third she's gnawing on a finger, glancing sideways guiltily, as if surprised with her hand in the till. In a fourth there must have been a defect in the film, because there's an effect of dappled light, falling not down on her but up, as if she's stand-ing on the edge of an illuminated swimming pool, at night.

After the ceremony Reenie was there, in respectable blue and a feather. She hugged me tightly, and said, "If only your mother was here." What did she mean? To applaud, or to call a halt to the proceedings? From her tone of voice, it could have been either. She cried then, I didn't. People cry at weddings for the same reason they cry at happy endings: because they so desper-ately want to believe in something they know is not credible. But I was beyond such childishness; I was breathing the high bleak air of disillusionment, or thought I was.

There was champagne, of course. There must have been: Winifred would not have omitted it. Others ate. Speeches were made, of which I remember nothing. Did we dance? I believe so. I didn't know how to dance, but I found myself on the dance floor, so some sort of stumbling-around must have occurred.

Then I changed into my going-away outfit. It was a two-piece suit, a light spring wool in pale green, with a demure hat to match. It cost a mint, said Winifred. I stood poised for departure, on the steps (what steps? The steps have vanished from memory), and threw my bouquet towards Laura. She didn't catch it. She stood there in her seashell-pink outfit, staring at me coldly, hands gripped together in front of her as if to restrain herself, and one of the bridesmaids – some Griffen cousin or other – grabbed it and made off with it greedily, as if it were food.

My father by that time had disappeared. Just as well, because when last seen he'd been rigid with drink. I expect he'd gone to finish the job.

Then Richard took me by the elbow and steered me towards the getaway car. No one was supposed to know our destination, which was assumed to be somewhere out of town – some secluded, romantic inn. In fact we were driven around the block to the side entrance of the Royal York Hotel, where we'd just had the wedding reception, and smuggled up in the elevator. Richard said that since we were taking the train to New York the next morning and Union Station was just across the street, why go out of our way?

About my bridal night, or rather my bridal afternoon – the sun was not yet set and the room was bathed, as they say, in a rosy glow, because Richard did not pull the curtains – I will tell very little. I didn't know what to expect; my only informant had been Reenie, who had led me to believe that whatever would happen would be unpleasant and most likely painful, and in this I was not deceived. She'd also implied that this disagreeable event or sensation would be nothing out of the ordinary – all women went through it, or all who got married – so I shouldn't make a fuss. *Grin and bear it* had been her words. She'd said there would be some blood, and there was. (But she hadn't said why. That part was a complete surprise.)

I did not yet know that my lack of enjoyment – my distaste, my suffering even – would be considered normal and even desirable by my husband. He was one of those men who felt that if a woman did not experience sexual pleasure this was all to the good, because then she would not be liable to wander off seeking it elsewhere. Perhaps such attitudes were common, at that period of time. Or perhaps not. I have no way of knowing.

Richard had arranged for a bottle of champagne to be sent up, at what he'd anticipated would be the proper moment. Also our dinners. I hobbled to the bathroom and locked myself in while the waiter was setting everything out, on a portable table with a white linen tablecloth. I was wearing the outfit Winifred had thought appropriate for the occasion, which was a night-gown of satin in a shade of salmon pink, with a delicate lace trim of cobweb grey. I tried to clean myself up with a wash-cloth, then wondered what should be done with this: the red on it was so visible, as if I'd had a nosebleed. In the end I put it into the wastepaper basket and hoped the hotel maid would think it had fallen in there by mistake.

Then I sprayed myself with Liù, a scent I found frail and wan. It was named, I had by this time discovered, after a girl in an opera – a slave girl, whose fate was to kill herself rather than betray the man she loved, who in his turn loved someone else. That was how things went, in operas. I did not find this scent auspicious, but I was worried that I smelled odd. I did smell odd. The oddness had come from Richard, but now it was mine. I hoped I hadn't made too much noise. Involuntary gasps, sharp intakes of breath, as when plunging into cold water.

The dinner was a steak, along with a salad. I ate mostly the salad. All the lettuce in hotels at that time was the same. It tasted like pale-green water. It tasted like frost.

The train trip to New York the next day was uneventful. Richard read the newspapers, I read magazines. The conversa-tions we had were not different in kind than those we'd had before the wedding. (I hesitate to call them conversations, because I did not talk much. I smiled and agreed, and did not listen.)

In New York, we had dinner at a restaurant with some friends of Richard's, a couple whose names I've forgotten. They were new money, without a doubt: so new it shrieked. Their clothes looked as if they'd covered themselves in glue, then rolled around in hundred-dollar bills. I wondered how they'd made it, this money; it had a fishy whiff.

These people didn't know Richard all that well, nor did they yearn to: they owed him something, that was all – for some unstated favour. They were fearful of him, a little deferential. I gathered this from the play of the cigarette lighters: who lit what for whom, and how quickly. Richard enjoyed their deference. He enjoyed having cigarettes lit for him, and, by extension, for me.

It struck me that Richard had wanted to go out with them not only because he wanted to surround himself with a small coterie of cringers, but because he didn't want to be alone with me. I could scarcely blame him: I had little to say. Nonetheless, he was now – in company – solicitous of me, placing my coat with tenderness over my shoulders, paying me small, cherishing attentions, keeping a hand always on me, lightly, somewhere. Every once in a while he'd scan the room, checking over the other men in it to see who was envying him. (Retrospect of course, on my part: at the time I recognized none of this.)

The restaurant was very expensive, and also very modern. I'd never seen anything like it. Things glittered rather than shone; there was bleached wood and brass trim and brash glass everywhere, and a great deal of lamination. Sculptures of stylized women in brass or steel, smooth as taffy, with eyebrows but no eyes, with streamlined haunches and no feet, with arms melting back into their torsos; white marble spheres; round mirrors like portholes. On every table, a single calla lily in a thin steel vase.

Richard's friends were even older than Richard, and the woman looked older than the man. She was wearing white mink, despite the spring weather. Her gown was white as well, a design inspired – she told us at some length – by ancient Greece, the Winged Victory of Samothrace to be precise. The pleats of this gown were bound around with gold cord under her breasts, and in a crisscross between them. I thought that if I had breasts that slack and droopy I'd never wear such a gown. The skin showing above the neckline was freckled and puckered, as were her arms. Her husband sat silently while she talked, his hands fisted together, his half-smile set in concrete; he looked wisely down at the tablecloth. *So this is marriage*, I thought: this shared tedium, this twitchiness, and those little powdery runnels forming to the sides of the nose.

"Richard didn't warn us you'd be this *young*," said the woman.

Her husband said, "It will wear off," and his wife laughed.

I considered the word *warn*: was I that dangerous? Only in the way sheep are, I now suppose. So dumb they jeopardize themselves, and get stuck on cliffs or cornered by wolves, and some custodian has to risk his neck to get them out of trouble.

Soon – after two days in New York, or was it three? – we crossed over to Europe on the *Berengeria*, which Richard said was the ship taken by everybody who was anybody. The sea wasn't rough for that time of year, but nevertheless I was sick as a dog. (Why dogs, in this respect? Because they look as if they can't help it. Neither could I.)

They brought me a basin, and cold weak tea with sugar but no milk. Richard said I should drink champagne because it was the best cure, but I didn't want to take the risk. He was more or less considerate, but also more or less annoyed, though he did say what a shame I was feeling ill. I said I didn't want to ruin his evening and he should go off and socialize, and so he did. The benefit to my seasickness was that Richard showed no inclination to climb into bed with me. Sex may go nicely with many things, but vomit isn't one of them.

The next morning Richard said I should make an effort to appear at breakfast, as having the right attitude was the war half won. I sat at our table and nibbled bread and drank water, and tried to ignore the cooking smells. I felt bodiless and flaccid and crepey-skinned, like a deflating balloon. Richard tended me intermittently, but he knew people, or seemed to know them, and people knew him. He got up, shook hands, sat down again. Sometimes he introduced me, sometimes not. He did not however know all of the people he wanted to know. This was clear by the way he was always gazing around, past me, past those he was talking with – over their heads.

I made a gradual recovery during the day. I drank ginger ale, which helped. I did not eat dinner, but I attended it. In the evening there was a cabaret. I wore the dress Winifred had chosen for such an event, dove grey with a chiffon cape in lilac. There were lilac sandals with high heels and open toes to match. I had not yet quite got the hang of such high heels: I teetered slightly. Richard said the sea air must have agreed with me; he said I had just the right amount of colour, a faint schoolgirl blush. He said I looked marvellous. He steered me to the table he'd reserved, and ordered a martini for me and one for himself. He said the martini would fix me up in no time flat.

I drank some of it, and after that Richard was no longer beside me, and there was a singer who stood in a blue spot-light. She had her black hair waved down over one eye, and was wearing a tubular black dress covered with big scaly sequins, which clung to her firm but prominent bottom and was held up by what looked like twisted string. I stared at her with fascination. I'd never been to a cabaret, or even to a nightclub. She wiggled her shoulders and sang "Stormy Weather" in a voice like a sultry groan. You could see halfway down her front.

People sat at their tables watching her and listening to her, and having opinions about her – free to like or dislike her, to be seduced by her or not, to approve or disapprove of her performance, of her dress, of her bottom. She however was not free. She had to go through with it – to sing, to wiggle. I wondered what she was paid for doing this, and whether it was worth it. Only if you were poor, I decided. The phrase *in the spotlight* has seemed to me ever since to denote a precise form of humiliation. *The spotlight* was something you should evidently stay out of, if you could.

After the singer, there was a man who played a white piano, very fast, and after him a couple, two professional dancers: a tango act. They were in black, like the singer. Their hair shone like patent leather in the spotlight, which was now an acid green. The woman had one dark curl glued to her forehead, and a large red flower behind one ear. Her dress gored out from mid-thigh but was otherwise like a stocking. The music was jagged, hobbled – like a four-legged animal lurching on three legs. A crippled bull with its head down, lunging.

As for the dance, it was more like a battle than a dance. The faces of the dancers were set, impassive; they eyed each other glitteringly, waiting for a chance to bite. I knew it was an act, I could see that it was expertly done; nonetheless, both of them looked wounded.

The third day came. In the early afternoon I walked on the deck, for the fresh air. Richard didn't come with me: he was expecting some important telegrams, he said. He'd had a lot of telegrams already; he would slit the envelopes with a silver paper knife, read the contents, then tear them up or tuck them away in his briefcase, which he kept locked.

I didn't especially want him to be there with me on the deck, but nonetheless I felt alone. Alone and therefore neglected, neglected and therefore unsuccessful. As if I'd been stood up, jilted; as if I had a broken heart. A group of English people in cream-coloured linen stared at me. It wasn't a hostile stare; it was bland, remote, faintly curious. No one can stare like the English. I felt rumpled and grubby, and of minor interest.

The sky was overcast; the clouds were a dingy grey, and sagged down in clumps like the stuffing from a saturated mattress. It was drizzling lightly. I wasn't wearing a hat, for fear it might blow off; I had only a silk scarf, knotted under my chin. I stood at the railing, looking over and down, at the slate-coloured waves rolling and rolling, at the ship's white wake scrawling its brief meaningless message. Like the clue to a hidden mishap: a trail of torn chiffon. Soot from the funnels blew down over me; my hair came unpinned and stuck to my cheeks in wet strands.

So this is the ocean, I thought. It did not seem as profound as it should. I tried to remember something I might have read about it, some poem or other, but could not. *Break, break, break.* Something began that way. It had cold grey stones in it. *Oh Sea.*

I wanted to throw something overboard. I felt it was called for. In the end I threw a copper penny, but I didn't make a wish.

VI

The Blind Assassin: The houndstooth suit

He turns the key. It's a bolt lock, a small mercy. He's in luck this time, he has the loan of a whole flat. A bachelorette, only one large room with a narrow kitchen counter, but its own bathroom, with a claw-footed tub and pink towels in it. Ritzy doings. It belongs to the girlfriend of a friend of a friend, out of town for a funeral. Four whole days of safety, or the illusion of it.

The drapes match the bedspread; they're a heavy nubbled silk, cherry-coloured, over wispy undercurtains. Keeping a little back from the window, he looks out. The view – what he can see through the yellowing leaves – is of Allan Gardens. A couple of drunks or hobos are passed out under the trees, one with his face under a newspaper. He himself has slept like that. Newspapers dampened by your breath smell like poverty, like defeat, like mildewed upholstery with dog hairs on it. There's a scattering of cardboard signs and crumpled papers on the grass, from last night – a rally, the comrades hammering away at their dogma and the ears of their listeners, making hay while the sun don't shine. Two disconsolate men picking up after them now, with steel-tipped sticks and burlap bags. At least it's work for the poor buggers.

She'll walk diagonally across the park. She'll stop, look too obviously around her to see if there's anyone watching. By the time she's done that, there will be.

On the epicene white-and-gold desk there's a radio the size and shape of half a loaf of bread. He turns it on: a Mexican trio, the voices like liquid rope, hard, soft, intertwining. That's where he should go, Mexico. Drink tequila. Go to the dogs, or go more to the dogs. Go to the wolves. Become a desperado.

He sets his portable typewriter on the desk, unlocks it, takes off the lid, rolls paper in. He's running out of carbons. He has time for a few pages before she arrives, if she arrives. She sometimes gets hung up, or intercepted. Or so she claims.

He'd like to lift her into the ritzy bathtub, cover her with suds. Wallow around in there with her, pigs in pink bubbles. Maybe he will.

What he's been working on is an idea, or the idea of an idea. It's about a race of extraterrestrials who send a spaceship to explore Earth. They're composed of crystals in a high state of organization, and they attempt to establish communications with those Earth beings they've assumed are like themselves: eyeglasses, windowpanes, Venetian paperweights, wine goblets, diamond rings. In this they fail. They send back a report to their homeland: *This planet contains many interesting relics of a once-flourishing but now-defunct civilization, which must have been of a superior order. We cannot tell what catastrophe has caused all intelligent life to become extinct. The planet currently harbours only a variety of viscous green filigree and a large number of eccentrically shaped globules of semi-liquid mud, which are tumbled hither and thither by the erratic currents of the light, transparent fluid that covers the planet's surface. The shrill squeaks and resonant groans produced by these must be ascribed to frictional vibration, and should not be mistaken for speech.*

It isn't a story though. It can't be a story unless the aliens invade and lay waste, and some dame bursts out of her jumpsuit. But an invasion would violate the premise. If the crystal beings think the planet has no life, why would they bother to land on it? For archeological reasons, perhaps. To take samples. All of a sudden thousands of windows are sucked from the skyscrapers of New York by an extraterrestrial vacuum. Thousands of bank presidents are sucked out as well, and fall screaming to their deaths. That would be fine.

No. Still not a story. He needs to write something that will sell. It's back to the never-fail dead women, slavering for blood. This time he'll give them purple hair, set them in motion beneath the poisonous orchid beams of the twelve moons of Arn. The best thing is to picture the cover illustration the boys will likely come up with, and then go on from there.

He's tired of them, these women. He's tired of their fangs, their litheness, their firm but ripe half-a-grapefruit breasts, their gluttony. He's tired of their red talons, their viperish eyes. He's tired of bashing in their heads. He's tired of the heroes, whose names are Will or Burt or Ned, names of one syllable; he's tired of their ray guns, their metallic skin-tight clothing. Ten cents a thrill. Still, it's a living, if he can keep up the speed, and beggars can hardly be choosers.

He's running out of cash again. He hopes she'll bring a cheque, from one of the P.O. boxes not in his name. He'll endorse it, she'll cash it for him; with her name, at her bank, she'll have no problems. He hopes she'll bring some postage stamps. He hopes she'll bring more cigarettes. He's only got three left.

He paces. The floor creaks. Hardwood, but stained where the radiator's leaked. This block of flats was put up before the war, for single business people of good character. Things were more hopeful then. Steam heat, never-ending hot water, tiled corridors – the latest of everything. Now it's seen better days. A few years ago when he was young, he'd known a girl who'd had a place here. A nurse, as he recalls: French letters in the night-table drawer. She'd had a two-ring burner, she'd cooked breakfast for him sometimes – bacon and eggs, buttery pancakes with maple syrup, he'd sucked it off her fingers. There was a stuffed and mounted deer's head, left over from the previous tenants; she'd dried her stockings by hanging them on the antlers.

They'd spend Saturday afternoons, Tuesday evenings, whenever she had off, drinking – scotch, gin, vodka, whatever there was. She liked to be quite drunk first. She didn't want to go to the movies, or out dancing; she didn't seem to want romance or any pretense of it, which was just as well. All she'd required of him was stamina. She liked to haul a blanket onto the bathroom floor; she liked the hardness of the tiles under her back. It was hell on his knees and elbows, not that he'd noticed at the time, his attention being elsewhere. She'd moan as if in a spotlight, tossing her head, rolling her eyes. Once he'd had her standing up, in her walk-in closet. A knee-trembler, smelling of mothballs, in among the Sunday crepes, the lambswool twin sets. She'd wept with pleasure. After dumping him she'd married a lawyer. A canny match, a white wedding; he'd read about it in the paper, amused, without rancour. *Good for her*, he'd thought. *The sluts win sometimes.*

Salad days. Days without names, witless afternoons, quick and profane and quickly over, and no longing in advance or after, and no words required, and nothing to pay. Before he got mixed up in things that got mixed up.

He checks his watch and then the window again, and here she comes, loping diagonally across the park, in a wide-brimmed hat today and a tightly belted houndstooth suit, handbag clutched under her arm, pleated skirt swinging, in her curious undulating stride, as if she's never got used to walking on her hind legs. It may be the high heels though. He's often wondered how they balance. Now she's stopped as if on cue; she gazes around in that dazed way she has, as if she's just been wakened from a puzzling dream, and the two guys picking up the papers look her over. *Lost something, miss?* But she comes on, crosses the street, he can see her in fragments through the leaves, she must be searching for the street number. Now she's coming up the front steps. The buzzer goes. He pushes the button, crushes out his cigarette, turns off the desk light, unlocks the door.

Hello. I'm all out of breath. I didn't wait for the elevator. She pushes the door shut, stands with her back against it.

Nobody followed you. I was watching. You've got cigarettes?

And your cheque, and a fifth of scotch, best quality. I pinched it from our well-stocked bar. Did I tell you we have a well-stocked bar?

She's attempting to be casual, frivolous even. She's not good at it. She's stalling, waiting to see what he wants. She'd never make the first move, she doesn't like to give herself away.

Good girl. He moves towards her, takes hold of her.

Am I a good girl? Sometimes I feel like a gun moll – doing your errands.

You can't be a gun moll, I don't have a gun. You watch too many movies.

Not nearly enough, she says, to the side of his neck. He could use a haircut. Soft thistle. She undoes his four top buttons, runs her hand in under his shirt. His flesh is so condensed, so dense. Fine-grained, charred. She's seen ashtrays carved out of wood like that.

That was lovely, she says. The bath was lovely. I never pictured you with pink towels. Compared to the usual, it's pretty opulent.

Temptation lurks everywhere, he says. The fleshpots beckon. I'd say she's an amateur tart, wouldn't you?

He'd wrapped her in one of the pink towels, carried her to the bed wet and slippery. Now they're under the nubbly cherry-coloured silk bedspread, the sateen sheets, drinking the scotch she's brought with her. It's a fine blend, smoky and warm, it goes down smooth as toffee. She stretches luxuriously, wondering only briefly who will wash the sheets.

She never manages to overcome her sense of transgression in these various rooms – the feeling that she's violating the private boundaries of whoever ordinarily lives in them. She'd like to go through the closets, the bureau drawers – not to take, only to look; to see how other people live. Real people; people more real than she is. She'd like to do the same with him, except that he has no closets, no bureau drawers, or none that are his. Nothing to find, nothing to betray him. Only a scuffed blue suitcase, which he keeps locked. It's usually under the bed.

His pockets are uninformative; she's been through them a few times. (It wasn't spying, she just wanted to know where things were and what they were, and where they stood.) Handkerchief, blue, with white border; spare change; two cigarette butts, wrapped in waxed paper – he must have been saving them up. A jackknife, old. Once, two buttons, from a shirt, she'd guessed. She hadn't offered to sew them back on because then he'd know she'd been snooping. She'd like him to think she's trustworthy.

A driver's licence, the name not his. A birth certificate, ditto. Different names. She'd love to go over him with a fine-toothed comb. Rummage around in him. Turn him upside down. Empty him out.

He sings gently, in an oily voice, like a radio crooner:

A smoke-filled room, a devil's moon, and you –
I stole a kiss, you promised me you would be true –
I slid my hand beneath your dress.
You bit my ear, we made a mess,
Now it is dawn – and you are gone –
And I am blue.

She laughs. Where'd you get that?

It's my tart song. It goes with the surroundings.

She's not a real tart. Not even an amateur. I don't expect she takes money. Most likely she gets rewarded in some other way.

A lot of chocolates. Would you settle for that?

It would have to be truckloads, she says. I'm moderately expensive. The bedspread's real silk, I like the colour – garish, but it's quite pretty. Good for the complexion, like pink candle-shades. Have you cooked up any more?

Any more what?

Any more of my story.

Your story?

Yes. Isn't it for me?

Oh yes, he says. Of course. I think of nothing else. It keeps me awake nights.

Liar. Does it bore you?

Nothing that pleases you could possibly bore me.

God, how gallant. We should have the pink towels more often. Pretty soon you'll be kissing my glass slipper. But go on, anyway.

Where was I?

The bell had rung. The throat was slit. The door was opening.

Oh. Right, then.

He says: The girl of whom we have been speaking has heard the door open. She backs against the wall, pulling the red brocade of the Bed of One Night tightly around herself. It has a brackish odour, like a salt marsh at low tide: the dried fear of those who have gone before her. Someone has come in; there's the sound of a heavy object being dragged along the floor. The door closes again; the room is dark as oil. Why is there no lamp, no candle?

She stretches her hands out in front of her to protect herself, and finds her left hand taken and held by another hand: held gently and without coercion. It's as if she's being asked a question.

She can't speak. She can't say, *I can't speak*.

The blind assassin lets his woman's veil fall to the floor. Holding the girl's hand, he sits down on the bed beside her. He still intends to kill her, but that can come later. He's heard about these impounded girls, kept hidden away from every-one until the last day of their lives; he's curious about her. In any case she's a gift of sorts, and all for him. To refuse such a gift would be to spit in the face of the gods. He knows he should move swiftly, finish the job, vanish, but there's lots of time for that still. He can smell the scent they've rubbed on her; it smells of funeral biers, those of young women who've died unwed. Wasted sweetness.

He won't be ruining anything, or nothing that's been bought and paid for: the fraudulent Lord of the Underworld must have been and gone already. Had he kept his rusty chainmail on? Most likely. Clanked into her like a ponderous iron key, turned himself in her flesh, wrenched her open. He remembers the feeling all too well. Whatever else, he will not do that.

He lifts her hand to his mouth and touches his lips to it, not a kiss as such but a token of respect and homage. Gracious and most golden one, he says – the beggar's standard address to a prospective benefactor – rumour of your extreme beauty has brought me here, though simply by being here my life is forfeit. I can't see you with my eyes, because I'm blind. Will you permit me to see you with my hands? It would be a last kindness, and perhaps for yourself as well.

He hasn't been a slave and a whore for nothing: he's learned how to flatter, how to lie plausibly, how to ingratiate himself. He puts his fingers on her chin, and waits until she hesitates, then nods. He can hear what she's thinking: *Tomorrow I'll be dead*. He wonders if she guesses why he's really here.

Some of the best things are done by those with nowhere to turn, by those who don't have time, by those who truly understand the word *helpless*. They dispense with the calculation of risk and profit, they take no thought for the future, they're forced at spearpoint into the present tense. Thrown over a precipice, you fall or else you fly; you clutch at any hope, however unlikely; however – if I may use such an overworked word – miraculous. What we mean by that is, *Against all odds*.

And so it is, this night.

The blind assassin begins very slowly to touch her, with one hand only, the right – the dexterous hand, the knife hand. He passes it over her face, down her throat; then he adds the left hand, the sinister hand, using both together, tenderly, as if picking a lock of the utmost fragility, a lock made of silk. It's like being caressed by water. She trembles, but not as before with fear. After a time she lets the red brocade fall away from around her, and takes his hand and guides it.

Touch comes before sight, before speech. It is the first language and the last, and it always tells the truth.

This is how the girl who couldn't speak and the man who couldn't see fell in love.

You surprise me, she says.

Do I? he says. Why? Though I like to surprise you. He lights a cigarette, offers her one; she shakes her head for no. He's smoking too much. It's nerves, despite his steady hands.

Because you said they fell in love, she says. You've sneered at that notion often enough – not realistic, bourgeois superstition, rotten at the core. Sickly sentiment, a high-flown Victorian excuse for honest carnality. Going soft on yourself?

Don't blame me, blame history, he says, smiling. Such things happen. Falling in love has been recorded, or at least those words have. Anyway, I said he was lying.

You can't wiggle out of it that way. The lying was only at first. Then you changed it.

Point granted. But there could be a more callous way of looking at it.

Looking at what?

This falling in love business.

Since when is it a business? she says angrily.

He smiles. That notion bother you? Too commercial? Your own conscience would flinch, is that what you're saying? But there's always a tradeoff, isn't there?

No, she says. There isn't. Not always.

You might say he grabbed what he could get. Why wouldn't he? He had no scruples, his life was dog eat dog and it always had been. Or you could say they were both young so they didn't know any better. The young habitually mistake lust for love, they're infested with idealism of all kinds. And I haven't said he didn't kill her afterwards. As I've pointed out, he was nothing if not self-interested.

So you've got cold feet, she says. You're backing down,

you're chicken. You won't go all the way. You're to love as a cock-teaser is to fucking.

He laughs, a startled laugh. Is it the coarseness of the words, is he taken aback, has she finally managed that? Restrain your language, young lady.

Why should I? You don't.

I'm a bad example. Let's just say they could indulge themselves – their emotions, if you want to call it that. They could roll around in their emotions – live for the moment, spout poetry out of both ends, burn the candle, drain the cup, howl at the moon. Time was running out on them. They had nothing to lose.

He did. Or he certainly thought he did!

All right then. *She* had nothing to lose. He blows out a cloud of smoke.

Not like me, she says, I guess you mean.

Not like you, darling, he says. Like me. I'm the one with nothing to lose.

She says, But you've got me. I'm not nothing.

The Toronto Star, August 28, 1935

SOCIETY SCHOOLGIRL FOUND SAFE
SPECIAL TO THE STAR

Police called off their search yesterday for fifteen-year-old society schoolgirl Laura Chase, missing for over a week, when Miss Chase was found safely lodged with family friends Mr. and Mrs. E. Newton-Dobbs at their summer residence in Muskoka. Well-known industrialist Richard E. Griffen, married to Miss Chase's sister, spoke to reporters by telephone on behalf of the family. "My wife and I are very relieved," he said. "It was a simple confusion, caused by a letter which was delayed in the post. Miss Chase made holiday arrangements of which she believed us to have been aware, as did her host and hostess. They do not read the newspapers while on vacation or this mix-up would never have occurred. When they returned to the city and became aware of the situation, they rang us immediately."

Questioned about rumours that Miss Chase had run away from home and had been located in curious circumstances at the Sunnyside Beach Amusement Park, Mr. Griffen said he did not know who was responsible for these malicious fabrications but he would make it his business to find out. "It was an ordinary misunderstanding, such as might happen to anybody," he stated. "My wife and I are grateful that she is safe, and sincerely thank the police, the newspapers, and the concerned public for their help." Miss Chase is said to have been unsettled by the publicity, and is refusing interviews.

Although no lasting harm was done, these are by no means the first serious difficulties to have been caused by faulty postal delivery. The public deserves a service it can rely on unquestioningly. Government officials should take note.

The Blind Assassin: Street walk

She walks along the street, hoping she looks like a woman entitled to be walking along the street. Or along this street. She
doesn't, though. She's dressed wrong, her hat is wrong, her coat
is wrong. She ought to have a scarf tied over her head and
under her chin, a baggy coat worn along the sleeves. She ought
to look drab and frugal.

The houses here are cheek by jowl. Servants' cottages once,
row on row, but there are fewer servants now, and the rich have
made other provisions. Sooty brick, two up, two down, privy
out back. Some have the remains of vegetable gardens on their
tiny front lawns – a blackened tomato vine, a wooden stake
with string dangling from it. The gardens couldn't have gone
well – it would have been too shady, the earth too cindery. But
even here the autumn trees have been lavish, the remaining
leaves yellow and orange and vermilion, and a deeper red like
fresh liver.

From inside the houses comes howling, barking, a rattle or
slam. Female voices raised in thwarted rage, the defiant yells of
children. On the cramped porches men sit on wooden chairs,
hands dangling from knees, out of work but not yet out of
house and home. Their eyes on her, their scowls, taking bitter
stock of her with her fur trim at wrists and neck, her lizard
handbag. It could be they are lodgers, crammed into cellars and
odd corners to help cover the rent.

Women hurry along, heads down, shoulders hunched, carrying brown paper bundles. Married, they must be. The word
braised comes to mind. They'll have been scrounging bones
from the butcher, they'll be toting home the cheap cuts, to be
served with flabby cabbage. Her shoulders are too far back, her

chin too far up, she doesn't wear that beaten-down look: when they raise their heads enough to focus on her, the glances are filthy. They must think she's a hooker, but in shoes like that what's she doing down here? Way below her league.

Here's the bar, on the corner where he said it would be. The beer parlour. Men are gathered in a clump outside it. None of them says anything to her as she goes past, they just stare as if from thickets, but she can hear the muttering, hatred and lust mixed in the throat, following her like the wash from a ship. Perhaps they've mistaken her for a church worker or some other sniffy do-gooder. Poking scrubbed fingers into their lives, asking questions, offering table scraps of patronizing help. But she's dressed too well for that.

She took a taxi, paid it off three blocks away, where there was more traffic. It's best not to become an anecdote: who'd take a cab, around here? Though she's an anecdote anyway. What she needs is a different coat, picked up at a rummage sale, crumpled into a suitcase. She could go into a hotel restaurant, leave her own coat at the check, slip into the powder room, change. Frump up her hair, smudge her lipstick. Emerge as a different woman.

No. It would never work. There's the suitcase, just to begin with; there's getting out of the house with it. *Where are you off to in such a hurry?*

And so she's stuck doing a cloak-and-dagger number without a cloak. Relying on her face alone, its guile. She's had enough practice by now, in smoothness, coolness, blankness. A lifting of both eyebrows, the candid, transparent stare of a double agent. A face of pure water. It's not the lying that counts, it's evading the necessity for it. Rendering all questions foolish in advance.

There is however some danger. For him too: more than there was, he's told her. He thinks he was spotted once, on the street: recognized. Some goon from the Red Squad, maybe. He'd walked through a crowded beer joint, out the back door.

She doesn't know whether to believe in it or not, this sort of danger: men in dark bulgy suits with their collars turned up, cars on the prowl. *Come with us. We're taking you in.* Bare rooms and harsh lights. It seems too theatrical, or else like things that occur only in fog, in black and white. Only in other countries, in other languages. Or if here, not to her.

If caught, she'd renounce him, before the cock crowed even once. She knows that, plainly, calmly. Anyway she'd be let off, her involvement viewed as frivolous dabbling or else a rebellious prank, and whatever turmoil might result would be covered up. She'd have to pay for it privately, of course, but with what? She's already bankrupt: you can't get blood from a stone. She'd close herself off, put up the shutters. Out to lunch, permanently.

Lately she's had the sense of someone watching her, though whenever she reconnoitres there's nobody there. She's being more careful; she's being as careful as she can. Is she afraid? Yes. Most of the time. But her fear doesn't matter. Or rather, it does matter. It enhances the pleasure she feels with him; also the sense that she's getting away with it.

The real danger comes from herself. What she'll allow, how far she's willing to go. But allowing and willing have nothing to do with it. Where she'll be pushed, then; where she'll be led. She hasn't examined her motives. There may not be any motives as such; desire is not a motive. It doesn't seem to her that she has any choice. Such extreme pleasure is also a humiliation. It's like being hauled along by a shameful rope, a leash around the neck. She resents it, her lack of freedom, and so she stretches out the time between, rationing him. She stands him up, fibs about why she couldn't make it – claims she didn't see the chalked markings on the park wall, didn't get the message – the new address of the non-existent dress shop, the postcard signed by an old friend she's never had, the telephone call for the wrong number.

But in the end, back she comes. There's no use resisting. She goes to him for amnesia, for oblivion. She renders herself up, is blotted out; enters the darkness of her own body, forgets her name. Immolation is what she wants, however briefly. To exist without boundaries.

Still, she finds herself wondering about things that never occurred to her at first. How does he do his laundry? One time there were socks drying on the radiator – he'd seen her looking, whipped them out of sight. He tidies things away before her visits, or at least he takes a swipe at it. Where does he eat? He's told her he doesn't like to be seen too often in one place. He must move around, from one eatery, one beanery, to another. In his mouth these words have a sleazy glamour. Some days he's more nervous, he keeps his head down, he doesn't go out; there are apple cores, in this or that room; there are bread crumbs on the floor.

Where does he get the apples, the bread? He's oddly reticent about such details – what goes on in his life when she's not there. Perhaps he feels it might diminish him in her eyes, to know too much. Too many sordid particulars. Perhaps he's right. (All those paintings of women, in art galleries, surprised at private moments. Nymph Sleeping. Susanna and the Elders. Woman Bathing, one foot in a tin tub – Renoir, or was it Degas? Both, both women plump. Diana and her maidens, a moment before they catch the hunter's prying eyes. Never any paintings called Man Washing Socks in Sink.)

Romance takes place in the middle distance. Romance is looking in at yourself, through a window clouded with dew.

Romance means leaving things out: where life grunts and snuffles, romance only sighs. Does she want more than that – more of him? Does she want the whole picture?

The danger would come from looking too closely and seeing too much – from having him dwindle, and herself along with him. Then waking up empty, all of it used up – over and done. She would have nothing. She would be *bereft*.

An old-fashioned word.

He hasn't come to meet her, this time. He said it was better not. She's been left to make her way alone. Tucked into the palm of her glove there's a square of folded paper, with cryptic directions, but she doesn't need to look at it. She can feel the slight glow of it against her skin, like a radium dial in the dark.

She imagines him imagining her – imagining her walking along the street, closer now, impending. Is he impatient, on edge, can he hardly wait? Is he like her? He likes to imply indifference – that he doesn't care whether she'll arrive or not – but it's just an act, one of several. For instance, he's no longer smoking ready-mades, he can't afford them. He rolls his own, with one of those obscene-looking pink rubber devices that turns out three at a time; he cuts them with a razor blade, then stows them in a Craven A package. One of his small deceptions, or vanities; his need for them makes her breath catch.

Sometimes she brings him cigarettes, handfuls of them – largesse, opulence. She nicks them out of the silver cigarette box on the glass coffee table, crams them into her purse. But she doesn't do this every time. It's best to keep him in suspense, it's best to keep him hungry.

He lies on his back, replete, smoking. If she wants avowals, she has to get them beforehand – make sure of them first, like a whore and her money. Meagre though they may be. *I've missed you*, he might say. Or: *I can't get enough of you*. His eyes shut, grinding his teeth to hold himself back; she can hear it against her neck.

Afterwards, she has to fish.

Say something.

Like what?

Like anything you like.

Tell me what you want to hear.

If I do that and then you say it, I won't believe you.

Read between the lines then.

But there aren't any lines. You don't give me any.

Then he might sing:

Oh, you put your dingus in, and you pull your dingus out,
And the smoke goes up the chimney just the same —

How's that for a line? he'll say.

You really are a bastard.

I've never claimed otherwise.

No wonder they resort to stories.

She turns left at the shoe repair, then a block along, then two houses. Then the small apartment building: The Excelsior. It must be named after the poem by Henry Wadsworth Longfellow. A banner with a strange device, a knight sacrificing all earthly concerns to scale the heights. The heights of what? Of armchair bourgeois pietism. How ridiculous, here and now.

The Excelsior is red brick with three storeys, four windows each floor, with wrought-iron balconies — more like ledges than balconies, no room for a chair. A cut above the neighbourhood once, now a place where people cling to the edges. On one balcony someone's improvised a clothesline; a greying dishcloth hangs on it like the flag of some defeated regiment.

She walks past the building, then crosses at the next corner. There she stops and glances down as if there's something caught on her shoe. Down, then back. There's nobody walking behind her, no slow car. A stout woman labouring up front steps, a string bag in either hand like ballast; two patched boys chasing a grubby dog along the sidewalk. No men here except three old porch vultures hunched over a shared newspaper.

She turns then and retraces her steps, and when she comes to the Excelsior she ducks into the alleyway beside it and hurries along, forcing herself not to run. The asphalt is uneven, her heels too high. This is the wrong place to turn an ankle. She feels more exposed now, caught in the glare, although there are no windows. Her heart's going hard, her legs are flimsy, silken. Panic has its hook into her, why?

He won't be there, says a soft voice in her head; a soft anguished voice, a plaintive cooing voice like a mourning dove's. He's gone away. He's been taken away. You'll never see him again. Never. She almost cries.

Silly, frightening herself like that. But there's a real part to it all the same. He could vanish more easily than she could: she's of a fixed address, he'd always know where to find her.

She pauses, lifts her wrist, breathes in the reassuring smell of perfumed fur. There's a metal door towards the back, a service door. She knocks lightly.

The door opens, he's there. She has no time to feel gratitude before he pulls her inside. They're on a landing; back stairs. No light except what comes through a window, somewhere above. He kisses her, hands to either side of her face. Sandpaper of his chin. He's shivering, but not with arousal, or not only.

She draws away. You look like a bandit. She's never seen a bandit; she's thinking of the ones in operas. The smugglers, in *Carmen*. Heavy on the burnt cork.

Sorry, he says. I had to decamp in a hurry. Could be a false alarm, but I had to leave some things behind.

Such as a razor?

Among the rest. Come on – it's down here.

The stairs are narrow: unpainted wood, a two-by-four as banister. At the bottom, a cement floor. The smell of coal dust, a piercing underground smell, like the damp stones of a cave.

It's in here. The janitor's room.

But you aren't the janitor, she says, laughing a little. Are you?

I am now. Or that's what the landlord thinks. He's dropped by a couple of times, early in the morning, to make sure I've stoked the furnace, but not too much. He wouldn't want hot tenants, they're too expensive; lukewarm's good enough. It's not much of a bed.

It's a bed, she says. Lock the door.

It doesn't lock, he says.

There's a small window, bars across it; the remains of a curtain. Rust-coloured light comes through it. They've propped a chair against the doorknob, a chair with most rungs missing, half matchwood already. Not much of a barrier. They're under the one mildewed blanket, with his coat and hers piled on top. The sheet doesn't bear thinking about. She can feel his ribs, trace the spaces between.

What are you eating?

Don't pester me.

You're too thin. I could bring something, some food.

You're not very dependable though, are you? I could starve to death waiting for you to turn up. Don't worry, I'll be out of here soon enough.

Where? You mean this room, or the city, or . . .

I don't know. Don't nag.

I'm interested, that's all. I'm concerned, I want . . .

Cut it out.

Well then, she says, I guess it's back to Zycron. Unless you want me to leave.

No. Stay a little. I'm sorry, but I've been under a strain. Where were we? I've forgotten.

He was deciding whether to cut her throat or love her forever.

Right. Yes. The usual choices.

He's deciding whether to cut her throat or love her forever, when – with the sensitive hearing conferred on him by his blindness – he detects a metallic noise of grinding and rasping. Chain link against chain link, shackles in motion. It's drawing nearer along the corridor. He already knows that the Lord of the Underworld hasn't yet made his purchased visitation: he could tell that by the state the girl had been in. A pristine state, as you might say.

What to do now? He could slip behind the door or under the bed, leave her to her fate, then reappear and finish the job he'll be paid for. But matters being as they are, he's reluctant to do that. Or he could wait until things are well underway and the courtier is deaf to the outside world, and slide out the door;

but then, the honour of the assassins as a group – as a guild, if you like – would be tarnished.

He takes the girl by the arm, and by placing her hand across her own mouth, he indicates the need for silence. Then he leads her away from the bed and stashes her behind the door. He checks to make sure the door is unlocked, as has been arranged. The man won't be expecting a sentry: in his deal with the High Priestess, he specified no witnesses. The temple sentry was to have made herself scarce when she heard him coming.

The blind assassin hauls the dead sentry out from under the bed and arranges her on the coverlet, with her scarf concealing the slash in her throat. She's not cold yet, and has stopped dripping. Too bad if the fellow has a bright candle; otherwise, in the night all cats are grey. Temple maidens are trained to manifest inertia. It might take the man – hampered as he is by his ponderous god costume, which traditionally includes a helmet and visor – some time to discover he's fucking the wrong woman, and a dead one at that.

The blind assassin pulls the brocade bedcurtains almost shut. Then he joins the girl, squeezing the two of them as flat as possible against the wall.

The heavy door groans open. The girl watches a glow advancing across the floor. The Lord of the Underworld can't see very well, evidently; he bumps into something, curses. He's fumbling now with the hangings of the bed. Where are you, my pretty one? he's saying. It won't surprise him when she doesn't answer, seeing that she is so conveniently mute.

The blind assassin begins to ease himself out from behind the door, and the girl with him. How do I get this damn thing off? the Lord of the Underworld is muttering to himself. The two of them creep around the door, then out into the hall, hand in hand, like children avoiding the grownups.

Behind them there's a shout, of rage or horror. One hand on the wall, the blind assassin begins to run. He pulls the torches from their sconces as he goes, hurls them behind him, hoping they will go out.

He knows the Temple inside out, by touch and smell; it's his business to know such things. He knows the city in the same way, he can run it like a rat in a maze – he knows its doorways, its tunnels, its boltholes and cul-de-sacs, its lintels, its ditches and gutters – even its passwords, most of the time. He knows which walls he can scale, where all the toeholds are. Now he pushes on a marble panel – it has a bas-relief of the Broken God on it, patron of fugitives – and they're in darkness. He knows this by the way the girl stumbles, and it occurs to him for the first time that by taking her with him he'll be slowed down. He'll be hampered by her ability to see.

On the other side of the wall, feet hammer past. He whispers, Take hold of my robe, adding, unnecessarily, Don't say a word. They're in the network of hidden tunnels that allows the High Priestess and her cohorts to learn so many valuable secrets from those who come to the Temple to meet or confess to the Goddess or pray, but they have to get out of it as quickly as possible. It is, after all, the first place the High Priestess will think to look. Nor can he take them out via the loosened stone in the outer wall by which he originally entered. The false Lord of the Underworld may know about that, having arranged for the killing and specified the time and place, and must by now have guessed the blind assassin's treachery.

Muffled by thick rock, a bronze gong sounds. He can hear it through his feet.

He leads the girl from wall to wall, and then down an abrupt, cramped staircase. She's whimpering with fear: cutting out her tongue hasn't stopped her capacity for tears. Pity, he thinks. He feels for the disused culvert he knows is there, lifts her up to it, offering his hands for a stirrup, then swings himself up beside her. Now they must worm their way along. The smell is not pleasant, but it's an old smell. Clotted human effluvium, gone to dust.

Now there's fresh air. He sniffs it, testing for the smoke of torches.

Are there stars? he asks her. She nods. No clouds then. Unfortunate. A couple of the five moons must be shining – he knows that from the time of month – and three more will shortly follow. The two of them will be clearly visible for the rest of the night, and in daylight they'll be incandescent.

The Temple won't want the story of their escape to become general knowledge – it would lead to loss of face, and riots might ensue. Some other girl will be tagged for the sacrifice: what with the veils, who's to know? But many will be hunting for them, on the hush but relentlessly.

He can put them into a hiding hole, but sooner or later they'd have to come out for food and water. Alone, he might get by, but not the two of them.

He could always ditch her. Or stab her, dump her in a well. No, he can't.

There's always the assassins' den. That's where they all go when off-duty, to exchange gossip and share loot and boast about their exploits. It's hidden audaciously right under the judgment room of the main palace, a deep cave lined with carpets – carpets the assassins were forced to make as children, and have stolen since. They know them by touch, and often sit on them, smoking the dream-inducing *fring* weed and running their fingers over the patterns, over the luxurious colours, remembering what these colours looked like when they could see.

But only the blind assassins are allowed into this cave. They form a closed society, into which strangers are brought only as plunder. Also, he's betrayed his calling by saving alive someone he's been paid to murder. They're professionals, the assassins; they pride themselves on completing their contracts, they don't stand for violations of their own code of conduct. They'd kill him without mercy, and her too after a while.

One of his fellows may well be hired to track them. Set a thief to catch a thief. Then, sooner or later, they'll be doomed. Her fragrance alone will give them away – they've perfumed her up to the gills.

He'll have to take her out of Sakiel-Norn – out of the city, out of familiar territory. It's a danger, but not as great a one as remaining. Perhaps he can get them down to the harbour, then aboard a ship. But how to sneak past the gates? All eight of them are locked and guarded, as is the nightly custom. Alone, he could scale the walls – his fingers and toes can grip like a gecko's – but with her it would be a catastrophe.

There's another way. Listening at every step, he leads her downhill, towards the side of the city nearest the sea. The waters of all the springs and fountains of Sakiel-Norn are collected into one canal, and this canal takes the water out beneath the city wall, through an arched tunnel. The water is higher than a man's head and the current is swift, so no one ever tries to get into the city that way. But out?

Running water will deaden the scent.

He himself can swim. It's one of the skills the assassins take care to learn. He assumes, correctly, that the girl can't. He tells her to remove all of her clothes and make them into a bundle. Then he sheds the Temple robe and ties his own clothes into the bundle with hers. He knots the cloth around his shoulders, then around her wrists, tells her that if the knots come undone she must not let go of him, no matter what. When they come to the archway, she must hold her breath.

The *nyerk* birds are stirring; he can hear their first croaking;

soon it will be light. Three streets away, someone is coming, steadily, deliberately, as if searching. He half leads, half pushes the girl into the cold water. She gasps, but does as she is told. They float along; he feels for the main current, listens for the rush and gurgle where the water enters the archway. Too early and they'll run out of breath, too late and he'll strike his head against the stone. Then he plunges.

Water is nebulous, it has no shape, you can pass your hand right through it; yet it can kill you. The force of such a thing is its momentum, its trajectory. What it collides with, and how fast. The same might be said about – but never mind that.

There's a long agonizing passage. He thinks his lungs will burst, his arms give out. He feels her dragging behind him, wonders if she's drowned. At least the current is with them. He scrapes against the tunnel wall; something tears. Cloth, or flesh?

On the other side of the archway they surface; she's coughing, he's laughing softly. He holds her head above the water, lying on his back; in this fashion they float down the canal for some distance. When he judges it's far enough and safe enough, he lands them, hauling her up the sloping stone embankment. He feels for the shadow of a tree. He's exhausted, but also elated, filled with a strange aching happiness. He has saved her. He has extended mercy, for the first time in his life. Who knows what may come of such a departure from his chosen path?

Is anyone around? he says. She pauses to look, shakes her head for no. Any animals? No, again. He hangs their clothes on the branches of the tree; then, in the fading light of the saffron and heliotrope and magenta moons, he gathers her up like silk, sinks into her. She's cool as a melon, and faintly salty, like a fresh fish.

They're lying in each other's arms, fast asleep, when three spies who've been sent ahead by the People of Desolation to scout

out the approaches to the city stumble across them. Brusquely they are awakened, then questioned by the one spy who speaks their language, though far from perfectly. This boy is blind, he tells the others, and the girl is mute. The three spies marvel at them. How could they have come here? Not out of the city, surely; all the gates are locked. It is as if they have appeared out of the sky.

The answer is obvious: they must be divine messengers. They are courteously allowed to dress in their now-dry clothing, mounted together on a spy's horse, and led off to be presented to the Servant of Rejoicing. The spies are enormously pleased with themselves, and the blind assassin knows better than to say very much. He's heard vague tales about these people and their curious beliefs concerning divine messengers. Such messengers are said to deliver their messages in obscure forms, and so he tries to remember all of the riddles and paradoxes and conundrums he has ever known: The way down is the way up. What goes on four legs at dawn, two at noon and three in the evening? Out of the eater comes forth meat, and out of the strong came forth sweetness. What's black and white and red all over?

That's not Zycronian, they didn't have newspapers.

Point taken. Scratch that. How about, More powerful than God, more evil than the Devil; the poor have it, the rich lack it, and if you eat it you die?

That's a new one.

Take a guess.

I give up.

Nothing.

She takes a minute to work it out. Nothing. Yes, she says. That should do it.

As they ride, the blind assassin keeps one arm around the girl. How to protect her? He has an idea, impromptu and born of desperation, but nevertheless it may work. He will affirm that both of them are indeed divine messengers, but of different kinds. He is the one who receives the messages from the Invincible One, but only she can interpret them. This she does with her hands, by making signs with her fingers. The method of reading of these signs has been revealed only to him. He will add, just in case they get any nasty ideas, that no man must be allowed to touch the mute girl in an improper way, or in any way at all. Except himself, of course. Otherwise she will lose the power.

It's foolproof, for as long as they'll buy it. He hopes she's quick on the uptake, and can improvise. He wonders if she knows any signs.

That's all for today, he says. I need to open the window.

But it's so cold.

Not for me it isn't. This place is like a closet. I'm suffocating.

She feels his forehead. I think you're coming down with something. I could go to the drugstore –

No. I never get sick.

What is it? What's wrong? You're worried.

I'm not worried as such. I never worry. But I don't trust what's happening. I don't trust my friends. My so-called friends.

Why? What are they up to?

Bugger all, he says. That's the problem.

Mayfair, February 1936

TORONTO HIGH NOON GOSSIP
BY YORK

The Royal York Hotel overflowed with exotically garbed revellers in mid-January at the season's third charity costume ball, given in aid of the Downtown Foundlings' Crèche. The theme this year – with a nod to last year's spectacular "Tamurlane in Samarkand" Beaux Arts Ball – was "Xanadu," and under the skilled direction of Mr. Wallace Wynant, the three lavish ballrooms were transformed into a "stately pleasure dome" of compelling brilliance, where Kubla Khan and his glittering entourage held court. Foreign potentates from Eastern realms and their retinues – harems, servants, dancing girls and slaves, as well as damsels with dulcimers, merchants, courtesans, fakirs, soldiers of all nations, and beggars galore – whirled gaily around a spectacular "Alph, the Sacred River" fountain, dyed a Bacchanalian purple by an overhead spotlight, beneath shimmering crystal festoons in the central "Cave of Ice."

Dancing went briskly forward as well in the two adjacent garden-bowers, each loaded with blossom, while a jazz orchestra in each ballroom kept up the "symphony and song." We did not hear any "ancestral voices prophesying war," as all was sweet accord, thanks to the firmly-guiding hand of Mrs. Winifred Griffen Prior, the Ball's convenor, ravishing in scarlet and gold as a Princess from Rajistan. Also on the reception committee were Mrs. Richard Chase Griffen, an Abyssinian maid in green and silver, Mrs. Oliver MacDonnell, in Chinese red, and Mrs. Hugh N. Hillert, imposing as a Sultaness in magenta.

He's in another place now, a room he's rented out near the Junction. It's above a hardware store. In its window is a sparse display of wrenches and hinges. It isn't doing too well; nothing around here is doing too well. Grit blows through the air, crumpled paper along the ground; the sidewalks are treacherous with ice, from packed snow nobody's shovelled.

In the middle distance trains mourn and shunt, their whistles trailing into the distance. Never hello, always goodbye. He could hop one, but it's a chance: they're patrolled, though you never know when. Anyway he's nailed in place right now – let's face it – because of her; although, like the trains, she's never on time and always departing.

The room is two flights up, back stairs with rubber treads, the rubber worn patchy, but at least it's a separate entrance. Unless you count the young couple with a baby on the other side of the wall. They use the same stairs, but he rarely sees them, they get up too early. He can hear them at midnight though, when he's trying to work; they go at it as if there's no tomorrow, their bed squeaking like rats. It drives him crazy. You'd think with one yelling brat they'd have called it quits, but no, on they gallop. At least they're quick about it.

Sometimes he sets his ear against the wall to listen. Any port-hole in a storm, he thinks. In the night all cows are cows.

He's crossed paths with the woman a couple of times, padded and kerchiefed like a Russian granny, labouring with parcels and baby buggy. They stash that thing on the downstairs landing, where it waits like some alien death trap, its black mouth gaping. He helped her with it once and she smiled at him, a stealthy smile, her little teeth bluish around the edges, like skim milk. *Does my typewriter bother you at night?* he'd ventured – hinting that he's awake then, that he overhears. *No, not at all.* Blank stare, dumb as a heifer. Dark circles under her eyes, downward lines etched from nose to mouth corners. He doubts the evening doings are her idea. Too fast, for one thing – the guy's in and out like a bank robber. She has *drudge* written all over her; she probably stares at the ceiling, thinks about mopping the floor.

His room has been created by dividing a larger room in two, which accounts for the flimsiness of the wall. The space is narrow and cold: there's a breeze around the window frame, the radiator clanks and drips but gives no heat. A toilet stashed in one chilly corner, old piss and iron staining the bowl a toxic orange, and a shower stall made of zinc, with a rubber curtain grimy with age. The shower is a black hose running up one wall, with a round head of perforated metal. The dribble of water that comes out of it is cold as a witch's tit. A Murphy bed, inexpertly installed so that he has to bust a gut prying it down; a plywood counter stuck together with furniture nails, painted yellow some time ago. A one-ring burner. Dinginess blankets everything like soot.

Compared to where he might be, it's a palace.

He's ditched his pals. Skipped out on them, left no address. It shouldn't have taken this long to arrange a passport, or the two passports he requires. He felt they were keeping him in the larder as insurance: if someone more valuable to them got caught, they could trade him in. Maybe they were thinking of turning him in anyway. He'd make a cute fall guy: he's expendable, he's never really fit their notions. A fellow-traveller who didn't travel far or fast enough. They disliked his erudition, such as it was; they disliked his skepticism, which they mistook for levity. *Just because Smith is wrong doesn't mean Jones is right,* he'd said once. They'd probably noted it down for future reference. They have their little lists.

Maybe they wanted their own martyr, their own one-man Sacco and Vanzetti. After he's been hanged by the neck until Red, villainous face in all the papers, they'll reveal some proof of his innocence – chalk up a few points of moral outrage. *Look what the system does! Outright murder! No justice!* They think like that, the comrades. Like a chess game. He'd be the pawn sacrifice.

He goes to the window, looks out. Icicles like brownish tusks depend outside the glass, taking their colour from the roofing. He thinks of her name, an electric aura circling it – a sexual buzz like blue neon. Where is she? She won't take a taxi, not right to the spot, she's too bright for that. He stares at the streetcar stop, willing her to materialize. Stepping down with a flash of leg, a high-heeled boot, best plush. *Cunt on stilts.* Why does he think like that, when if any other man said that about her he'd hit the bastard?

She'll be wearing a fur coat. He'll despise her for it, he'll ask her to keep it on. Fur all the way through.

Last time he saw her there was a bruise on her thigh. He wished he'd made it himself. *What's this? I bumped into a door.* He always knows when she's lying. Or he thinks he knows. Thinking he knows can be a trap. An ex-professor once told him he had a diamond-hard intellect and he'd been flattered at the time. Now he considers the nature of diamonds. Although sharp and glittering and useful for cutting glass, they shine with reflected light only. They're no use at all in the dark.

Why does she keep arriving? Is he some private game she's playing, is that it? He won't let her pay for anything, he won't be bought. She wants a love story out of him because girls do, or girls of her type who still expect something from life. But there must be another angle. The wish for revenge, or for punishment. Women have curious ways of hurting someone else. They hurt themselves instead; or else they do it so the guy doesn't even know he's been hurt until much later. Then he finds out. Then his dick falls off. Despite those eyes, the pure line of her throat, he catches a glimpse in her at times of something complex and smirched.

Better not to invent her in her absence. Better to wait until she's actually here. Then he can make her up as she goes along.

He has a bridge table, flea-market vintage, and one folding chair. He sits down at the typewriter, blows on his fingers, rolls in paper.

In a glacier located in the Swiss Alps (or the Rocky Mountains, better, or on Greenland, even better), some explorers have found – embedded in a flow of clear ice – a space vehicle. It's shaped like a small dirigible, but pointed at the ends like an okra pod. An eerie glow comes from it, shining up through the ice. What colour is this glow? Green is best, with a yellow tinge to it, like absinthe.

The explorers melt the ice, using what? A blowtorch they happen to have with them? A large fire made from nearby trees? If trees, better to move it back to the Rocky Mountains. No trees in Greenland. Perhaps a huge crystal could be employed, which would magnify the rays of the sun. The Boy Scouts – of which he had briefly been one – were taught to use this method to start fires. Out of sight of the Scoutmaster, a jovial, mournful pink-faced man fond of sing-songs and hatchets, they'd held their magnifying glasses trained on their bare arms to see who could stand it longest. They'd set fire to pine needles that way, and scraps of toilet paper.

No, the giant crystal would be too impossible.

The ice is gradually melted. X, who will be a dour Scot,

warns them not to meddle with it as no good will come, but Y, who is an English scientist, says they must add to the store of human knowledge, whereas Z, an American, says they stand to make millions. B, who is a girl with blonde hair and a puffy, bludgeoned-looking mouth, says it is all very thrilling. She is a Russian and is thought to believe in Free Love. X, Y, and Z have not put this to the test, though all would like to – Y subconsciously, X guiltily, and Z crudely.

He always calls his characters by letters at first, then fills the names in afterwards. Sometimes he consults the telephone book, sometimes the inscriptions on tombstones. The woman is always B, which stands for Beyond Belief, Bird Brain, or Big Boobs, depending on his mood. Or Beautiful Blonde, of course.

B sleeps in a separate tent and is in the habit of forgetting her mittens, and wandering around at night contrary to orders. She comments on the beauty of the moon, and on the harmonic qualities of wolf howls; she's on first-name terms with the sled dogs, talks to them in Russian baby talk, and claims (despite her official scientific materialism) that they have souls. This will be a nuisance if they run out of food and have to eat one, X has concluded in his pessimistic Scottish way.

The glowing pod-like structure is freed from the ice, but the explorers have only a few minutes to examine the material from which it is made – a thin metal alloy unknown to man – before it vaporizes, leaving a smell of almonds, or patchouli, or burnt sugar, or sulphur, or cyanide.

Revealed to view is a form, humanoid in shape, obviously male, dressed in a skin-tight suit the greenish-blue of peacock feathers, with a sheen like beetles' wings. No. Too much like fairies. Dressed in a skin-tight suit the greenish-blue of a gas flame, with a sheen like gasoline spilled on water. He is still embedded in ice, which must have formed inside the pod. He has light-green skin, slightly pointed ears, thin chiselled lips, and large eyes, which are open. They are mostly pupil, as in owls. His hair is a darker green, and lies in thick coils over his skull, which comes to a noticeable point on top.

Unbelievable. A being from Outer Space. Who knows how long he has lain there? Decades? Centuries? Millennia?

Surely he is dead.

What are they to do? They hoist up the block of ice that encases him, and engage in a conference. (X says they should leave now, and call the authorities; Y wants to dissect him on the spot, but is reminded that he might vaporize, like the spaceship; Z is all for getting him out to civilization on a sled, then packing him in dry ice and selling him to the highest bidder; B points out that their sled dogs are taking an unhealthy interest and have begun to whine, but she is disregarded due to her excessive, Russian, female way of putting things.) Finally – by now it's dark, and the Northern Lights are behaving in a peculiar fashion – it is decided to put him into B's tent. B will have to sleep in the other tent, along with the three men, which will provide some opportunities for voyeurism by candlelight, as B certainly knows how to fill an alpine climbing outfit and a sleeping bag as well. During the night they will take four-hour watches, turn and turn about. In the morning they will cast lots in order to reach a final decision.

All goes well through the watches of X, Y and Z. Then it is the turn of B. She says she has an uncanny feeling, a hunch that all will not go well, but she is in the habit of saying this and is ignored. Newly wakened by Z, who has watched with libidinous urges while she has stretched and clambered out of her sleeping bag and then wiggled into her padded outdoor suit, she takes her place in the tent with the frozen being. The flickering of the candle puts her into a drowsy state; she finds herself wondering what the green man would be like in a romantic situation – he has attractive eyebrows, although he is so thin. She nods off to sleep.

The creature encased in ice begins to glow, softly at first, then more strongly. Water runs silently onto the floor of the tent. Now the ice is gone. He sits up, then stands. Without a sound he approaches the sleeping girl. The dark-green hair on his head stirs, coil by coil, then lengthens, tentacle – it now appears – by tentacle. One tentacle twines itself around the girl's throat, another around her ample charms, a third tightens itself across her mouth. She awakens as if from a nightmare, but it is no nightmare: the space being's face is close to hers, his cold tentacles hold her in an implacable grip; he is gazing at her with unprecedented longing and desire, with sheer naked need. No mortal man has ever looked at her with such intensity. She struggles briefly, then surrenders to his embrace.

Not that she has much of a choice.

The green mouth opens, revealing fangs. They approach her neck. He loves her so much he'll assimilate her – make her part of himself, forever. He and she will become one. She understands this wordlessly, because among other things this gent has the gift of telepathic communication. *Yes*, she sighs.

He rolls himself another cigarette. Will he let B be eaten and drunk in this fashion? Or will the sled dogs heed her plight, break loose from their tethers, tear in through the canvas, rip this guy to pieces, tentacle by tentacle? Will one of the others – he favours Y, the cool English scientist – come to her rescue? Will a fight ensue? That might be good. *Fool! I could have taught you everything!* the alien will beam at Y telepathically, just before he dies. His blood will be a non-human colour. Orange would be good.

Or perhaps the green fellow will exchange intravenous fluids with B, and she will become like him – a perfected, greenish version of herself. Then there will be two of them, and they will crush the others to jelly, decapitate the dogs, and set out to conquer the world. The rich, tyrannical cities must be destroyed, the virtuous poor set free. *We are the Flail of the Lord*, the pair of them will announce. They will now be in possession of the Death Ray, put together from the spaceman's knowledge and some wrenches and hinges looted from a nearby hardware store, so who will argue?

Or else the alien is not drinking B's blood at all – he's injecting himself into her! His own body will shrivel up like a grape, his dry, wrinkled skin will turn to mist, and in the morning not a trace of him will be left. The three men will come upon B, rubbing her eyes sleepily. *I don't know what happened*, she will say, and since she never does, they will believe this. *Maybe we've all been hallucinating*, they will say. *It's the North, the Northern Lights – they addle men's brains. They thick men's blood with cold.* They will not catch the ultra-intelligent alien green gleam in B's eyes, which were green to begin with anyway. The dogs will know, however. They will smell the change. They will growl with their ears back, they will howl plaintively, they will no longer be her friends. *What's got into those dogs?*

It could go so many ways.

The struggle, the fight, the rescue. The death of the alien. Clothes will be torn off in the process. They always are.

Why does he crank out this junk? Because he needs to – otherwise he'd be stony flat broke, and to seek other employment at this juncture would bring him further out in the open than would be at all prudent. Also because he can. He has a facility for it. Not everyone does: many have tried, many failed. He had bigger ambitions once, more serious ones. To write a man's life the way it really is. To go in at the ground level, the level of starvation pay and bread and dripping and slag-faced penny-ante whores and boots in the face and puke in the gutter. To expose the workings of the system, the machinery, the way it keeps you alive just so long as you've got some kick left in you, how it uses you up, turns you into a cog or a souse, crushes your face into the muck one way or another.

The average working man wouldn't read that kind of thing, though – the working man the comrades think is so inherently noble. What those guys want is his stuff. Cheap to buy, value for a dime, fast-paced action, with lots of tits and ass. Not that you can print the words *tits and ass*: the pulps are surprisingly prudish. Breasts and bottom are as far as they'll go. Gore and bullets, guts and screams and writhing, but no full frontal nudity. No *language*. Or maybe it's not prudishness, maybe they just don't want to be closed down.

He lights a cigarette, he prowls, he looks out the window. Cinders darken the snow. A streetcar grinds past. He turns away, he prowls, nests of words in his head.

He checks his watch: she's late again. She's not coming.

VII

The steamer trunk

The only way you can write the truth is to assume that what you set down will never be read. Not by any other person, and not even by yourself at some later date. Otherwise you begin excusing yourself. You must see the writing as emerging like a long scroll of ink from the index finger of your right hand; you must see your left hand erasing it.

Impossible, of course.

I pay out my line, I pay out my line, this black thread I'm spinning across the page.

Yesterday a package arrived for me: a fresh edition of *The Blind Assassin*. This copy is merely a courtesy: no money will result, or not for me. The book is now in the public domain and anyone at all can publish it, so Laura's estate won't be seeing any of the proceeds. That's what happens a set number of years after the death of the author: you lose control. The thing is out there in the world, replicating itself in God knows how many forms, without any say-so from me.

Artemesia Press, this outfit's called; it's English. I think they're the ones who wanted me to write an introduction, which I refused to do, of course. Probably run by a bunch of women, with a name like that. I wonder which Artemesia they have in mind – the Persian lady general from Herodotus who turned tail when the battle was going against her, or the Roman matron who ate the ashes of her dead husband so her body could become his living sepulchre? Probably the raped Renaissance painter: that's the only one of them that gets remembered now.

The book is on my kitchen table. *Neglected masterpieces of the twentieth century*, it says in italic script under the title. Laura was a "modernist," we are told on the inside flap. She was "influenced" by the likes of Djuna Barnes, Elizabeth Smart, Carson McCullers – authors I know for a fact that Laura never read. The cover design isn't too bad, however. Shades of washed-out brownish purple, a photographic look: a woman in a slip, at a window, seen through a net curtain, her face in shadow. Behind her, a segment of a man – the arm, the hand, the back of the head. Appropriate enough, I suppose.

I decided it was time for me to phone my lawyer. Or not my real lawyer. The one I used to consider mine, the one who handled that business with Richard, who battled Winifred so heroically, though in vain – that one died several decades ago. Ever since then I have been passed from hand to hand within the firm, like some ornate silver teapot fobbed off on each new generation as a wedding gift, but that nobody ever uses.

"Mr. Sykes, please," I said to the girl who answered. Some receptionist or other, I suppose. I imagined her fingernails, long and maroon and pointed. But perhaps these are the wrong kind of fingernails for a receptionist of today. Perhaps they are ice blue.

"I'm sorry, Mr. Sykes is in a meeting. Who may I say is calling?"

They might as well use robots. "Mrs. Iris Griffen," I said, in my best diamond-cutting voice. "I'm one of his oldest clients."

This did not open any doors. Mr. Sykes was still in a meeting. He is a busy lad, it appears. But why do I think of him as a lad? He must be in his mid-fifties – born, perhaps, in the same year Laura died. Has she really been dead that long, the time it's taken to grow and ripen a lawyer? Another of those things that must be true because everyone else agrees they are, although they don't seem so to me.

"May I tell Mr. Sykes what it concerns?" said the receptionist.

"My will," I said. "I'm considering writing one. He's often
told me that I should." (A lie, but I wanted to establish in her
easily distracted brain the fact that Mr. Sykes and I were as
close as two peas in a pod.) "That, and some other matters. I
ought to come into Toronto soon, to consult him. Perhaps
he could give me a call, when he can spare a minute."

I imagined Mr. Sykes receiving the message; I imagined the
tiny chill that would run down the back of his neck as he tried
to place my name, and then succeeded. Goose feet on his
grave. It's what you feel – even I feel – when coming across
those small items in the paper concerning folks once famous
or glamorous or notorious, and long thought dead. Yet it
appears they continue to live on, in some shrivelled, darkened
form, encrusted with years, like beetles under a stone.

"Of course, Mrs. Griffen," said the receptionist. "I'll make
sure he gets back to you." They must take lessons – elocution
lessons – to achieve just the right blend of consideration and
contempt. But why am I complaining? It's a skill I perfected,
once, myself.

I set down the phone. No doubt there will be some
eyebrow-raising among Mr. Sykes and his youthful, balding,
Mercedes-driving, tubby-bellied cronies: *What can the old bat
possibly have to leave?*

What, that is, worth mentioning?

In one corner of my kitchen there's a steamer trunk, stuck with
tattered labels. It's part of the matched luggage set from my
trousseau – clear yellow calfskin once, dingy now, the steel
bindings marred and grimy. I keep it locked, the key sunk deep
in a sealer jar filled with bran cereal. Coffee and sugar tins
would be too obvious.

I wrestled with the jar lid – I must think of some better, easier hiding place – and finally got it open, and extracted the key. I knelt with some difficulty, turned the key in the lock, lifted the lid.

I hadn't opened this trunk for some time. The singed, autumn-leaf smell of old paper rose to greet me. There were all of the notebooks with their cheap cardboard covers, like pressed sawdust. Also the typescript, held together by a criss-cross of ancient kitchen string. Also the letters to the publishers – from me, of course, not from Laura, she was dead by then – and the corrected proofs. Also the hate mail, until I stopped saving it.

Also five copies of the first edition, with the dust jackets still in mint condition – tawdry, but dust jackets were then, in the years just after the war. The colours are a garish orange, a flat purple, a lime green, printed on flimsy paper, with an awful drawing – a faux Cleopatra type with bulbous green breasts and kohl-rimmed eyes and purple necklaces from navel to chin and an enormous, pouting orange mouth, rising up like a genie from the writhing smoke of a purple cigarette. Acid is eating into the pages, the virulent cover fading like the feathers of a stuffed tropical bird.

(I received six free copies – the author's copies, they were called – but I gave one of them to Richard. I don't know what became of it. I expect he tore it up, which was what he always did with pieces of paper he didn't want. No – I remember now. It was found on the boat with him, on the galley table, beside his head. Winifred sent it back to me with a note: *Now look what you've done!* I threw it out. I didn't want anything near me that had ever touched Richard.)

I've often wondered what to do with all of this – this cache of odds and ends, this tiny archive. I can't bring myself to sell it, but I can't bring myself to discard it either. If I do nothing, the choice will be left to Myra, tidying up after me. After her first moments of shock – supposing she begins to read – there will no doubt be some ripping and shredding. Then a struck match and none the wiser. She'd interpret that as loyalty: it's what Reenie would have done. In the old days trouble was kept in the family, which is still the best place for it, not that there's ever a best place for trouble. Why stir everything up again after that many years, with all concerned tucked, like tired children, so neatly into their graves?

Perhaps I should leave this trunk and its contents to a university, or else to a library. It would at least be appreciated there, in a ghoulish way. There are more than a few scholars who'd like to get their claws into all this waste paper. *Material*, they'd call it – their name for loot. They must think of me as a fusty old dragon crouched on an ill-gotten hoard – some gaunt dog-in-the-manger, some desiccated, censorious wardress, a prim-lipped keeper of the keys, guarding the dungeon in which starved Laura is chained to the wall.

For years they've bombarded me with letters, wanting Laura's own letters – wanting manuscripts, mementoes, interviews, anecdotes – all the grisly details. To these importunate missives I used to compose tersely worded replies:

"Dear Miss W., In my view your plan for a 'Commemoration Ceremony' at the bridge which was the scene of Laura Chase's tragic death is both tasteless and morbid. You must be out of your mind. I believe you are suffering from auto-intoxication. You should try an enema."

"Dear Ms. X., I acknowledge your letter concerning your proposed thesis, though I can't say that its title makes a great deal of sense to me. Doubtless it does to you or you would not have come up with it. I cannot give you any help. Also you do not deserve any. 'Deconstruction' implies the wrecking ball, and 'problematize' is not a verb."

"Dear Dr. Y., Concerning your study of the theological implications of *The Blind Assassin*: my sister's religious beliefs were strongly held but were scarcely what is called conventional. She did not like God or approve of God or claim to understand God. She said she loved God, and as with human beings that was a different thing. No, she was not a Buddhist. Don't be fatuous. I suggest you learn to read."

"Dear Professor Z., I have noted your opinion that a biography of Laura Chase is long overdue. She may well be, as you say, 'among our most important female mid-century writers.' I wouldn't know. But my co-operation in what you call 'your project' is out of the question. I have no wish to satisfy your lust for phials of dried blood and the severed fingers of saints.

Laura Chase is not your 'project.' She was my sister. She would not have wished to be pawed over after her death, whatever that pawing over might euphemistically be termed. Things written down can cause a great deal of harm. All too often, people don't consider that."

"Dear Miss W., This is your fourth letter on the same subject. Stop pestering me. You are a drone."

For decades I took a grim satisfaction in this venomous doodling. I enjoyed licking the stamps, then dropping the letters like so many hand grenades into the shiny red box, with the sense of having settled the hash of some earnest, greedy snoop. But lately I've stopped answering. Why needle strangers? They don't give a hoot what I think of them. For them I'm only an appendage: Laura's odd, extra hand, attached to no body – the hand that passed her on, to the world, to them. They see me as a repository – a living mausoleum, a *resource*, as they term it. Why should I do them any favours? As far as I'm concerned they're scavengers – hyenas, the lot of them; jackals on the scent of carrion, ravens hunting for road-kill; corpse flies. They want to pick through me as if I'm a boneheap, looking for scrap metal and broken pottery, for shards of cuneiform and scraps of papyrus, for curios, lost toys, gold teeth. If they ever suspected what I've got stashed away here, they'd jimmy the locks, they'd break and enter, they'd knock me over the head and make off with the boodle, and feel more than justified.

No. Not a university then. Why give them the satisfaction?

Perhaps my steamer trunk should go to Sabrina, despite her decision to remain incommunicado, despite – this is where it festers – her persistent neglect of me. Nevertheless, blood is thicker than water, as anyone knows who has tasted both. These things are hers by right. You might even say they are her inheritance: she is, after all, my granddaughter. She is also Laura's grandniece. Surely she will want to inform herself about her origins, once she gets around to it.

But no doubt Sabrina would reject such a gift. She's an adult now, I keep reminding myself. If she has anything to ask me, anything to say to me at all, she'll let me know.

But why doesn't she? What can be taking her so long? Is her silence a form of revenge, for something or someone? Not for Richard, surely. She never knew him. Not for Winifred, from whom she ran away. For her mother then – for poor Aimee?

How much can she possibly remember? She was only four. Aimee's death was not my fault.

Where is Sabrina now, and what can she be seeking? I picture her as a thinnish girl, with a hesitant smile, a little ascetic; lovely though, with her grave eyes blue as Laura's, her long dark hair coiled like sleeping serpents around her head. She won't have a veil, though; she'll have sensible sandals, or even boots, the soles worn down. Or has she assumed a sari? Girls of her sort do.

She's on some mission or other – feeding the Third World poor, soothing the dying; expiating the sins of the rest of us. A fruitless task – our sins are a bottomless pit, and there's lots more where they came from. But that's God's point, she'd doubtless argue – the fruitlessness. He's always liked futility. He thinks it's noble.

She takes after Laura in that respect: the same tendency towards absolutism, the same refusal to compromise, the same scorn for the grosser human failings. To get away with that, you have to be beautiful. Otherwise it seems mere peevishness.

The Fire Pit

The weather remains unseasonably warm. Balmy, kindly, dry and bright; even the sun, so pale and thin usually at this time of year, is full and mellow, the sunsets lush. The brisk, smiley-face folks on the weather channel say it's due to some distant, dusty catastrophe – an earthquake, a volcano? Some new, murderous Act of God. *No cloud without a silver lining*, is their motto. And no silver lining without a cloud.

Yesterday Walter drove me into Toronto for the appointment with the lawyer. It's a place he never goes if he can help it, but Myra put him up to it. That was after I said I'd be taking the bus. Myra wouldn't hear of it. As everyone knows, there's only one bus, and it leaves in the dark and returns in it. She said that when I got off the bus at night, the motorists would never see me and I'd be squashed like a bug. Anyway, I shouldn't be going to Toronto by myself, because, as everyone also knows, it's populated entirely by crooks and thugs. Walter, she said, would take care of me.

Walter wore a red baseball cap for the trip; between the back of it and the top of his jacket collar his bristly neck bulged out like a biceps. His eyelids were creased as knees. "I would of took the pickup," he said, "built like a brick shit-house, give the buggers something to think about before ramming into me. Only there's a few springs gone, so it's not such a smooth ride." According to him, the drivers in Toronto were all crazy. "Well, you'd have to be crazy to go there, eh?" he said.

"We're going there," I pointed out.

"But only the once. Like we used to tell the girls, once don't count."

"And did they believe you, Walter?" I said, stringing him along as he likes to be strung.

"Sure. Dumb as a stump. Specially the blondes." I could feel him grinning.

Built like a brick shithouse. That used to be said about women. It was meant as a compliment, in the days when not everyone had a brick shit-house: only wooden ones, flimsy and smelly and easy to push over.

As soon as he'd got me into the car and buckled me up, Walter turned on the radio: electric violins wailing, twisted romance, the four-square beat of heartbreak. Trite suffering, but suffering nonetheless. The entertainment business. What voyeurs we have all become. I leaned back against the pillow provided by Myra. (She'd provisioned us as if for an ocean voyage – she'd packed a lap rug, tuna sandwiches, brownies, a thermos of coffee.) Out the window was the Jogues River, pursuing its sluggish course. We crossed it and turned north, past streets of what used to be workers' cottages and are now what is known as "starter homes," then a few small businesses: an auto wrecker, a foundering health-food emporium, an orthopedic shoe outlet with a green neon foot flashing on and off as if walking all by itself in one place. Then a miniature shopping mall, five stores, of which only one had managed to get the Christmas tinsel up yet. Then Myra's beauty parlour, The Hair Port. There was a picture of a crop-headed person in the window, whether male or female I really couldn't say.

Then a motel that used to be called Journeys End. I suppose they were thinking of "Journeys end in lovers meeting," but not everyone could be expected to get the reference: it might have come across as too sinister, a building all entrances but no exits, reeking of aneurysms and thromboses and emptied bottles of sleeping pills and gun wounds to the head. Now it's called simply Journeys. How wise to have changed it. So much more inconclusive, so much less terminal. So much better to travel than to arrive.

We passed a few more franchises – smiling chickens offering platters of their own fried body parts, a grinning Mexican wielding tacos. The town water tank loomed up ahead, one of those huge bubbles of cement that dot the rural landscape like comic-strip voice balloons emptied of words. Now we'd hit open country. A metal silo lifted out of a field like a conning tower; by the roadside, three crows pecked at a furry burst lump of groundhog. Fences, more silos, a huddle of damp cows; a stand of dark cedar, then a patch of swamp, the summer's bulrushes already ragged and balding.

It began to drizzle. Walter turned the windshield wipers on. To their soothing lullaby, I went to sleep.

When I woke up, my first thought was, Did I snore? If so, had my mouth been open? How unsightly, and therefore how humiliating. But I couldn't bring myself to ask. In case you're wondering, vanity never ends.

We were on the eight-lane freeway, close to Toronto. That was according to Walter: I couldn't see, because we were stuck behind a swaying farm truck top-heavy with crates of white geese, bound no doubt for market. Their long, doomed necks and frantic heads poked out here and there through the slats, their beaks opened and closed, uttering their tragic and ludicrous cries, drowned out by the racket of wheels. Feathers stuck to the windshield, the car filled with the smell of goose shit and gas fumes.

The truck had a sign on it that said, If You're Close Enough To Read This You're Too Close. When it finally turned off, there was Toronto up ahead, an artificial mountain of glass and concrete rising from the flat lakeside plain, all crystals and spires and giant shining slabs and sharp-edged obelisks, floating in an orange-brown haze of smog. It looked like something I'd never seen before – something that had grown up overnight, or that wasn't really there at all, like a mirage.

Black flakes flew past as if a mound of paper up ahead were smouldering. Anger vibrated in the air like heat. I thought of drive-by shootings.

The lawyer's office was near King and Bay. Walter got lost, then couldn't find parking. We had to walk five blocks, Walter propelling me by the elbow. I didn't know where we were, because everything has changed so much. It changes every time I go there, which is not often, and the cumulative effect is devastating – as if the city's been bombed level, then built again from scratch.

The downtown I remember – drab, Calvinistic, with white men in dark overcoats marching in lockstep on the sidewalks, interspersed with the occasional woman, in regulation high heels, gloves and hat, clutch purse under the arm, eyes front – is simply gone, but then it's been gone for some time. Toronto is no longer a Protestant city, it's a mediaeval one: the crowds clogging the street are many-hued, the clothing vivid. Hot-dog stands with yellow umbrellas, pretzel-sellers, hawkers of earrings and woven bags and leather belts, beggars hung with crayoned Out of Work signs: among them they've staked out the territory. I passed a flute player, a trio with electric guitars, a man with a kilt and bagpipes. At any moment I expected jugglers or fire-eaters, lepers in procession, with hoods and iron bells. There was a blare of noise; an iridescent film clung to my glasses like oil.

At last we made it as far as the lawyer's. When I first consulted this firm, back in the 1940s, it was located in one of those sooty red-brick Manchester-shaped office buildings, with a mosaic-tiled lobby and stone lions, and gold lettering on the wooden doors with their pebble-glass inserts. The elevator was the kind that had a crisscross grille of metal bars within the cage itself; stepping into it was like going briefly to jail. A woman in a navy-blue uniform and white gloves ran it, calling out the numbers, which reached only to ten.

Now the law firm is housed in a plate-glass tower, in an office suite fifty floors up. Walter and I ascended in the gleaming elevator, with its plastic marble interior and its smell of car upholstery and its crush of suited people, men and women both, all with the averted eyes and vacant faces of lifelong servants. People who see only what they're paid to see. The law office itself had a reception area that might as well have been that of a five-star hotel: a flower arrangement of eighteenth-century density and ostentation, thick mushroom-coloured wall-to-wall, an abstract painting composed of pricey smudges.

The lawyer arrived, shook hands, murmured, gestured: I was to accompany him. Walter said he would wait for me, right where he was. He stared with some alarm at the young, polished receptionist, with her black suit, mauve scarf and nacreous fingernails; she stared, not at him, but at his checked shirt and his immense, pod-like rubber-soled boots. Then he sat down on the two-bum sofa, into which he sank immediately as if into a pile of marshmallows; his knees jack-knifed, his pant legs shot up, revealing thick red loggers' socks. In front of him, on a suave coffee table, was an array of business magazines, advising him on how to maximize his investment dollar. He picked up the issue on mutual funds: in his vast paw it looked like a Kleenex. His eyes were rolling around in his head like a steer's at a stampede.

"I won't be long," I said, to calm him. I was in fact somewhat longer than I'd thought. Well, they bill by the minute, these lawyers, just like the cheaper whores. I kept expecting to hear a knock on the door, and an irritated voice: *Hey in there. Whatcha waiting for? Get it up, get it in and get it out!*

When I'd finished my business with the lawyer, we made our way back to the car and Walter said he'd take me to lunch. He knew a place, he said. I expect Myra had put him up to this: *For Heaven's sakes make sure she eats something, at that age they eat like a bird, they don't even know when they're running out of steam, she could die of starvation in the car.* Also he may have been hungry: he'd devoured all of Myra's carefully packed sand-wiches while I was sleeping, and the brownies into the bargain.

The place he knew was called The Fire Pit, he said. He'd eaten there the last time, maybe two-three years ago, and it had been more or less decent, considering. Considering what? Considering that it was in Toronto. He'd had the double cheese-burger with all the trimmings. They did barbecued ribs there, and specialized in grilled things generally.

I remembered this eatery myself, from over a decade ago – back in the days when I'd been keeping an eye on Sabrina, after that first time she'd run away. I used to hang around her school at day's end, positioning myself on park benches, in spots where I might waylay her – no, where I might have been recognized by her, though there was scant chance of that. I'd hide behind an opened newspaper, like some obsessed, pathetic flasher, filled similarly with hopeless yearning for a girl who'd doubt-less flee me as if I were a troll.

I wanted only to let Sabrina know I was there; that I existed; that I wasn't what she'd been told. That I could be a refuge for her. I knew she would need one, already needed one, because I knew Winifred. Nothing ever came of it though. She never spotted me, I never revealed myself. When it came to the point, I was too cowardly.

One day I tracked her to The Fire Pit. It appeared to be a

place where the girls – the girls of that age, from that school – hung out at lunchtime, or when they were skipping classes. The sign outside its door was red, the window edges decorated with scallops of yellow plastic meant to be flames. I was alarmed by the Miltonic audacity of the name: could they possibly have known what they were invoking?

Hurl'd headlong flaming from th'Ethereal Sky
With hideous ruin and combustion down.
. . . A fiery Deluge, fed
With ever-burning Sulphur unconsum'd.

No. They didn't know. The Fire Pit was Hell only for the meat.

The interior had hanging lamps with stained-glass shades, and mottled, fibrous plants in earthen pots – a sixties feel. I took the booth next to the one where Sabrina was sitting with two school friends, all of them wearing the same lumpy boyish uniforms, those blanket-like kilts with matching ties that Winifred always found so prestigious. The three girls had done their best to spoil the effect – drooping socks, shirts partly untucked, ties askew. They were chewing gum as if it were a religious duty, and talking in that bored, too-loud way girls of that age seem always to have mastered.

The three of them were beautiful, in the way all girls of that age are beautiful. It can't be helped, that sort of beauty, nor can it be conserved; it's a freshness, a plumpness of the cells, that's unearned and temporary, and that nothing can replicate. None of them was satisfied with it, however; already they were making attempts to alter themselves, to improve and distort and diminish, to cram themselves into some impossible, imaginary mould, plucking and pencilling away at their faces. I didn't blame them, having done the same once myself.

I sat there peering at Sabrina from under the brim of my floppy sun hat and eavesdropping on their trivial chatter, which they threw up in front of themselves like camouflage. None was saying what was on her mind, none trusted the others – quite rightly, as casual treachery is a daily affair at that age. The other two were blondes; Sabrina alone was dark and glossy as a mulberry. She wasn't really listening to her friends, or looking at them either. Behind the studied blankness of her gaze, revolt must have been simmering. I recognized that surliness, that stubbornness, that captive-princess indignation, which must be kept hidden until enough weapons have been collected. Watch your back, Winifred, I thought with satisfaction.

Sabrina didn't notice me. Or she did notice me, but she didn't know who I was. There was some glancing from the three of them, some whispering and giggling; I remember the sort of thing. *Shrivelled-up frump*, or the modern version of it. I expect my hat was the object of it. It was a long way from being fashionable, that hat. For Sabrina that day I was merely an old woman – an older woman – a nondescript older woman, not yet decrepit enough to be remarkable.

After the three of them had left, I went to the washroom. On the cubicle wall was a poem:

I love Darren yes I do
Meant for me not for you
If you try to take my place
I swear to God I'll smash your face.

Young girls have become more forthright than they used to be, although no better at punctuation.

When Walter and I finally located The Fire Pit, which wasn't (he said) where he'd left it, there was plywood nailed across the windows, an official notice of some kind stapled to it. Walter snuffled around the locked-up door like a dog that's misplaced a bone. "Looks like it's closed," he said. He stood for a long moment, hands in his pockets. "They're always changing things," he said. "You can't keep up with it."

After some casting about and a few false leads, we settled for a greasy spoon of sorts on Davenport, with vinyl seats and juke-boxes at the tables, stocked with country music and a sprinkling of old Beatles and Elvis Presley songs. Walter put on "Heartbreak Hotel," and we listened to it while we ate our hamburgers and drank our coffee. Walter insisted on paying – Myra again, without a doubt. She must have slipped him a twenty.

I ate only half of my hamburger. I couldn't manage the whole thing. Walter ate the other half, slotting it into his mouth in one bite as if mailing it.

On the way out of the city, I asked Walter to drive me past my old house – the house where I'd once lived with Richard. I remembered the way perfectly, but when I reached the house itself I didn't at first recognize it. It was still angular and grace-less, squinty-windowed, ponderous, a dense brown like stewed tea, but ivy had grown up over the walls. The fake-chalet half-timbering, once cream-coloured, had been painted apple green, and the heavy front door as well.

Richard was against ivy. There had been some when we'd first moved in, but he'd pulled it down. It ate away at the brick-work, he said; it got into the chimneys, it encouraged rodents. This was when he was still coming up with reasons for what he thought and did, and was still presenting them as reasons for what I myself should think and do. It was before he'd thrown reasons to the wind.

I caught a glimpse of myself back then, in a straw hat, a pale-yellow dress, cotton because of the heat. It was late summer, the year after my marriage; the ground was like brick. At Winifred's instigation I had taken up gardening: I needed to have a hobby, she said. She'd decided I should start with a rock garden, because even if I killed the plants the rocks would still be there. *Not much you can do to kill a rock*, she'd joked. She'd sent over what she called three reliable men, who were to do the digging and the arranging of the rocks, so that I could then plant things.

There were already some rocks in the garden, ordered by Winifred: small ones, larger ones like slabs, strewn at random or piled like fallen dominoes. We were all standing there, the three reliable men and myself, looking at this jumbled heap of stone. They had their caps on, their jackets off, their shirt sleeves rolled up, their braces in plain view; they were waiting for my instructions, but I didn't know what to tell them.

I'd still wanted to change something back then – do something myself, make something, from whatever unpromising materials. I still thought I might. But I'd known nothing whatsoever about gardening. I'd felt like crying, but cry once and it's all over: if you cry, the reliable men will despise you, and then they will not be reliable any more.

Walter levered me out of the car, then waited silently, a little behind me, ready to catch me if I should topple. I stood on the sidewalk and looked at the house. The rock garden was still there, though much neglected. Of course it was winter, so therefore hard to tell, but I doubted that anything grew in it any more, except perhaps some dragon's blood, which will grow anywhere.

There was a large dumpster standing in the driveway, full of shattered wood, slabs of plaster: renovations were going on. Either that or there had been a fire: an upstairs window was smashed. Street people camp out in such houses, according to Myra: leave a house untenanted, in Toronto anyway, and they're into it like a shot, having their drug parties or whatever. Satanic cults, she's heard. They'll make bonfires on the hardwood floors, they'll plug up the toilets and crap in the sinks, they'll steal the faucets, the fancy doorknobs, anything they can sell. Though sometimes it's only kids who do the smashing-up, for fun. The young have a talent for it.

The house looked unowned, transient, like a picture in a real-estate flyer. It no longer seemed connected with me in any way. I tried to recall the sound of my footsteps, in winter boots on the dry creaking snow, walking quickly home, late, concocting excuses; the inky portcullis of the doorway; the way the light from the street lamps fell on the snowbanks, ice blue at the edges and spotted with the yellow Braille of dog pee. The shadows were different back then. My uncalm heart, my breath unscrolling, white smoke in the freezing air. The hectic warmth of my fingers; the rawness of my mouth under my fresh lipstick.

There was a fireplace in the living room. I used to sit in front of it, with Richard, the light flickering on us, and on our glasses, each with its coaster to protect the veneer. Six in the evening, martini time. Richard liked to sum up the day: that's what he called it. He'd had a habit of putting his hand on the back of my neck – resting it there, just keeping it there lightly while he conducted the summing up. *Summing up* was what judges did before a case went to the jury. Is that how he saw himself? Perhaps. But his inner thoughts, his motives, were frequently obscure to me.

This was one source of the tension between us: my failure to understand him, to anticipate his wishes, which he set down to my wilful and even aggressive lack of attention. In reality it was also bafflement, and later, fear. As we went on, he became less and less like a man for me, with a skin and working parts, and more and more like a gigantic tangle of string, which I was doomed as if by enchantment to try every day to unravel. I never did succeed.

I stood outside my house, my former house, waiting to have an emotion of any kind at all. None came. Having experienced both, I am not sure which is worse: intense feeling, or the absence of it.

From the chestnut tree on the lawn a pair of legs was dangling, a woman's legs. I thought for a moment they were real legs, clambering down, escaping, until I looked more closely. It was a pair of pantyhose, stuffed with something – toilet paper, no doubt, or underwear – and thrown out of the upstairs window during some Satanic rite or adolescent prank or homeless revel. Caught in the branches.

It must have been my own window these disembodied legs had been thrown from. My former window. I pictured myself gazing out of that window, long ago. Plotting how I might slip out that way, unnoticed, and climb down through the tree – easing my shoes off, swinging myself over the sill, reaching one stockinged foot down and then the next, clinging on to the handholds. I hadn't done it though.

Gazing out the window. Hesitating. Thinking, How lost to myself I have become.

Postcards from Europe

The days darken, the trees turn glum, the sun rolls downhill towards the winter solstice, but still it isn't winter. No snow, no sleet, no howling winds. It's ominous, this delay. A dun-coloured hush pervades us.

Yesterday I walked as far as the Jubilee Bridge. There's been talk of rust, of corrosion, of structural weaknesses; there's been talk of tearing it down. Some nameless, faceless developer lusts to put condos on the public property adjoining it, says Myra – it's prime land because of the view. Views are worth more than potatoes these days, not that there were ever any potatoes in that exact spot. Rumour has it that a wad of dirty money has changed hands under the table to facilitate the deal, which I'm sure is what happened too when this bridge was first erected, ostensibly to honour Queen Victoria. Some contractor or other must have paid off Her Majesty's elected representatives in order to get the job, and we continue to respect the old ways in this town: *Make a buck no matter what.* Those are the old ways.

Strange to think that ladies in ruffles and bustles once strolled over this bridge and leaned on this filigreed railing, to take in the now-costly, soon-to-be-private view: the tumult of the water below, the picturesque limestone cliffs to the west, the factories alongside going full tilt fourteen hours a day, filled with subservient cap-tugging yokels and twinkling in the dusk like gas-lit gambling casinos.

I stood on the bridge and stared over the side, at the water upstream, smooth as taffy, dark and silent, all menacing potential. On the other side were the cascades, the whirlpools, the white noise. It's a fair distance down. I became conscious of my heart, and of dizziness. Also of breathlessness, as if I were in over my head. But over my head in what? Not water; something thicker. Time: old cold time, old sorrow, settling down in layers like silt in a pond.

For instance:

Richard and myself, sixty-four years ago, coming down the gangway of the *Berengeria* on the far shore of the Atlantic Ocean, his hat at a jaunty angle, my gloved hand resting lightly on his arm – the newly wedded couple on their honeymoon.

Why is a honeymoon called that? *Lune de miel*, moon of honey – as if the moon itself is not a cold and airless and barren sphere of pockmarked rock, but soft, golden, luscious – a luminous candied plum, the yellow kind, melting in the mouth and sticky as desire, so achingly sweet it makes your teeth hurt. A warm floodlight floating, not in the sky, but inside your own body.

I know about all of that. I remember it very well. But not from my honeymoon.

The emotion I recall most clearly from that eight weeks – could it have been only nine? – was anxiety. I was worried that Richard was finding the experience of our marriage – by which I meant the part of it that took place in the dark and could not be spoken about – as disappointing as I did. Although this did not appear to be the case: he was affable enough to me at first, at least in daylight. I concealed this anxiety of mine as well as I could, and took frequent baths: I felt I was becoming addled inside, like an egg.

After we'd docked at Southampton, Richard and I travelled to London by train, where we stayed at Brown's Hotel. We had breakfast served in the suite, for which I would put on a negligée, one of the three selected for me by Winifred: ashes of roses, bone with dove-grey lace, lilac with aquamarine – pale, watery colours that were easy on the morning face. Each had the satin mules to match, trimmed with dyed fur or swan's-down. I assumed this was what grown-up women wore in the mornings. I'd seen pictures of such ensembles (but where? Could they have been advertisements, for a brand of coffee perhaps?) – the man in suit and tie, his hair combed slickly back, the woman in her negligée looking just as groomed, one hand lifted, holding the silver coffee pot with its curved spout, the two of them smiling woozily at each other across the butter dish.

Laura would have sneered at these outfits. She'd already sneered when she'd seen them being packed. Though it wasn't sneering exactly: Laura was incapable of true sneering. She lacked the necessary cruelty. (The necessary deliberate cruelty, that is. Her cruelties were accidental – by-products of whatever lofty notions may have been going through her head.) Her reaction had been more like amazement – like disbelief. She'd run her hand over the satin with a little shiver, and I'd felt the cold oiliness, the slipperiness of the fabric, in the ends of my own fingers. Like lizard skin. "You're going to *wear* these?" she'd said.

On those summer mornings in London – for it was summer by then – we would eat our breakfasts with the curtains half-drawn against the clarity of the sun. Richard would have two boiled eggs, two thick rashers of bacon and a grilled tomato, with toast and marmalade, the toast brittle, cooled in a toast rack. I would have half a grapefruit. The tea would be dark, tannic, like swamp water. This was the correct, the English way to serve it, said Richard.

Not much would be said, apart from the obligatory "Sleep well, darling?" and "Mmm – you?" Richard would have the newspapers delivered, along with the telegrams. There were always several of these. He would scan the papers, then open the telegrams, read them, fold them carefully once and then

again, place them in a pocket. Or else he would rip them into
shreds. He never crumpled them up and tossed them into a
wastebasket, and if he had done that I might not have dug them
out and read them, or not at that period of my life.

I supposed all of them were for him: I had never been sent a
telegram, and could think of no reason why I might receive
one.

Richard had various engagements during the day. I assumed
they were with business associates. He hired a car and driver for
me, and I was taken out to see what in his view ought to be
seen. Most of the things I inspected were buildings, others were
parks. Others were statues, erected outside the buildings or
inside the parks: statesmen with their tummies sucked in and
their chests stuck out, the front leg bent, clutching scrolls of
paper; military men on horseback. Nelson on his column,
Prince Albert on his throne with a quartet of exotic women
roiling and wallowing around his feet, spewing out fruit and
wheat. These were supposed to be the Continents, over which
Prince Albert, though dead, still held sway, but he paid no
attention to them; he sat stern and silent under his ornate,
gilded cupola, gazing into the distance, his mind on higher
things.

"What did you see today?" Richard would ask at dinner, and
I would dutifully recite, ticking off one building or park or
statue after another: the Tower of London, Buckingham Palace,
Kensington, Westminster Abbey, the Houses of Parliament. He
did not encourage the visiting of museums, apart from the
Natural History Museum. I wonder, now, why it was that he
thought the sight of so many large stuffed animals would be
conducive to my education? For it had become evident that this
is what all of these visits were aimed at – my education. Why
should the stuffed animals have been better for me, or better for
his idea of what I should become, than a roomful of paintings,

for instance? I think I know, but perhaps I am wrong. Perhaps the stuffed animals were more or less like a zoo – something you'd take a child to, for an outing.

I did go to the National Gallery, though. The concièrge at the hotel suggested it, once I'd run out of buildings. It wore me out – it was like a department store, so many bodies crowded against the walls, so much dazzle – but at the same time it was exhilarating. I had never seen so many naked women in one place. There were naked men as well, but they were not quite so naked. There was also a lot of fancy dress. Perhaps these are primary categories, like women and men: naked and clothed. Well, God thought so. (Laura, as a child: *What does God wear?*)

At all of these places the car and driver would wait, and I would walk briskly in, through whatever gate or door, trying to look purposeful; trying not to look so lonely and empty. Then I would stare and stare, so I would have something to say later. But I could not really make sense out of what I was seeing. Buildings are only buildings. There's nothing much to them unless you know about architecture, or else about what once happened there, and I did not know. I lacked the talent for overviews; it was as if my eyes were right up against whatever I was supposed to be looking at, and I would come away only with textures: roughness of brick or stone, smoothness of waxed wooden banisters, harshness of mangy fur. The striations of horn, the warm gleam of ivory. Glass eyes.

In addition to these educational excursions, Richard encouraged me to go shopping. I found the shop clerks intimidating, and bought little. On other occasions I had my hair done. He did not want me to get it cut or marcelled, and so I didn't. A simple style was best for me, he said. It suited my youth.

Sometimes I would just amble around, or sit on park benches, waiting until it was time to go back. Sometimes a man would sit down beside me, and try to begin a conversation. Then I would leave.

I spent a lot of time changing my costumes. Diddling with straps, with buckles, with the tilt of hats, the seams on stockings. Worrying about the appropriateness of this or that, for this or that hour of the day. No one to hook me up at the neckline or tell me what I looked like from the back and whether I was all tucked in. Reenie used to do that, or Laura. I missed them, and tried not to.

Filing my nails, soaking my feet. Yanking out hairs, or shaving them off: it was necessary to be sleek, devoid of bristles. A topography like wet clay, a surface the hands would glide over.

Honeymoons were said to allow the new couple the time to get to know each other better, but as the days went by I felt I knew Richard less and less. He was effacing himself, or was it concealment? Withdrawal to a vantage point. I myself however was taking shape – the shape intended for me, by him. Each time I looked in the mirror a little more of me had been coloured in.

After London we went to Paris, by channel boat and then by train. The shape of the days in Paris was much the same as those in London, although the breakfasts were different: a hard roll, strawberry jam, coffee with hot milk. The meals were succulent; Richard made quite a fuss over them, and especially over the wines. He kept saying we weren't in Toronto, a fact that was self-evident to me.

I saw the Eiffel Tower but did not go up it, having a dislike of heights. I saw the Panthéon, and Napoleon's tomb. I did not see Notre Dame, because Richard did not favour churches, or at least not Catholic ones, which he considered enervating. Incense in particular he considered stultifying to the brain.

The French hotel had a bidet, which Richard explained to me with the trace of a smirk after he caught me washing my feet in it. I thought, They do understand something the others don't, the French. They understand the anxiety of the body. At least they admit it exists.

We stayed at the Lutetia, which was to become the Nazi headquarters during the war, but how were we to know that? I would sit in the hotel café for morning coffee, because I was afraid to go anywhere else. I had the idea that if I lost sight of the hotel I would never be able to get back to it. I knew by then that whatever French I had been taught by Mr. Erskine was next to useless: *Le coeur a ses raisons que la raison ne connaît point* would not get me any more hot milk.

An old walrus-faced waiter attended to me; he had the knack of pouring the coffee and the hot milk from two jugs, held high in the air, and I found this entrancing, as if he were a child's magician. One day he said to me – he had some English – "Why are you sad?"

"I'm not sad," I said, and began to cry. Sympathy from strangers can be ruinous.

"You should not be sad," he said, gazing at me with his melancholy, leathery walrus eyes. "It must be the love. But you are young and pretty, you will have time to be sad later." The French are connoisseurs of sadness, they know all the kinds. This is why they have bidets. "It is criminal, the love," he said, patting my shoulder. "But none is worse."

The effect was a little spoiled the next day, when he propositioned me, or I think that is what it was: my French wasn't good enough to tell. He wasn't so old after all – forty-five, perhaps. I should have accepted. He was wrong about the sadness, though: far better to have it while you're young. A sad pretty girl inspires the urge to console, unlike a sad old crone. But never mind that part.

Then we went to Rome. Rome seemed familiar to me – at least I had a context for it, provided long ago by Mr. Erskine and his Latin lessons. I saw the Forum, or what was left of it, and the Appian Way, and the Coliseum, looking like a mouse-eaten cheese. Various bridges, various well-worn angels, grave and pensive. I saw the Tiber flowing along, yellow as jaundice. I saw St. Peter's, though only from the outside. It was very big. I suppose I ought to have seen Mussolini's Fascist troops in their black uniforms, marching around and roughing people up – were they doing that yet? – but I did not see them. That sort of thing tends to be invisible at the time unless you yourself happen to be the object of it. Otherwise you see it only later, in newsreels, or else in films made long after the event.

In the afternoons I would order a cup of tea – I was getting the hang of ordering things, I was figuring out what tone to use with waiters, how to keep them at a safe distance. While drinking the tea I would write postcards. My postcards were to Laura and to Reenie, and several to Father. They had photographs on them of the buildings I had been taken to visit – picturing, in tiny sepia detail, what I ought to have seen. The messages I wrote on them were fatuous. To Reenie: *The weather is wonderful. I am enjoying it.* To Laura: *Today I saw the Coliseum, where they used to throw the Christians to the lions. You would have been interested.* To Father: *I hope you are in good health. Richard sends his regards.* (This last was not true, but I was learning which lies, as a wife, I was automatically expected to tell.)

Towards the end of the time allotted for our honeymoon we spent a week in Berlin. Richard had some business there, which had to do with the handles of shovels. One of Richard's firms made shovel handles, and the Germans were short of wood. There was a lot of digging to be done, and more projected, and Richard could supply the shovel handles at a price that undercut his competitors.

As Reenie used to say, *Every little bit helps*. As she also used to say, *Business is business and then there's funny business*. But I knew nothing about business. My task was to smile.

I have to admit I enjoyed Berlin. Nowhere had I been so blonde. The men were exceptionally polite, although they did not look behind themselves when striding through swinging doors. Hand-kissing covered a multitude of sins. It was in Berlin that I learned to perfume my wrists.

I memorized the cities through their hotels, the hotels through their bathrooms. Dressing, undressing, lying in the water. But enough of these travel notes.

We returned to Toronto via New York, in mid-August, in a heat wave. After Europe and New York, Toronto seemed squat and cramped. Outside Union Station there was a mist of bituminous fumes, from where they were fixing the potholes. A hired car met us and took us past the streetcars and their dust and clanging, then past the ornate banks and the department stores, then up the slant of land into Rosedale and the shade of chestnuts and maples.

We stopped in front of the house Richard had bought for us by telegram. He'd picked it up for a song, he said, after the previous owner had managed to bankrupt himself. Richard liked to say he picked things up for a song, which was odd, because he never sang. He never even whistled. He was not a musical person.

The house was dark on the outside, festooned with ivy, its tall, narrow windows turned inward. The key was under the mat, the front hall smelled of chemicals. Winifred had been redecorating during our absence, and the work was not quite finished: there were painters' cloths down still in the front rooms, where they'd stripped off the old Victorian wallpaper. The new colours were pearly, pale – the colours of luxurious indifference, of cool detachment. Cirrus clouds tinged by a faint sunset, drifting high above the vulgar intensities of birds and flowers and such. This was the setting proposed for me, the rarefied air I was to waft around in.

Reenie would be scornful of this interior – of its gleaming emptiness, its pallor. *This whole place looks like a bathroom.* But at the same time she'd be frightened by it, as I was. I called up Grandmother Adelia: she'd know what to do. She'd recognize the new-money attempt to make an impression; she'd be polite, but dismissive. *My, it's certainly modern,* she might say. She'd make short work of Winifred, I thought, but it brought me no solace: I was now of the tribe of Winifred myself. Or I was partly.

And Laura? Laura would smuggle in her coloured pencils, her tubes of pigment. She'd spill something on this house, break something, deface at least a small corner of it. She'd make her mark.

A note from Winifred was propped against the telephone in the front hall. "Hi kids! Welcome home! I got them to finish the bedroom first! I hope you love it – so snazzy! Freddie."

"I didn't know Winifred was doing this," I said.

"We wanted it to be a surprise," said Richard. "We didn't want you to get bogged down in details." Not for the first time, I felt like a child excluded by its parents. Genial, brutal parents, up to their necks in collusion, determined on the rightness of their choices, in everything. I could tell already that my birthday presents from Richard would always be something I didn't want.

I went upstairs to freshen up, at Richard's suggestion. I must have looked as if I needed it. Certainly I felt sticky and wilted. ("Dew's off the rose," was his comment.) My hat was a wreck;

I flung it onto the vanity. I splashed my face with water, and blotted it on one of the white monogrammed towels Winifred had set out. The bedroom looked out over the back garden, where nothing had been done. I kicked off my shoes, threw myself down on the endless cream-coloured bed. It had a canopy, with muslin draped around as if on safari. This, then, was where I was to grin and bear it – the bed I hadn't quite made, but now must lie in. And this was the ceiling I would be staring up at from now on, through the muslin fog, while earthly matters went on below my throat.

The telephone beside the bed was white. It rang. I picked it up. It was Laura, in tears. "Where have you been?" she sobbed. "Why didn't you come back?"

"What do you mean?" I said. "This is when we were supposed to come back! Calm down, I can't hear you."

"You never answered!" she wailed.

"What on earth are you talking about?"

"Father's dead! He's dead, he's dead – we sent five telegrams! Reenie sent them!"

"Just a minute. Slow down. When did this happen?"

"A week after you left. We tried to phone, we phoned all the hotels. They said they'd tell you, they promised! Didn't they tell you?"

"I'll be there tomorrow," I said. "I didn't know. Nobody told me anything. I didn't get any telegrams. I never got them."

I couldn't take it in. What had happened, what had gone wrong, why had Father died, why hadn't I been notified? I found myself on the floor, on the bone-grey carpet, crouching down over the telephone, curled around it as if it were something precious and fragile. I thought of my postcards from Europe, arriving at Avilion with their cheerful, trivial messages. They were probably still on the table in the front hall. *I hope you are in good health.*

"But it was in the papers!" Laura said.

"Not where I was," I said. "Not those papers." I didn't add that I'd never bothered with the papers anyway. I'd been too stupefied.

It was Richard who'd collected the telegrams, on the ship and at all our hotels. I could see his meticulous fingers, opening the envelopes, reading, folding the telegrams into quarters, stowing them away. I couldn't accuse him of lying – he'd never said anything about them, these telegrams – but it was the same as lying. Wasn't it?

He must have told them at the hotels not to put through any calls. Not to me, and not while I was there. He'd been keeping me in the dark, deliberately.

I thought I might be sick, but I wasn't. After a time I went downstairs. *Lose your temper and you lose the fight*, Reenie used to say. Richard was sitting on the back verandah with a gin and tonic. So thoughtful of Winifred to lay in a supply of gin, he'd already said, twice. Another gin was poured ready, waiting for me on the low white glass-topped wrought-iron table. I picked it up. Ice chimed against the crystal. That was how my voice needed to sound.

"Good lord," said Richard, looking at me. "I thought you were freshening up. What happened to your eyes?" They must have been red.

"Father's dead," I said. "They sent five telegrams. You didn't tell me."

"*Mea culpa*," said Richard. "I know I ought to have, but I wanted to spare you the worry, darling. There was nothing to be done, and no way we could get back in time for the funeral, and I didn't want things to be ruined for you. I guess I was selfish, too – I wanted you all to myself, if only for a little while. Now sit down and buck up, and have your drink, and forgive me. We'll deal with all this in the morning."

The heat was dizzying; where the sun hit the lawn it was a blinding green. The shadows under the trees were thick as tar. Richard's voice came through to me in staccato bursts, like Morse code: I heard only certain words.

Worry. Time. Ruined. Selfish. Forgive me.

What could I say to that?

The eggshell hat

Christmas has come and gone. I tried not to notice it. Myra, however, would not be denied. She gave me a little plum pudding she'd boiled herself, made of molasses and caulking compound and decorated with halved maraschino rubber cherries, bright red, like the pasties on an old-style stripper, and a two-dimensional painted wooden cat with a halo and angel wings. She said these cats had been all the rage at The Gingerbread House, and she thought they were pretty cute, and she had one left over, and it was just a hairline crack that you could hardly see at all, and it would sure look nice on the wall over my stove.

Good position, I told her. Angel above, and a carnivorous angel too – high time they came clean on that subject! Oven below, as in all the most reliable accounts. Then there's the rest of us in between, stuck in Middle Earth, on the level of the frying pan. Poor Myra was baffled, as she always is by theological discourse. She likes her God plain – plain and raw, like a radish.

The winter we'd been waiting for arrived on New Year's Eve – a hard freeze, followed by an enormous fall of snow the next day. Outside the window it swirled down, bucket after bucket of it, as if God were dumping laundry flakes in the finale of a children's pageant. I turned on the weather channel to get the full panorama – roads closed, cars buried, power lines down, merchandising brought to a standstill, workmen in bulky suits waddling around like outsized children bundled up for play. Throughout their presentation of what they euphemistically termed "current conditions," the young anchorfolk kept their perky optimism, as they habitually do through every disaster imaginable. They have the footloose insouciance of troubadours or fun-fair gypsies, or insurance salesmen, or stock-market gurus – making overblown predictions in the full knowledge that none of what they're telling us may actually come true.

Myra called to ask if I was all right. She said Walter would be over as soon as the snow stopped, to dig me out.

"Don't be silly, Myra," I said. "I'm quite capable of digging myself out." (A lie – I had no intention of lifting a finger. I was well supplied with peanut butter, I could wait it out. But I felt like company, and threats of action on my part usually speeded up the arrival of Walter.)

"Don't you touch that shovel!" said Myra. "Hundreds of old – of people your age die of heart attacks from snow shovelling every year! And if the electricity goes off, watch where you put the candles!"

"I'm not senile," I snapped. "If I burn the house down it will be on purpose."

Walter appeared, Walter shovelled. He'd brought a paper sack of doughnut holes; we ate them at the kitchen table, me cautiously, Walter wholesale, but contemplatively. He's a man for whom chewing is a form of thinking.

What came back to me then was the sign that used to be in the window of the Downyflake Doughnut stand, at the Sunnyside Amusement Park, in – what was it? – the summer of 1935:

As you ramble on through life, Brother,
Whatever be your goal,
Keep your eye upon the doughnut,
And not upon the hole.

A paradox, the doughnut hole. Empty space, once, but now they've learned to market even that. A minus quantity; *nothing*, rendered edible. I wondered if they might be used – metaphorically, of course – to demonstrate the existence of God. Does naming a sphere of nothingness transmute it into being?

The next day I ventured out, among the cold, splendid dunes. Folly, but I wanted to participate – snow is so attractive, until it gets porous and sooty. My front lawn was a lustrous avalanche, with an Alpine tunnel cut through it. I made it out to the sidewalk, so far so good, but a few houses farther north of me the neighbours had not been so assiduous as Walter about their shovelling, and I got trapped in a drift, and floundered, slipped, and fell. Nothing was broken or sprained – I didn't think it was – but I couldn't get up. I lay there in the snow, pawing with my arms and legs, like a turtle on its back. Children do that, but deliberately – flapping like birds, making angels. For them it's joy.

I was beginning to fret about hypothermia when two strange men levered me up and carted me back to my door. I hobbled into the front room and collapsed onto the sofa, my overshoes and coat still on. Scenting disaster from afar as is her habit, Myra arrived, bearing half-a-dozen turgid cupcakes left over from some family starch-fest. She made me a hot-water bottle and some tea, and the doctor was summoned, and both of them fussed around, giving out a stream of helpful advice and hearty, hectoring tut-tuts, and mightily pleased with themselves.

Now I'm grounded. Also enraged at myself. Or not at myself – at this bad turn my body has done me. After having imposed itself on us like the egomaniac it is, clamouring about its own needs, foisting upon us its own sordid and perilous desires, the body's final trick is simply to absent itself. Just when you need it, just when you could use an arm or a leg, suddenly the body has other things to do. It falters, it buckles under you; it melts away as if made of snow, leaving nothing much. Two lumps of coal, an old hat, a grin made of pebbles. The bones dry sticks, easily broken.

It's an affront, all of that. Weak knees, arthritic knuckles, varicose veins, infirmities, indignities – they aren't ours, we never wanted or claimed them. Inside our heads we carry ourselves perfected – ourselves at the best age, and in the best light as well: never caught awkwardly, one leg out of a car, one still in, or picking our teeth, or slouching, or scratching our noses or bums. If naked, seen gracefully reclining through a gauzy mist, which is where movie stars come in: they assume such poses for us. They are our younger selves as they recede from us, glow, turn mythical.

As a child, Laura would say: *In Heaven, what age will I be?*

Laura was standing on the front steps of Avilion, between the two stone urns where no flowers had been planted, waiting for us. Despite her tallness, she looked very young, very fragile and alone. Also peasant-like, pauperish. She was wearing a pale-blue housedress printed with faded mauve butterflies – mine, three summers before – and no shoes whatsoever. (Was this some new mortification of the flesh, or was it simple eccentricity, or had she simply forgotten?) Her hair was in a single braid, coming down over her shoulder, like the stone nymph's at our lily pool.

God knows how long she'd been there. We hadn't been able to say exactly when we'd arrive, because we'd come down by car, which was possible at that time of year: the roads were not flooded or axle-deep in mud, and some were even paved by then.

I say *we*, because Richard came with me. He said he wouldn't think of sending me off to face such a thing alone, not at a time like this. He was more than solicitous.

He drove us himself, in his blue coupé – one of his newest

toys. In the trunk behind us were our two suitcases, the small ones, just for overnight – his maroon leather, mine lemon-sherbet yellow. I was wearing an eggshell linen suit – frivolous to mention it, no doubt, but it was from Paris and I was very keen on it – and I knew it would be wrinkled at the back once we arrived. Linen shoes, with stiff fabric bows and peek-a-boo toes. My matching eggshell hat rode on my knees like a delicate gift box.

Richard was a jumpy driver. He didn't like to be interrupted – he said it ruined his concentration – and so we made the trip in silence, more or less. The trip took over four hours, which now takes less than two. The sky was clear, and bright and depthless as metal; the sun poured down like lava. The heat wavered up off the asphalt; the small towns were closed against the sun, their curtains drawn. I remember their singed lawns and white-pillared porches, and the lone gas stations, the pumps like cylindrical one-armed robots, their glass tops like brimless bowler hats, and the cemeteries that looked as if no one else would ever be buried in them. Once in a while we'd hit a lake, with a smell of dead minnows and warm waterweed coming off it.

As we drove up, Laura did not wave. She stood waiting while Richard brought the car to a stop and clambered out and walked around to open the door on my side. I was swinging my legs sideways, both knees together as I'd been taught, and reaching for Richard's proffered hand, when Laura suddenly came to life. She ran down the steps and took hold of my other arm and hauled me out of the car, ignoring Richard completely, and threw her arms around me and clutched on to me as if she were drowning. No tears, just that spine-cracking embrace.

My eggshell hat fell out onto the gravel and Laura stepped on it. There was a crackling sound, an intake of breath from

Richard. I said nothing. In that instant I no longer cared about the hat.

Arms around each other's waists, Laura and I went up the steps into the house. Reenie loomed in the kitchen door at the far end of the hall, but she knew enough to leave us alone right then. I expect she turned her attention to Richard – distracted him with a drink or something. Well, he would have wanted to look over the premises and have a stroll around the grounds, now that he'd effectively inherited them.

We went straight up to Laura's room and sat down on her bed. We held on tightly to each other's hands – left in right, right in left. Laura wasn't weeping, as on the telephone. Instead she was calm as wood.

"He was in the turret," said Laura. "He'd locked himself in."

"He always did that," I said.

"But this time he didn't come out. Reenie left the trays with his meals on them outside the door as usual, but he wasn't eating anything, or drinking anything either – or not that we could tell. So then we had to kick down the door."

"You and Reenie?"

"Reenie's boyfriend came – Ron Hincks – the one she's going to marry. He kicked it down. And Father was lying on the floor. He must have been there for at least two days, the doctor said. He looked awful."

I hadn't realized that Ron Hincks was Reenie's boyfriend – indeed her fiancé. How long had that been going on, and how had I missed it?

"Was he dead, is that what you're saying?"

"I didn't think so at first, because his eyes were open. But he was dead all right. He looked . . . I can't tell you how he looked. As if he was listening, to something that had startled him. He looked *watchful*."

"Was he shot?" I don't know why I asked this.

"No. He was just dead. It was put in the paper as natural causes – *suddenly, of natural causes*, is what it said – and Reenie told Mrs. Hillcoate that it was natural causes all right, because drinking certainly was like second nature to Father, and judging from all the empty bottles he'd downed enough booze to choke a horse."

"He drank himself to death," I said. It wasn't a question. "When was this?"

"It was right after they announced the permanent closing of the factories. That's what killed him. I know it was!"

"What?" I said. "What permanent closing? Which factories?"

"All of them," said Laura. "All of ours. Everything of ours in town. I thought you must have known about it."

"I didn't know," I said.

"Ours have been merged in with Richard's. Everything's been moved to Toronto. It's all Griffen-Chase Royal Consolidated, now." No more *Sons*, in other words. Richard had made a clean sweep of them.

"So that means no jobs," I said. "None here. It's finished. Wiped out."

"They said it was a matter of costs. After the button factory was burned – they said it would take too much to rebuild it."

"Who is *they*?"

"I don't know," said Laura. "Wasn't it Richard?"

"That wasn't the deal," I said. Poor Father – trusting to handshakes and words of honour and unspoken assumptions. It was becoming clear to me that this was not the way things worked any more. Maybe it never had been.

"What deal?" said Laura.

"Never mind."

I'd married Richard for nothing, then – I hadn't saved the factories, and I certainly hadn't saved Father. But there was

Laura, still; she wasn't out on the street. I had to think of that. "Did he leave anything – any letter, any note?"

"No."

"Did you look?"

"Reenie looked," said Laura in a small voice; which meant that she herself hadn't been up to it.

Of course, I thought. Reenie would have looked. And if she had in fact found anything like that, she would have burned it.

Besotted

Father wouldn't have left a note though. He would have been aware of the implications. He wouldn't have wanted a verdict of suicide, because, as it turned out, he'd had some life insurance: he'd been paying into it for years, so no one could accuse him of having fixed it up at the last minute. He'd tied up the money – it was to go straight into a trust, so that only Laura could touch it, and only after she was twenty-one. He must already have distrusted Richard by then, and concluded that leaving any of it to me would have done no good. I was still a minor, and I was Richard's wife. The laws were different then. What was mine was his, to all intents and purposes.

As I've said, I got Father's medals. What were they for? Courage. Bravery under fire. Noble gestures of self-sacrifice. I suppose I was expected to live up to them.

Everyone in town came to the funeral, said Reenie. Well, almost everyone, because there was considerable bitterness in some quarters; but still, he'd been well respected, and by that time they'd known it wasn't him shut down the factories for good like that. They'd known he'd had no part in it – he couldn't stop it, that was all. It was the big interests did him in.

Everyone in town felt sorry for Laura, said Reenie. (*But not for me* was left unspoken. In their view, I'd ended up with the spoils. Such as they were.)

Here are the arrangements Richard made:

Laura would come to live with us. Well, of course she would have to: she couldn't remain at Avilion all by herself, she was only fifteen.

"I could stay with Reenie," said Laura, but Richard said that was out of the question. Reenie was getting married; she wouldn't have time to look after Laura. Laura said she didn't need to be looked after, but Richard only smiled.

"Reenie could come to Toronto," said Laura, but Richard said she didn't want to. (Richard didn't want her to. He and Winifred had already engaged what they considered to be a suitable staff for the running of his household – people who knew the ropes, he said. Which meant they knew Richard's ropes, and Winifred's ropes as well.)

Richard said he had already discussed things with Reenie, and had come to a satisfactory arrangement. Reenie and her new husband would act as custodians for us, he said, and would oversee the repairs – Avilion was falling to pieces, so there were a lot of repairs to be done, beginning with the roof – and that way they would be on hand to prepare the house for us whenever requested, because it was to serve as a summer abode. We would come down to Avilion to go boating and so forth, he said, in the tone of an indulgent uncle. That way, Laura and I would not be deprived of our ancestral home. He said *ancestral home* with a smile. Wouldn't we like that?

Laura did not thank him. She stared at his forehead, with the cultivated blankness she had once used on Mr. Erskine, and I saw we were in for trouble.

Richard and I would return to Toronto by car, he continued, once things were in place. First he needed to meet with Father's lawyers, an occasion at which we need not be present: it would be too harrowing for us, considering recent events, and he wanted to spare us as much as possible. One of these lawyers was a connection by marriage on our mother's side, said Reenie privately – a second cousin's husband – so he'd surely keep an eye out.

Laura would remain at Avilion until she and Reenie had packed up her things; then she would come in to the city on the train, and would be met at the station. She would live with us in our house – there was a spare bedroom that would suit her perfectly, once it had been redecorated. And she would attend – at last – a proper school. St. Cecilia's was the one he had picked, in consultation with Winifred, who knew about such things. Laura might need some extra lessons, but he was sure all of that would work out as time went by. In this way she would be able to gain the benefits, the advantages . . .

"The advantages of what?" said Laura.

"Of your position," said Richard.

"I don't see that I have any position," said Laura.

"What exactly do you mean by that?" said Richard, less indulgently.

"It's Iris who has the position," said Laura. "She's the Mrs. Griffen. I'm just extra."

"I realize you are understandably upset," said Richard stiffly, "considering the unfortunate circumstances, which have been difficult for everyone, but there's no need to be unpleasant. It isn't easy for Iris and myself, either. I am only trying to do the best for you that I can."

"He thinks I'll be in the way," Laura said to me that evening, in the kitchen, where we had gone to seek refuge from Richard. It was upsetting for us to watch him making his lists – what was to be discarded, what repaired, what replaced. To watch, and to be silent. *He acts like he owns the place*, Reenie had said indignantly. *But he does*, I'd replied.

"In the way of what?" I said. "I'm sure that isn't what he meant."

"In the way of him," said Laura. "In the way of the two of you."

"It will all work out for the best," said Reenie. She said this as if by rote. Her voice was exhausted, devoid of conviction, and I saw that there was no further help to be expected from her. In the kitchen that night she looked old, and rather fat, and also defeated. As would presently appear, she was already pregnant with Myra. She'd allowed herself to be swept off her feet. *It's dirt that gets swept, and it's into the dustbin*, she used to say, but she'd violated her own maxims. Her mind must have been on other things, such as whether she would make it to the altar, and if not, what then? Bad times, without a doubt. There were no walls then between sufficiency and disaster: if you slipped you fell, and if you fell you flailed and thrashed and went under. She'd be hard put to make another chance for herself, because even if she went away to have the baby and then gave it up, word would get around and people in town would never forget a thing like that. She might as well hang out a sign: there'd be a lineup around the block. Once a woman was loose, it was seen to that she stayed that way. *Why buy a cow when milk's free*, she must have been thinking.

So she'd given up on us, she'd given us over. For years she'd done what she could, and now she had no more power.

Back in Toronto, I waited for Laura to arrive. The heat wave continued. Sultry weather, damp foreheads, a shower before gin and tonics on the back verandah, overlooking the sere garden. The air like wet fire; everything limp or yellow. There was a fan in the bedroom that sounded like an old man with a wooden foot climbing the stairs: a breathless wheezing, a clunk, a wheezing. In the heavy, starless nights I stared up at the ceiling while Richard went on with what he was doing.

He was besotted with me, he said. *Besotted* – as if he were drunk. As if he would never feel the way he did about me if he were sober and in his right mind.

I looked at myself in the mirror, wondering, What is it about me? What is it that is so besotting? The mirror was full-length: in it I tried to catch the back view of myself, but of course you never can. You can never see yourself the way you are to someone else – to a man looking at you, from behind, when you don't know – because in a mirror your own head is always cranked around over your shoulder. A coy, inviting pose. You can hold up another mirror to see the back view, but then what you see is what so many painters have loved to paint – Woman Looking In Mirror, said to be an allegory of vanity. Though it is unlikely to be vanity, but the reverse: a search for flaws. *What is it about me?* can so easily be construed as *What is wrong with me?*

Richard said women could be divided into apples and pears, according to the shapes of their bottoms. I was a pear, he said, but an unripe one. That was what he liked about me – my greenness, my hardness. In the bottom department, I think he meant, but possibly all the way through.

After my showers, my removal of bristles, my brushings and combings, I was now careful to remove any hairs from the floor. I would lift the little wads of hair from the drains of tub or sink and flush them down the toilet, because Richard had casually remarked that women were always leaving hair around. Like shedding animals, was the implication.

How did he know? How did he know, about the pears and the apples and the shed hair? Who were these women, these other women? Aside from a surface curiosity, I did not much care.

I tried to avoid thinking about Father, and the way he had died, and what he might have been up to before that event, and about how he must have felt, and about everything Richard had not seen fit to tell me.

Winifred was a very busy bee. Despite the heat she looked cool, swathed in light and airy draperies like some parody of a fairy godmother. Richard kept saying how marvellous she was and how much work and bother she was sparing me, but she made me increasingly nervous. She was in and out of the house constantly; I never knew when she might appear, popping her head around the door with a brisk smile. My only refuge was the bathroom, because there I could turn the lock without seeming unduly rude. She was overseeing the rest of the decoration, ordering the furniture for Laura's room. (A dressing table with a frilled skirt, in a pink floral print, with curtains and bedspread to match. A mirror with a white curlicue frame, picked out in gold. It was just the thing for Laura, didn't I agree? I didn't, but there was no point in saying so.)

She was also planning the garden; she'd already sketched out several designs – just a few little ideas, she said, thrusting the pieces of paper at me, then withdrawing them, replacing them carefully in the folder already bulging with her other little ideas. A fountain would be lovely, she said – something French, but it would have to be authentic. Didn't I think?

I wished Laura would come. The date of her arrival had been postponed three times now – she wasn't packed yet, she'd had a cold, she'd lost the ticket. I talked to her on the white phone; her voice was restrained, remote.

The two servants had been installed, a grouchy cook-housekeeper and a large jowly man who was passed off as the gardener/chauffeur. Their name was Murgatroyd, and they were said to be husband and wife, but they looked like brother and sister. They regarded me with distrust, which I reciprocated. During the days, when Richard was at his office and Winifred was ubiquitous, I tried to get away from the house as much as I could. I would say I was going downtown – shopping, I'd say, which was an acceptable version of how I should be spending my time. I would have myself dropped off at Simpsons department store by the chauffeur, telling him I would take a taxi home. Then I would go inside, make a quick purchase: stockings and gloves were always convincing as evidence of my zeal. Then I would walk the length of the store and exit by the opposite door.

I resumed my former habits – the aimless wandering, the examination of display windows, of theatre posters. I even went to the movies, by myself; I was no longer susceptible to groping men, who had lost their aura of demonic magic, now that I knew what they had in mind. I wasn't interested in more of the same – the same obsessive clutching and fumbling. *Keep your hands to yourself or I'll scream* worked well enough as long as you were prepared to follow it up. They seemed to know I was. Joan Crawford was my favourite movie star at that time. Wounded eyes, lethal mouth.

Sometimes I went to the Royal Ontario Museum. I looked at suits of armour, stuffed animals, antique musical instruments. This did not take me very far. Or I would go to Diana Sweets for a soda or a cup of coffee: it was a genteel tea room across from the department stores, much patronized by ladies, and I was unlikely to be bothered by stray men there. Or I would walk through Queen's Park, quickly and with purpose. If too slowly, a man was bound to appear. *Flypaper*, Reenie used to call some young woman or other. *She has to scrape them off.* Once, a man exposed himself, right in front of me, at eye level. (I'd made the mistake of sitting on a secluded bench, on the grounds of the university.) He wasn't a tramp either, he was quite well dressed. "I'm sorry," I said to him. "I'm just not interested." He looked so disappointed. Most likely he'd wanted me to faint.

In theory I could go wherever I liked, in practice there were invisible barriers. I kept to the main streets, the more prosperous areas: even within those confines, there were not really very many places where I felt unconstrained. I watched other people – not the men so much, the women. Were they married?

Where were they going? Did they have jobs? I couldn't tell much from looking at them, except the price of their shoes.

I felt as if I'd been picked up and set down in a foreign country, where everyone spoke a different language.

Sometimes there would be couples, arm in arm – laughing, happy, amorous. Victims of an enormous fraud, and at the same time its perpetrators, or so I felt. I stared at them with rancour.

Then one day – it was a Thursday – I saw Alex Thomas. He was on the other side of the street, waiting for the light to change. It was Queen Street, at Yonge. He was the worse for wear – he had on a blue shirt, like a worker, and a battered hat – but it was him all right. He looked illuminated, as if a shaft of light were falling on him from some invisible source, rendering him frighteningly visible. Surely everyone else on the street was looking at him too – surely they all knew who he was! Any minute now they would recognize him, they'd shout, they'd give chase.

My first impulse was to warn him. But then I knew that the warning must be for both of us, because whatever trouble he was involved in, I was suddenly involved in it as well.

I could have paid no attention. I could have turned away. That would have been wise. But such wisdom was not available to me then.

I stepped down off the curb and began to cross towards him. The light changed again: I was stranded in the middle of the street. Cars honked their horns; there were shouts; the traffic surged. I didn't know whether to go back or forward.

He turned then, and at first I was not sure he could see me. I stretched out my hand, like a drowning person beseeching rescue. In that moment I had already committed treachery in my heart.

Was this a betrayal, or was it an act of courage? Perhaps both. Neither one involves forethought: such things take place in an instant, in an eyeblink. This can only be because they have been rehearsed by us already, over and over, in silence and darkness; in such silence, such darkness, that we are ignorant of them ourselves. Blind but sure-footed, we step forward as if into a remembered dance.

Sunnyside

Three days after this, Laura was due to arrive. I had myself driven down to Union Station to meet the train, but she wasn't on it. She wasn't at Avilion either: I phoned Reenie to check, provoking an outburst: she'd always known something like this would happen, just because of the way Laura was. She'd gone with Laura to the train, she'd shipped off the trunk and everything as instructed, she'd taken every precaution. She should have accompanied her all the way, and now look! Some white slaver had made off with her.

Laura's trunk turned up on schedule, but Laura herself appeared to have vanished. Richard was more upset than I would have predicted. He was afraid she'd been spirited away by unknown forces – people who had it in for him. It could be the Reds, or else an unscrupulous business rival: such twisted men existed. Criminals, he hinted, who were in cahoots with all sorts of folks – folks who'd stop at nothing to assert undue influence on him, because of his growing political connections. Next thing you knew we'd get a blackmail note.

He was suspicious of many elements, that August; he said we had to keep a sharp lookout. There had been a big march on Ottawa, in July – thousands, tens of thousands of men who claimed to be unemployed, and who were demanding jobs and fair pay, egged on by subversives bent on overthrowing the government.

"I bet young what's-his-name was mixed up in it," said Richard, looking at me narrowly.

"Young who?" I said, glancing out the window.

"Pay attention, darling. Laura's pal. The dark one. The young thug who burned down your father's factory."

"It didn't burn down," I said. "They put it out in time. Anyway, they never proved it."

"He skedaddled," said Richard. "Ran like a rabbit. That's proof enough for me."

The marchers on Ottawa had been trapped through a clever backroom stratagem suggested – or so he said – by Richard himself, who moved in high circles these days. The leaders of the march had been decoyed to Ottawa for "official talks," and the whole kit and kaboodle had been stalled in Regina. The talks came to nothing, as planned, but then there had been riots: the subversives had stirred things up, the crowd had gone out of control, men had been killed and injured. It was the Communists who were behind it, because they had a finger in every dubious pie, and who was to say that waylaying Laura was not one of the pies?

I thought Richard was working himself up unduly. I was upset too, but I believed Laura had merely wandered off – been distracted somehow. That would be more like her. She'd got off at the wrong station, forgotten our telephone number, lost her way.

Winifred said we should check the hospitals: Laura might have been taken ill, or had an accident. But she was not in a hospital.

After two days of worrying we informed the police, and soon after that, despite Richard's precautions, the story hit the papers. Reporters besieged the sidewalk outside our house. They took pictures, if only of our doors and windows; they telephoned; they begged for interviews. What they wanted was a scandal. "Prominent Socialite Schoolgirl in Love Nest." "Union Station Site of Grisly Remains." They wanted to be told that Laura had run away with a married man, or had been abducted by anarchists, or had been found dead in a checked suitcase in the baggage room. Sex or death, or both together – that was what they had in mind.

Richard said we should be gracious but uninformative. He said there was no point in antagonizing the newspapers unduly, because reporters were vindictive little vermin who would hold a grudge for years and pay you back later, when you were least expecting it. He said he would handle things.

First he put it about that I was on the brink of collapse, and asked that my privacy and my delicate health be respected. That made the reporters back off some; they assumed of course that I was pregnant, which still counted for something in those days, and was also thought to scramble a woman's brain. Then he let it be known that there would be a reward for information, though he did not say how much. On the eighth day there was an anonymous phone call: Laura was not dead, but was working in a waffle booth at the Sunnyside Amusement Park. The caller claimed to have recognized her, from the description of her that was in all the papers.

It was decided that Richard and I would drive down together to reclaim her. Winifred said Laura was most likely in a state of delayed shock, considering Father's unseemly death and her discovery of the body. Anyone would be disturbed after such an ordeal, and Laura was a girl with a nervous temperament. Most likely she hardly knew what she was doing or saying. Once we got her back, she must be given a strong sedative and carted off to the doctor.

But the most important thing, said Winifred, was that not a word of all this must leak out. A fifteen-year-old running away from home like that – it would reflect badly on the family. People might think she'd been mistreated, and this could become a serious impediment. To Richard and his future political prospects, was what she meant.

Sunnyside was where people went in summer, then. Not

people like Richard and Winifred – it was too rowdy for them, too sweaty. Merry-go-rounds, Red Hots, root beer, shooting galleries, beauty contests, public bathing: in a word, vulgar diversions. Richard and Winifred would not have wished to be in such close proximity to other people's armpits, or to those who counted their money in dimes. Though I don't know why I'm being so holier-than-thou, because I wouldn't have wanted it either.

It's all gone now, Sunnyside – swept away by twelve lanes of asphalt highway sometime in the fifties. Dismantled long ago, like so much else. But that August it was still in full swing. We drove down in Richard's coupé, but we had to leave the car at some distance because of the traffic, and the throngs jostling along the sidewalks and the dusty roads.

It was a foul day, torrid and hazy; hotter than the hinges of Hades, as Walter would say now. Above the lakeshore there was an invisible but almost palpable fog, composed of stale perfume and the oil from tanned bare shoulders, mixed with the steam from the cooking wieners and the burnt tang of spun sugar. Walking into the crowd was like sinking into a stew – you became an ingredient, you took on a certain flavour. Even Richard's forehead was damp, beneath the brim of his Panama.

From overhead came the squealing of metal on metal, and an ominous rumbling, and a chorus of female screams: the roller coaster. I had never been on one, and gaped up at it until Richard said, "Close your mouth, darling, you'll catch flies." I heard an odd story later – who from? Winifred, no doubt; it was the sort of thing she used to toss out to show she knew what really went on in life, in low life, behind the scenes. The story was that girls who'd got themselves in trouble – Winifred's term, as if these girls had managed the trouble all by themselves – that these troubled girls would go on the roller coaster at Sunnyside, hoping to start an abortion that way.

Winifred laughed: *Of course it didn't work*, she said, *and if it had, what would they have done? With all the blood, I mean? Way up in the air like that? Just imagine!*

What I pictured when she said this was those red streamers they used to toss from ocean liners at the moment of sailing, cascading down over the spectators below; or a series of lines, long thick lines of red, scrolling out from the roller coaster and from the girls in it like paint thrown from a bucket. Like long scrawls of vermilion cloud. Like skywriting.

Now I think: but if writing, what kind of writing? Diaries, novels, autobiographies? Or simply graffiti: *Mary Loves John*. But John does not love Mary, or not enough. Not enough to save her from emptying herself out like that, scribbling all over everyone in such red, red letters.

An old story.

But on that August day in 1935 I had not yet heard about abortions. If the word had been said in my presence, which it was not, I would have had no idea what it meant. Not even Reenie had mentioned it: dark hints about kitchen-table butchers was about as far as she had gone, and Laura and I – hiding on the back stairs, eavesdropping – had thought she was talking about cannibalism, which we'd found intriguing.

The roller coaster screamed past, the shooting gallery made a noise like popcorn. Other people laughed. I found myself becoming hungry, but could not suggest a snack; it would not have been apropos right then, and the food was beyond the pale. Richard was frowning like destiny; he held me by the elbow, steering me through the crowd. He had his other hand in his pocket: this place, he said, was bound to be crawling with light-fingered thieves.

We made our way to the waffle booth. Laura was not in view, but Richard did not wish to speak with Laura first, he knew better than that. He liked to fix things from the top down, always, if possible. So he asked to have a private word with the waffle-booth owner, a large dark-chinned man who reeked of stale butter. The man knew at once why Richard was there. He stepped away from his booth, casting a furtive glance back over his shoulder.

Was the waffle-booth owner aware that he'd been harbouring a juvenile runaway? asked Richard. God forbid! said the man, in horror. Laura had got round him – said she was nineteen. She was a hard worker though, she'd worked like a horse, keeping the joint clean, lending a hand with the waffles when things got real busy. Where had she been sleeping? The man was vague about that. Someone around here had given her a bed, but it wasn't him. Nor was there any funny business, we had to believe it, or not that he knew about. She was a good girl and he was a happily married man, unlike some around here. He'd felt sorry for her – thought maybe she was in some kind of trouble. He had a soft spot for nice kids like her. Matter of fact, it was him who'd made the call, and not just for the reward either; he'd figured she'd be better off back with her family, right?

Here he looked at Richard expectantly. Money changed hands, though somehow – I gathered – not quite so much money as the man had expected. Then Laura was summoned. She didn't protest. She took one look at us and decided against it. "Thanks for everything, anyway," she said to the waffle man. She shook hands with him. She didn't realize he'd cashed her in.

Richard and I each held one of her elbows; we walked her back through Sunnyside. I felt like a traitor. Richard installed her in the car, between the two of us. I put a steadying arm around her shoulder. I was angry with her, but knew I had to be comforting. She smelled of vanilla, and of hot sweet syrup, and of unwashed hair.

Once we got her into the house, Richard summoned Mrs. Murgatroyd and ordered up a glass of iced tea for Laura. She didn't drink it though; she sat in the dead centre of the sofa, knees together, rigid, stony-faced, her eyes like slate.

Did she have any idea of how much anxiety and commotion she had caused? said Richard. No. Did she care? No answer. He certainly hoped she wouldn't try anything of the kind again. No answer. Because he now stood *in loco parentis*, so to speak, and he had a responsibility towards her, and he had every intention of fulfilling that responsibility, whatever it might cost him. And since nothing was a one-way street, he expected her to realize that she had a responsibility towards him as well – towards *us*, he added – which was to behave herself, and to do as required, within reason. Did she understand that?

"Yes," said Laura. "I understand what you mean."

"I certainly hope so," said Richard. "I certainly hope you do, young lady."

The *young lady* made me nervous. It was a reproach, as if there were something wrong with being young, and also with being a lady. If so, it was a reproach that included me. "What did you eat?" I said, for a distraction.

"Candy apples," said Laura. "Doughnuts from the Downyflake Doughnuts, they were cheaper the second day. The people there were really nice. Red Hots."

"Oh dear," I said, with a weak, deprecating little smile at Richard.

"That's what other people eat," said Laura, "in real life," and I began to see, a little, what the attraction of Sunnyside must have been for her. It was *other people* – those people who had always been and who would continue to be *other*, insofar as Laura was concerned. She longed to serve them, these other people. She longed, in some way, to join them. But she never could. It was the soup kitchen in Port Ticonderoga all over again.

"Laura, why did you do it?" I said as soon as we were alone. (*How did you do it?* had a simple answer: she'd got off the train in London and changed her ticket for a later train. At least she hadn't gone to some other city: we might never have found her then.)

"Richard killed Father," she said. "I can't live in his house. It's wrong."

"That's not really fair," I said. "Father died because of an unfortunate combination of circumstances." I felt ashamed of myself for saying that: it sounded like Richard.

"It may not be fair but it's true. Underneath, it's true," she said. "Anyway, I wanted a job."

"But why?"

"To show that we – to show that I could. That I, that we didn't have to . . ." She looked away from me, chewed on her finger.

"Have to what?"

"You know," she said. "All of this." She waved her hand at the frilled dressing table, the matching floral curtains. "I went to the nuns first. I went to the Star of the Sea Convent."

Oh God, I thought, not the nuns again. I thought we'd put paid to the nuns. "And what did they say?" I asked, in a kindly, disinterested manner.

"It was no good," said Laura. "They were very nice to me, but they said no. It wasn't just not being a Catholic. They said I didn't have a true vocation, I was just evading my duties. They said if I wanted to serve God, I should do it in the life to which he has called me." A pause. "But what life?" she said. "I have no life!"

She cried then, and I put my arms around her, the time-worn gesture from when she was little. *Just stop howling.* If I'd had a lump of brown sugar I would have given it to her, but we were well past the brown-sugar stage by then. Sugar was not going to help.

"How can we ever get out of here?" she wailed. "Before it's too late?" At least she had the sense to be frightened; she had more sense than I did. But I thought it was just adolescent melodrama. "Too late for what?" I asked her gently. A deep breath was all that was called for; a deep breath, some calm, some stocktaking. There was no need to panic.

I thought I could cope with Richard, with Winifred. I thought I could live like a mouse in the castle of the tigers, by creeping around out of sight inside the walls; by staying quiet, by keeping my head down. No: I give myself too much credit. I didn't see the danger. I didn't even know they were tigers. Worse: I didn't know I might become a tiger myself. I didn't know Laura might become one, given the proper circumstances. Anyone might, for that matter.

"Look on the bright side," I said to Laura in my best soothing tone. I patted her back. "I'll get you a cup of warm milk and then you can have a good long sleep. You'll feel better tomorrow." But she cried and cried, and would not be comforted.

Xanadu

Last night I dreamt I was wearing my costume from the Xanadu ball. I was supposed to be an Abyssinian maiden – the damsel with the dulcimer. It was green satin, that costume: a little bolero jacket with gold spangle trim, showing a lot of cleavage and midriff; green satin undershorts, translucent pantaloons. Lots of fake gold coins, worn as necklaces and looped over the forehead. A small, jaunty turban with a crescent pin. A nose veil. Some tawdry circus designer's idea of the East.

I thought I looked pretty nifty in it, until I realized, looking down at my drooping belly, my enlarged blue-veined knuckles, my shrivelled arms, that I was not the age I was then, but the age I am now.

I wasn't at the ball, however. I was all alone, or so it seemed at first, in the ruined glass conservatory at Avilion. Empty pots were strewn here and there; others, not empty, filled with dry earth and dead plants. One of the stone sphinxes was lying on the floor, tipped on its side, defaced with Magic Marker – names, initials, crude drawings. There was a hole in the glass roof. The place stank of cat.

The main house behind me was dark, deserted, everyone in it gone away. I'd been left behind in this ridiculous fancy dress. It was night, with a fingernail moon. By its light I could see that there was indeed a single plant left alive: a glossy sort of bush, with one white flower. *Laura*, I said. From over in the shadows, a man laughed.

Not much of a nightmare, you'd say. Wait till you try it. I woke up desolate.

Why does the mind do such things? Turn on us, rend us, dig

the claws in. If you get hungry enough, they say, you start eating your own heart. Maybe it's much the same.

Nonsense. It's all chemicals. I need to take steps, about these dreams. There must be a pill.

More snow today. Just looking out the window at it makes my fingers ache. I write at the kitchen table, as slowly as if engraving. The pen is heavy, hard to push, like a nail scratching on cement.

Autumn, 1935. The heat receded, the cold advanced. Frost on fallen leaves, then on leaves that were not fallen. Then on windows. I took joy in such details then. I liked breathing in. The space inside my lungs was all my own.

Meanwhile, things continued.

What was now referred to by Winifred as "Laura's little escapade" was covered up as much as possible. Richard told Laura if she talked about it to anyone else, especially anyone at her school, he would be bound to hear about it and would consider it a personal affront, as well as an attempt at sabotage. He'd fixed things up with the press: an alibi had been provided by the Newton-Dobbses, a couple of his highly placed pals – the Mr. was something in one of the railroads – who were prepared to swear that Laura had been with them at their place in Muskoka the whole time. It had been a last-minute holiday arrangement, and Laura thought the Newton-Dobbses had telephoned us and the Newton-Dobbses thought Laura had, and it was all a simple misunderstanding, and they hadn't realized Laura had been considered missing because while on vacation they never paid any attention to the news.

A likely story. But people believed it, or had to pretend they did. I suppose the Newton-Dobbses were spreading the real story around among their twenty closest friends, hush-hush and for your ears only, which was what Winifred would have done in their place, gossip being a commodity like any other. But at least it never hit the papers.

Laura was bundled up in an itchy kilt and a plaid tie and sent off to St. Cecilia's. She made no secret of detesting it. She said she didn't have to go there; she said that now she'd got one job she could get another one. She said these things to me, when Richard was present. She would not speak directly to him.

She was chewing her fingers, she was not eating enough, she was too thin. I became very worried about her, as I was expected to become, and, in fairness, as I should have been. But Richard said he was tired of this hysterical nonsense, and as for a job, he didn't want to hear anything more about it. Laura was far too young to be out on her own; she would get involved in something unsavoury, because the woods were full of those who made a business of preying on silly young girls like her. If she didn't like her school, she could be sent to another one, far away, in a different city, and if she ran away from that one he would put her into a Home for Wayward Girls along with all the other moral delinquents, and if that didn't do the trick there was always a clinic. A private clinic, with bars on the windows: if it was sackcloth and ashes she wanted, that would certainly fill the bill. She was a minor, he was in authority, and make no mistake about it, he would do exactly as he said. As she knew — as everyone knew — he was a man of his word.

His eyes tended to bulge out when he was angry, and they were bulging out now, but he said all of this in a calm, believable tone, and Laura believed him, and was intimidated. I tried to intervene — these threats were too harsh, he didn't understand about Laura and the way she took things literally — but he told me to keep out of it. What was needed was a firm hand. Laura had been mollycoddled enough. It was time for her to shape up.

Over the weeks, an uneasy truce was established. I tried to

arrange things in the house so that the two of them never collided. Ships in the night, was what I hoped for.

Winifred had put in her oar over this, of course. She must have told Richard to take a stand, because Laura was the kind of girl who would bite the hand that fed her unless a muzzle was applied.

Richard consulted Winifred about everything, because she was the one who sympathized with him, propped him up, encouraged him generally. She was the one who propped him up socially, who promoted his interests in what she considered the right quarters. When would he make his bid for Parliament? Not quite yet, she'd whisper into whatever ear she was bending – the time was not yet ripe – but soon. They'd both decided that Richard was the man of the future, and that the woman standing behind him – didn't every successful man have one of those? – was her.

It certainly wasn't me. Our relative positions were now clear, hers and mine; or they'd always been clear to her, but they were now becoming clear to me as well. She was necessary to Richard, I on the other hand could always be replaced. My job was to open my legs and shut my mouth.

If that sounds brutal, it was. But it wasn't out of the ordinary.

Winifred had to keep me busy during daylight hours: she didn't want me loopy with boredom, she didn't want me going off the deep end. She put a good deal of thought into cooking up meaningless tasks for me, then rearranging my time and space so I would be at liberty to perform them. These tasks were never too exacting, because she made no secret of her opinion that I was a bit of a dumb bunny. I in my turn did nothing to discourage this view.

Thus the Downtown Foundlings' Crèche charity ball, of which she was the convenor. She put me on the list of organizers, not only to keep me hopping but because it would reflect well on Richard. "Organizers" was a joke, she didn't think I was capable of organizing my own shoelaces, so what cinder-sweeping chore could I be given? Envelope-addressing, she decided. She was right, I could do that. I was even good at it. I didn't have to think about it, and could spend the mental time elsewhere. ("Thank the Lord she has *one* talent," I could hear her telling the Billies and Charlies, at bridge. "Oh, I forgot – two!" Gales of laughter.)

The Downtown Foundlings' Crèche, in aid of slum children, was Winifred's best thing, or at least the charity ball was. It was a costume ball – such functions mostly were, because people at that time liked costumes. They liked them almost as much as they liked uniforms. Both served the same end: to avoid being who you were, you could pretend to be someone else. You could become bigger and more powerful, or more alluring and mysterious, just by putting on exotic clothes. Well, there was something to it.

Winifred had a committee for the ball, but everyone knew she made all the big decisions herself. She held the hoops, others jumped through them. It was she who'd picked the theme for 1936 – "Xanadu." The rival Beaux Arts Ball had recently done "Tamurlane in Samarkand," and it had been a great success. Eastern themes couldn't miss, and surely everyone had been made to memorize "Kubla Khan" at school, so even lawyers – even doctors – even *bankers* would know what Xanadu was. Their wives would know as a matter of course.

In Xanadu did Kubla Khan
A stately pleasure-dome decree:
Where Alph, the sacred river, ran
Through caverns measureless to man
    Down to a sunless sea.

Winifred had the entire poem typed out and mimeographed and distributed to our committee – to get the ideas percolating, she said – and any suggestions from us were more than welcome, though we knew she had the entire thing mapped out in her head already. The poem would appear on the engraved invitation as well – gold lettering, with a gold-and-cerulean border of Arabic writing. Did anyone understand such writing? No, but it looked just lovely.

These functions were by invitation only. You were invited and then you paid through the nose, but the circle was very tight. Who was on the list became a matter of anxious anticipation, though only for those in doubt about their status. To expect an invitation and then not to receive one was a foretaste of Purgatory. I expect many tears were shed over such things, but in secret – in that world, you could never let it appear that you cared.

The beauty of Xanadu was (said Winifred, after she had read out the poem in her whisky voice – read it excellently, I'll give her that) – the *beauty* of it was that with such a theme you could be as revealing or concealing as you might wish. The corpulent could swathe themselves in rich brocades, the svelte could come as slave girls or Persian dancers and show off everything but the kitchen sink. Gauzy skirts, bangles, tinkling ankle chains – the scope was practically infinite, and of course men loved to dress up as pashas and pretend they had harems. Though she doubted that she could talk anyone into playing the eunuchs, she added, to appreciative tittering.

Laura was too young for this ball. Winifred was planning a début for her, a rite of passage that had not yet taken place, and until it did she was not considered eligible. However, she took quite an interest in the proceedings. I was very relieved to have her once more taking an interest in something. Certainly she was not taking an interest in her schoolwork: her marks had been abysmal.

Correction: it wasn't the proceedings she took an interest in, it was the poem. I knew it already, from Miss Violence, from Avilion, but Laura hadn't bothered much about it then. Now she read it over and over.

What was a demon-lover, she wanted to know? Why was the sea sunless, why was the ocean lifeless? Why did the sunny pleasure-dome have caves of ice? What was Mount Abora, and why was the Abyssinian maid singing about it? Why were the ancestral voices prophesying war?

I didn't know the answers to any of these questions. I know all of them now. Not the answers of Samuel Taylor Coleridge – I'm not sure he had any answers, since he was hopped up on drugs at the time – but my own answers. Here they are, for what they're worth.

The sacred river is alive. It flows to the lifeless ocean, because that's where all things that are alive end up. The lover is a demon-lover because he isn't there. The sunny pleasure-dome has caves of ice because that's what pleasure-domes have – after a while they become very cold, and after that they melt, and then where are you? All wet. Mount Abora was the Abyssinian maid's home, and she was singing about it because she couldn't get back to it. The ancestral voices were prophesying war because ancestral voices never shut up, and they hate to be wrong, and war is a sure thing, sooner or later.

Correct me if I'm wrong.

The snow fell, softly at first, then in hard pellets that stung the skin like needles. The sun set in the afternoon, the sky changed from washed blood to skim milk. Smoke poured from the chimneys, from the furnaces stoked with coal. The bread-wagon horses left piles of steaming brown buns on the street which then froze solid. Children threw them at one another. The clocks struck midnight, over and over, every midnight a deep blue-black riddled with icy stars, the moon white bone. I looked out the bedroom window, down to the sidewalk, through the branches of the chestnut tree. Then I turned out the light.

The Xanadu ball was the second Saturday in January. My costume had come that morning, in a box with armfuls of tissue paper. The smart thing to do was to rent your costume from Malabar's, because to have one specially made would be displaying too much of an effort. Now it was almost six o'clock and I was trying it on. Laura was in my room: she would often do her homework there, or make a show of doing it. "What are you supposed to be?" she said.

"The Abyssinian Maid," I said. What I would do for a dulcimer I wasn't yet sure. Perhaps a banjo, with ribbons added. Then I remembered that the only banjo I knew about was back at Avilion, in the attic, left over from my dead uncles. I would have to skip the dulcimer.

I didn't expect Laura to tell me I looked pretty, or nice even. She never did that: *pretty* and *nice* were not categories of thought for her. This time she said, "You aren't very Abyssinian. Abyssinians aren't supposed to be blonde."

"I can't help the colour of my hair," I said. "It's Winifred's fault. She should have chosen Vikings or something."

"Why are they all afraid of him?" said Laura.

"Afraid of who?" I said. (I hadn't considered the fear in this poem, only the pleasure. The *pleasure-dome*. The pleasure-dome was where I really lived now – where I had my true being, unknown to those around me. With walls and towers girdled round, so nobody else could get in.)

"Listen," she said. She recited, with her eyes closed:

> Could I revive within me
> Her symphony and song,
> To such a deep delight 'twould win me,
> That with music loud and long,
> I would build that dome in air,
> That sunny dome! those caves of ice!
> And all who heard should see them there,
> And all should cry, Beware! Beware!
> His flashing eyes, his floating hair!
> Weave a circle round him thrice,
> And close your eyes with holy dread,
> For he on honey-dew hath fed,
> And drunk the milk of Paradise.

"See, they're afraid of him," she said, "but why? Why *Beware*?"

"Really, Laura, I have no idea," I said. "It's just a poem. You can't always tell what poems mean. Maybe they think he's crazy."

"It's because he's too happy," said Laura. "He's drunk the milk of Paradise. It frightens people when you're too happy, in that way. Isn't that why?"

"Laura, don't keep *at* me," I said. "I don't know everything, I'm not a professor."

Laura was sitting on the floor, in her school kilt. She sucked on her knuckle, staring up at me, disappointed. I was disappointing her frequently of late. "I saw Alex Thomas the other day," she said.

I turned away quickly, adjusted my veil in the mirror. It was a fairly poor effect, the green satin: some Hollywood vamp in a desert movie. I comforted myself with the thought that everyone else would look equally faux. "Alex Thomas? Really?" I said. I should have displayed more surprise.

"Well, aren't you glad?"

"Glad about what?"

"Glad he's alive," she said. "Glad they haven't caught him."

"Of course I'm glad," I said. "But don't say anything to anyone. You wouldn't want them to track him down."

"You don't need to tell me that. I'm not a baby. That's why I didn't wave at him."

"Did he see you?" I said.

"No. He was just walking along the street. He had his coat collar up and his scarf over his chin, but I knew it was him. He had his hands in his pockets."

At the mention of hands, of pockets, a sharp pang went through me. "What street was this?"

"Our street," she said. "He was on the other side, looking at the houses. I think he was looking for us. He must know we live around here."

"Laura," I said, "have you still got a crush on Alex Thomas? Because if you do, you should try to get over it."

"I don't have a crush on him," she said with scorn. "I never had a crush. *Crush* is a horrible word. It really stinks." She'd become less pious since going to school, and her language had become a good deal stronger. *Stinks* was in the ascendant.

"Whatever you want to call it, you should give it up. It's just not possible," I said gently. "It will only make you unhappy."

Laura put her arms around her knees. "Unhappy," she said. "What on earth do you know about *unhappy*?"

VIII

He's moved again, which is just as well. She hated that place out by the Junction. She didn't like going there, and in any case it was so far, and so cold then: every time she got to it her teeth were chattering. She hated the narrow cheerless room, the stink of old cigarettes because you couldn't open the stuck window, the sordid little shower in the corner, that woman she'd meet on the stairs – a woman like a downtrodden peasant in some musty old novel, you kept expecting to see her with a bundle of sticks on her back. The sullen insolent stare she'd give, as if picturing exactly what would go on behind his door once it was closed. A stare of envy, but also of spite.

Good riddance to all of that.

Now the snow has melted, though a few grey smudges of it remain in the shadows. The sun is warm, there's the smell of damp earth and stirring roots and the sodden vestiges of last winter's discarded newspapers, blurred and illegible. In the better sections of the city the daffodils are out, and, in a few front gardens where there's no shade, there are tulips, red and orange. A note of promise, as the gardening column says; though even now, in late April, it snowed the other day – big white sloppy flakes, a freakish blizzard.

She's hidden her hair under a kerchief, worn a navy blue coat, the closest she could get to sombre. He said it would be best. In the nooks and corners down here, tomcat scents and vomit, the reek of crated chickens. Horse dung on the road, from the mounted policemen who keep an eye out, not for thieves but for agitators – nests of foreign Reds, whispering together like rats in straw, six to a bed no doubt, sharing their women, incubating their warped, intricate plots. Emma

Goldman, exiled from the States, is said to live somewhere nearby.

Blood on the sidewalk, a man with a bucket and brush. She steps fastidiously around the wet pink puddle. It's a region of kosher butchers; also of tailors, of wholesale furriers. And sweatshops, no doubt. Rows of immigrant women hunched over machines, their lungs filling with lint.

The clothes on your back come off somebody else's, he'd said to her once. Yes, she'd replied lightly, but I look better in them. Then added with some anger, What do you want me to *do*? What do you want *me* to do? Do you seriously think I have any power?

She stops at a greengrocer's, buys three apples. Not very good apples, last season's, their skins softly wrinkling, but she feels she needs a peace offering of some kind. The woman takes one of the apples away from her, points out a punky brown spot, substitutes a better apple. All this without speaking. Meaningful nods and gap-toothed smiles.

Men in long black coats, wide black hats, small quick-eyed women. Shawls, long skirts. Broken verbs. They don't look directly at you but they don't miss much. She's conspicuous, a giantess. Her legs right out in the open.

Here's the button store, just where he said. She stops a moment to look in the window. Fancy buttons, satin ribbons, braid, rickrack, sequins – raw material for the dreamland adjectives of fashion copy. Someone's fingers, right around here, must have sewn the ermine trim on her white chiffon evening cape. The contrast of fragile veil and rank animal pelt, that's what appeals to the gentlemen. Delicate flesh, then the shrubbery.

His new room is above a baker's. Around to the side, up the stairs, in a haze of a smell she likes. But dense, overpowering – yeast fermenting, going straight to her head like warm helium. She hasn't seen him for too long. Why has she kept away?

He's there, he opens the door.

I brought you some apples, she says.

After a while the objects of this world take shape around her once more. There's his typewriter, precarious on the tiny washstand. The blue suitcase is beside it, topped with the displaced washbasin. Shirt crumpled on the floor. Why is it that tumbled cloth always signifies desire? With its wrenched, impetuous forms. The flames in paintings look like that – like orange fabric, hurled and flung.

They lie in the bed, an enormous carved mahogany structure that almost fills the room. Wedding furniture once, from far away, meant to last a lifetime. *Lifetime*, what a stupid word it seems right now; durability, how useless. She cuts an apple up with his pocket knife, feeds him segments.

If I didn't know better I'd think you were trying to seduce me.

No – I'm just keeping you alive. I'm fattening you up to eat later.

That's a perverse thought, young lady.

Yes. It's yours. Don't tell me you've forgotten the dead women with azure hair and eyes like snake-filled pits? They'd have you for breakfast.

Only if permitted. He reaches for her again. Where have you been keeping yourself? It's been weeks.

Yes. Wait. I need to tell you something.

Is it urgent? he says.

Yes. Not really. No.

The sun declines, the shadows of the curtains move across the bed. Voices on the street outside, unknown languages. I will always remember this, she tells herself. Then: Why am I thinking about memory? It's not *then* yet, it's now. It's not over.

I've thought out the story, she says. I've thought out the next part of it.

Oh? You've got your own ideas?

I've always had my own ideas.

Okay. Let's hear them, he says, grinning.

All right, she says. The last we knew, the girl and the blind man were being taken off to see the Servant of Rejoicing, leader of the barbarian invaders called the People of Desolation, because the two of them were suspected of being divine messengers. Correct me if I'm wrong.

You really pay attention to this stuff? he says wonderingly. You really remember it?

Of course I do. I remember every word you say. They arrive at the barbarian camp, and the blind assassin tells the Servant of Rejoicing he has a message for him from the Invincible One, only it must be delivered in private, with just the girl there. That's because he doesn't want to let her out of his sight.

He can't see. He's blind, remember?

You know what I mean. So the Servant of Rejoicing says that's fine.

He wouldn't just say *That's fine*. He'd make a speech.

I can't do those parts. The three of them go into a tent apart from the others, and the assassin says here's the plan. He will tell them how to get into the city of Sakiel-Norn without any siege or loss of life, I mean their lives. They should send a couple of men, he'll give them the password for the gate – he knows the passwords, remember – and once they're inside, these men should go to the canal and float a rope down it, under the archway. They should tie their end of it to something or other – a stone pillar or something – and then at night a group of soldiers can pull themselves into the city hand over hand by the rope, underwater, and overpower the guard, and open all eight of the gates, and then bingo.

Bingo? he says, laughing. That's not a very Zycronian word.

Well, Bob's your uncle then. After that, they can kill everyone to their heart's content, if that's what they want to do.

A smart trick, he said. Very crafty.

Yes, she said, it's in Herodotus, or something like that is. The fall of Babylon, I think it was.

You've got a surprising amount of bric-à-brac in your head, he says. But I suppose there's a tradeoff? Our two young folks can't go on posing as divine messengers. It's too risky. Sooner or later they'd make a slip, they'd fail, and then they'd be killed. They have to get away.

Yes. I've thought of that. Before the password and the directions are handed over, the blind man says that the two of them must be taken to the foothills of the western mountains, with ample food supplies and so on. He'll say they have to make a sort of pilgrimage there – go up a mountain, get more divine instructions. Only then will he hand over the goods, by which he means the password. That way, if the barbarian attack fails, the two of them will be somewhere none of the citizens of Sakiel-Norn will ever think to follow them.

But they'll be killed by the wolves, he says. And if not by them, by the dead women with curvaceous figures and ruby-red lips. Or she'll be killed, and he'll be forced to fulfill their unnatural desires till the cows come home, poor fellow.

No, she says. That's not what will happen.

Oh no? Says who?

Don't say *oh no*. Says me. Listen – it's this way. The blind assassin hears all rumours, and so he knows the real truth about those women. They aren't actually dead at all. They just put those stories around so they'll be left in peace. Really they're escaped slaves, and other women who've run away to avoid being sold by their husbands or fathers. They aren't all women either – some are men, but they're kind and friendly men. All of them live in caves and herd sheep, and have their own veg-etable gardens. They take turns lurking around the tombs and frightening travellers – howling at them, and so forth – in order to keep up appearances.

In addition to that, the wolves aren't really wolves, they're just sheepdogs who've been trained to impersonate wolves. Really they're very tame, and very loyal.

So these people will take the two fugitives in, and once they've heard their sad story they'll be really nice to them. Then the blind assassin and the girl with no tongue can live in one of the caves, and sooner or later they'll have children who can see and speak, and they'll be very happy.

Meanwhile, all their fellow-citizens are being slaughtered? he says, grinning. You're endorsing treachery to one's country? You've traded the general social good for private contentment?

Well, those were the people that were going to kill them. Their fellow citizens.

Only a few had those intentions – the elite, the top cards in the deck. You'd condemn the rest along with them? You'd have our twosome betray their own people? That's pretty selfish of you.

It's history, she says. It's in *The Conquest of Mexico* – what's his name, Cortez – his Aztec mistress, that's what she did. It's in the Bible too. The harlot Rahab did the same thing, at the fall of Jericho. She helped Joshua's men, and she and her family were spared.

Point taken, he says. But you've broken the rules. You can't just change the undead women into a bunch of folkloric pas-toralists at whim.

You never actually put these women into the story, she says. Not directly. You only told rumours about them. Rumours can be false.

He laughs. True enough. Now here's my version. In the camp of the People of Joy, everything happens as you've said, although with better speeches. Our two young folks are taken to the foothills of the western mountains and left there among the tombs, and then the barbarians proceed to enter the city as per instructions, and they loot and destroy, and massacre the inhabitants. Not one escapes alive. The King is hanged from a tree, the High Priestess is disembowelled, the plotting courtier perishes along with the rest. The innocent slave children, the guild of blind assassins, the sacrificial girls in the Temple – all die. An entire culture is wiped from the universe. No one is left alive who knows how to weave the marvellous carpets, which you'll have to admit is a shame.

Meanwhile the two young people, hand in hand with wandering steps and slow, through the western mountains take their solitary way. They are secure in the faith that they'll soon be discovered by the benevolent vegetable-gardeners, and taken in. But, as you say, rumours don't have to be true, and the blind assassin has got hold of the wrong rumour. The dead women really are dead. Not only that, the wolves really are wolves, and the dead women can whistle them up at will. Our two romantic leads are wolf meat before you can say Jack Robinson.

You're certainly an incurable optimist, she says.

I'm not incurable. But I like my stories to be true to life, which means there have to be wolves in them. Wolves in one form or another.

Why is that so true to life? She turns away from him onto her back, stares up at the ceiling. She's miffed because her own version has been trumped.

All stories are about wolves. All worth repeating, that is. Anything else is sentimental drivel.

All of them?

Sure, he says. Think about it. There's escaping from the wolves, fighting the wolves, capturing the wolves, taming the wolves. Being thrown to the wolves, or throwing others to the wolves so the wolves will eat them instead of you. Running with the wolf pack. Turning into a wolf. Best of all, turning into the head wolf. No other decent stories exist.

I think they do, she says. I think the story about you telling me the story about wolves isn't about wolves.

Don't bet on it, he says. I have a wolf side to me. Come over here.

Wait. There's something I have to ask you.

Okay, shoot, he says lazily. His eyes are closed again, his hand is across her.

Are you ever unfaithful to me?

Unfaithful. What a quaint word.

Never mind my choice of vocabulary, she says. Are you?

No more than you are to me. He pauses. I don't think of it as unfaithfulness.

What do you think of it as? she asks, in a cold voice.

Absent-mindedness, on your part. You close your eyes and forget where you are.

And on yours?

Let's just say you're first among equals.

You really are a bastard.

I'm only telling the truth, he says.

Well, maybe you shouldn't.

Don't get up on your hind legs, he says. I'm only fooling. I couldn't stand to lay a finger on any other woman. I'd sick up.

There's a pause. She kisses him, draws back. I have to go away, she says carefully. I needed to tell you. I didn't want you to wonder where I was.

Away where? What for?

We're going on the maiden voyage. All of us, the whole entourage. He says we can't miss it. He says it's the event of the century.

The century's only a third finished. And even so, I'd have thought that little spot was reserved for the Great War. Champagne by moonlight can hardly compete with millions dead in the trenches. Or how about the influenza epidemic, or . . .

He means the social event.

Oh, pardon me, ma'am. I stand corrected.

What's the matter? I'll only be gone a month – well, more or less. Depending on the arrangements.

He says nothing.

It's not as if I *want* to.

No. I don't suppose you do. Too many seven-course meals to eat, and far too much dancing. A gal could get all wore out.

Don't be like that.

Don't tell me how to be! Don't join the chorus line of folks with plans for my improvement. I'm fucking tired of it. I'll be what I am.

I'm sorry. I'm sorry, I'm sorry, I'm sorry.

I hate it when you grovel. But Jesus you're good at it. I bet you get a lot of practice, on the home front.

Maybe I should leave.

Leave if you feel like it. He rolls over, his back to her. Do whatever you fucking well feel like doing. I'm not your keeper. You don't have to sit up and beg and whine and wag your tail for me.

You don't understand. You don't even try. You don't understand at all what it's like. It's not as if I *enjoy* it.

Right.

Mayfair, July 1936

IN SEARCH OF AN ADJECTIVE
BY J. HERBERT HODGINS

. . . No more beautiful ship ever crossed the sea lanes. She has the lithe, streamlined beauty of the greyhound in her outward construction and she is outfitted, in her interior, with a lavishness of detail and a superiority of décor that make her a masterpiece of comfort, efficiency and luxury. The new ship is a Waldorf-Astoria hotel, afloat.

I have searched for the proper adjective. She has been called marvellous, thrilling, magnificent, regal, stately, majestic and superb. All of these words describe her with a certain feeling of accuracy. But each word, in itself, accounts for no more than a single phase of this "greatest achievement in the history of British shipbuilding." The *Queen Mary* is impossible of description: she must be seen and "felt," and her unique shipboard life participated in.

. . . There was dancing each evening, of course, in the Main Lounge, and here it was difficult to imagine one was at sea. The music, the dance floor, the smartly dressed crowd was typical of a hotel ballroom in any one of a half dozen cities in the world. You saw all of the newest gowns decreed by London and Paris, fresh and crisp from their bandboxes. You saw, too, the latest conceits in accessories: charming little hand bags; billowing evening capes of which there were many smart versions to accent colour schemes; luxurious wraps and capelets in fur. The bouffant gown carried off top honours, whether in taffeta or net. Where the pencil silhouette was favoured, the frock was invariably accompanied by an elaborate tunic of taffeta or printed satin. Chiffon capes were many and varied. But all fell from the shoulders in flowing military fashion. One lovely young woman with a Dresden china face under a coiffure of white hair wore a lilac chiffon cape over a full-flowing grey gown. A tall blonde in a watermelon pink gown wore a white chiffon cape trimmed with ermine tails.

In the evenings there's dancing, smooth glittery dancing on a slippery floor. Induced hilarity: she can't avoid it. Everywhere around, the flashbulbs pop: you can never tell where they're aiming, or when a picture will appear in the paper, of you, with your head thrown back, all your teeth showing.

In the mornings her feet are sore.

In the afternoons she takes refuge in memory, lying in a deck chair, behind her sunglasses. She refuses the swimming pool, the quoits, the badminton, the endless, pointless games. Pastimes are for passing the time and she has her own pastime.

The dogs go round and round the deck on the ends of their leashes. Behind them are the top-grade dog-walkers. She pretends to be reading.

Some people write letters, in the library. For her there's no point. Even if she sent a letter, he moves around so much he might never get it. But someone else might.

On calm days the waves do what they are hired to do. They lull. The sea air, people say – oh, it's so good for you. Just take a deep breath. Just relax. Just let go.

Why do you tell me these sad stories? she says, months ago. They're lying wrapped in her coat, fur side up, his request. Cold air blows through the cracked window, streetcars clang past. Just a minute, she says, there's a button pressing into my back.

That's the kind of stories I know. Sad ones. Anyway, taken to its logical conclusion, every story is sad, because at the end everyone dies. Birth, copulation, and death. No exceptions, except maybe for the copulation part of it. Some guys don't even get that far, poor sods.

But there can be happy parts in between, she said. In between the birth and the death – can't there? Though I guess if you believe in Heaven that could be a happy story of sorts – dying, I mean. With flights of angels singing you to your rest and so forth.

Yeah. Pie in the sky when you die. No thanks.

Still, there can be happy parts, she says. Or more of them than you ever put in. You don't put in many.

You mean, the part where we get married and settle down in a little bungalow and have two kids? That part?

You're being vicious.

Okay, he says. You want a happy story. I can see you won't leave it alone until you get one. So here goes.

It was the ninety-ninth year of what was to become known as the Hundred Years' War, or the Xenorian Wars. The Planet Xenor, located in another dimension of space, was populated by a super-intelligent but super-cruel race of beings known as the Lizard Men, which wasn't what they called themselves. In appearance they were seven feet tall, scaly, and grey. Their eyes had vertical slits, like the eyes of cats or snakes. So tough was their hide that ordinarily they didn't have to wear clothing, except for short pants made of carchineal, a flexible red metal unknown on Earth. These protected their vital parts, which were also scaly, and enormous I might add, but at the same time vulnerable.

Well, thank heaven something was, she says, laughing.

I thought you'd like that. Anyway, their plan was to capture a large number of Earth women and breed a super-race, half-human, half-Xenorian Lizard Man, which would be better equipped for life on the various other habitable planets of the universe than they were – able to adjust to strange atmospheres, eat a variety of foods, resist unknown diseases, and so on – but which would also have the strength and the extraterrestrial intelligence of the Xenorians. This super-race would spread out through space and conquer it, eating the inhabitants of the different planets en route, because the Lizard Men needed room for expansion and a new source of protein.

The space fleet of the Lizard Men of Xenor had launched its first attack on Earth in the year 1967, scoring devastating hits on major cities in which millions had perished. Amid widespread panic, the Lizard Men had made parts of Eurasia and South America their slave colonies, appropriating the younger women for their hellish breeding experiments and burying the corpses of the men in enormous pits, after eating the parts of them they preferred. They liked the brains and the hearts especially, and the kidneys, grilled lightly.

But the Xenorian supply lines had been cut by rocket fire from hidden Earth installations, thus depriving the Lizard Men of the vital ingredients for their zorch-ray death guns, and Earth had rallied and struck back – not only with her own fighting forces, but with clouds of gas made from the poison of the rare Iridis *hortz* frog once used by the Nacrods of Ulinth to tip their arrows, and to which, it had been discovered by Earth scientists, the Xenorians were particularly susceptible. Thus the odds had been evened out.

Also their carchineal shorts were flammable, if you could hit them dead on with a missile that was hot enough already. Earth snipers with bull's-eye aim, using long-range phosphorus-bullet guns, were the heroes of the day, although retaliations against them were severe, and involved electrical tortures previously unknown and excruciatingly painful. The Lizard Men did not take kindly to having their private parts burst into flame, which was understandable.

Now, by the year 2066, the alien Lizard Men had been beaten back into yet another dimension of space, where Earth fighter pilots in their small, quick two-man harry-craft were pursuing them. Their ultimate goal was to wipe out the Xenorians entirely, keeping perhaps a few dozen for display in specially fortified zoos, with windows of unbreakable glass. The Xenorians however were not giving up without a fight to the death. They still had a viable fleet, and a few tricks left up their sleeves.

They had sleeves? I thought they were naked on top.

Judas Priest, don't be so picky. You know what I mean.

Will and Boyd were two old buddies – two scarred and battle-seasoned harry-craft veterans of three years' standing. This was a long time in the harry-craft service, where losses ran high. Their courage was said by their commanders to exceed their judgment, though so far they had got away with their rash behaviour, raid after daring raid.

But as our story opens, a Xenorian zorch-craft had closed in on them, and now they were shot to hell and limping badly. The zorch-rays had put a hole in their fuel tank, knocked out their link with Earth control, and melted their steering gear, giving Boyd a nasty scalp wound in the process, whereas Will was bleeding into his spacesuit from an unknown site in mid-section.

Looks like we're for it, said Boyd. Screwed, blued and tat-tooed. This thing's gonna go kablooey any minute now. I just wish we'd of had the time to blast a few hundred more of the scaly sons of guns to kingdom come, is all.

Yeah, ditto. Well, mud in your eye, old pal, said Will. It looks like you've got some running down in there anyway – red mud. Your toes are leaking. Ha, ha.

Ha, ha, said Boyd, grimacing in pain. Some joke. You always had a bum sense of humour.

Before Will could reply, the ship spun out of control and went into a dizzying spiral. They'd been seized by a gravity field, but of which planet? They had no idea where they were. Their artificial-gravity system was kaput, and so the two men blacked out.

When they awoke, they couldn't believe their eyes. They were no longer in the harry-craft, nor in their tight-fitting metallic spacesuits. Instead they were wearing loose green robes of some shining material, and reclining on soft golden sofas in a bower of leafy vines. Their wounds were healed, and Will's third finger on the left hand, blown off in a previous raid, had grown back. They felt suffused with health and well-being.

Suffused, she murmurs. My, my.

Yeah, us guys like a fancy word now and then, he says, talking out of the side of his mouth like a movie gangster. It gives the joint a bit of class.

So I imagine.

To proceed. I don't get it, said Boyd. You think we're dead?

If we're dead I'll settle for dead, said Will. This is all right, all righty.

I'll say.

Just then Will gave a low whistle. Coming towards them were two of the peachiest dames they had ever seen. Both had hair the colour of a split-willow basket. They were wearing long garments of a purplish-blue hue, which fell in tiny pleats and rustled as they moved. It reminded Will of nothing more than the little paper skirts they put around the fruit in snooty Grade-A grocery stores. Their arms and feet were bare; each had a strange headdress of fine red netting. Their skin was a succulent golden pink. They walked with an undulating motion, as if they'd been dipped in syrup.

Our greetings to you, men of Earth, said the first.

Yes, greetings, said the second. We have long expected you. We have tracked your advent on our interplanetary tele-camera.

Where are we? said Will.

You are on the Planet of Aa'A, said the first. The word sounded like a sigh of repletion, with a small gasp in the middle of it of the kind babies make when they turn over in their sleep. It also sounded like the last breath of the dying.

How did we get here? said Will. Boyd was speechless. He was running his eyes over the lush ripe curves on display before him. I'd like to sink my teeth into a piece of that, he was thinking.

You fell from the sky, in your craft, said the first woman. Unfortunately it has been destroyed. You will have to stay here with us.

That won't be hard to take, said Will.

You will be well cared for. You have earned your reward. For in protecting your world against the Xenorians, you are also protecting ours.

Modesty must draw a veil over what happened next.

Must it?

I'll demonstrate in a minute. It merely needs to be added that Boyd and Will were the only men on Planet Aa'A, so of course these women were virgins. But they could read minds, and each could tell in advance what Will and Boyd might desire. So very soon the most outrageous fantasies of the two friends had been realized.

After that there was a delicious meal of nectar, which, the men were told, would stave off age and death; then there was a stroll in the lovely gardens, which were filled with unimagin-able flowers; then the two were taken to a large room full of pipes, from which they could select any pipe they wanted.

Pipes? The kind you smoke?

To go with the slippers, which were issued to them next.

I guess I walked into that one.

You sure did, he said, grinning.

It got better. One of the girls was a sexpot, the other was more serious-minded and could discuss art, literature, and philosophy, not to mention theology. The girls seemed to know which was required of them at any given moment, and would switch around according to the moods and inclinations of Boyd and Will.

And so the time passed in harmony. As the perfect days went by, the men learned more about the Planet of Aa'A. First, no meat was eaten on it, and there were no carnivorous animals, though there were lots of butterflies and singing birds. Need I add that the god worshipped on Aa'A took the form of a huge pumpkin?

Second, there was no birth as such. These women grew on trees, on a stem running into the tops of their heads, and were picked when ripe by their predecessors. Third, there was no death as such. When the time came, each of the Peach Women – to call them by the names by which Boyd and Will soon referred to them – would simply disorganize her molecules, which would then be reassembled via the trees into a new, fresh woman. So the very latest woman was, in substance as well as in form, identical with the very first.

How did they know when the time had come? To disorganize their molecules?

First, by the soft wrinkles their velvety skin would develop when overripe. Second, by the flies.

The flies?

The fruit flies that would hover in clouds around their headdresses of red netting.

This is your idea of a happy story?

Wait. There's more.

★

After some time this existence, wonderful though it was, began to pall on Boyd and Will. For one thing, the women kept checking up on them to make sure they were happy. This can get tedious for a fellow. Also, there was nothing these babes wouldn't do. They were completely shameless, or without shame, whichever. On cue they would display the most whorish behaviour. Slut was hardly the word for them. Or they could become shy and prudish, cringing, modest; they would even weep and scream – that too was on order.

At first Will and Boyd found this exciting, but after a while it began to irritate.

When you hit the women, no blood came out, only juice. When you hit them harder, they dissolved into sweet mushy pulp, which pretty soon became another Peach Woman. They didn't appear to experience pain, as such, and Will and Boyd began to wonder whether they experienced pleasure either. Had all the ecstasy been a put-on show?

When questioned about this, the gals were smiling and evasive. You could never get to the bottom of them.

You know what I'd like right about now? said Will one fine day.

The same thing I'd like, I bet, said Boyd.

A great big grilled steak, rare, dripping with blood. A big stack of French fries. And a nice cold beer.

Ditto. And then a rip-roaring dogfight with those scaly sons of guns from Xenor.

You got the idea.

They decided to go exploring. Despite having been told that Aa'A was the same in every direction, and that they would only find more trees and more bowers and more birds and butterflies and more luscious women, they set out towards the west. After a long time and no adventures whatsoever, they came up against an invisible wall. It was slippery, like glass, but soft and yielding when you pushed on it. Then it would spring back into shape. It was higher than they could possibly reach or climb. It was like a huge crystal bubble.

I think we're trapped inside a big transparent tit, said Boyd.

They sat down at the foot of the wall, overcome by a profound despair.

This joint is peace and plenty, said Will. It's a soft bed at night and sweet dreams, it's tulips on the sunny breakfast table, it's the little woman making coffee. It's all the loving you ever dreamed of, in every shape and form. It's everything men think they want when they're out there, fighting in another dimension of space. It's what other men have given their lives for. Am I right?

You said a mouthful, said Boyd.

But it's too good to be true, said Will. It must be a trap. It may even be some devilish mind-device of the Xenorians, to keep us from being in the war. It's Paradise, but we can't get out of it. And anything you can't get out of is Hell.

But this isn't Hell. It's happiness, said one of the Peach Women who was materializing from the branch of a nearby tree. There's nowhere to go from here. Relax. Enjoy yourselves. You'll get used to it.

And that's the end of the story.

That's it? she says. You're going to keep those two men cooped up in there forever?

I did what you wanted. You wanted happiness. But I can keep them in or let them out, depending how you want it.

Let them out, then.

Outside is death. Remember?

Oh. I see. She turns on her side, pulls the fur coat over her, slides her arm around him. You're wrong about the Peach Women though. They aren't the way you think.

Wrong how?

You're just wrong.

The Mail and Empire, September 19, 1936

GRIFFEN WARNS OF REDS IN SPAIN
SPECIAL TO THE MAIL AND EMPIRE

In a spirited address to the Empire Club last Thursday, prominent industrialist Richard E. Griffen, of Griffen-Chase Royal Consolidated, warned of potential dangers threatening world order and the peaceful conduct of international commerce due to the ongoing civil conflict in Spain. The Republicans, he said, were taking their orders from the Reds, as had already been shown by their seizure of property, the slaughter of peaceful civilians, and the atrocities committed against religion. Many churches had been desecrated and burnt, and the murder of nuns and priests had become an everyday occurrence.

The intervention of the Nationalists headed by General Franco was a reaction only to be expected. Indignant and courageous Spaniards of every class had rallied to defend tradition and civil order, and the world would look on with anxiety as to the outcome. A triumph for the Republicans would mean a more aggressive Russia, and many smaller countries might well find themselves under threat. Of the continental countries, only Germany and France, and to some extent Italy, were strong enough to resist the tide.

Mr. Griffen strongly urged that Canada follow the lead of Britain, France and the United States, and distance itself from this conflict. The policy of non-intervention was a sound one and should be adopted immediately, as Canadian citizens should not be asked to risk their lives in this foreign fray. However there was already an underground stream of die-hard Communists heading for Spain from our continent, and although they should be prohibited by law from doing so, the country should be thankful that an opportunity had arisen whereby it might purge itself of disruptive elements at no cost to the tax-payer.

Mr. Griffen's remarks were roundly applauded.

The Blind Assassin: The Top Hat Grill

The Top Hat Grill has a neon sign with a red top hat and a blue glove lifting it. Up comes the hat, up it comes again; it never comes down. No head under it though, only one eye, winking. A man's eye, opening, closing; a conjurer's eye; a sly, headless joke.

The top hat is the classiest thing about the Top Hat Grill. Still, here they are, sitting at one of its booths, out in public like real people, each with a hot beef sandwich, the meat grey on bread white and soft and flavourless as an angel's buttock, the brown gravy thick with flour. Canned peas on the side, a delicate greyish green; French fries limp with grease. At the other booths sit lone disconsolate men with the pink, apologetic eyes and the faintly grimy shirts and shiny ties of bookkeepers, and a few battered couples making the most Friday-night whoopee they can afford, and some trios of off-duty whores.

I wonder if he goes with any of the whores, she thinks. When I'm not around. Then: How do I know they're whores?

It's the best thing here, he says, for the money. He means the hot beef sandwich.

You've tried the other things?

No, but you get an instinct.

It's quite good really, of its kind.

Spare me the party manners, he says, but not too rudely. His mood isn't what you'd call genial, but he's alert. Keyed up about something.

He hadn't been like that when she'd returned from her travels. He'd been taciturn, and vengeful.

Long time no see. Come for the usual?

The usual what?

The usual wham-bam.

Why do you feel the need to be so crude?

It's the company I keep.

What she'd like to know at the moment is why they're eating out. Why they aren't in his room. Why he's throwing caution to the winds. Where he got the money.

He answers the last question first, even though she hasn't asked it.

The beef sandwich you see before you, he says, is courtesy of the Lizard Men of Xenor. Here's to them, the vile scaly beasts, and to all that sail in them. He lifts his glass of Coca-Cola; he's spiked it with rum, from his flask. (No cocktails, I'm afraid, he'd said while opening the door for her. This joint's dry as a witch's thingamajig.)

She lifts her own glass. The Lizard Men of Xenor? she says. The same ones?

The very same. I committed it to paper, I sent it off two weeks ago, they snapped it up. The cheque came in yesterday.

He must have gone to the P.O. box himself, cashed the cheque too, he's been doing that lately. He's had to, she's been away too much.

You're happy with it? You seem happy.

Yeah, sure . . . it's a masterpiece. Plenty of action, plenty of gore on the floor. Beautiful dames. He grins. Who could resist?

Is it about the Peach Women?

Nope. No Peach Women in this one. It's a whole other plot.

He thinks: What happens when I tell her? Game over or eternal vows, and which is worse? She's wearing a scarf, of a wispy, floating material, some sort of pinkish orange. *Watermelon* is the word for that shade. Sweet crisp liquid flesh. He remembers the first time he saw her. All he could picture inside her dress then was mist.

What's got into you? she says. You seem very . . . Have you been drinking?

No. Not much. He pushes the pale-grey peas around on his plate. It's finally happened, he says. I'm on my way. Passport and all.

Oh, she says. Just like that. She tries to keep the dismay out of her voice.

Just like that, he says. The comrades got in touch. They must've decided I'm more use to them over there than back here. Anyway, after that endless beating around the bush, all of a sudden they can't wait to see the last of me. One more pain out of their ass.

You'll be safe, travelling? I thought . . .

Safer than staying here. But the word is nobody's looking too hard for me any more. I get the feeling the other side wants me to scram as well. Less complicated for them that way. I won't tell anybody which train I'll be on though. I'm not interested in being pushed off it with a hole in my head and a knife in my back.

What about crossing the border? You always said . . .

The border's like tissue paper right now, if you're going out, that is. The customs fellows know what's going on all right, they know there's a pipeline straight from here to New York, then across to Paris. It's all organized, and everyone's name is Joe. The cops have been given their orders. Look the other way, they've been told. They know which side their bread is buttered on. They don't give a hoot in hell.

I wish I could come with you, she says.

So that's why the dinner out. He wanted to break it to her some place where she wouldn't carry on. He's hoping she won't make a scene in public. Weeping, wailing, tearing her hair. He's counting on it.

Yeah. I wish you could too, he says. But you can't. It's rough over there. He hums in his head:

Stormy weather,
Don't know why, got no buttons on my fly,
Got a zipper . . .

Get a grip, he tells himself. He feels an effervescence in his
head, like ginger ale. Sparkling blood. It's as if he's flying –
looking down at her from the air. Her lovely distressed face
wavers like a reflection in a troubled pool; already dissolving,
and soon it will be into tears. But despite her sorrow, she's
never been so luscious. A soft and milky glow surrounds her;
the flesh of her arm, where he's held it, is firm and plumped.
He'd like to grab hold of her, haul her up to his room, fuck her
six ways to Sunday. As if that would fix her in place.

I'll wait for you, she says. When you come back I'll just walk
out the front door, and then we can go away together.

Would you really leave? Would you leave him?

Yes. For you, I would. If you wanted. I'd leave everything.

Slivers of neon light come in through the window above
them, red, blue, red. She imagines him wounded; it would be
one way of making him stay put. She'd like him locked up, tied
down, kept for her alone.

Leave him now, he says.

Now? Her eyes widen. Right now? Why?

Because I can't stand you being with him. I can't stand the
idea of it.

It doesn't mean anything to me, she says.

It does to me. Especially after I'm gone, when I can't see
you. It'll drive me crazy – thinking about it will.

But I wouldn't have any money, she says in a wondering
voice. Where would I live? In some rented room, all by myself?
Like you, she thinks. What would I live on?

You could get a job, he says helplessly. I could send you some
money.

You don't have any money, none to speak of. And I can't *do* anything. I can't sew, I can't type. There's another reason too, she thinks, but I can't tell him that.

There must be some way. But he doesn't urge her. Maybe it wouldn't be such a bright idea, her out on her own. Out there in the big bad world, where every guy from here to China could take a crack at her. If anything went wrong, he'd have only himself to blame.

I think I'd better stay put, don't you? That's the best thing. Until you come back. You will come back, won't you? You'll come back safe and sound?

Sure, he says.

Because if you don't, I don't know what I'll do. If you got yourself killed or anything I'd go completely to pieces. She thinks: I'm talking like a movie. But how else can I talk? We've forgotten how else.

Shit, he thinks. She's working herself up. Now she'll cry. She'll cry and I'll sit here like a lump, and once women start crying there's no way to make them stop.

Come on, I'll get your coat, he says grimly. This is no fun. We don't have much time. Let's go back to the room.

IX

The laundry

March at last, and a few grudging intimations of spring. The trees are still bare, the buds still hard, cocooned, but in places where the sun hits there's meltdown. Dog doings unfreeze, then wane, their icy lacework sallow with wornout pee. Slabs of lawn come to light, sludgy and bestrewn. Limbo must look like this.

Today I had something different for breakfast. Some new kind of cereal flake, brought over by Myra to pep me up: she's a sucker for the writing on the backs of packages. These flakes, it says in candid lettering the colours of lollipops, of fleecy cotton jogging suits, are not made from corrupt, overly commercial corn and wheat, but from little-known grains with hard-to-pronounce names – archaic, mystical. The seeds of them have been rediscovered in pre-Columbian tombs and in Egyptian pyramids; an authenticating detail, though not, when you come to think of it, all that reassuring. Not only will these flakes whisk you out like a pot scrubber, they murmur of renewed vitality, of endless youth, of immortality. The back of the box is festooned with a limber pink intestine; on the front is an eyeless jade mosaic face, which those in charge of publicity have surely not realized is an Aztec burial mask.

In honour of this new cereal I forced myself to sit down properly at the kitchen table, with place setting and paper napkin complete. Those who live alone slide into the habit of vertical eating: why bother with the niceties when there's no one to share or censure? But laxity in one area may lead to derangement in all.

★

Yesterday I decided to do the laundry, to thumb my nose at God by working on a Sunday. Not that he gives two hoots what day of the week it is: in Heaven, as in the subconscious – or so we're told – there is no time. But really it was to thumb my nose at Myra. I shouldn't be making the bed, says Myra; I shouldn't be carrying heavy baskets of soiled clothing down the rickety steps to the cellar, where the ancient, frantic washing machine is located.

Who does the laundry? Myra, by default. *While I'm here I might as well just pop in a load*, she'll say. Then we both pretend she hasn't done it. We conspire in the fiction – or what is rapidly becoming the fiction – that I can fend for myself. But the strain of make-believe is beginning to tell on her.

Also she's getting a bad back. She wants to arrange for a woman, some nosy hired stranger, to come in and do all that. Her excuse is my heart. She has somehow found out about it, about the doctor and his nostrums and his prophecies – I suppose from his nurse, a chemical redhead with a mouth that flaps at both ends. This town is a sieve.

I told Myra that what I do with my dirty linen is my own business: I will stave off the generic *woman* for as long as possible. How much of this is embarrassment, on my part? Quite a lot. I don't want anyone else poking into my insufficiencies, my stains and smells. It's all right for Myra to do it, because I know her and she knows me. I am her cross to bear: I am what makes her so good, in the eyes of others. All she has to do is say my name and roll her eyes, and indulgence is extended to her, if not by the angels, at least by the neighbours, who are a damn sight harder to please.

Don't misunderstand me. I am not scoffing at goodness, which is far more difficult to explain than evil, and just as complicated. But sometimes it's hard to put up with.

Having made my decision – and having anticipated Myra's

bleats of distress upon discovering the stack of washed and folded towels, and my own smug grin of triumph – I set about my laundering escapade. I delved about in the hamper, narrowly saving myself from toppling into it head first, and fished out what I thought I could carry, avoiding nostalgia for the undergarments of yesteryear. (How lovely they were! They don't make things like that any more, not with self-covered buttons, not hand-stitched. Or perhaps they do, but I never see them, and couldn't afford them anyway, and wouldn't fit into them. Such things have waists.)

Into the plastic basket went my selections, and off I set, step by step, sideways down the stairs, like Little Red Riding Hood on her way to Granny's house via the underworld. Except that I myself am Granny, and I contain my own bad wolf. Gnawing away, gnawing away.

The main floor, so far so good. Along the hall into the kitchen, then on with the cellar light and the jittery plunge into the dank. Almost at once, trepidation set in. Places in this house that I could once negotiate with ease have become treacherous: the sash windows are poised like traps, ready to fall on my hands, the stepstool threatens to collapse, the top shelves of the cupboards are booby-trapped with precarious glassware. Halfway down the cellar stairs I knew I shouldn't have tried it. The angle was too steep, the shadows too dense, the smell too sinister, like freshly poured cement concealing some deftly poisoned spouse. On the floor at the bottom there was a pool of darkness, deep and shimmering and wet as a real pool. Perhaps it was a real pool; perhaps the river was welling up through the floor, as I have seen happen on the weather channel. Any of the four elements may become displaced at any time: fire may break from the earth, earth liquefy and tumble about your ears, air beat against you like a rock, dashing the roof from over your head. Why not then a flood?

I heard a gurgling, which may or may not have been coming from inside me; I felt my heart gulping in my chest with panic. I knew the water was a quirk, of eye or ear or mind; still, better not to descend. I dropped the laundry on the cellar stairs, abandoning it. Perhaps I might go back and pick it up later, perhaps not. Someone would. Myra would, lips tightening. Now I'd done it, now I would have *the woman* foisted on me for sure. I turned, half fell, grasped the banister; then pulled myself back up, one step at a time, to the sane bland daylight of the kitchen.

Outside the window it was grey, a uniform spiritless grey, the sky as well as the porous, aging snow. I plugged in the electric kettle; soon it began its lullaby of steam. Things have gone pretty far when you've come to feel that it's your utensils that are taking care of you and not the other way around. Still, I was comforted.

I made a cup of tea, drank it, then rinsed out the cup. I can still wash my own dishes, at any rate. Then I put the cup away, on the shelf with the other cups, Grandmother Adelia's hand-painted patterns, lilies with lilies, violets with violets, like patterns matched with like. My cupboards at least have not gone haywire. But the image of the cast-away items of laundry fallen on the cellar steps was bothering me. All those tatters, those crumpled fragments, like shed white skins. Though not entirely white. A testament to something: blank pages my body's been scrawling on, leaving its cryptic evidence as it slowly but surely turns itself inside out.

Perhaps I should make a try at gathering these things up, then stowing them away in their hamper, and none the wiser. *None* means Myra.

I have been overcome, it seems, by a lust for tidiness.

Better late than never, says Reenie.

Oh Reenie. How I wish you were here. Come back and take care of me!

She won't, though. I will have to take care of myself. Myself and Laura, as I solemnly promised to do.

Better late than never.

Where am I? *It was winter.* No, I've done that.

It was spring. The spring of 1936. That was the year everything began to fall apart. Continued to fall apart, that is, in a more serious fashion than it was doing already.

King Edward abdicated in that year; he chose love over ambition. No. He chose the Duchess of Windsor's ambition over his own. That's the event people remember. And the Civil War began, in Spain. But those things didn't happen until months later. What was March known for? Something. Richard rattling his paper at the breakfast table, and saying, *So he's done it.*

There were just the two of us at breakfast, that day. Laura did not eat breakfast with us, except on weekends, and then she avoided it as much as possible by pretending to sleep in. On weekdays she ate by herself in the kitchen, because she had to go to school. Or not by herself: Mrs. Murgatroyd would have been present. Mr. Murgatroyd then drove her to school and picked her up, because Richard didn't like the idea of her walking. What he really didn't like was the idea that she might go astray.

She had lunch at the school, and took flute lessons there on Tuesdays and Thursdays, because a musical instrument was mandatory. The piano had been tried, but had come to nothing. Likewise the cello. Laura was averse to practising, we were told, although in the evenings we were sometimes treated to the sorrowful, off-key wailing of her flute. The false notes sounded deliberate.

"I'll speak to her," said Richard.

"We can scarcely complain," I said. "She's only doing what you require."

Laura was no longer overtly rude to Richard. But if he entered a room, she would leave it.

Back to the morning paper. Since Richard was holding it up between us, I could read the headline. *He* was Hitler, who had marched into the Rhineland. He'd broken the rules, he'd crossed the line, he'd done the forbidden thing. *Well*, said Richard, *you could see it coming a mile away, but the rest of them got caught with their pants down. He's thumbing his nose at them. He's a smart fellow. Sees a weak point in the fence. Sees a chance and he takes it. You've got to hand it to him.*

I agreed, but did not listen. Not listening was the only way I had, during those months, of keeping my balance. I had to blot out the ambient noise: like a tightrope walker crossing Niagara Falls, I could not afford to look around me, for fear of slipping. What else can you do when what you are thinking about every waking moment is so far removed from the life you're supposedly living? From what's right there on the table, which that morning was a bud vase with a paper-white narcissus in it, picked from the bowl of forced bulbs sent over by Winifred. *So lovely to have at this time of year*, she'd said. *So fragrant. Like a breath of hope.*

Winifred thought I was innocuous. Put another way, she thought I was a fool. Later – ten years into the future – she was to say, over the phone because we no longer met in person, "I used to think you were stupid, but really you're evil. You've always hated us because your father went bankrupt and burned down his own factory, and you held it against us."

"He didn't burn it down," I would say. "Richard did. Or he fixed it."

"That is a malicious lie. Your father was stony flat broke, and if it wasn't for the insurance on that building you wouldn't have had a bean! We pulled the two of you out of the swamp, you and your dopey sister! If it wasn't for us, you would've been out walking the streets instead of sitting around on your bottoms like the silver-plated spoiled brats you were. You always had everything handed to you, you never had to make an effort, you never showed one moment of gratitude to Richard. You didn't lift one finger to help him out, not once, ever."

"I did what you wanted. I kept my mouth shut. I smiled. I was the window-dressing. But Laura was going too far. He should have left Laura out of it."

"All of that was just spite, spite, spite! You owed us everything, and you couldn't stand it. You had to get back at him! You killed him dead between the two of you, just as if you'd put a gun to his head and pulled the trigger."

"Who killed Laura, then?"

"Laura killed herself, as you know perfectly well."

"I could say the same of Richard."

"That is a slanderous lie. Anyway, Laura was crazy as a coot. I don't know how you could ever have believed a word she said, about Richard or anything else. Nobody in their right mind would have!"

I couldn't say another word, and so I hung up on her. But I was powerless against her, because by then she had a hostage. She had Aimee.

In 1936, however, she was still affable enough, and I was still her protégée. She continued to haul me around from function to function – Junior League meetings, political bun-fests, committees for this and that – and to park me on chairs and in corners, while she did the necessary socializing. I could see now that she was for the most part not liked, but merely tolerated, because of her money, and her boundless energy: most of the women in those circles were content to let Winifred do the lion's share of whatever work might be involved.

Every now and then, one of them would sidle up to me and remark that she had known my grandmother – or, if younger, that she wished she'd known her, back in those golden days before the Great War, when true elegance had still been possible. This was a password: it meant that Winifred was an *arriviste* – new money, brash and vulgar – and that I should be standing up for some other set of values. I would smile vaguely, and say that my grandmother had died long before I was born. In other words, they couldn't expect any kind of opposition to Winifred from me.

And how is your clever husband? they would say. *When may we expect the big announcement?* The big announcement had to do with Richard's political career, not yet formally begun but considered imminent.

Oh, I would smile, *I expect I'll be the first to know.* I did not believe this: I expected to be the last.

Our life – Richard's and mine – had settled into what I then supposed would be its pattern forever. Or rather there were two lives, a daytime one and a nighttime one: they were distinct, and also invariable. Placidity and order and everything in its place, with a decorous and sanctioned violence going on underneath everything, like a heavy, brutal shoe tapping out the rhythm on a carpeted floor. Every morning I would take a shower, to get rid of the night; to wash off the stuff Richard wore on his hair – some kind of expensive perfumed grease. It rubbed off all over my skin.

Did it bother him that I was indifferent to his nighttime activities, even repelled by them? Not at all. He preferred conquest to cooperation, in every area of life.

Sometimes – increasingly, as time went by – there were bruises, purple, then blue, then yellow. It was remarkable how easily I bruised, said Richard, smiling. A mere touch would do it. He had never known a woman to bruise so easily. It came from being so young and delicate.

He favoured thighs, where it wouldn't show. Anything overt might get in the way of his ambitions.

I sometimes felt as if these marks on my body were a kind of code, which blossomed, then faded, like invisible ink held to a candle. But if they were a code, who held the key to it?

I was sand, I was snow – written on, rewritten, smoothed over.

The ashtray

I've been to see the doctor again. Myra drove me there: in view of the black ice caused by a thaw followed by a freeze, it was too slippery for me to walk, she said.

The doctor tapped my ribs and eavesdropped on my heart, and frowned and then cancelled his frown, and then – having already made up his mind about it – asked me how I was feeling. I believe he has done something to his hair; surely he used to be thinner on top. Has he been indulging in the gluing on of strands across his scalp? Or worse, transplantation? Aha, I thought. Despite your jogging and the hairiness of your legs, the shoe of aging is beginning to pinch. Soon you'll regret all that sun-tanning. Your face will look like a testicle.

Nonetheless he was offensively jocular. At least he doesn't say, *How are we today?* He never calls me *we*, the way some of them do: he does understand the importance of the first person singular.

"I can't sleep," I told him. "I dream too much."

"Then if you're dreaming, you must be sleeping," he said, intending a witticism.

"You know what I mean," I said sharply. "It's not the same. The dreams wake me up."

"You've been drinking coffee?"

"No," I lied.

"Must be a bad conscience." He was writing out a prescription, no doubt for sugar pills. He chuckled to himself: he thought he'd been quite funny. After a certain point, the ravages of experience reverse themselves; we put on innocence with advancing age, at least in the minds of others. What the doctor sees when he looks at me is an ineffectual and therefore blameless old biddy.

Myra sat reading out-of-date magazines in the waiting room while I was in the inner sanctum. She tore out an article on coping with stress, and another one on the beneficial effects of raw cabbage. These were for me, she said, pleased with her helpful *trouvailles*. She is always diagnosing me. My corporeal health is of almost as much interest to her as my spiritual health: she is especially proprietary about my bowels.

I told her I could hardly be said to suffer from stress, as there was no stress in a vacuum. As for raw cabbage, it bloated me up like a dead cow, so I would skip the beneficial effects. I said I had no wish to go through life, or what remained of it, stinking like a barrel of sauerkraut and sounding like a truck horn.

Crude references to bodily functions usually put a stop to Myra. She drove the rest of the way home in silence, with a smile hardening on her face like plaster of Paris.

Sometimes I am ashamed of myself.

To the task at hand. *At hand* is appropriate: sometimes it seems to me that it's only my hand writing, not the rest of me; that my hand has taken on a life of its own, and will keep on going even if severed from the rest of me, like some embalmed, enchanted Egyptian fetish or the dried rabbit claws men used to suspend from their car mirrors for luck. Despite the arthritis in my fingers, this hand of mine has been displaying an unusual amount of friskiness lately, as if tossing restraint to the dogs. Certainly it's been writing down a number of things it wouldn't be allowed to if subject to my better judgment.

Turn the pages, turn the pages. Where was I? April 1936.

In April we got a call from the headmistress of St. Cecilia's, where Laura was attending school. It concerned Laura's behaviour, she said. It was not a matter that could best be discussed over the telephone.

Richard was tied up with business affairs. He proposed Winifred as my escort, but I said I was sure it was nothing; I myself would handle things, and would let him know if there was anything of importance. I made an appointment to see the headmistress, whose name I have forgotten. I dressed in a manner I hoped would intimidate her, or at least remind her of Richard's standing and influence: I believe I wore a cash-mere coat trimmed with wolverine – warm for the season, but impressive – and a hat with a dead pheasant on it, or parts of one. The wings, the tail, and the head, which was fitted with beady little red glass eyes.

The headmistress was a greying female shaped like a wooden clothes rack – brittle bones with damp-looking textiles draped on them. She was sitting in her office, barricaded behind her oak desk, her shoulders up to her ears with terror. A year earlier I would have been as frightened of her as she was of me, or rather of what I represented: a big wad of money. Now however I had gained assurance. I had watched Winifred in action, I had practised. Now I could raise one eyebrow at a time.

She smiled nervously, displaying plump yellow teeth like the kernels on a half-eaten cob of corn. I wondered what Laura had been doing: it must have been something, to have worked her up to the point of confrontation with absent Richard and his unseen power. "I'm afraid we can't really continue with Laura," she said. "We have done our best, and we are aware that there are mitigating circumstances, but considering everything we do have to think of our other pupils, and I am afraid Laura is simply too disruptive an influence."

I had learned, by then, the value of making other people explain themselves. "I'm sorry, but I don't know what you are talking about," I said, barely moving my lips. "What mitigating circumstances? What disruptive influence?" I kept my hands still in my lap, my head high and slightly tilted, the best angle for the pheasant hat. I hoped she would feel stared at by four eyes and not just by two. Though I had the benefit of wealth, hers was her age and position. It was hot in the office. I'd slung my coat over the back of the chair, but even so I was sweating like a stevedore.

"She is calling God into question," she said, "in the Religious Knowledge class, which I have to say is the only subject in which she appears to take any interest whatsoever. She went so far as to produce an essay entitled, 'Does God Lie?' It was very unsettling to the entire class."

"And what answer did she arrive at?" I asked. "About God?" I was surprised, though I didn't show it: I'd thought Laura had been slackening off on the God question, but apparently not.

"An affirmative one." She looked down at her desk, where Laura's essay was spread out in front of her. "She cites – it's right here – First Kings, chapter twenty-two – the passage in which God deceives King Ahab. 'Now therefore, behold, the Lord hath put a lying spirit in the mouth of all these thy prophets.' Laura goes on to say that if God did this once, how do we know he didn't do it more than once, and how can we tell the false prophecies apart from the true ones?"

"Well, that's a logical conclusion, at any rate," I said. "Laura knows her Bible."

"I dare say," said the headmistress, exasperated. "The Devil can quote Scripture to his purpose. She does proceed to remark that although God lies, he doesn't cheat – he always sends a true prophet as well, but people don't listen. In her opinion God is like a radio broadcaster and we are faulty radios, a comparison I find disrespectful, to say the least."

"Laura doesn't mean to be disrespectful," I said. "Not about God, at any rate."

The headmistress ignored this. "It's not so much the specious arguments she makes, as the fact that she saw fit to pose the question in the first place."

"Laura likes to have answers," I said. "She likes to have answers on important matters. I am sure you'll agree that God is an important matter. I don't see why that should be considered disruptive."

"The other students find it so. They believe she's – well, showing off. Challenging established authority."

"As Christ did," I said, "or so some people thought at the time."

She did not make the obvious point that such things may have been all very well for Christ but they were not appropriate in a sixteen-year-old girl. "You don't quite understand," she said. She actually wrung her hands, an operation I studied with interest, having never seen it before. "The others think she's – they think she's being *funny*. Or some of them do. Others think she's a Bolshevik. The rest just consider her odd. In any case, she attracts the wrong kind of attention."

I began to see her point. "I don't expect Laura intends to be funny," I said.

"But it's so hard to tell!" We looked across her desk at each other for a moment of silence. "She has quite a following, you know," said the headmistress, with a touch of envy. She waited for me to absorb this, then went on. "It's also a question of her absences. I understand there are health problems, but . . ."

"What health problems?" I said. "There's nothing wrong with Laura's health."

"Well, I assumed, considering all of the doctor's appointments . . ."

"What doctor's appointments?"

"You didn't authorize them?" She produced a sheaf of letters. I recognized the notepaper, which was mine. I looked through them: I hadn't written them, but they were signed with my name.

"I see," I said, gathering up my wolverine coat and my handbag. "I will have to speak to Laura. Thank you for your time." I shook the ends of her fingers. It went without saying, now, that Laura would have to be withdrawn from the school.

"We did try our best," said the poor woman. She was practically weeping. Another Miss Violence, this one. A hired drudge, well-meaning but ineffectual. No match for Laura.

That evening, when Richard asked how my interview had gone, I told him about Laura's disruptive effect on her classmates. Instead of being angry he seemed amused, and close to admiring. He said Laura had backbone. He said a certain amount of rebelliousness showed get-up-and-go. He himself had disliked school and had made life difficult for the teachers, he said. I didn't think this had been Laura's motive, but I didn't say so.

I didn't mention the false doctor notes to him: that would have set the cat among the pigeons. Bothering teachers was one thing, playing hookey would have been quite another. It smacked of delinquency.

"You shouldn't have forged my handwriting," I said to Laura privately.

"I couldn't forge Richard's. It's too different from ours. Yours was a lot easier."

"Handwriting is a personal thing. It's like stealing."

She did look chagrined, for a moment. "I'm sorry. I was only borrowing. I didn't think you'd mind."

"I suppose there's no point in wondering why you did it?"

"I never asked to be sent to that school," said Laura. "They didn't like me any more than I liked them. They didn't take me seriously. They aren't serious people. If I'd had to be there all the time, I really would have got sick."

"What were you doing," I said, "when you weren't at school? Where did you go?" I was worried that she might have been meeting someone – meeting a man. She was getting to be the age for it.

"Oh, here and there," said Laura. "I went downtown, or I sat in parks and things. Or I just walked around. I saw you, a couple of times, but you didn't see me. I guess you were going shopping." I felt a surge of blood to the heart, then a constriction: panic, like a hand squeezing me shut. I must have gone pale.

"What's wrong?" said Laura. "Don't you feel well?"

That May we crossed to England on the *Berengeria*, then returned to New York on the maiden voyage of the *Queen Mary*. The *Queen* was the largest and most luxurious ocean liner ever built, or that's what was written in all the brochures. It was an epoch-making event, said Richard.

Winifred came with us. Also Laura. Such a voyage would do her a lot of good, said Richard: she'd been looking pinched and weedy, she'd been at loose ends ever since her abrupt departure from school. The trip would be an education for her, of the kind a girl like her could really use. Anyway, we could scarcely leave her behind.

The public couldn't get enough of the *Queen Mary*. It was described and photographed within an inch of its life, and decorated that way too, with strip lighting and plastic laminates and fluted columns and maple burr – costly veneers everywhere. But it wallowed like a pig, and the second-class deck overlooked the first-class one, so you couldn't walk about there without a railing-full of impecunious gawkers checking you over.

I was seasick the first day out, but after that I was fine. There was a lot of dancing. I knew how to dance by then; well enough, but not too well. (*Never do anything too well*, said Winifred, *it shows you're trying*.) I danced with men other than Richard – men he knew through his business, men he'd introduce me to.

Take care of Iris for me, he would say to these men, smiling, patting them on the arm. Sometimes he would dance with other women, the wives of the men he knew. Sometimes he would go out to have a cigarette or take a turn around the deck, or that's what he'd say he was doing. I thought instead that he was sulking, or brooding. I'd lose track of him for an hour at a time. Then he'd be back, sitting at our table, watching me dance well enough, and I'd wonder how long he'd been there.

He was disgruntled, I decided, because this trip wasn't working out for him the way he'd planned. He couldn't get dinner reservations he wanted at the Verandah Grill, he wasn't meeting the people he'd wanted to meet. He was a big potato on his own stomping ground, but on the *Queen Mary* he was a very small potato indeed. Winifred was a small potato too: her sprightliness was wasted. More than once I saw her cut dead, by women she'd sidled up to. Then she'd slink back to what she called "our crowd," hoping no one had noticed.

Laura did not dance. She didn't know how, she had no interest in it; anyway she was too young. After dinner she'd shut herself up in her cabin; she said she was reading. On the third day of the voyage, at breakfast, her eyes were swollen and red.

At mid-morning I went looking for her. I found her in a deck chair with a plaid rug pulled up to her neck, listlessly watching a game of quoits. I sat down next to her. A brawny young woman strode by with seven dogs, each on its own leash; she was wearing shorts despite the chilliness of the weather, and had tanned brown legs.

"I could get a job like that," said Laura.

"A job like what?"

"Walking dogs," she said. "Other people's dogs. I like dogs."

"You wouldn't like the owners."

"I wouldn't be walking the owners." She had her sunglasses on, but was shivering.

"Is anything the matter?" I said.

"No."

"You look cold. I think you're coming down with something."

"There's nothing wrong with me. Don't fuss."

"Naturally I'm concerned."

"You don't have to be. I'm sixteen. I can tell if I'm ill."

"I promised Father I'd take care of you," I said stiffly. "And Mother too."

"Stupid of you."

"No doubt. But I was young, I didn't know any better. That's what young is."

Laura took off her sunglasses, but she didn't look at me. "Other people's promises aren't my fault," she said. "Father fobbed me off on you. He never did know what to do with me – with us. But he's dead now, they're both dead, so it's all right. I absolve you. You're off the hook."

"Laura, what *is* it?"

"Nothing," she said. "But every time I just want to think – to sort things out – you decide I'm sick and start nagging at me. It drives me nuts."

"That's hardly fair," I said. "I've tried and tried, I've always given you the benefit of the doubt, I've given you the utmost . . ."

"Let's leave it alone," she said. "Look, what a silly game! I wonder why they call them quoits?"

I put all this down to old grief – to mourning, for Avilion and all that had happened there. Or could she still be mooning over Alex Thomas? I should have asked her more, I should have insisted, but I doubt that even then she would have told me what was really bothering her.

The thing I recall most clearly from the voyage, apart from Laura, was the looting that went on, all over the ship, on the day we sailed into port. Everything with the *Queen Mary* name or monogram on it went into a handbag or a suitcase – writing paper, silverware, towels, soap dishes, the works – anything not chained to the floor. Some people even unscrewed the faucet handles, and the smaller mirrors, and doorknobs. The first-class passengers were worse than the others; but then, the rich have always been kleptomaniacs.

What was the rationale for all this pillaging? Souvenirs. These people needed something to remember themselves by. An odd thing, souvenir-hunting: *now* becomes *then* even while it is still now. You don't really believe you're there, and so you nick the proof, or something you mistake for it.

I myself made off with an ashtray.

The man with his head on fire

Last night I took one of the pills the doctor prescribed for me. It put me to sleep all right, but then I dreamed, and this dream was no improvement on the kind I'd been having without benefit of medication.

I was standing on the dock at Avilion, with the broken, greenish ice of the river tinkling all around like bells, but I wasn't wearing a winter coat – only a cotton print dress covered with butterflies. Also a hat made of plastic flowers in lurid colours – tomato red, a hideous lilac – that was lit up from inside by tiny light bulbs.

Where's mine? said Laura, in her five-year-old's voice. I looked down at her, but then we were not children any longer. Laura had grown old, like me; her eyes were little dried raisins. This was horrifying to me, and I woke up.

It was three in the morning. I waited until my heart had stopped protesting, then groped my way downstairs and made myself a hot milk. I should have known better than to rely on pills. You can't buy unconsciousness quite so cheaply.

But to continue.

Once off the *Queen Mary*, our family party spent three days in New York. Richard had some business to conclude; the rest of us could sightsee, he said.

Laura did not want to go to the Rockettes, or up to the top of the Statue of Liberty or the Empire State Building. Nor did she want to shop. She just wanted to walk around and look at things on the street, she said, but that was too dangerous a thing for her to do by herself, said Richard, so I went with her. She was not lively company – a relief after

Winifred, who was determined to be as lively as was humanly possible.

After that we spent several weeks in Toronto, while Richard caught up on his affairs. After that we went to Avilion. We would go sailing there, said Richard. His tone implied that this was the only thing the place was good for; also that he was happy to make the sacrifice of his own time in order to indulge our whims. Or, more gently put, to please us – to please me, but to please Laura too.

It seemed to me that he'd come to regard Laura as a puzzle, one that it was now his business to solve. I'd catch him looking at her at odd moments, in much the same way as he looked at the stock-market pages – searching out the grip, the twist, the handle, the wedge, the way in. According to his view of life, there was such a grip or twist for everything. Either that, or a price. He wanted to get Laura under his thumb, he wanted her neck under his foot, however lightly placed. But Laura didn't have that kind of neck. So after each of his attempts he was left standing with one leg in the air, like a bear-hunter posing in a picture from which the slain bear has vanished.

How did Laura do it? Not by opposing him, not any longer: by this time she avoided clashing with him head-on. She did it by stepping back, and turning away, and throwing him off balance. He was always lunging in her direction, always grabbing, always grabbing air.

What he wanted was her approval, her admiration even. Or simply her gratitude. Something like that. With some other young girl he might have tried presents – a pearl necklace, a cashmere sweater – things that sixteen-year-olds were supposed to long for. But he knew better than to foist anything of this sort on Laura.

Blood from a stone, I thought. He'll never figure her out. And she doesn't have a price, because there's nothing he has that she wants. In any contest of wills, with anyone at all, I was still betting on Laura. In her own way she was stubborn as a pig.

I did think she'd jump at the chance to spend some time at Avilion – she'd been so reluctant to leave it – but when the plan was mentioned, she seemed indifferent. She was unwilling to give Richard credit for anything, or this was my reading. "At least we'll see Reenie," was all she said.

"I regret to say that Reenie is no longer in our employ," said Richard. "She was asked to leave."

When was that? A while ago. A month, several months? Richard was vague. It was a question, he said, of Reenie's husband, who had been drinking too much. Therefore the repairs to the house had not been carried out in what any reasonable person would consider a timely and satisfactory manner, and Richard did not see any point in paying out good money for laziness, and for what could only be termed insubordination.

"He didn't want her here at the same time as us," said Laura. "He knew she'd take sides."

We were wandering around on the main floor of Avilion. The house itself appeared to have dwindled in size; the furniture was covered with dust cloths, or what was left of the furniture – some of the bulkier, darker pieces had been removed, on Richard's orders I suppose. I could imagine Winifred saying that nobody should be expected to live with a sideboard festooned with such chunky, unconvincing wooden grapes. The leather-bound books were still in the library, but I had a feeling that they might not be there much longer. The portraits of the prime ministers with Grandfather Benjamin had been deleted: someone – Richard, no doubt – must finally have noticed their pastel faces.

Avilion had once had an air of stability that amounted to intransigence – a large, dumpy boulder plunked down in the middle of the stream of time, refusing to be moved for anybody – but now it was dog-eared, apologetic, as if it were about to collapse in on itself. It no longer had the courage of its own pretensions.

So demoralizing, said Winifred, how dusty everything was, and there were mice in the kitchen, she'd seen the droppings, and silverfish as well. But the Murgatroyds were arriving later that day, by train, along with a couple of other, newer servants who'd been added to our entourage, and then everything would soon be shipshape, except of course (she said with a laugh) the ship itself, by which she meant the *Water Nixie*. Richard was down in the boathouse right now, looking her over. She was supposed to have been scraped down and repainted under the supervision of Reenie and Ron Hincks, but this was yet another thing that had not taken place. Winifred failed to see what Richard wanted with that old tub – if Richard really longed to sail, he should scuttle that old dinosaur of a boat and buy a new one.

"I suppose he thinks it has sentimental value," I said. "For us, I mean. Laura and me."

"And does it?" said Winifred, with that amused smile of hers.

"No," said Laura. "Why would it? Father never took us sailing in it. Only Callie Fitzsimmons." We were in the dining room; at least the long table was still there. I wondered what decision Richard, or rather Winifred, would make about Tristan and Iseult and their glassy, outmoded romance.

"Callie Fitzsimmons came to the funeral," said Laura. We were alone together; Winifred had gone upstairs for what she called her beauty rest. She put cotton pads dampened with witch hazel on her eyes for this, and covered her face with a preparation of expensive green mud.

"Oh? You didn't tell me."

"I forgot. Reenie was furious with her."

"For coming to the funeral?

"For not coming earlier. She was quite rude to her. She said, 'You're an hour too late and a dime too short.'"

"But she hated Callie! She always hated it when she came to stay! She thought she was a slut!"

"I guess she hadn't been enough of a slut to suit Reenie. She'd been lazy at it, she'd fallen down on the job."

"Of being a slut?"

"Well, Reenie felt she ought to have followed through. At least she should have been there, when Father was in such difficulties. Taken his mind off things."

"Reenie said all that?"

"Not exactly, but you could tell what she meant."

"What did Callie do?"

"Pretended she didn't understand. After that, she did what everyone does at funerals. Cried and told lies."

"What lies?" I said.

"She said even if they didn't always see eye to eye from a political point of view, Father was a fine, fine person. Reenie said *political point of view my fanny*, but behind her back."

"I think he tried to be," I said. "Fine, I mean."

"Well, he didn't try hard enough," said Laura. "Don't you remember what he used to say? That we'd been *left on his hands*, as if we were some kind of a smear."

"He tried as hard as he could," I said.

"Remember the Christmas he dressed up as Santa Claus? It was before Mother died. I'd just turned five."

"Yes," I said. "That's what I mean. He tried."

"I hated it," said Laura. "I always hated those kinds of surprises."

We'd been told to wait in the cloak room. The double doors to the hall had gauzy curtains on the inside, so we couldn't see through into the square front hall, which had a fireplace, in the old manner; that was where the Christmas tree had been set up. We were perched on the cloak-room settee, with the oblong mirror behind it. Coats were hanging on the long rack – Father's coats, Mother's coats, and the hats too, above them – hers with large feathers, his with small ones. There was a smell of rubber overshoes, and of fresh pine resin and cedar from the garlands wreathed around the front-stair banisters, and of wax on warm floorboards, because the furnace was on: the radiators hissed and clanked. From under the windowsill came a cold draught, and the pitiless, uplifting scent of snow.

There was a single overhead light in the room; it had a yellow silk shade. In the glass doors I could see us reflected: our royal blue velvet dresses with the lace collars, our white faces, our pale hair parted in the middle, our pale hands folded in our laps. Our white socks, our black Mary Janes. We'd been taught to sit with one foot crossed over the other – never the knees – and that is how we were sitting. The mirror rose behind us like a glass bubble coming out of the tops of our heads. I could hear our breathing, going in and out: the breath of waiting. It sounded like someone else breathing – someone large but invisible, hiding inside the muffling coats.

All at once the double doors swung open. There was a man in red, a red giant towering upwards. Behind him was the night darkness, and a blaze of flame. His face was covered with white smoke. His head was on fire. He lurched forward: his arms were outstretched. Out of his mouth came a sound of hooting, or of shouting.

I was startled for a moment, but I was old enough to know what it was supposed to be. The sound was meant to be laughter. It was only Father, pretending to be Santa Claus, and he wasn't burning – it was only the tree lit up behind him, it was only the wreath of candles on his head. He had his red brocade dressing gown on, backwards, and a beard made out of cotton batten.

Mother used to say he never knew his own strength: he never knew how big he was in relation to everyone else. He wouldn't have known how frightening he might seem. He was certainly frightening to Laura.

"You screamed and screamed," I said now. "You didn't understand he was just pretending."

"It was worse than that," said Laura. "I thought he was pretending the rest of the time."

"What do you mean?"

"That this was what he was really like," said Laura patiently. "That underneath, he was burning up. All the time."

The Water Nixie

This morning I slept in, exhausted after a night of dark wanderings. My feet were swollen, as if I'd been walking long distances over hard ground; my head felt porous and damp. It was Myra knocking at the door that woke me up. "Rise and shine," she trilled through the letter slot. Out of perversity, I didn't answer. Maybe she'd think I was dead – croaked in my sleep! No doubt she was already fussing over which of my floral prints she'd lay me out in, and was planning the eats for the post-funeral reception. It wouldn't be called a wake, nothing so barbaric. A wake was to wake you up, because it's just as well to make sure the dead are really dead before you shovel the mulch over them.

I smiled at that. Then I remembered Myra had a key. I thought of pulling the sheet up over my face to give her at least a minute of pleasurable horror, but decided better not. I levered myself upright and out of the bed, and pulled on my dressing gown.

"Hold your horses," I called down the stairwell.

But Myra was already inside, and with her was *the woman*: the cleaning woman. She was a hefty creature with a Portuguese look to her: no way to stave her off. She set to work at once with Myra's vacuum cleaner – they'd thought of everything – while I followed her around like a banshee, wailing, *Don't touch that! Leave that there! I can do that myself! Now I'll never find anything!* At least I got to the kitchen ahead of them, and had time to shove my pile of scribbled pages into the oven. They'd be unlikely to tackle that on the first day of cleaning. In any case it's not too dirty, I never bake anything.

"There," said Myra, when the woman had finished. "All clean and tidy. Doesn't that make you feel better?"

She'd brought me a fresh do-dad from The Gingerbread House – an emerald-green crocus planter, only a little bit chipped, in the shape of a coyly smiling girl's head. The crocuses are supposed to grow out through the holes in the top and burst into a *halo of bloom*, her words exactly. All I have to do is water it, says Myra, and pretty soon it'll be cute as a button.

God works in his mysterious ways his wonders to perform, as Reenie used to say. Could it be that Myra is my designated guardian angel? Or is she instead a foretaste of Purgatory? And how do you tell the difference?

On our second day at Avilion, Laura and I went off to see Reenie. It wasn't hard to find out where she was living: everyone in town knew. Or the people in Betty's Luncheonette did, because that's where she was working now, three days a week. We didn't tell Richard and Winifred where we were going, because why add to the unpleasant atmosphere around the breakfast table? We could not be absolutely prohibited, but we would be certain to attract an annoying measure of subdued scorn.

We took the teddy bear I'd bought for Reenie's baby, at Simpsons, in Toronto. It wasn't a very cuddly teddy bear – it was stern and tightly stuffed and stiff. It looked like a minor civil servant, or a civil servant of those days. I don't know what they look like now. Most likely they wear jeans.

Reenie and her husband were living in one of the small limestone row-house cottages originally built for the factory workmen – two floors, pointed roof, privy at the back of the narrow garden – not so very far from where I live now. They had no telephone, so we could not alert Reenie to the fact that we were coming. When she opened the door and saw the two of us standing there, she smiled broadly, and then began to cry.

After a moment, so did Laura. I stood holding the teddy bear, feeling left out because I wasn't crying too.

"Bless you," said Reenie to both of us. "Come in and see the baby."

We went along the linoleum-floored corridor into the kitchen. Reenie had painted it white and added yellow curtains, the same shade of yellow as the curtains at Avilion. I noticed a set of canisters, white as well, with yellow stencilling: Flour, Sugar, Coffee, Tea. I didn't need to be told that Reenie had done these decorations herself. Those, and the curtains, and anything else she could lay her hands on. She was making the best of it.

The baby – that's you, Myra, you have now entered the story – was lying in a wicker laundry basket, staring at us with round, unblinking eyes that were even bluer than babies' eyes usually are. I have to say she looked like a suet pudding, but then most babies do.

Reenie insisted on making us a cup of tea. We were young ladies now, she said; we could have real tea, and not just milk with a little tea in it, the way we used to. She had gained weight; the undersides of her arms, once so firm and strong, wobbled a little, and as she walked across to the stove she almost waddled. Her hands were puffy, the knuckles dimpled.

"You eat for two and then you forget to stop," she said. "See my wedding ring? I couldn't get it off unless they cut it off. I'll have to be buried in it." She said this with a sigh of complacency. Then the baby began to fuss, and Reenie picked it up and set it on her knee, and looked across the table at us almost defiantly. The table (plain, cramped, with an oilcloth covering printed in yellow tulips) was like a great chasm – on one side of it the two of us, on the other, immensely far away now, Reenie and her baby, with no regrets.

Regrets for what? For her abandonment of us. Or that is what it felt like to me.

There was something odd in Reenie's manner, not towards the baby but towards us in relation to it – almost as if we'd found her out. I've since wondered – and you'll have to excuse me for mentioning it, Myra, but really you shouldn't be reading this, and curiosity killed the cat – I've since wondered whether this baby's father was not Ron Hincks at all, but Father himself. There was Reenie, the only servant left at Avilion, after I'd gone off on my honeymoon, and all around Father's head the towers were crashing down. Wouldn't she have applied herself to him like a poultice, in the same spirit in which she'd bring him a cup of warm soup or a hot-water bottle? Comfort, against the cold and dark.

In that case, Myra, you are my sister. Or my half-sister. Not that we'll ever know, or I myself will never know. I suppose you could have me dug up, and take a sample of my hair or bone or whatever they use, and send it off to be analysed. But I doubt that you'd go that far. The only other possible proof would be Sabrina – you could get together, compare snippets of yourselves. But in order for that to happen, Sabrina would have to come back, and God only knows whether she ever will. She could be anywhere. She could be dead. She could be at the bottom of the sea.

I wonder if Laura knew about Reenie and Father, if indeed there was anything to know. I wonder if that is among the many things she knew, but never told. Such a thing is entirely possible.

The days at Avilion did not pass quickly. It was still too hot, it was still too humid. The water levels in the two rivers were low: even the Louveteau's rapids were sluggish, and an unpleasant smell was coming off the Jogues.

I stayed inside the house most of the time, sitting in the leather-backed chair in Grandfather's library with my legs over its arm. The husks of last winter's dead flies were still encrusting the windowsills: the library was not a top priority for Mrs. Murgatroyd. Grandmother Adelia's portrait was still presiding.

I spent the afternoons with her scrapbooks, with their clippings about teas and the visiting Fabians, and the explorers with their magic lantern shows and their accounts of quaint native customs. I don't know why anyone found it strange that they decorated the skulls of their ancestors, I thought. We do that too.

Or I would leaf through old society magazines, remembering how I'd once envied the people in them; or I'd ferret through the poetry books with their tissue-thin gilt-edged pages. The poems that used to entrance me in the days of Miss Violence now struck me as overdone and sickly. *Alas, burthen, thine, cometh, aweary* – the archaic language of unrequited love. I was irritated with such words, which rendered the unhappy lovers – I could now see – faintly ridiculous, like poor moping Miss Violence herself. Soft-edged, blurry, soggy, like a bun fallen into the water. Nothing you'd want to touch.

Already my childhood seemed far away – a remote age, faded and bittersweet, like dried flowers. Did I regret its loss, did I want it back? I didn't think so.

Laura didn't stay inside. She rambled around the town, the way we used to do. She wore a yellow cotton dress of mine from the summer before, and the hat that went with it. Seeing her from behind gave me a peculiar sensation, as if I were watching myself.

Winifred made no secret of the fact that she was bored stiff. She went swimming every day, from the small private beach beside the boathouse, though she never went in over her depth: mostly she just splashed around, wearing a giant magenta coolie hat. She wanted Laura and me to join her, but we declined. Neither of us could swim very well, and also we knew what sorts of things used to be dumped into the river, and possibly still were. When she wasn't swimming or sunbathing, Winifred wandered around the house making notes and sketches, and lists of imperfections – the wallpaper in the front hall really had to be replaced, there was dry rot under the stairs – or else she took naps in her room. Avilion seemed to drain her energy. It was reassuring to know that something could.

Richard talked on the telephone a lot, long distance; or else he'd go into Toronto for the day. The rest of the time he diddled around with the *Water Nixie*, supervising the repairs. It was his goal to get the thing floated, he said, before we had to leave.

He had the papers delivered every morning. "Civil war in Spain," he said one day at lunch. "Well, it's been a long time coming."

"That's unpleasant," said Winifred.

"Not for us," said Richard. "As long as we keep out of it. Let the Commies and the Nazis kill each other off – they'll both jump into the fray soon enough."

Laura had skipped lunch. She was down on the dock, by herself, with only a cup of coffee. She was frequently down there: it made me nervous. She would lie on the dock, trailing one arm in the water, gazing into the river as if she'd dropped something and was looking for it down at the bottom. The water was too dark though. You couldn't see much. Only the occasional clutch of silvery minnows, flitting about like a pick-pocket's fingers.

"Still," said Winifred. "I wish they wouldn't. It's very dis-agreeable."

"We could use a good war," said Richard. "Maybe it will pep things up – put paid to the Depression. I know a few fellows who are counting on it. Some folks are going to make a lot of money." I was never told anything about Richard's financial position, but I'd come to believe lately – from various hints and indications – that he didn't have as much money as I'd once thought. Or he no longer had it. The restoration of Avilion had been halted – *postponed* – because Richard had been unwilling to spend any more. That was according to Reenie.

"Why will they make money?" I said. I knew the answer perfectly well, but I'd drifted into the habit of asking naive questions just to see what Richard and Winifred would say. The sliding moral scale they applied to almost every area of life had not yet ceased to hold my attention.

"Because that's the way things are," said Winifred shortly. "By the by, your pal got arrested."

"What pal?" I said, too quickly.

"That Callista woman. Your father's old light o'love. The one who thinks of herself as an artist."

I resented her tone, but didn't know how to counter it. "She was awfully good to us when we were kids," I said.

"Of course she would have been, wouldn't she?"

"I liked her," I said.

"No doubt. She got hold of me a couple of months ago – tried to get me to buy some dreadful painting or mural or something – a bunch of ugly women in overalls. Not anyone's first choice for the dining room."

"Why would they arrest her?"

"The Red Squad, some roundup or other at a pinko party. She called here – she was quite frantic. She wanted to speak to you. I didn't see why you should be involved, so Richard went all the way into town and bailed her out."

"Why would he do that?" I said. "He hardly knows her."

"Oh, just out of the goodness of his heart," said Winifred, smiling sweetly. "Though he's always said those people are more trouble in jail than out of it, haven't you, Richard? They howl their heads off, in the press. Justice this, justice that. Maybe he was doing the prime minister a favour."

"Is there any more coffee?" said Richard.

This meant Winifred should drop the subject, but she went on. "Or maybe he felt he owed it to your family. I suppose you might consider her a sort of family heirloom, like some old crock that gets passed down from hand to hand."

"I think I'll join Laura on the dock," I said. "It's such a beautiful day."

Richard had been reading the paper all through my conversation with Winifred, but now he looked up quickly. "No," he said, "stay here. You encourage her too much. Leave her alone and she'll get over it."

"Over what?" I said.

"Whatever's eating her," said Richard. He'd turned his head to look at her out the window, and I noticed for the first time that there was a thinning spot at the back of his head, a round of pink scalp showing through his brown hair. Soon he would have a tonsure.

"Next summer we'll go to Muskoka," said Winifred. "I can't say this little vacation experiment has been a raging success."

Towards the end of our stay I decided to visit the attic. I waited until Richard was occupied on the telephone and Winifred was lying in a deck chair on our little strip of sand with a damp washcloth across her eyes. Then I opened the door to the attic stairs, closing it behind me, and went up as quietly as I could.

Laura was already there, sitting on one of the cedar chests. She'd got the window open, which was a mercy: otherwise the place would have been stifling. There was a musky scent of old cloth and mouse droppings.

She turned her head, not quickly. I hadn't startled her. "Hello," she said. "There's bats living up here."

"I'm not surprised," I said. There was a large paper grocery bag beside her. "What've you got there?"

She began to take things out – various bits and pieces, bric-à-brac. The silver teapot that was my grandmother's, and three china cups and saucers, hand-painted, from Dresden. A few monogrammed spoons. The nutcracker shaped like an alligator, a lone mother-of pearl cuff link, a tortoiseshell comb with missing teeth, a broken silver lighter, a cruet stand minus the vinegar.

"What're you doing with these things?" I said. "You can't take them back to Toronto!"

"I'm hiding them. They can't lay waste to everything."

"Who can't?"

"Richard and Winifred. They'd just throw these things out anyway; I've heard them talking about worthless junk. They'll make a clean sweep, sooner or later. So I'm saving a few things, for us. I'll leave them up here in one of the trunks. That way they'll be safe, and we'll know where they are."

"What if they notice?" I said.

"They won't notice. There's nothing really valuable. Look," she said, "I found our old school exercise books. They were still here, in the same place we left them. Remember when we brought them up here? For him?"

Alex Thomas never needed a name, for Laura: he was always *he, him, his.* I'd thought for a while that she'd given him up, or given up the idea of him, but it was obvious now that she hadn't.

"It's hard to believe we did it," I said. "That we hid him up here, that we weren't found out."

"We were careful," said Laura. She thought for a moment, then smiled. "You never really believed me, about Mr. Erskine," she said. "Did you?"

I suppose I should have lied outright. Instead I compromised. "I didn't like him. He was horrible," I said.

"Reenie believed me, though. Where do you think he is?"

"Mr. Erskine?"

"You know who." She paused, turned to look out the window again. "Do you still have your picture?"

"Laura, I don't think you should dwell on him," I said. "I don't think he's going to turn up. It's not in the cards."

"Why? Do you think he's dead?"

"Why would he be dead?" I said. "I don't think he's dead. I just think he's gone somewhere else."

"Anyway they haven't caught him, or we would have heard about it. It would have been in the papers," said Laura. She gathered up the old exercise books and slid them into her paper bag.

We lingered on at Avilion longer than I'd thought we would, and certainly longer than I wanted: I felt hemmed in there, locked up, unable to move.

The day before we were due to leave, I came down to breakfast, and Richard wasn't there; only Winifred, who was eating an egg. "You missed the big launch," she said.

"What big launch?"

She gestured at our view, which was of the Louveteau on one hand, the Jogues on the other. I was surprised to see Laura on the *Water Nixie*, sailing away downriver. She was sitting up in the bow, like a figurehead. Her back was towards us. Richard was at the wheel. He was wearing some awful white sailor hat.

"At least they haven't sunk," said Winifred, with a hint of acid.

"Didn't you want to go?" I said.

"No, actually." There was an odd tone to her voice, which I mistook for jealousy: she did so like being in on the ground floor, in any project of Richard's.

I was relieved: maybe Laura would unbend a little now, maybe she would let up on the deep-freeze campaign. Maybe she would start treating Richard as if he were a human being instead of something that had crawled out from under a rock. That would certainly make my own life easier, I thought. It would lighten the atmosphere.

It didn't, however. If anything, the tension increased, though it had reversed itself: now it was Richard who would leave the room whenever Laura came into it. It was almost as if he was afraid of her.

"What did you say to Richard?" I asked her one evening when we were all back in Toronto.

"What do you mean?"

"That day you went sailing with him, on the *Water Nixie*."

"I didn't say anything to him," she said. "Why would I?"

"I don't know."

"I never say anything to him," said Laura, "because I have nothing to say."

The chestnut tree

I look back over what I've written and I know it's wrong, not because of what I've set down, but because of what I've omitted. What isn't there has a presence, like the absence of light.

You want the truth, of course. You want me to put two and two together. But two and two doesn't necessarily get you the truth. Two and two equals a voice outside the window. Two and two equals the wind. The living bird is not its labelled bones.

Last night I woke abruptly, my heart pounding. From the window there was a clinking sound: someone was throwing pebbles against the glass. I climbed out of bed and groped my way towards the window, and raised the sash higher and leaned out. I didn't have my glasses on, but I could see well enough. There was the moon, almost full, spider-veined with old scars, and below it the ambient sub-orange glow cast up into the sky by the street lights. Beneath me was the sidewalk, patchy with shadow and partially hidden by the chestnut tree in the front yard.

I was aware that there shouldn't be a chestnut tree there: that tree belonged elsewhere, a hundred miles away, outside the house where I had once lived with Richard. Yet there it was, the tree, its branches spread out like a hard thick net, its white-moth flowers glimmering faintly.

The glassy clinking came again. There was a shape there, bending over: a man, foraging in the garbage cans, shuffling the wine bottles in the desperate hope that there might be something left in one of them. A street drunk, impelled by emptiness and thirst. His movements were stealthy, invasive, as if he was not hunting, but spying – sifting through my discarded trash for evidence against me.

Then he straightened and moved sideways into the fuller light, and looked up. I could see the dark eyebrows, the hollows of the eye sockets, the smile a white slash across the dark oval of his face. At the V below his throat there was pallor: a shirt. He lifted his hand, moved it to the side. A wave of greeting, or else departure.

Now he was walking away, and I couldn't call after him. He knew I couldn't call. Now he was gone.

I felt a choking pressure around the heart. *No, no, no, no*, said a voice. Tears were running down my face.

But I'd said that out loud – too loudly, because Richard was awake now. He was standing right behind me. He was about to put his hand on my neck.

This was when I woke up really. I lay with my wet face, eyes open, staring at the grey blank of the ceiling, waiting for my heart to slow down. I don't cry often any more, when awake; only a few dry tears now and then. It's a surprise to find I've been doing it.

When you're young, you think everything you do is disposable. You move from now to now, crumpling time up in your hands, tossing it away. You're your own speeding car. You think you can get rid of things, and people too – leave them behind. You don't yet know about the habit they have, of coming back.

Time in dreams is frozen. You can never get away from where you've been.

There really was a clinking sound, glass against glass. I climbed out of bed – out of my real, single bed – and made my way over to the window. Two raccoons were pawing through the neighbours' Blue Box across the street, turning over the bottles and cans. Scavengers, at home in the junkyard. They looked up at me, alert, unalarmed, their small thieves' masks black in the moonlight.

Good luck to you, I thought. Take what you can, while you can get it. Who cares if it belongs to you? Just don't get caught.

I went back to bed and lay in the heavy darkness, listening to the sound of breathing I knew was not there.

X

The Blind Assassin: Lizard Men of Xenor

For weeks she trolls the racks. She goes to the nearest drug-store, buys some emery boards or an orange stick, something minor, then strolls past the magazines, not touching and careful not to be seen looking, but riffling through the titles with her eyes, on the lookout for his name. One of his names. She knows them by now, or most of them: she used to cash the cheques.

Wonder Stories. Weird Tales. Astounding. She scans them all.

At last she spots something. This must be it: *Lizard Men of Xenor. First Thrilling Episode in the Annals of the Zycronian Wars.* On the cover, a blonde in a quasi-Babylonian getup, a white robe tightly cinched under her unlikely breasts by a gold-link belt, her throat wound in lapis jewellery, a crescent moon in silver sprouting from her head. She's wet-lipped, open-mouthed, big-eyed, in the grip of two creatures with three-fingered claws and eyes with vertical pupils. They're wearing nothing but red shorts. Their faces are flattened disks, their skin is covered with scales, a pewtery teal in hue. They shine slickly, as if basted; under their grey-blue hide their muscles bulge and gleam. The teeth in their lipless mouths are numerous and needle-sharp.

She'd know them anywhere.

How to get hold of a copy? Not in this store, where she's recognized. It would never do to start rumours, by strange behaviour of any kind at all. On her next shopping trip she makes a detour to the train station and locates the magazine at the newsstand there. One thin dime; she pays with her gloves on, rolls the magazine up quickly, caches it in her handbag. The newsie looks at her strangely, but then men do.

She hugs the magazine to her all the way back in the taxi, smuggles it up the stairs, locks herself in the bathroom with it. Her hands, she knows, will tremble turning the pages. It's a story of the kind bums read on boxcars, or school-age boys by the light of a flashlight. Factory watchmen at midnight, to keep themselves awake; salesmen in their travellers' hotels after a fruitless day, tie off, shirt open, feet up, whisky in the toothbrush glass. Police, on a dull evening. None of them will find the message that will surely be concealed some- where within the print. It will be a message meant only for her.

The paper's so soft it almost falls apart in her hands.

Here in the locked bathroom, spread out on her knees in hard print, is Sakiel-Norn, city of a thousand splendours – its gods, its customs, its wondrous carpet-weaving, its enslaved and maltreated children, the maidens about to be sacrificed. Its seven seas, its five moons, its three suns; the western mountains and their sinister tombs, where wolves howl and beautiful undead women lurk. The palace coup stretches its tentacles, the King bides his time, guessing at the forces deployed against him; the High Priestess pockets her bribes.

Now it's the night before the sacrifice; the chosen one waits in the fatal bed. But where is the blind assassin? What's become of him, and his love for the innocent girl? He must be keeping that part for later, she decides.

Then, sooner than she's expecting it, the ruthless barbarians attack, spurred on by their monomaniac leader. But they've just made their way inside the city gates when there's a surprise: three spaceships make a landing on the flat plain to the east. They're shaped like fried eggs or Saturn cut in half, and they come from Xenor. Out of them burst the Lizard Men, with their rippling grey muscles and their metallic bathing trunks and their advanced weaponry. They have ray guns, electric lassoes, one-man flying machines. All sorts of newfangled gadgets.

The sudden invasion changes things for the Zycronians. Barbarians and urbanites, incumbents and rebels, masters and slaves – all forget their differences and make common cause. Class barriers dissolve – the Snilfards discard their ancient titles along with their face masks, and roll up their sleeves, manning the barricades alongside the Ygnirods. All salute to each other by the name of *tristok*, which means (roughly), *he with whom I have exchanged blood*, that is to say, comrade or brother. The women are taken to the Temple and locked into it for their own safety, the children as well. The King takes charge. The barbarian forces are welcomed into the city because of their prowess in battle. The King shakes hands with the Servant of Rejoicing, and they decide to share command. *A fist is more than the sum of its fingers*, says the King, quoting an archaic proverb. In the nick of time the eight heavy gates of the city swing shut.

The Lizard Men achieve an initial success in the outlying fields, gained by the element of surprise. They capture a few likely women, who are shut up in cages and drooled at through the bars by dozens of Lizard soldiers. But then the Xenorian army suffers a setback: the ray guns on which they rely don't work very well on the planet of Zycron due to a difference in gravitational forces, the electric lassoes are efficient only at close quarters, and the inhabitants of Sakiel-Norn are now on the other side of a very thick wall. The Lizard Men don't have enough one-man flying machines to transport a sufficient assault force to take the city. Projectiles rain down from the ramparts on any Lizard Man who gets close enough: the Zycronians have discovered that the Xenorians' metal pants are inflammable at high temperatures, and are hurling balls of burning pitch.

The leader of the Lizards has a screaming tantrum, and five Lizard scientists bite the dust: Xenor is evidently not a democracy. Those left alive set to work to solve the technical problems. Given enough time and the proper equipment, they claim, they can dissolve the walls of Sakiel-Norn. They can also develop a gas that will render the Zycronians unconscious. Then they will be able to have their wicked way at leisure.

That's the end of the fist instalment. But what's happened to the love story? Where are the blind assassin and the tongueless girl? The girl has been all but forgotten in the confusion – she was last seen hiding under the red brocade bed – and the blind man has never turned up at all. She riffles back through the pages: maybe she's missed something. But no, the two of them have simply vanished.

Perhaps it will turn out all right, in the next thrilling episode. Perhaps he'll send word.

She knows there's something demented about this expectation of hers – he won't send a message to her, or if he does, this is not how it will arrive – but she can't free herself of it. It's hope that spins these fantasies, it's longing that raises these mirages – hope against hope, and longing in a vacuum. Perhaps her mind is slipping, perhaps she's going off the tracks, perhaps she is coming unhinged. *Unhinged*, like a broken door, like a rammed gate, like a rusting strongbox. When you're unhinged, things make their way out of you that should be kept inside, and other things get in that ought to be shut out. The locks lose their powers. The guards go to sleep. The passwords fail.

She thinks, Perhaps I've been forsaken. It's an outworn word, forsaken, but it describes her plight exactly. Forsaking her is something he might be imagined as doing. On impulse he might die for her, but living for her would be quite different. He has no talent for monotony.

Despite her better judgment she waits and watches, month after month. She haunts the drugstores, the train station, every chance newsstand. But the next thrilling episode never appears.

Mayfair, May 1937

TORONTO HIGH NOON GOSSIP
BY YORK

April gambolled in like a lamb this year, and taking a cue
from his sprightly kick-up-your-heels mood, the Spring
season was all aflutter with the gay bustle of arrivals and
departures. Mr. and Mrs. Henry Ridelle have returned
from a winter sojourn in Mexico, Mr. and Mrs. Johnson
Reeves have motored back from their Florida hideaway in
Palm Beach, and Mr. and Mrs. T. Perry Grange are back
from their cruise amongst the sunny Caribbean isles,
while Mrs. R. Westerfield and her daughter Daphne have
set out for a visit to France, and to Italy as well,
"Mussolini permitting," while Mr. and Mrs. W.
McClelland are off to fabled Greece. The Dumont
Fletchers passed an exciting London season and made their
entrance upon our local stage once more, just in time for
the Dominion Drama Festival, at which Mr. Fletcher was
an adjudicator.

Meanwhile, an entrance of another kind was celebrated
in the lilac and silver setting of the Arcadian Court, where
Mrs. Richard Griffen (formerly Miss Iris Montfort
Chase) was glimpsed at a luncheon party given by her
sister-in-law, Mrs. Winifred "Freddie" Griffen Prior.
Young Mrs. Griffen, as lovely as ever and one of last
season's most important brides, was wearing a smart
ensemble of sky-blue silk with a chapeau of Nile green,
and was receiving congratulations on the arrival of a
daughter, Aimee Adelia.

The Pleiades were all abuzz over the advent of their visiting star, Miss Frances Homer, the celebrated monologuist, who, at Eaton Auditorium, again presented her Women of Destiny series, in which she portrays women of history and the influence they brought to bear upon the lives of such momentous world figures as Napoleon, Ferdinand of Spain, Horatio Nelson and Shakespeare. Miss Homer sparkled with wit and vivacity as Nell Gywn; she was dramatic as Queen Isabella of Spain; her Josephine was a delightful vignette; and her Lady Emma Hamilton was a poignant bit of acting. Altogether it was a picturesque and charming entertainment.

The evening concluded with a buffet supper for the Pleiades and their guests at the Round Room, lavishly hosted by Mrs. Winifred Griffen Prior.

Letter from BellaVista

Office of the Director,
The BellaVista Sanctuary,
Arnprior, Ontario
May 12, 1937

Mr. Richard E. Griffen,
President and Chairman of the Board,
Griffen-Chase Royal Consolidated Industries Ltd.,
20 King Street West,
Toronto, Ontario

Dear Richard:

It was a pleasure to meet with you in February – although in such regrettable circumstances – and to shake your hand again after so many years. Our lives have certainly taken us in different directions since those "good old golden rule days."

On a more sober note, I am sorry to report that the condition of your young sister-in-law, Miss Laura Chase, has not improved; if anything it has worsened somewhat. The delusions from which she suffers are well entrenched. In our opinion, she remains a danger to herself and must be kept under constant observation, with sedation when necessary. No more windows have been broken, though there has been an incident involving a pair of scissors; however, we will do our utmost to prevent a recurrence.

We continue to do all in our power. Several new treatments are available that we hope to use with positive effect, in particular the "electro-shock therapy," for which we will have the equipment soon. With your permission we will add this to the insulin treatment. We have firm hopes for an eventual improvement, although it is our prognosis that Miss Chase will never be strong.

Distressing though it may be, I must request that you and your wife refrain from visiting or even from sending letters to Miss Chase at present, as contact with either of you is sure to have a disruptive effect upon the treatment. As you are aware, you yourself are the focus of Miss Chase's more persistent fixations.

I will be in Toronto this Wednesday week, and look forward to a private conversation with you – at your offices, as your young wife, being a new mother, ought not to be unduly troubled with such disturbing matters. At that time I will ask you to sign the necessary forms of consent relative to the treatments we propose.

I take the liberty of enclosing this past month's bill for your prompt consideration.

Yours sincerely,

Dr. Gerald P. Witherspoon, Director

She feels heavy and soiled, like a bag of unwashed laundry. But at the same time flat and without substance. Blank paper, on which – just discernible – there's the colourless imprint of a signature, not hers. A detective could find it, but she herself can't be bothered. She can't be bothered looking.

She hasn't given up hope, just folded it away: it's not for daily wear. Meanwhile the body must be tended. There's no point in not eating. It's best to keep your wits about you, and nourishment helps with that. Small pleasures too: flowers to fall back on, the first tulips for instance. No use going distracted. Running down the street barefoot, shouting *Fire!* The fact that there is no fire is sure to be noticed.

The best way of keeping a secret is to pretend there isn't one. *So kind*, she says to the telephone. *But so sorry. I can't make it then. I'm tied up.*

On some days – clear warm days especially – she feels buried alive. The sky is a dome of blue rock, the sun a round hole in it through which the light of the real day shines mockingly. The other people buried with her don't know what's happened: only she knows. If she were to voice this knowledge, they'd shut her away forever. Her only chance is to go on as if everything is proceeding normally, meanwhile keeping an eye on the flat blue sky, watching out for the large crack that is bound to appear in it eventually. After which he might come down through it on a rope ladder. She'll make her way to the roof, jump for it. The ladder will be drawn up with the two of them clinging to it, clinging to each other, past turrets and towers and spires, out through the crack in the fake sky, leaving the others down below on the lawn, gawking with their mouths open.

Such omnipotent and childish plots.

Under the blue stone dome it rains, it shines, it blows, it clears. Amazing to consider how all these naturalistic weather effects are arranged.

There's a baby in the vicinity. Its cries come to her intermittently, as if borne on the wind. Doors open and close, the sound of its tiny, immense rage waxes and wanes. Amazing how they can roar. Its wheezy breathing is quite close at times, the sound harsh and soft, like silk tearing.

She lies on her bed, sheets over or under her depending on the time of day. She prefers a white pillow, white as a nurse and lightly starched. Several pillows to prop her up, a cup of tea to anchor her so she won't drift off. She holds it in her hands, and if it hits the floor she'll wake. She doesn't do this all the time, she's far from lazy.

Reverie intrudes at intervals.

She imagines him imagining her. This is her salvation.

In spirit she walks the city, traces its labyrinths, its dingy mazes: each assignation, each rendezvous, each door and stair and bed. What he said, what she said, what they did, what they did then. Even the times they argued, fought, parted, agonized, rejoined. How they'd loved to cut themselves on each other, taste their own blood. We were ruinous together, she thinks. But how else can we live, these days, except in the midst of ruin?

Sometimes she wants to put a match to him, have done with him; finish with that endless, useless longing. At the very least, daily time and the entropy of her own body should take care of it – wear her threadbare, wear her out, erase that place in her brain. But no exorcism has been enough, nor has she tried very hard at it. Exorcism is not what she wants. She wants that terrified bliss, like falling out of an airplane by mistake. She wants his famished look.

The last time she'd seen him, when they'd gone back to his room – it was like drowning: everything darkened and roared, but at the same time it was very silvery, and slow, and clear.

This is what it means, to be in thrall.

Perhaps he carries an image of her always with him, as if in a locket; or not an image exactly, more like a diagram. A map, as if for treasure. What he'll need to get back.

First there's the land, thousands of miles of it, with an outer circle of rock and mountains, ice-covered, fissured and wrinkled; then forest tangled with windfall, a matted pelt of it, dead wood rotting under moss; then the odd clearing. Then heaths and windswept steppes and dry red hills where war goes forward. Behind the rocks, at ambush within the parched canyons, the defenders crouch. They specialize in snipers.

Next come the villages, with squalid hovels and squinting urchins and women lugging bundles of sticks, the dirt roads murky with pig-wallow. Then the railroad tracks running into the towns, with their stations and depots, their factories and warehouses, their churches and marble banks. Then the cities, vast oblongs of light and dark, tower upon tower. The towers are sheathed in adamant. No: something more modern, more believable. Not zinc, that's poor women's washtubs.

The towers are sheathed in steel. Bombs are made there, bombs fall there also. But he bypasses all of that, comes through it unscathed, all the way to this city, the one containing her, its houses and steeples encircling her where she sits in the most inward, the most central tower of them all, which doesn't even resemble a tower. It's camouflaged: you could be forgiven for confusing it with a house. She's the tremulous heart of everything, tucked into her white bed. Locked away from danger, but she is the point of it all. The point of it all is to protect her. That's what they spend their time doing – protecting her from everything else. She looks out the window, and nothing can get at her, and she can get at nothing.

She's the round O, the zero at the bone. A space that defines itself by not being there at all. That's why they can't reach her, lay a finger on her. That's why they can't pin anything on her. She has such a good smile, but she doesn't stand behind it.

He wants to think of her as invulnerable. Standing in her lighted window, behind her a locked door. He wants to be right there, under the tree, looking up. Taking courage, he climbs the wall, hand over hand past vine and ledge, happy as a crook; he crouches, raises the window, steps down in. The radio's gently on, dance music swelling and fading. It drowns out footsteps. There's not a word between them, and so begins again the delicate, painstaking ransack of the flesh. Muffled, hesitating and dim, as if underwater.

You've led a sheltered life, he'd said to her once.

You could call it that, she'd said.

But how can she ever get out of it, her life, except through him?

The Globe and Mail, May 26, 1937

RED VENDETTA IN BARCELONA
PARIS. SPECIAL TO THE GLOBE AND MAIL

Although news from Barcelona is heavily censored, word has got through to our correspondent in Paris of clashes between rival Republican factions in that city. The Stalin-backed Communists, well armed by Russia, are rumoured to be carrying out purges against the rival POUM, the extremist Trotskyists who have made common cause with the Anarchists. The heady early days of Republican rule have given way to an atmosphere of suspicion and fear, as Communists accuse the POUM of "fifth-column" treachery. Open street fighting has been observed, with city police siding with the Communists. Many POUM members are said to be in jail or in flight. Several Canadians may have been caught in the crossfire, but these reports remain unverified.

Elsewhere in Spain, Madrid continues to be held by the Republicans, but Nationalist forces under General Franco are making significant gains.

The Blind Assassin: Union Station

She bends her neck, rests her forehead on the edge of the table. Imagines his advent.

It's dusk, the station lights are on, his face is haggard in them. Somewhere nearby there's a coast, ultramarine: he can hear the cries of gulls. He swings aboard the train through clouds of hissing steam, hoists his duffel bag onto the rack; then he slumps into the seat, takes out the sandwich he's bought, unwraps it from the crumpled paper, tears it apart. He's almost too tired to eat.

Beside him is an elderly woman who's knitting something red, a sweater. He knows what she's knitting because she tells him; she'd tell him all about it if allowed, about her children, about her grandchildren; no doubt she's got snapshots, but hers is not a story he wishes to hear. He can't think about children, having seen too many dead ones. It's the children that stay with him, even more than the women, more than the old men. They were always so unexpected: their sleepy eyes, their waxy hands, the fingers lax, the tattered rag doll soaked with blood. He turns away, gazes at his face in the night window, hollow-eyed, framed by his wet-looking hair, the skin greenish black, bleared with soot and the dark shapes of trees rushing past behind it.

He clambers past the old woman's knees into the aisle, stands between cars, smokes, tosses the butt, pisses into the void. He senses himself going the same way – off into nothingness. He could fall away here and never be found.

Marshland, a dimly seen horizon. He returns to his seat. The train is chilly and damp or overheated and muggy; he either sweats or shivers, perhaps both: he burns and freezes, as in love.

The bristly upholstery of the seat back is musty and comfort-less, and rasps against his cheek. At last he sleeps, mouth open, head fallen to the side, against the dirty glass. In his ears is the ticking of the knitting needles, and under that the clacking of the wheels along the iron rails, like the workings of some relentless metronome.

Now she imagines him dreaming. She imagines him dream-ing of her, as she is dreaming of him. Through a sky the colour of wet slate they fly towards each other on dark invisible wings, searching, searching, doubling back, drawn by hope and longing, baffled by fear. In their dreams they touch, they inter-twine, it's more like a collision, and that is the end of the flying. They fall to earth, fouled parachutists, botched and cindery angels, love streaming out behind them like torn silk. Enemy groundfire comes up to meet them.

A day passes, a night, a day. At a stop he gets out, buys an apple, a Coca-Cola, a half-pack of cigarettes, a newspaper. He should have brought a mickey or even a whole bottle, for the oblivion that's in it. He looks out through the rain-blurred windows at the long flat fields unrolling like stubbled rugs, at the clumps of trees; his eyes cross with drowsiness. In the evening there's a lingering sunset, receding westward as he approaches, wilting from pink to violet. Night falls with its fitfulness, its starts and stops, the iron screams of the train. Behind his eyes is redness, the red of tiny hoarded fires, of explosions in the air.

He wakes as the sky grows lighter; he can make out water on one side, flat and shoreless and silvery, the inland lake at last. On the other side of the tracks are small discouraged houses, laundry drooping on the lines in their yards. Then an encrusted brick smokestack, a blank-eyed factory with a tall chimney; then another factory, its many windows reflecting palest blue.

•

She imagines him descending into the early morning, walking through the station, through the long vaulted hall lined with pillars, across the marble floor. Echoes float there, blurred loudspeaker voices, their messages obscure. The air smells of smoke – the smoke of cigarettes, of trains, of the city itself, which is more like dust. She too is walking through this dust or smoke; she's poised to open her arms, to be lifted up by him into the air. Joy clutches her by the throat, indistinguishable from panic. She can't see him. Dawn sun comes in through the tall arched windows, the smoky air ignites, the floor glimmers. Now he's in focus, at the far end, each detail distinct – eye, mouth, hand – though tremulous, like a reflection on a shivering pool.

But her mind can't hold him, she can't fix the memory of what he looks like. It's as if a breeze blows over the water and he's dispersed, into broken colours, into ripples; then he reforms elsewhere, past the next pillar, taking on his familiar body. Around him is a shimmering.

The shimmering is his absence, but it appears to her as light. It's the simple daily light by which everything around her is illuminated. Every morning and night, every glove and shoe, every chair and plate.

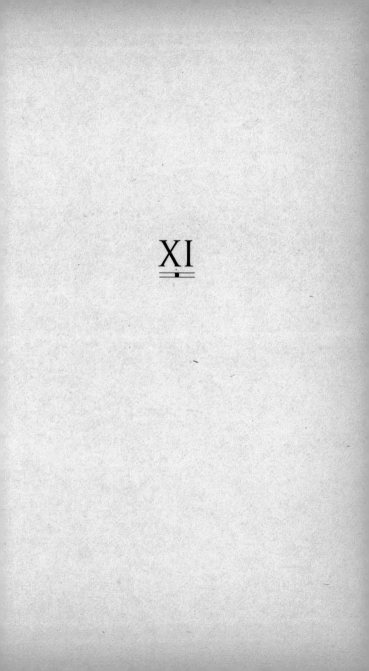

XI

The cubicle

From here on in, things take a darker turn. But then, you knew they would. You knew it, because you already know what happened to Laura.

Laura herself didn't know it, of course. She had no thought of playing the doomed romantic heroine. She became that only later, in the frame of her own outcome and thus in the minds of her admirers. In the course of daily life she was frequently irritating, like anyone. Or dull. Or joyful, she could be that as well: given the right conditions, the secret of which was known only to her, she could drift off into a kind of rapture. It's her flashes of joy that are most poignant for me now.

And so in memory she rambles through her mundane activities, to the outward eye nothing very unusual – a bright-haired girl walking up a hill, intent on thoughts of her own. There are many of these lovely, pensive girls, the landscape is cluttered with them, there's one born every minute. Most of the time nothing out of the ordinary happens to them, these girls. This and that and the other, and then they get older. But Laura has been singled out, by you, by me. In a painting she'd be gathering wildflowers, though in real life she rarely did anything of the kind. The earth-faced god crouches behind her in the forest shade. Only we can see him. Only we know he will pounce.

I've looked back over what I've set down so far, and it seems inadequate. Perhaps there is too much frivolity in it, or too many things that might be taken for frivolity. A lot of clothes, the styles and colours outmoded now, shed butterflies' wings. A lot of dinners, not always very good ones. Breakfasts, picnics, ocean voyages, costume balls, newspapers, boating on the river. Such items do not assort very well with tragedy. But in life, a tragedy is not one long scream. It includes everything that led up to it. Hour after trivial hour, day after day, year after year, and then the sudden moment: the knife stab, the shell-burst, the plummet of the car from the bridge.

It's April now. The snowdrops have come and gone, the crocuses are up. Soon I'll be able to take up residence on the back porch, at my mousy, scarred old wooden table, at least when it's sunny. No ice on the sidewalks, and so I have begun to walk again. The winter months of inactivity have weakened me; I can feel it in my legs. Nevertheless I am determined to repossess my former territories, revisit my watering holes.

Today, with the aid of my cane and with several pauses along the way, I managed to make it as far as the cemetery. There were the two Chase angels, not obviously any the worse for wear after their winter in the snow; there were the family names, only slightly more illegible, but that might be my eyesight. I ran my fingers along these names, along the letters of them; despite their hardness, their tangibility, they appeared to soften under my touch, to fade, to waver. Time has been at them with its sharp invisible teeth.

Someone had cleared away last autumn's soggy leaves from Laura's grave. There was a small bunch of white narcissi, already wilted, the stems wrapped in aluminum foil. I scooped it up and chucked it into the nearest bin. Who do they think appreciates these offerings of theirs, these worshippers of Laura? More to the point, who do they think picks up after them? Them and their floral trash, littering the precincts with the tokens of their spurious grief.

I'll give you something to cry about, Reenie would say. If we'd been her real children she would have slapped us. As it was, she never did, so we never found out what this threatening *something* might be.

On my return journey I stopped at the doughnut shop. I must have looked as tired as I felt, because a waitress came over right away. Usually they don't serve tables, you have to stand at the counter and carry things yourself, but this girl – an oval-faced girl, dark-haired, in what looked like a black uniform – asked me what she could bring me. I ordered a coffee and, for a change, a blueberry muffin. Then I saw her talking to another girl, the one behind the counter, and I realized that she wasn't a waitress at all, but a customer, like myself: her black uniform wasn't even a uniform, only a jacket and slacks. Silver glittered on her somewhere, zippers perhaps: I couldn't make out the details. Before I could thank her properly she was gone.

So refreshing, to find politeness and consideration in girls of that age. Too often (I reflected, thinking of Sabrina) they display only thoughtless ingratitude. But thoughtless ingratitude is the armour of the young; without it, how would they ever get through life? The old wish the young well, but they wish them ill also: they would like to eat them up, and absorb their vitality, and remain immortal themselves. Without the protection of surliness and levity, all children would be crushed by the past – the past of others, loaded onto their shoulders. Selfishness is their saving grace.

Up to a point, of course.

The waitress in her blue smock brought the coffee. Also the muffin, which I regretted almost immediately. I couldn't make much of an inroad into it. Everything in restaurants is becoming too big, too heavy – the material world manifesting itself as huge damp lumps of dough.

After I'd drunk as much of the coffee as I could manage, I set off to reclaim the washroom. In the middle cubicle, the writings I remembered from last autumn had been painted over, but luckily this season's had already begun. At the top right-hand corner, one set of initials coyly declared its love for another set, as is their habit. Underneath that, printed neatly in blue:

Good judgment comes from experience. Experience comes from bad judgment.

Under that, in purple ballpoint cursive: *For an experienced girl call Anita the Mighty Mouth, I'll take you to Heaven*, and a phone number.

And, under that, in block lettering, and red Magic Marker: *The Last Judgment is at hand. Prepare to meet thy Doom and that means you Anita.*

Sometimes I think – no, sometimes I play with the idea – that these washroom scribblings are in reality the work of Laura, acting as if by long distance through the arms and hands of the girls who write them. A stupid notion, but a pleasing one, until I take the further logical step of deducing that in this case they must all be intended for me, because who else would Laura still know in this town? But if they are intended for me, what does Laura mean by them? Not what she says.

At other times I feel a strong urge to join in, to contribute; to link my own tremulous voice to the anonymous chorus of truncated serenades, scrawled love letters, lewd advertisements, hymns and curses.

The Moving Finger writes, and, having writ,
Moves on; nor all your Piety nor Wit
    Shall lure it back to cancel half a Line,
Nor all your Tears blot out a Word of it.

Ha, I think. That would make them sit up and bark.

Some day when I'm feeling better I'll go back there and actually write the thing down. They should all be cheered by it, for isn't it what they want? What we all want: to leave a message behind us that has an effect, if only a dire one; a message that cannot be cancelled out.

But such messages can be dangerous. Think twice before you wish, and especially before you wish to make yourself into the hand of fate.

(*Think twice*, said Reenie. Laura said, *Why only twice?*)

The kitten

September came, then October. Laura was back at school, a different school. The kilts there were grey and blue rather than maroon and black; otherwise this school was much the same as the first, so far as I could see.

In November, just after she'd turned seventeen, Laura announced that Richard was wasting his money. She would continue to attend the school if he demanded it, she would place her body at a desk, but she wasn't learning anything useful. She stated this calmly and without rancour, and surprisingly enough Richard gave in. "She doesn't really need to go to school anyway," he said. "It's not as if she'll ever have to work for a living."

But Laura had to be busied with something, just as I did. She was enlisted in one of Winifred's causes, a volunteer organization called The Abigails, which had to do with hospital visiting. The Abigails were a perky group: girls of good family, training to be future Winifreds. They dressed up in dairy-maid pinafores with tulips appliquéd on their bibs and traipsed around to hospital wards, where they were supposed to talk to the patients, read to them perhaps, and cheer them up – how, it was not specified.

Laura proved to be adept at this. She did not like the other Abigails, that goes without saying, but she took to the pinafore. Predictably, she gravitated to the poverty wards, which the other Abigails tended to avoid because of their stench and outrageousness. These wards were filled with derelicts: old women with dementia, impecunious veterans down on their luck, noseless men with tertiary syphilis and the like. Nurses were in short supply in these realms, and soon Laura was setting her hand to tasks that were strictly speaking none of her business. Bedpans and vomit did not throw her for a loop, it appeared, nor did the swearing and raving and general carryings-on. This was not the situation Winifred had intended, but pretty soon it was the one we were stuck with.

The nurses thought Laura was an angel (or some of them did; others simply thought she was in the way.) According to Winifred, who tried to keep an eye on things and had her spies, Laura was said to be especially good with the hopeless cases. It didn't seem to register on her that they were dying, said Winifred. She treated their condition as ordinary, as normal even, which – Winifred supposed – they must have found calming after a fashion, although a sane person wouldn't. To Winifred, this facility or talent of Laura's was another sign of her fundamentally bizarre nature.

"She must have nerves of ice," said Winifred. "I certainly couldn't do it. I couldn't *bear* it. Think of the squalor!"

Meanwhile, plans were afoot for Laura's début. These plans had not yet been shared with Laura: I'd led Winifred to expect that the reaction from her would not be positive. In that case, said Winifred, the whole thing would have to be arranged, then presented as a *fait accompli*; or, even better, the début could be dispensed with altogether if its primary object had already been accomplished, the primary object being a strategic marriage.

We were having lunch at the Arcadian Court; Winifred had invited me there, just the two of us, to devise a stratagem for Laura, as she put it.

"Stratagem?" I said.

"You know what I mean," said Winifred. "Not disastrous." The best that could be hoped for Laura, all things considered – she continued – was that some nice rich man would bite the bullet and propose to her, and march her off to the altar. Better still, some nice, rich, stupid man, who wouldn't even see there was a bullet to be bitten until it was too late.

"What bullet did you have in mind?" I asked. I wondered if this was the scheme Winifred herself had been following when she'd bagged the elusive Mr. Prior. Had she concealed her bullet-like nature until the honeymoon and then sprung it on him too suddenly? Is that why he was never seen, except in photographs?

"You have to admit," said Winifred, "that Laura is more than a little odd." She paused to smile at someone over my shoulder, and to waggle her fingers in greeting. Her silver bangles clanked; she was wearing too many of them.

"What do you mean?" I asked mildly. Collecting Winifred's explanations of what she meant had become a reprehensible hobby of mine.

Winifred pursed her lips. Her lipstick was orange, her lips were beginning to pleat. Nowadays we would say it was too much sun, but people had not yet made that connection, and Winifred liked to be bronzed; she liked the metallic patina. "She's not to every man's taste. She comes out with some very odd things. She lacks – she lacks *caution*."

Winifred was wearing her green alligator shoes, but I no longer judged them elegant; instead I judged them garish. Much about Winifred that I'd once found mysterious and alluring I now found obvious, merely because I knew too much. Her high gloss was chipped enamel, her sheen was varnish. I'd looked behind the curtain, I'd seen the strings and pulleys, I'd seen the wires and corsets. I'd developed tastes of my own.

"Such as what?" I asked. "What odd things?"

"Yesterday she told me that marriage wasn't important, only love. She said Jesus agreed with her," said Winifred.

"Well, that's her attitude," I said. "She doesn't make any

bones about it. But she doesn't mean sex, you know. She doesn't mean *eros*."

When there was something Winifred didn't understand, she either laughed at it or ignored it. This she ignored. "They all mean sex, whether they know it or not," she said. "An attitude like that could get a girl like her in a lot of trouble."

"She'll grow out of it in time," I said, although I didn't think so.

"None too soon. Girls with their head in the clouds are the worst by far – men take advantage. All we need is some greasy little Romeo. That would cook her goose."

"What do you suggest, then?" I said, gazing at her blankly. I used this blank look of mine to conceal irritation or even anger, but it only encouraged Winifred.

"As I said, marry her off to some nice man who doesn't know which end is up. Then she can fool around with the love stuff later, if that's what she wants. As long as she does it on the Q.T., nobody will say boo."

I dabbled around in the remains of my chicken pot pie. Winifred had picked up a good many slangy expressions lately. I suppose she thought they were up-to-date: she'd reached the age at which being up-to-date would have begun to concern her.

Obviously she didn't know Laura. The idea of Laura doing anything like that on the Q.T. was difficult for me to grasp. Right out on the sidewalk in full daylight was more like it. She'd want to defy us, rub our noses in it. Elope, or something equally melodramatic. Show the rest of us what hypocrites we were.

"Laura will have money, when she's twenty-one," I said.

"Not enough," said Winifred.

"Maybe it will be enough for Laura. Maybe she just wants to lead her own life," I said.

"Her own life!" said Winifred. "Just think what she'd do with it!"

There was no point in trying to deflect Winifred. She was like a meat cleaver in mid-air. "Have you got any candidates?" I said.

"Nothing firm, but I'm working on it," said Winifred briskly. "There's a few people who wouldn't mind having Richard's connections."

"Don't go to too much trouble," I murmured.

"Oh, but if I don't," said Winifred brightly, "what then?"

"I hear you've been rubbing Winifred the wrong way," I said to Laura. "Getting her all stirred up. Teasing her about Free Love."

"I never said Free Love," said Laura. "I only said marriage was an outworn institution. I said it had nothing to do with love, that's all. Love is giving, marriage is buying and selling. You can't put love into a contract. Then I said there was no marriage in Heaven."

"This isn't Heaven," I said. "In case you haven't noticed. Anyway, you certainly put the wind up her."

"I was just telling the truth." She was pushing back her cuticles with my orange stick. "I guess now she'll start introducing me to people. She's always putting her oar in."

"She's just afraid you might ruin your life. If you go in for love, I mean."

"Did getting married keep your life from being ruined? Or is it too soon to tell?"

I ignored the tone. "What do you think, though?"

"You've got a new perfume. Did Richard give it to you?"

"Of the marriage idea, I mean."

"Nothing." Now she was brushing her long blonde hair, with my hairbrush, seated at my vanity table. She'd been taking more interest in her personal appearance lately; she'd begun to dress quite stylishly, both in her own clothes and in mine.

"You mean, you don't think much of it?" I asked.

"No. I don't think about it at all."

"Perhaps you should," I said. "Perhaps you should give at least a minute of thought to your future. You can't always just keep ambling along, doing . . ." I wanted to say *doing nothing*, but this would have been a mistake.

"The future doesn't exist," said Laura. She'd acquired the habit of talking to me as if I was the younger sister and she was the elder one; as if she had to spell things out for me. Then she said one of her odd things. "If you were a blindfolded tightrope walker crossing Niagara Falls on a high wire, what would you pay more attention to – the crowds on the far shore, or your own feet?"

"My feet, I suppose. I wish you wouldn't use my hairbrush. It's unsanitary."

"But if you paid too much attention to your feet, you'd fall. Or too much attention to the crowds, you'd fall too."

"So what's the right answer?"

"If you were dead, would this hairbrush still be yours?" she said, looking at her profile out of the sides of her eyes. This gave her, in reflection, a sly expression, which was unusual for her. "Can the dead own things? And if not, what makes it 'yours' now? Your initials on it? Or your germs?"

"Laura, stop teasing!"

"I'm not teasing," said Laura, setting the hairbrush down. "I'm thinking. You can never tell the difference. I don't know why you listen to anything Winifred has to say. It's like listening to a mousetrap. One without a mouse in it," she added.

She'd become different lately: she'd become brittle, insouciant, reckless in a new way. She was no longer open about her defiances. I suspected her of taking up smoking, behind my back: I'd smelled tobacco on her once or twice. Tobacco, and something else: something too old, too knowing. I ought to have been more alert to the changes taking place in her, but I had a good many other things on my mind.

I waited until the end of October to tell Richard that I was pregnant. I said I'd wanted to be sure. He expressed conventional joy, and kissed my forehead. "Good girl," he said. I was only doing what was expected of me.

One benefit was that he now left me scrupulously alone at night. He didn't want to damage anything, he said. I told him that was very thoughtful of him. "And you're on gin rations from now on. I won't allow any naughtiness," he said, wagging his finger at me in a way I found sinister. He was more alarming to me during his moments of levity than he was the rest of the time; it was like watching a lizard gambol. "We'll have the very best doctor," he added. "No matter what it costs." Putting things on a commercial footing was reassuring to both of us. With money in play, I knew where I stood: I was the bearer of a very expensive package, pure and simple.

Winifred, after her first little scream of genuine fright, made an insincere fuss. Really she was alarmed. She guessed (rightly) that being the mother of a son and heir, or even just an heir, would give me more status with Richard than I'd had so far, and a good deal more than I was entitled to. More for me, and less for her. She would be on the lookout for ways to whittle me down to size: I expected her to appear any minute with detailed plans for decorating the nursery.

"When may we expect the blessed event?" she asked, and I could see I was in for a prolonged dose of coy language from her. It would now be *the new arrival* and *a present from the stork* and *the little stranger*, nonstop. Winifred could get quite elfish and finicky about subjects that made her nervous.

"In April, I think," I said. "Or March. I haven't seen a doctor yet."

"But you must *know*," she said, arching her eyebrows.

"It's not as if I've done this before," I said crossly. "It's not as if I was *expecting* it. I wasn't paying attention."

I went to Laura's room one evening to tell her the same news. I knocked at the door; when she didn't answer, I opened it softly, thinking she might be asleep. She wasn't though. She was kneeling beside her bed, in her blue nightgown, with her head down and her hair spreading as if blown by an unmoving wind, her arms flung out as if she'd been thrown there. At first I thought she must be praying, but she wasn't, or not that I could hear. When she noticed me at last, she got up, as matter-of-factly as if she'd been dusting, and sat on the frilled bench of her vanity table.

As usual, I was struck by the relationship between her surroundings, the surroundings Winifred had chosen for her – the dainty prints, the ribbon rosebuds, the organdies, the flounces – and Laura herself. A photograph would have revealed only harmony. Yet to me the incongruity was intense, almost surreal. Laura was flint in a nest of thistledown.

I say *flint*, not *stone*: a flint has a heart of fire.

"Laura, I wanted to tell you," I said. "I'm going to have a baby."

She turned towards me, her face smooth and white as a porcelain plate, the expression sealed inside it. But she didn't seem surprised. Nor did she congratulate me. Instead she said, "Remember the kitten?"

"What kitten?" I said.

"The kitten Mother had. The one that killed her."

"Laura, it wasn't a kitten."

"I know," said Laura.

Beautiful view

Reenie is back. She's none too pleased with me. *Well, young lady. What do you have to say for yourself? What did you do to Laura? Don't you ever learn?*

There is no answer to such questions. The answers are so entangled with the questions, so knotted and many-stranded, that they aren't really answers at all.

I'm on trial here. I know it. I know what you'll soon be thinking. It will be much the same as what I myself am thinking: Should I have behaved differently? You'll no doubt believe so, but did I have any other choices? I'd have such choices now, but now is not then.

Should I have been able to read Laura's mind? Should I have known what was going on? Should I have seen what was coming next? Was I my sister's keeper?

Should is a futile word. It's about what didn't happen. It belongs in a parallel universe. It belongs in another dimension of space.

On a Wednesday in February, I made my way downstairs after my mid-afternoon nap. I was napping a lot by then: I was seven months' pregnant, and having trouble sleeping through the night. There was some concern too about my blood pressure; my ankles were puffy, and I'd been told to lie with my feet up for as much as I could. I felt like a huge grape, swollen to bursting with sugar and purple juice; I felt ugly and cumbersome.

It was snowing that day, I remember, great soft wet flakes: I'd looked out the window after I'd levered myself to my feet, and seen the chestnut tree, all white, like a giant coral.

Winifred was there, in the cloud-coloured living room. That wasn't unheard of − she came and went as if she owned the place − but Richard was there too. Usually at that time of day he was at his office. Each of them had a drink in hand. Each looked morose.

"What is it?" I said. "What's wrong?"

"Sit down," said Richard. "Over here, beside me." He patted the sofa.

"This is going to be a shock," said Winifred. "I'm sorry it had to happen at such a delicate time."

She did the talking. Richard held my hand and looked at the floor. Every now and then he would shake his head, as if he found her story either unbelievable or all too true.

Here is the essence of what she said:

Laura had finally snapped. Snapped, she said, as if Laura was a bean. "We ought to have got help sooner for the poor girl, but we did think she was settling down," she said. However, today at the hospital where she'd been doing her charity visiting, she had gone out of control. Luckily there was a doctor present, and another one − a specialist − had been summoned. The upshot of it was that Laura had been declared a danger to herself and to others, and unfortunately Richard had been forced to commit her to the care of an institution.

"What are you telling me? What did she do?"

Winifred had on her pitying look. "She threatened to harm herself. She also said some things that were − well, she's clearly suffering from delusions."

"What did she say?"

"I'm not sure I should tell you."

"Laura is my sister," I said. "I'm entitled to know."

"She accused Richard of trying to kill you."

"In those words?"

"It was clear what she meant," said Winifred.

"No, please tell me exactly."

"She called him a lying, treacherous slave-trader, and a degenerate Mammon-worshipping monster."

"I know she has extreme views at times, and she does tend to express herself in a direct manner. But you can't put someone in the loony bin just for saying something like that."

"There was more," said Winifred darkly.

Richard, by way of soothing me, said that it wasn't a standard institution – not a Victorian norm. It was a private clinic, a very good one, one of the best. The BellaVista Clinic. They would take excellent care of her there.

"What is the view?" I said.

"Pardon?"

"BellaVista. It means *beautiful view*. So what is the view? What will Laura see when she looks out the window?"

"I hope this isn't your idea of a joke," said Winifred.

"No. It's very important. Is it a lawn, a garden, a fountain, or what? Or some sort of squalid alleyway?"

Neither of them could tell me. Richard said he was sure it would be natural surroundings of one kind or another. BellaVista, he said, was outside the city. There were landscaped grounds.

"Have you been there?"

"I know you're upset, darling," he said. "Maybe you should have a nap."

"I just had a nap. Please tell me."

"No, I haven't been there. Of course I haven't."

"Then how do you know?"

"Now really, Iris," said Winifred. "What does it matter?"

"I want to see her." I had a hard time believing that Laura had suddenly fallen to pieces, but then I was so used to Laura's quirks that I no longer found them strange. It would have been easy for me to have overlooked the slippage – the telltale signs of mental frailty, whatever they might have been.

According to Winifred, the doctors had advised us that seeing Laura was out of the question for the time being. They'd been most emphatic about it. She was too deranged, not only that, she was violent. Also there was my own condition to be considered.

I started to cry. Richard handed me his handkerchief. It was lightly starched, and smelled of cologne.

"There's something else you should know," said Winifred. "This is most distressing."

"Perhaps we should leave that item till later," said Richard in a subdued voice.

"It's very painful," said Winifred, with false reluctance. So of course I insisted on knowing right then and there.

"The poor girl claims she's pregnant," said Winifred. "Just like you."

I stopped crying. "Well? Is she?"

"Of course not," said Winifred. "How could she be?"

"Who is the father?" I couldn't quite picture Laura making up such a thing, out of whole cloth. I mean, who does she imagine it is?

"She refuses to say," said Richard.

"Of course she was hysterical," said Winifred, "so it was all jumbled up. She appeared to believe that the baby you're going to have is actually hers, in some way she was unable to explain. Of course she was raving."

Richard shook his head. "Very sad," he murmured, in the hushed and solemn tone of an undertaker: muffled, like a thick maroon carpet.

"The specialist – the *mental* specialist – said that Laura must be insanely jealous of you," said Winifred. "Jealous of everything about you – she wants to be living your life, she wants to be you, and this is the form it's taken. He said you ought to be kept out of harm's way." She took a tiny sip of her drink. "Haven't you had your own suspicions?"

You can see what a clever woman she was.

Aimee was born in early April. In those days they used ether, and so I was not conscious during the birth. I breathed in and blacked out, and woke up to find myself weaker and flatter. The baby was not there. It was in the nursery, with the rest of them. It was a girl.

"There's nothing wrong with it, is there?" I said. I was very anxious about this.

"Ten fingers, ten toes," said the nurse briskly, "and no more of anything else than there ought to be."

The baby was brought in later in the afternoon, wrapped in a pink blanket. I'd already named her, in my head. Aimee meant *one who was loved*, and I certainly hoped she would be loved, by someone. I had doubts about my own capacity to love her, or to love her as much as she'd need. I was spread too thin as it was: I did not think there would be enough of me left over.

Aimee looked like any newborn baby – she had that squashed face, as if she'd hit a wall at high speed. The hair on her head was long and dark. She squinted up at me through her almost-shut eyes, a distrustful squint. What a beating we take when we get born, I thought; what a bad surprise it must be, that first, harsh encounter with the outside air. I did feel sorry for the little creature; I vowed to do the best for her that I could.

While we were examining each other, Winifred and Richard arrived. The nurse at first mistook them for my parents. "No, this is the proud papa," said Winifred, and they all had a laugh. The two of them were toting flowers, and an elaborate layette, all fancy crocheting and white satin bows.

"Adorable!" said Winifred. "But my goodness, we were expecting a blonde. She's awfully dark. Look at that hair!"

"I'm sorry," I said to Richard. "I know you wanted a boy."

"Next time, darling," said Richard. He did not seem at all perturbed.

"That's only the birth hair," said the nurse to Winifred. "A lot of them have that, sometimes it's all down their back. It falls out and the real hair grows in. You can thank your stars she doesn't have teeth or a tail, the way some of them do."

"Grandfather Benjamin was dark," I said, "before his hair turned white, and Grandmother Adelia as well, and Father, of course, though I don't know about his two brothers. The blonde side of the family was my mother's." I said this in my usual conversational tone, and was relieved to see that Richard was paying no attention.

Was I grateful that Laura wasn't there? That she was shut up somewhere far away, where I couldn't reach her? Also where she couldn't reach me; where she couldn't stand beside my bed like the uninvited fairy at the christening, and say, *What are you talking about?*

She would have known, of course. She would have known right away.

Brightly shone the moon

Last night I watched a young woman set fire to herself: a slim young woman, dressed in gauzy flammable robes. She was doing it as a protest against some injustice or other; but why did she think this bonfire she was making of herself would solve anything? *Oh, don't do that*, I wanted to say to her. *Don't burn up your life. Whatever it's for, it's not worth it*. But it was worth it to her, obviously.

What possesses them, these young girls with a talent for self-immolation? Is it what they do to show that girls too have courage, that they can do more than weep and moan, that they too can face death with panache? And where does the urge come from? Does it begin with defiance, and if so, of what? Of the great leaden suffocating order of things, the great spike-wheeled chariot, the blind tyrants, the blind gods? Are these girls reckless enough or arrogant enough to think that they can stop such things in their tracks by offering themselves up on some theoretical altar, or is it a kind of testifying? Admirable enough, if you admire obsession. Courageous enough, too. But completely useless.

I worry about Sabrina, that way. What is she up to, over there at the ends of the earth? Has she been bitten by the Christians, or the Buddhists, or is there some other variety of bat inhabiting her belfry? *Inasmuch as ye do it unto the least of these, ye do it unto Me*. Are those the words on her passport to futility? Does she want to atone for the sins of her money-ridden, wrecked, deplorable family? I certainly hope not.

Even Aimee had a bit of that in her, but in her it took a slower, more devious form. Laura went over the bridge when

Aimee was eight, Richard died when she was ten. These events can't help but have affected her. Then, between Winifred and myself, she was pulled to pieces. Winifred wouldn't have won that battle now, but she did then. She stole Aimee away from me, and try as I might, I could never get her back.

No wonder that when Aimee came of age and got her hands on the money Richard had left her she jumped ship, and turned to various chemical forms of comfort, and flayed herself with one man after another. (Who, for instance, was Sabrina's father? Hard to say, and Aimee never did. Spin the wheel, she'd say, and take your pick.)

I tried to keep in touch with her. I kept hoping for a reconciliation – she was my daughter after all, and I felt guilty about her, and I wanted to make it up to her – to make up for the morass her childhood had become. But by then she'd turned against me – against Winifred too, which was some consolation at least. She wouldn't let either of us near her, or near Sabrina – especially not Sabrina. She didn't want Sabrina polluted by us.

She moved house frequently, restlessly. A couple of times she was tossed out on the street, for non-payment of rent; she was arrested for causing a disturbance. She was hospitalized on several occasions. I suppose you'd have to say she became a confirmed alcoholic, although I hate that term. She had enough money so she never had to get a job, which was just as well because she couldn't have held one down. Or maybe it wasn't just as well. Things might have been different if she hadn't been able to drift; if she'd had to concentrate on her next meal, instead of dwelling on all the injuries she felt we'd done her. An unearned income encourages self-pity in those already prone to it.

The last time I went to see Aimee, she was living in a slummy row house near Parliament Street, in Toronto. A child

I guessed must be Sabrina was squatting in the square of dirt beside the front walk – a grubby mop-headed ragamuffin wearing shorts but no T-shirt. She had an old tin cup and was shovelling grit into it with a bent spoon. She was a resourceful little creature: she asked me for a quarter. Did I give her one? Most likely. "I am your grandmother," I said to her, and she stared up at me as if I was crazy. Doubtless she'd never been told of the existence of such a person.

I got an earful from one of the neighbours, that time. They seemed like decent people, or decent enough to feed Sabrina when Aimee would forget to come home. Kelly was their last name, as I recall. They were the ones who called the police when Aimee was found at the bottom of the stairs with her neck broken. Fallen or pushed or jumped, we'll never know.

I should have snatched Sabrina up, that day, and made off with her. Headed for Mexico. I would have done so if I'd known what was going to happen – that Winifred would snaffle her and lock her away from me, just as she'd done with Aimee.

Would Sabrina have been better off with me than with Winifred? What must it have been like for her, growing up with a rich, vindictive, festering old woman? Instead of a poor vindictive festering one, namely myself. I would have loved her, though. I doubt Winifred ever did. She just hung on to Sabrina to spite me; to punish me; to show she'd won.

But I did no baby-snatching that day. I knocked on the door, and when there was no answer I opened it and walked in, then climbed the steep, dark, narrow stairs to Aimee's second-floor apartment. Aimee was in the kitchen, sitting at the small round table, looking at her hands, which were holding a coffee mug with a smile button on it. She had the cup right up close to her eyes and was turning it this way and that. Her face was pallid, her hair straggly. I can't say I found her very attractive. She was

smoking a cigarette. Most likely she was under the influence of
some drug or other, mixed with alcohol; I could smell it in the
room, along with the old smoke, the dirty sink, the unscrubbed
garbage pail.

I tried to talk to her. I began gently, but she wasn't in the
mood for listening. She said she was tired of it, of all of us.
Most of all she was tired of the feeling that things were being
hidden from her. The family had covered it up; no one would
tell her the truth; our mouths opened and closed and words
came out, but they were not words that led to anything.

She'd figured it out anyway, though. She'd been robbed,
she'd been deprived of her heritage, because I wasn't her real
mother and Richard hadn't been her real father. It was all there
in Laura's book, she said.

I asked her what on earth she meant. She said it was obvious:
her real mother was Laura, and her real father was that man, the
one in *The Blind Assassin*. Aunt Laura had been in love with
him, but we'd thwarted her – disposed of this unknown lover
somehow. Scared him off, bought him off, run him off, whatever; she'd lived in Winifred's house long enough to see how
things were done by people like us. Then, when Laura turned
out to be pregnant by him, we'd sent her away to cover up the
scandal, and when my own baby had died at birth, we'd stolen
the baby from Laura and adopted it, and passed it off as our own.

She was not at all coherent, but this was the gist of it. You
can see how appealing it must have been for her, this fantasy:
who wouldn't want to have a mythical being for a mother,
instead of the shop-soiled real kind? Given the chance.

I said she was quite wrong, she'd got things all mixed up, but
she didn't listen. No wonder she'd never felt happy with
Richard and me, she said. We'd never behaved like her real
parents, because in fact we weren't her real parents. And no
wonder Aunt Laura had thrown herself off a bridge – it was

because we'd broken her heart. Laura had probably left a note for Aimee explaining all of this, for her to read when she was older, but Richard and I must have destroyed it.

No wonder I'd been such a terrible mother, she continued. I'd never really loved her. If I had, I would have put her before everything else. I would have considered her feelings. I wouldn't have left Richard.

"I may not have been a perfect mother," I said. "I'm willing to admit that, but I did the best I could under the circumstances — circumstances about which you actually know very little." What was she doing with Sabrina? I went on. Letting her run around like that outside the house with no clothes on, filthy as a beggar; it was neglect, the child could disappear at any moment, children disappeared all the time. I was Sabrina's grandmother, I would be more than willing to take her in, and . . .

"You aren't her grandmother," said Aimee. She was crying by now. "Aunt Laura is. Or she was. She's dead, and you killed her!"

"Don't be stupid," I said. This was the wrong response: the more vehemently you deny such things, the more they are believed. But you often give the wrong response when you're frightened, and Aimee had frightened me.

When I said the word *stupid*, she began to scream at me. I was the stupid one, she said. I was dangerously stupid, I was so stupid I didn't even know how stupid I was. She used a number of words I won't repeat here, then picked up the smile-button coffee mug and threw it at me. Then she came at me, unsteadily; she was howling, great heart-rending sobs. Her arms were outstretched, in a threatening manner, I believed. I was upset, shaken. I retreated backwards, clutching the banister, dodging other items — a shoe, a saucer. When I got to the front door I fled.

Perhaps I should have stretched out my own arms. I should have hugged her. I should have cried. Then I should have sat down with her and told her this story I'm now telling you. But I didn't do that. I missed the chance, and I regret it bitterly.

It was only three weeks after this that Aimee fell down the stairs. I mourned her, of course. She was my daughter. But I have to admit I mourned the self she'd been at a much earlier age. I mourned what she could have become; I mourned her lost possibilities. More than anything, I mourned my own failures.

After Aimee was dead, Winifred got her claws into Sabrina. Possession is nine-tenths of the law, and she was on the scene first. She whisked Sabrina off to her tarted-up mansionette in Rosedale, and faster than you could blink she'd had herself declared the official guardian. I considered fighting, but it would just have been the battle over Aimee all over again – one I was doomed to lose.

When Winifred took charge of Sabrina I wasn't yet sixty; I could still drive then. From time to time I would make the trip into Toronto and shadow Sabrina, like a private eye in an old detective story. I'd hang around outside her primary school – her new primary school, her new exclusive primary school – just to catch a glimpse of her, and to assure myself that, despite everything, she was all right.

I was in the department store, for instance, the morning Winifred took her to Eaton's to get her some party shoes, a few months after she'd acquired her. No doubt she bought Sabrina's other clothes without consulting her – that would have been her way – but shoes do need to be tried on, and for some reason Winifred had not entrusted this chore to the hired help.

It was the Christmas season – the pillars in the store were twined with fake holly, wreaths of gold-sprayed pine cones and red velvet ribbon hung over the doorways like prickly haloes – and Winifred got trapped in the carol singing, much to her annoyance. I was in the next aisle over. My wardrobe wasn't what it used to be – I was wearing an old tweed coat and a kerchief pulled down over my forehead – and although she looked right at me, she didn't see me. She probably saw a cleaning lady, or an immigrant bargain-hunter.

She was done up to the nines as usual, but despite this she was looking quite tatty. Well, she must have been pushing seventy, and after a certain age her style of maquillage does tend to make you look mummified. She shouldn't have stuck to the orange lipstick, it was too harsh for her.

I could see the powdery furrows of exasperation between her eyebrows, the clamped muscles of her rouged jaw. She was hauling Sabrina along by one arm, trying to push her way through the chorus of bulky, winter-coated shoppers; she must have hated the enthusiastic, uncooked quality of the singing.

Sabrina on the other hand wanted to hear the music. She was dragging down, making herself a dead weight in the way children do – resistance without the appearance of it. Her arm was straight up, as if she was a good girl answering a question in school, but she was scowling like an imp. It must have hurt, what she was doing. Taking a stance, making a declaration. Holding out.

The song was "Good King Wenceslas." Sabrina knew the words: I could see her little mouth moving. "'Brightly shone the moon that night, though the frost was cruel,'" she sang. "'When a poor man came in sight, gathering winter fu-u-el.'"

It's a song about hunger. I could tell Sabrina understood it – she must still have remembered that, being hungry. Winifred gave her arm a jerk, and looked around nervously. She didn't see me, but she sensed me, the way a cow in a well-fenced field will sense a wolf. Even so, cows aren't like wild animals; they're used to being protected. Winifred was skittish, but she wasn't frightened. If I crossed her mind at all, she doubtless thought of me as being somewhere far away, mercifully out of sight, in the outer darkness to which she had consigned me.

I had an overpowering urge then to snatch Sabrina up in my arms and run away with her. I could imagine Winifred's quavering wail as I barged my way through the stolid carollers, yelling so comfortably about the bitter weather.

I would have held on to her tightly, I wouldn't have stumbled, I wouldn't have let her fall. But also I wouldn't have got far. They'd have been after me in a shot.

I went out onto the street by myself then, and walked and walked, head down, collar up, along the downtown sidewalks. The wind was coming in off the lake and the snow was whirling down. It was daytime, but because of the low clouds and the snow the light was dim; the cars were churning slowly past along the unploughed streets, their red tail lights receding from me like the eyes of hunchbacked beasts running backwards.

I was clutching a package – I've forgotten what I'd bought – and I had no gloves. I must have dropped them in the store, among the feet of the crowd. I hardly missed them. Once I could walk through blizzards with my hands bare and never feel it. It's love or hate or terror, or just plain rage, that can do that for you.

I used to have a daydream about myself – still have it, come to that. A ridiculous-enough daydream, though it's often through such images that we shape our destinies. (You'll notice how easily I slip into inflated language like *shape our destinies*, once I wander off in this direction. But never mind.)

In this daydream, Winifred and her friends, wreaths of money on their heads, are gathered around Sabrina's frilly white bed while she sleeps, discussing what they will bestow upon her. She's already been given the engraved silver cup from Birks, the nursery wallpaper with the frieze of domesticated bears, the starter pearls for her single-strand pearl necklace, and all the other golden gifts, perfectly *comme il faut*, that will turn to coal when the sun rises. Now they're planning the ortho-dontist and the tennis lessons and the piano lessons and the dancing lessons and the exclusive summer camp. What hope has she got?

At this moment, I appear in a flash of sulphurous light and a puff of smoke and a flapping of sooty leather wings, the unin-vited black-sheep godmother. *I too wish to bestow a gift,* I cry. *I have the right!*

Winifred and her crew laugh and point. *You? You were ban-ished long ago! Have you looked in a mirror lately? You've let yourself go, you look a hundred and two. Go back to your dingy old cave! What can you possibly have to offer?*

I offer the truth, I say. *I'm the last one who can. It's the only thing in this room that will still be here in the morning.*

Weeks went by, and Laura did not return. I wanted to write to her, telephone her, but Richard said that would be bad for her. She did not need to be interrupted, he said, by a voice from the past. She needed to concentrate her attention on her immediate situation – on the treatment at hand. That is what he'd been told. As for the nature of this treatment, he wasn't a doctor, he didn't pretend to understand such things. Surely they were best left to the experts.

I tortured myself with visions of her, imprisoned, struggling, trapped in a painful fantasy of her own making, or trapped in another fantasy, equally painful, which was not hers at all but those of the people around her. And when did the one become the other? Where was the threshold, between the inner world and the outer one? We each move unthinkingly through this gateway every day, we use the passwords of grammar – *I say, you say, he and she say, it, on the other hand, does not say* – paying for the privilege of sanity with common coin, with meanings we've agreed on.

But even as a child, Laura never quite agreed. Was this the problem? That she held firm for *no* when *yes* was the thing required? And vice versa, and vice versa.

Laura was doing well, I was told: she was making progress. Then she was not doing so well, she'd had a relapse. Progress in what, a relapse to what? It should not be gone into, it would disturb me, it was important for me to conserve my energies, as a young mother should do. "We'll have you well again in no time flat," said Richard, patting my arm.

"But I'm not really sick," I said.

"You know what I mean," he said. "Back to normal." He

gave a fond smile, a leer almost. His eyes were getting smaller, or the flesh around them was moving in, which gave him a cunning expression. He was thinking about the time when he could be back where he belonged: on top. I was thinking that he would squeeze the breath out of me. He was putting on weight; he was eating out a lot; he was making speeches, at clubs, at weighty gatherings, substantial gatherings. Ponderous gatherings, at which weighty, substantial men met and pondered, because – everyone suspected it – there was heavy weather ahead.

All that speech-making can bloat a man up. I've watched the process, many times now. It's those kinds of words, the kind they use in speeches. They have a fermenting effect on the brain. You can see it on television, during the political broadcasts – the words coming out of their mouths like bubbles of gas.

I decided to be as sickly as I could for as long as possible.

I fretted and fretted about Laura. I turned Winifred's story about her this way and that, looking at it from every angle. I couldn't quite believe it, but I couldn't disbelieve it either.

Laura had always had one enormous power: the power to break things without meaning to. Nor had she ever been a respecter of territories. What was mine was hers: my fountain pen, my cologne, my summer dress, my hat, my hairbrush. Had this catalogue expanded to include my unborn baby? However, if she was suffering from delusions – if she'd only been inventing things – why was it she'd invented precisely that?

But suppose on the other hand that Winifred was lying. Suppose Laura was as sane as she ever was. In that case, Laura had been telling the truth. And if Laura had been telling the truth, then Laura was pregnant. If there really was going to be a baby, what would become of it? And why hadn't she told me about it, instead of telling some doctor, some stranger? Why hadn't she asked me for help? I thought that over for some time. There could have been a good many reasons. My delicate condition would just have been one of them.

As for the father, whether imagined or real, there was only one man who was at all possible. It must be Alex Thomas.

But it couldn't be. How could it?

I no longer knew how Laura would have answered these questions. She had become unknown to me, as unknown as the inside of your own glove is unknown when your hand is inside it. She was with me all the time, but I couldn't look at her. I could only feel the shape of her presence: a hollow shape, filled with my own imaginings.

Months went by. It was June, then July, then August. Winifred said I was looking white and drained. I should spend more time outside, she said. If I would not take up tennis or golf, as she'd repeatedly suggested – it might do something about that little tummy of mine, which ought to be seen to before it became chronic – I could at least work on my rock garden. It was an occupation that accorded well with motherhood.

I was not fond of my rock garden, which was mine in name only, like so much else. (Like "my" baby, come to think of it: surely a changeling, surely something left by the gypsies; surely my real baby – one that cried less and smiled more, and was not so pungent – had been spirited away.) The rock garden was similarly resistant to my ministrations; nothing I did to it pleased it at all. Its rocks made a good show – there was a lot of pink granite, along with the limestone – but I couldn't get anything to grow in it.

I contented myself with books – *Perennials for the Rock Garden*, *Desert Succulents for Northern Climes*, and the like. I went through such books, making lists – lists of what I might plant, or else lists of what I had indeed already planted; what ought to have been growing, but was not. Dragon's blood, snow-on-the-mountain, hen-and-chickens. I liked the names, but didn't care much for the plants themselves.

"I don't have a green thumb," I said to Winifred. "Not like you." My pretense of incompetence had now become second nature to me, I scarcely had to think about it. Winifred on her part had ceased to find my fecklessness altogether convenient.

"Well, of course you have to make *some* effort," she would say. At which I would produce my dutiful lists of dead plants.

"The rocks are pretty," I said. "Can't we just call it a sculpture?"

I thought of setting off on my own to see Laura. I could leave Aimee with the new nursemaid, whom I thought of as Miss Murgatroyd – all our servants were Murgatroyds to my mind, they were all in cahoots. But no, the nursemaid would alert Winifred. I could defy them all; I could sneak off one morning, take Aimee with me; we could go on the train. But the train to where? I didn't know where Laura was – where she had been stashed away. The BellaVista Clinic was said to be up north somewhere, but *up north* covered a lot of territory. I rummaged around in Richard's desk, the one in his study at the house, but found no letters from this clinic. He must have been keeping them at the office.

One day Richard came home early. He seemed quite disturbed. Laura was no longer at BellaVista, he said.

How could that be? I asked.

A man had arrived, he said. This man claimed to be Laura's lawyer, or acting on her behalf. He was a trustee, he said – a trustee of Miss Chase's trust fund. He'd challenged the authority by which she had been placed in BellaVista. He had threatened legal action. Did I know anything about these proceedings?

No, I did not. (I kept my hands folded in my lap. I expressed surprise, and mild interest. I did not express glee.) And then what happened? I asked.

The director of BellaVista had been absent, the staff had been confused. They had let her go, in custody of this man. They had judged that the family would wish to avoid undue publicity. (The lawyer had threatened some of this.)

Well, I said, I guess they did the right thing.

Yes, said Richard, no doubt; but was Laura *compos mentis*? For her own good, for her own *safety*, we should at least determine that. Although on the surface of things she'd appeared calmer, the staff at BellaVista had their doubts. Who knew what danger to herself or others she might pose if allowed to run around at large?

I didn't happen by any chance to know where she was?

I did not.

I hadn't heard from her?

I had not.

I wouldn't hesitate to inform him, in that eventuality?

I would not hesitate. Those were my very words. It was a sentence without an object, and therefore not technically a lie.

I let a judicious amount of time go past, and then I set off to Port Ticonderoga, on the train, to consult Reenie. I invented a telephone call: Reenie was not in good health, I explained to Richard, and she wanted to see me again before something happened. I gave the impression that she was at death's door. She'd appreciate a photograph of Aimee, I said; she'd want to have a chat about old times. It was the least I could do. After all, she'd practically brought us up. Brought me up, I corrected, to divert Richard's attention away from the thought of Laura.

I arranged to see Reenie at Betty's Luncheonette. (She had a telephone by then, she was holding her own in the world.) That would be best, she said. She was still working there, part-time, but we could meet after her hours were up. Betty's had new owners, she said; the old owners wouldn't have liked her sitting out front like a paying customer, even if she was paying, but the new ones had figured out that they needed all the paying customers they could get.

Betty's had gone severely downhill. The striped awning was gone, the dark booths looked scratched and tawdry. The smell was no longer of fresh vanilla, but of rancid grease. I was over-dressed, I realized. I shouldn't have worn my white fox neck-piece. What had been the point of showing off, under the circumstances?

I didn't like the look of Reenie: she was too puffy, too yellow, she was breathing a little too heavily. Perhaps she really wasn't in good health: I wondered if I should ask. "Good to take the weight off my feet," she said as she subsided into the booth across from me.

Myra – how old were you, Myra? You must have been three or four, I've lost count – Myra was with her. Her cheeks were red with excitement, her eyes were round and slightly bulged out, as if she were being gently strangled.

"I've told her all about you," said Reenie fondly. "The both of you." Myra wasn't too interested in me, I have to say, but she was intrigued by the foxes around my neck. Children of that age usually like furry animals, even if dead.

"You've seen Laura," I said, "or talked with her?"

"Least said, soonest mended," said Reenie, glancing around her, as if even here the walls might have ears. I saw no need for such caution.

"I suppose it was you who organized the lawyer?" I said.

Reenie looked wise. "I did what was required," she said.

"Anyways, that lawyer was your mother's second cousin's husband, he was family in a way. So he saw the point of it, once I knew what was going on, that is."

"How did you know?" I was saving *what did you know* for later.

"She wrote me," said Reenie. "Said she wrote you, but never got an answer. She wasn't allowed to be mailing any letters as such, but the cook helped her out. Laura sent her the money for it afterwards, and a little extra."

"I didn't get any letter," I said.

"That's what she figured. She figured they'd seen to that."

I knew who was meant by *they*. "I suppose she came here," I said.

"Where else would she go?" said Reenie. "The poor creature. After all she'd been through."

"What had she been through?" I very much wanted to know; at the same time I dreaded it. Laura could be fabricating, I told myself. Laura could be suffering from delusions. That couldn't be ruled out.

Reenie had ruled it out, however: no matter what story Laura had told her, she'd believed it. I doubted that it was the same story I'd heard. I doubted especially that there had been a baby in it, in any shape or form. "There's children present, so I won't go into it," she said. She nodded at Myra, who was gobbling up a slice of grisly pink cake and staring at me as if she wanted to lick me. "If I told you all of it you wouldn't sleep at night. The only comfort is that you had no part in it. That's what she said."

"She said that?" I was relieved to hear it. Richard and Winifred had been cast as the monsters then, and I'd been excused – on the grounds of moral feebleness, no doubt. Though I could tell Reenie hadn't entirely forgiven me for having been so careless as to let all of this happen. (Once Laura had gone off the bridge, she forgave me even less. In her view I must have had something to do with it. She was cool to me after that. She died begrudgingly.)

"She oughtn't to have been put in such a place at all, a young girl like her," said Reenie. "No matter what. Men walking around with their trousers undone, all kinds of goings-on. Shameful!"

"Will they bite?" said Myra, reaching for my foxes.

"Don't touch that," said Reenie. "With your sticky little fingers."

"No," I said. "They're not real. See, they have glass eyes. They only bite their own tails."

"She said, if only you'd known, you'd never have left her in there," said Reenie. "Supposing you'd known. She said whatever else, you weren't heartless." She frowned sideways, at the glass of water. She had her doubts on that score. "Potatoes was what they ate there, mostly," she said. "Mashed and boiled, she said. Skimped on the food, took the bread out of the mouths of the poor nutcases and loony birds in there. Lining their own pockets, is my guess."

"Where has she gone? Where is she now?"

"That's between you and me and the doorpost," said Reenie. "She said it was better for you not to know."

"Did she seem – was she . . ." Was she visibly crazy, I wanted to ask.

"She was the same as she always was. No more, no less. She wasn't like a loony bird, if that's what you mean," said Reenie. "Thinner – she needs to get some meat back on her bones – and not so much talk about God. I only hope he stands by her now, for a change."

"Thank you, Reenie, for all you've done," I said.

"No need to thank me," said Reenie stiffly. "I only did what was right."

Meaning I hadn't. "Can I write to her?" I was fumbling for my handkerchief. I felt like crying. I felt like a criminal.

"She said best not. But she wanted me to say she left you a message."

"A message?"

"She left it before they took her off to that place. You'd know where to find it, she said."

"Is that your own hankie? Have you got a cold?" said Myra, noting my snifflings with interest.

"If you ask too many questions your tongue will fall out," said Reenie.

"No it won't," said Myra complacently. She began humming off-key, and kicking her fat legs against my knees, under the table. She had a cheerful confidence, it appeared, and was not easily frightened – qualities in her I've often found irritating, but have come to be grateful for. (Which may be news to you, Myra. Accept it as a compliment while you have the chance. They're thin on the ground.)

"I thought you might like to see a picture of Aimee," I said to Reenie. I had at least this one achievement I could show, to redeem myself in her eyes.

Reenie took the photo. "My, she's a dark little thing, isn't she?" she said. "You never know who a child will favour."

"I want to see too," said Myra, grabbing with her sugary paws.

"Quick then, and off we go. We're late for your Dad."

"No," said Myra.

"Be it ever so humble, there's no place like home," Reenie sang, scrubbing pink icing off Myra's little snout with a paper napkin.

"I want to stay here," said Myra, but her coat was pulled on, her knitted wool hat was flumped down over her ears, and she was hauled sideways out of the booth.

"Take care of yourself," said Reenie. She didn't kiss me.

I wanted to throw my arms around her, and howl and howl. I wanted to be comforted. I wanted it to be me that was going with her.

"'There's no place like home,'" Laura said one day, when she was eleven or twelve. "Reenie sings that. I think it's stupid."

"How do you mean?" I said.

"Look." She wrote it out as an equation. *No place = home. Therefore, home = no place. Therefore home does not exist.*

Home is where the heart is, I thought now, gathering myself together in Betty's Luncheonette. I had no heart any more, it had been broken; or not broken, it simply wasn't there any more. It had been scooped neatly out of me like the yolk from a hard-boiled egg, leaving the rest of me bloodless and congealed and hollow.

I'm heartless, I thought. Therefore I'm homeless.

The message

Yesterday I was too tired to do much more than lie on the sofa. As is becoming my no doubt slovenly habit, I watched a daytime talk show, the kind on which they spill the beans. It's the fashion now, bean-spilling: people spill their own beans and also those of other people, they spill every bean they have and even some they don't have. They do this out of guilt and anguish, and for their own pleasure, but mostly because they want to display themselves and other people want to watch them do it. I don't exempt myself: I relish these grubby little sins, these squalid family tangles, these cherished traumas. I enjoy the expectation with which the top is wrenched off the can of worms as if from some amazing birthday present, and then the sense of anticlimax in the watching faces: the forced tears and skimpy, gloating pity, the cued and dutiful applause. *Is that all there is?* they must be thinking. *Shouldn't it be less ordinary, more sordid, more epic, more truly harrowing, this flesh wound of yours? Tell us more! Couldn't we please crank up the pain?*

I wonder which is preferable – to walk around all your life swollen up with your own secrets until you burst from the pressure of them, or to have them sucked out of you, every paragraph, every sentence, every word of them, so at the end you're depleted of all that was once as precious to you as hoarded gold, as close to you as your skin – everything that was of the deepest importance to you, everything that made you cringe and wish to conceal, everything that belonged to you alone – and must spend the rest of your days like an empty sack flapping in the wind, an empty sack branded with a bright fluorescent label so that everyone will know what sort of secrets used to be inside you?

I carry no brief, for better or for worse.

Loose Lips Sink Ships, said the wartime poster. Of course the ships will all sink anyway, sooner or later.

After indulging myself in this way, I wandered into the kitchen, where I ate half of a blackening banana and two soda crackers. I wondered if something – food of some sort – had fallen down behind the garbage can – there was a meaty smell – but a quick check revealed nothing. Perhaps this odour was my own. I can't overcome the notion that my body smells like cat food, despite whatever stagnant scent I sprayed on myself this morning – Tosca, was it, or Ma Griffe, or perhaps Je Reviens? I still have a few odds and ends of that sort kicking around. Grist for the green garbage bags, Myra, when you get around to them.

Richard used to give me perfume, when he felt I needed mollifying. Perfume, silk scarves, small jewelled pins in the shapes of domestic animals, of caged birds, of goldfish. Winifred's tastes, not for herself but for me.

On the train coming back from Port Ticonderoga, and then for weeks afterwards, I pondered Laura's message, the one Reenie said she'd left for me. She must have known, then, that whatever she was planning to say to the strange doctor at the hospital might have repercussions. She must have known it was a risk, and so she'd taken precautions. Somehow, somewhere, she'd left some word, some clue for me, like a dropped handkerchief or a trail of white stones in the woods.

I pictured her writing this message, in the way she always set about writing. No doubt it would be in pencil, a pencil with a chewed end. She often chewed her pencils; as a child her mouth had smelled of cedar, and if it was a coloured pencil her lips would be blue or green or purple. She wrote slowly; her script was childish, with round vowels and closed o's, and long, wavery stems on her g's and her y's. The dots on the i's and j's were circular, placed far to the right, as if the dot were a small black balloon tethered to its stem by an invisible thread; the cross-strokes of the t's were one-sided. I sat beside her in spirit, to see what she would do next.

She'd have reached the end of her message, then put it into an envelope and sealed it, and then hidden it, the way she'd hidden her bundle of bits and scraps at Avilion. But where could she have put this envelope? Not at Avilion: she hadn't been anywhere near there, not just before she was taken away.

No, it must be in the house in Toronto. Somewhere no one else would look – not Richard, not Winifred, not any of the Murgatroyds. I searched in various places – the bottoms of drawers, the backs of cupboards, the pockets of my winter coats, my supply of handbags, my winter mittens even – but found nothing.

Then I remembered coming upon her once, in Grandfather's study, when she was ten or eleven. She'd had the family Bible spread out in front of her, a great leathery brute of a thing, and was snipping sections out of it with Mother's old sewing scissors.

"Laura, what are you doing?" I said. "That's the Bible!"

"I'm cutting out the parts I don't like."

I uncrumpled the pages she'd tossed into the wastebasket: swathes of *Chronicles*, pages and pages of *Leviticus*, the little snippet from St. Matthew in which Jesus curses the barren fig tree. I remembered now that Laura had been indignant about that fig tree, in her Sunday-school days. She'd been furious that Jesus had been so spiteful towards a tree. *We all have our bad days*, Reenie had commented, briskly whipping up egg whites in a yellow bowl.

"You shouldn't be doing this," I said.

"It's only paper," said Laura, continuing to snip. "Paper isn't important. It's the words on them that are important."

"You'll get in big trouble."

"No, I won't," she said. "No one ever opens it. They only look in the front, for the births, the marriages and the deaths."

She was right, too. She was never found out.

That memory was what led me to pull out my wedding album, where the photographs of that event were stored. Certainly this volume was of scant interest to Winifred, nor had Richard ever been found leafing fondly through it. Laura must have known that, she must have known it would be safe. But what — she must have thought — would lead me ever to look into it myself?

If I'd been searching for Laura, I would have. She'd know that. There were a lot of pictures of her in there, stuck to the brown pages with black triangles at the corners; pictures of her scowling and gazing at her feet, dressed in her bridesmaid's outfit.

I found the message, although it was not in words. Laura had gone to town on my wedding with the hand-tinting materials, the little tubes of paint she'd nicked from Elwood Murray's newspaper office back in Port Ticonderoga. She must have had them squirrelled away all this time. For a person who claimed such disdain for the material world, she was very bad at throwing things out.

She'd altered only two of the photographs. The first was a group shot of the wedding party. In this, the bridesmaids and groomsmen had been covered over with a thick coat of indigo — eliminated from the picture altogether. I had been left, and Richard, and Laura herself, and Winifred, who had been a matron of honour. Winifred had been coloured a lurid green, as had Richard. I had been given a wash of aqua blue. Laura herself was a brilliant yellow, not only her dress, but her face and hands as well. What did it mean, this radiance? For radiance it was, as if Laura was glowing from within, like a glass lamp or a girl made of phosphorus. She wasn't looking straight ahead, but sideways, as if the focus of her attention was not in the picture at all.

The second was the formal shot of bride and groom, taken in front of the church. Richard's face had been painted grey, such a dark grey that the features were all but obliterated. The hands were red, as were the flames that shot up from around and somehow from inside the head, as if the skull itself were burning. My wedding gown, the gloves, the veil, the flowers – these trappings Laura had not bothered with. She'd dealt with my face, however – bleached it so that the eyes and the nose and mouth looked fogged over, like a window on a cold, wet day. The background and even the church steps beneath our feet had been entirely blacked out, leaving our two figures floating as if in mid-air, in the deepest and darkest of nights.

The Globe and Mail, October 7, 1938

GRIFFEN LAUDS MUNICH ACCORD
SPECIAL TO THE GLOBE AND MAIL

In a vigorous and hard-hitting speech entitled "Minding Our Own Business," delivered at the Wednesday meeting of the Empire Club in Toronto, Mr. Richard E. Griffen, President and Chairman of Griffen-Chase-Royal Consolidated Industries Ltd., praised the outstanding efforts of the British Prime Minister, Mr. Neville Chamberlain, which have resulted in last week's Munich Accord. It was significant, said Mr. Griffen, that all parties in the British House of Commons cheered the news, and he hoped that all parties in Canada would also cheer, as this accord would put paid to the Depression and would usher in a new "golden era" of peace and prosperity. It also went to show the value of statesmanship and diplomacy as well as positive thinking and plain old hard-headed business sense. "If everyone gives a little," he said, "then everyone stands to gain a lot."

In reply to questions about the status of Czecho-Slovakia under the Accord, he stated that in his opinion the citizens of that country had been guaranteed sufficient safe-guards. A strong, healthy Germany, he claimed, was in the interests of the West, and of business in particular, and would serve to "keep Bolshevism at bay, and away from Bay Street." The next thing to be desired was a bilateral trade treaty, and he was assured that this was in progress. Attention could now be turned away from sabre-rattling to the provision of goods for the consumer, thus creating jobs and prosperity where they are most needed – "in our own backyard." The seven lean years, he stated, would now be followed by seven fat ones, and golden vistas could be seen stretching all the way through the '40's.

Mr. Griffen is rumoured to be in consultation with leading members of the Conservative Party, and to be eyeing the position of helmsman. His speech was roundly applauded.

Mayfair, June 1939

ROYAL STYLE AT
ROYAL GARDEN PARTY
BY CYNTHIA FERVIS

Five thousand honoured guests of Their Excellencies, Lord and Lady Tweedsmuir, stood spellbound along the garden walks at His Majesty's birthday party at Government House in Ottawa, as Their Majesties made their gracious rounds.

At half-past four they emerged from Government House by the Chinese Gallery. The King was in morning dress; the Queen chose beige, with soft fur and pearls and a large slightly uptilted hat, her face delicately flushed, her warm blue eyes smiling. All were charmed by her entrancing manner.

Walking behind Their Majesties were the Governor General and Lady Tweedsmuir, His Excellency a gracious and genial host, Her Excellency poised and beautiful. Her all-white ensemble, enhanced by fox furs from Canada's Arctic, was set off by a splash of turquoise in her hat. Presented to Their Majesties were Colonel and Mrs. F. Phelan, of Montreal; she wore a printed silk, on which bloomed small vivid flowers, and her smart hat had a large clear brim of Cellophane. Brigadier General and Mrs. W. H. L. Elkins and Miss Joan Elkins, and Mr. and Mrs. Gladstone Murray were similarly honoured.

Mr. and Mrs. Richard Griffen were singled out; her cape was of silver fox, the furs placed on black chiffon in the form of rays, worn over an orchid costume. Mrs. Douglas Watts wore chartreuse chiffon with a brown velvet jacket, Mrs. F. Reid was trim and lovely in an organdie and Valenciennes lace gown.

No whisper of tea was heard until the King and Queen had waved farewell, and the cameras had clicked and flashed, and all voices had been raised in *God Save the King*. After that the birthday cakes held centre stage . . . enormous white cakes, with snowy icing. The cake served to the King indoors was ornamented not only with roses, shamrocks and thistles, but also with flocks of miniature sugar doves with white pennants in their beaks, the fitting symbols of peace and hope.

It's mid-afternoon, cloudy and humid, everything sticky: her white cotton gloves are already smudged just from holding the railing. The world heavy, a solid weight; her heart pushes against it as if pushing against stone. The sultry air holds out against her. Nothing budges.

But then the train comes in, and she waits at the gate as is required of her, and like a promise fulfilled he comes through it. He sees her, comes towards her, they touch each other quickly, then shake hands as if distantly related. She kisses him briefly on the cheek, because it's a public place and you never know, and they walk up the slanted ramp into the marble station. She feels new with him, nervous; she's barely had a chance to look at him. Certainly he's thinner. What else?

I had the hell of a time getting back. I didn't have much money. It was tramp steamers all the way.

I would have sent you some money, she says.

I know. But I had no address.

He leaves his duffel at the baggage check, carries only the small suitcase. He'll pick up the bag later, he says, but right now he doesn't want to be hampered. People come and go around them, footsteps and voices; they stand irresolute; they don't know where to go. She should have thought, she should have arranged something, because of course he has no room, not yet. At least she's got a flask of scotch, tucked into her handbag. She did remember that.

They have to go somewhere so they go to a hotel, a cheap one he remembers. It's the first time they've done this and it's a risk, but as soon as she sees the hotel she knows that no one in it would expect them to be anything but unmarried; or if married, not to each other. She's worn her summer-weight raincoat from two seasons before, pulled a scarf over her head. The scarf is silk but it was the worst she could do. Maybe they'll think he's paying her. She hopes so. That way she's unremarkable.

On the stretch of sidewalk outside it there's broken glass, vomit, what looks like drying blood. Don't step in it, he says.

There's a bar on the ground floor, although it's called a Beverage Room. Men Only, Ladies and Escorts. Outside there's a red neon sign, the letters vertical, and a red arrow coming down and bending so that the arrowhead points at the door. Two of the letters are dead so it reads Be rage Room. Small bulbs like Christmas lights flash off and on, running down the sign like ants going down a drainpipe.

Even at this hour there are men hanging around, waiting for the place to open. He takes her elbow as they go past, hurries her a little. Behind them one of the men makes a noise like a tomcat yowling.

For the hotel part of things there's a separate door. The black-and-white mosaic tiling of the entranceway surrounds what was once perhaps a red lion, but it's been chewed away as if by stone-eating moths and so it's now more like a mangled polyp. The ochre-yellow linoleum floor hasn't been scrubbed for some time; splotches of dirt bloom on it like grey pressed flowers.

He signs the register, pays; while he does this she stands, hoping she looks bored, keeping her face still, eyes above the glum desk clerk, watching the clock. It's plain, assertive, without pretensions to grace, like a railway clock: utilitarian. *This is the time*, it says, *only one layer of it, there is no other.*

He has the key now. Second floor. There's a tiny coffin of an elevator but she can't stand the thought of it, she knows what it will smell like, dirty socks and decaying teeth, and she can't stand to be in there face to face with him, so close and in that smell. They walk up the stairs. A carpet, once dark blue and red. A pathway strewn with flowers, worn down now to the roots.

I'm sorry, he said. It could be better.

What you get is what you pay for, she says, intending brightness; but it's the wrong thing to say, he may think she's commenting on his lack of money. It's good camouflage though, she says, trying to fix it. He doesn't answer this. She's talking too much, she can hear herself, and what she's saying is not at all beguiling. Is she different from what he remembers, is she much changed?

In the hallway there's wallpaper, no longer any colour. The doors are dark wood, gouged and gored and flayed. He finds the number, the key turns. It's a long-shafted old-fashioned key, as if for an ancient strongbox. The room is worse than any of the furnished rooms they'd been in before: those had made at least a surface pretense of being clean. A double bed covered by a slippery spread, imitation quilted satin, a dull yellowy pink like the sole of a foot. One chair, with a leaking upholstered seat that appears to be stuffed with dust. An ashtray of chipped brown glass. Cigarette smoke, spilled beer, and under that another more disturbing smell, like underclothes long unwashed. There's a transom over the door, its bumpy glass painted white.

She peels off her gloves, drops them onto the chair along with her coat and scarf, digs the flask out of her handbag. No glasses in sight, they'll have to swig.

Does the window open? she says. We could use some fresh air.

He goes over, hoists the sash. A thick breeze pushes in. Outside, a streetcar grinds past. He turns, still at the window, leaning backwards, his hands behind him on the sill. With the light behind him, all she can see is his outline. He could be anybody.

Well, he says. Here we are again. He sounds bone tired. It occurs to her that he may not want to do anything in this room but sleep.

She goes over to him, slips her arms around his waist. I found the story, she says.

What story?

Lizard Men of Xenor. I looked everywhere for it, you should have seen me poking around the newsstands, they must have thought I was crazy. I looked and looked.

Oh, that, he says. You read that piece of tripe? I'd forgotten.

She won't show dismay. She won't show too much need. She won't say it was a clue that proved his existence; a piece of evidence, however absurd.

Of course I read it. I kept waiting for the next episode.

Never wrote it, he says. Too busy getting shot at, from both sides. Our bunch was caught in the middle. I was on the run from the good guys. What a shambles.

Belatedly his arms come around her. He smells malted. He rests his head on her shoulder, the sandpaper of his cheek against the side of her neck. She has him safe, at least for the moment.

God I need a drink, he says.

Don't go to sleep, she says. Don't go to sleep yet. Come to bed.

He sleeps for three hours. The sun moves, the light dims. She knows she ought to go, but she can't bear to do that, or to wake him either. What excuse will she present, once she gets back? She invents an old lady tumbling down stairs, an old lady needing rescue; she invents a taxi, a trip to the hospital. How could she leave her to fend for herself, the poor old soul? Lying on the sidewalk without a friend in the world. She'll say she knows she should have phoned, but there wasn't a phone nearby, and the old lady was in such pain. She steels herself for the lecture she'll get, about minding her own business; the shake of the head, because what can be done about her? When will she ever learn to leave well enough alone?

Downstairs the clock is clicking off the minutes. There are voices in the corridor, the sound of hurrying, rapid pulse of shoes. It's an in and out business. She lies awake beside him, listening to him sleeping, wondering where he's gone. Also how much she should tell him – whether she should tell him everything that's happened. If he asks her to go away with him, then she'll have to tell. Otherwise perhaps better not. Or not yet.

When he wakes up he wants another drink, and a cigarette.

I guess we shouldn't do this, she says. Smoking in bed. We'll catch on fire. Burn ourselves up.

He says nothing.

What was it like? she says. I read the papers, but that's not the same.

No, he says. It's not.

I was so worried you might get killed.

I almost did, he said. The funny thing is, it was hell but I got used to it, and now I can't get used to this. You've put on a bit of weight.

Oh, am I too fat?

No. It's nice. Something to hang on to.

It's full dark now. From down below the window, where the beverage room empties onto the street, come snatches of off-key song, shouts, laughter; then the sound of glass shattering. Someone's smashed a bottle. A woman screams.

Some celebration they're having.

What are they celebrating?

War.

But there isn't a war. It's all over.

They're celebrating the next one, he says. It's on the way. Everyone's denying it up there in cloud cuckoo land, but down at ground level you can smell it coming. With Spain shot to hell for target practice, they'll start in on the serious business pretty soon. It's like thunder in the air, and they're excited by it. That's why all the bottle-smashing. They want to get a head start.

Oh, surely not, she says. There can't be another one. They've made pacts and everything.

Peace in our time, he says scornfully. Fucking bullshit. What they're hoping is that Uncle Joe and Adolf will tear each other to pieces, and get rid of the Jews for them into the bargain, while they sit on their bums and make money.

You're as cynical as ever.

You're as naive.

Not quite, she says. Let's not argue. It won't be settled by us. But this is more like him, more like the way he was, and so she feels a little better.

No, he says. You're right. It won't be settled by us. We're small potatoes.

But you'll go anyway, she says. If it starts up again. Whether you're a small potato or not.

He looks at her. What else can I do?

He doesn't know why she's crying. She tries not to. I wish you'd been wounded, she says. Then you'd have to stay here.

And a fat lot of good that would do you, he says. Come here.

Leaving, she can scarcely see. She walks by herself a little, to calm down, but it's dark and there are too many men on the sidewalk, and so she takes a taxi. Sitting in the back seat, she repairs her mouth, powders her face. When they stop, she rummages in her purse, she pays the taxi, goes up the stone steps and through the arched entranceway, and closes the thick oak door. In her head she's rehearsing: *Sorry I'm late, but you wouldn't believe what happened to me. I've had quite a little adventure.*

How did the war creep up? How did it gather itself together? What was it made from? What secrets, lies, betrayals? What loves and hatreds? What sums of money, what metals?

Hope throws a smokescreen. Smoke gets in your eyes and so no one is prepared for it, but suddenly it's there, like an out-of-control bonfire – like murder, only multiplied. It's in full spate.

The war takes place in black and white. For those on the sidelines that is. For those who are actually in it there are many colours, excessive colours, too bright, too red and orange, too liquid and incandescent, but for the others the war is like a newsreel – grainy, smeared, with bursts of staccato noise and large numbers of grey-skinned people rushing or plodding or falling down, everything elsewhere.

She goes to the newsreels, in the movie theatres. She reads the papers. She knows herself to be at the mercy of events, and she knows by now that events have no mercy.

She's made up her mind. She's determined now, she'll sacrifice everything and everyone. Nothing and nobody will stand in her way.

This is what she'll do. She has it all planned out. She'll leave the house one day as if it's any other day. She'll have money, money of some description. This is the unclear part, but surely something will be possible. What do other people do? They go to the pawnshop, and that's what she will have done as well. She'll get the money by pawning things: a gold watch, a silver spoon, a fur coat. Bits and pieces. She'll pawn them little by little and they won't be missed.

It won't be enough money but it will have to be enough. She'll rent a room, an inexpensive room but not too dingy – nothing a coat of paint won't brighten up. She'll write a letter saying she isn't coming back. They'll send emissaries, ambassadors, then lawyers, they'll threaten, they'll penalize, she'll be afraid all the time but she'll hold firm. She'll burn all her bridges except the bridge to him, even though the bridge to him is so tenuous. *I'll be back*, he said, but how could he be sure? You can't guarantee such a thing.

She'll live on apples and soda crackers, on cups of tea and glasses of milk. Cans of baked beans and corned beef. Also on fried eggs when available, and slices of toast, which she'll eat at the corner café where the newsboys and early drunks also eat. Veterans will eat there too, more and more of them as the months go past: men missing hands, arms, legs, ears, eyes. She'll wish to talk with them, but she won't because any interest from her would be sure to be misunderstood. Her body as usual would get in the way of free speech. Therefore she will only eavesdrop.

In the café the talk will be about the end of the war, which everyone says is coming. It will only be a matter of time, they'll say, before it'll all be mopped up and the boys will be back. The men who say this will be strangers to one another, but they'll exchange such comments anyway, because the prospect of victory will make them talkative. There will be a different feeling in the air, part optimism, part fear. Any day now the ship will come in, but who can tell what might be on it?

Her apartment will be above a grocery store, with a kitchenette and a small bathroom. She will buy a house plant – a begonia, or else a fern. She will remember to water this plant and it will not die. The woman running the grocery store will be dark-haired and plump and motherly, and will talk about her thinness and the need for her to eat more, and about what should be done for a chest cold. Perhaps she will be Greek; Greek, or something like it, with big arms and a centre part in her hair, and a bun at the back. Her husband and son will be overseas; she'll have pictures of them, framed in painted wood, hand-tinted, beside the cash register.

Both of them – she and this woman – will spend a lot of time listening: for footsteps, a telephone call, a knock on the door. It's hard to sleep under these circumstances: they'll discuss remedies for sleeplessness. Occasionally the woman will press an apple into her hand, or an acid-green candy from the glass container of them on the counter. Such gifts will be more comforting to her than their low price would suggest.

How will he know where to reclaim her? Now that her bridges have been burned. He'll know, however. He'll find out somehow, because journeys end in lovers meeting. They should. They must.

She'll sew curtains for the windows, yellow curtains, the colour of canaries or the yolks of eggs. Cheerful curtains, like sunshine. Never mind that she doesn't know how to sew, because the woman downstairs will help her. She'll starch the curtains and hang them up. She'll get down on her knees with a whisk and clean out the mouse droppings and dead flies under the kitchen sink. She'll repaint a set of canisters she'll find in a junk store, and stencil on them: Tea, Coffee, Sugar, Flour. She will hum to herself while doing this. She'll buy a new towel, a whole set of new towels. Also sheets, these are important, and pillowcases. She'll brush her hair a lot.

These are the joyful things she will do, while waiting for him.

She'll buy a radio, a small tinny secondhand one, at the pawnshop; she'll listen to the news, to keep up with current events. Also she'll have a telephone: a telephone will be necessary in the long run, although no one will call her on it, not yet. Sometimes she'll pick it up just to listen to it purr. Or else there will be voices on it, having a conversation on the party line. Mostly it will be women, exchanging the details of meals and weather and bargains and children, and of men who are somewhere else.

None of this happens, of course. Or it does happen, but not so you would notice. It happens in another dimension of space.

The Blind Assassin: The telegram

The telegram is delivered in the usual way, by a man in a dark uniform whose face brings no glad tidings. When they're hired for the job they teach them that expression, remote but doleful, like a dark blank bell. The closed coffin look.

The telegram comes in a yellow envelope with a glassine window, and it says the same thing telegrams like that always say – the words distant, like the words of a stranger, an intruder, standing at the far end of a long empty room. There aren't many words, but every word is distinct: *inform*, *loss*, *regret*. Careful, neutral words, with a hidden question behind them: *What did you expect?*

What's this about? Who is this? she says. Oh. I remember. It's him. That man. But why did they send it to me? I'm scarcely the next of kin!

Kin? says one of them. Did he have any? It's meant to be a witticism.

She laughs. It's nothing to do with me. She crumples up the telegram, which she assumes they've read on the sly before passing it on to her. They read all of the mail; that goes without saying. She sits down, a little too abruptly. I'm sorry, she says. I feel quite strange all of a sudden.

Here you go. This'll buck you up. Drink it down, that's the ticket.

Thank you. It's nothing to do with me, but still it's a shock. It's like someone walking on your grave. She shivers.

Easy does it. You look a little green. Don't take it personally.

Perhaps it was a mistake. Perhaps they got the addresses mixed.

Could have done. Or perhaps it was his own doing. Perhaps it was his idea of a joke. He was an odd duck, as I recall.

Odder than we thought. What a filthy rotten thing to do! If he was alive you could sue him for mischief.

Perhaps he was trying to make you feel guilty. That's what they do, his kind. Envious, all of them. Dog in the manger. Don't let it worry you.

Well, it's not a very nice thing, no matter how you look at it.

Nice? Why would it be nice? He was never what you'd call *nice*.

I suppose I could write to the superior officer. Demand an explanation.

Why would he know anything about it? It wouldn't have been him, it was some functionary on this end of things. They just use what's written down in the records. He'd say it was a snafu, by no means the first, from what I hear.

Anyway, no sense in making a fuss. It would just draw attention, and no matter what you do you'll never find out why he did it.

Not unless the dead walk. Their eyes are bright, all watching her, alert. What are they afraid of? What are they afraid she'll do?

I wish you wouldn't use that word, she says fretfully.

What word? Oh. She means *dead*. Might as well call a spade a spade. No sense not. Now, don't be . . .

I don't like spades. I don't like what they're used for – digging holes in the ground.

Don't be morbid.

Get her a handkerchief. It's no time to badger her. She should go upstairs, have a little rest. Then she'll be right as rain.

Don't let it upset you.

Don't take it to heart.

Forget it.

In the night she wakes abruptly, her heart pounding. She slips out of bed and makes her way silently towards the window, and raises the sash higher and leans out. There's the moon, almost full, spider-veined with old scars, and below it the ambient sub-orange glow cast up into the sky by the street lights. Beneath is the sidewalk, patchy with shadow and partially hidden by the chestnut tree in the yard, its branches spread out like a hard thick net, its white-moth flowers glimmering faintly.

There's a man, looking up. She can see the dark eyebrows, the hollows of the eye sockets, the smile a white slash across the oval of his face. At the V below his throat there's pallor: a shirt. He lifts his hand, motions: he wants her to join him – slip out of the window, climb down through the tree. She's afraid though. She's afraid she'll fall.

Now he's on the windowsill outside, now he's in the room. The flowers of the chestnut tree flare up: by their white light she can see his face, the skin greyish, half-toned; two-dimensional, like a photograph, but smudged. There's a smell of burning bacon. He isn't looking at her, not at her exactly; it's as if she is her own shadow and he's looking at that. At where her eyes would be if her shadow could see.

She longs to touch him, but she hesitates: surely if she were to take him in her arms he would blur, then dissolve, into shreds of cloth, into smoke, into molecules, into atoms. Her hands would go right through him.

I said I would come back.

What's happened to you? What's wrong?

Don't you know?

★

Then they're outside, on the roof it seems, looking down on the city, but it isn't any city she's ever seen. It's as if one huge bomb has fallen on it, it's all in flames, everything burning at once – houses, streets, palaces, fountains and temples – exploding, bursting like fireworks. There's no sound. It burns silently, as if in a picture – white, yellow, red and orange. No screams. No people in it; the people must be dead already. Beside her he flickers in the flickering light.

Nothing will be left of it, he says. A heap of stones, a few old words. It's gone now, it's erased. Nobody will remember.

But it was so beautiful! she says. Now it seems to her like a place she's known; she's known it very well, she's known it like the back of her hand. In the sky three moons have risen. Zycron, she thinks. Beloved planet, land of my heart. Where once, long ago, I was happy. All gone now, all destroyed. She can't bear to look at the flames.

Beautiful for some, he says. That's always the problem.

What went wrong? Who did this?

The old woman.

What?

L'histoire, cette vieille dame exaltée et menteuse.

He shines like tin. His eyes are vertical slits. He isn't what she remembers. Everything that made him singular has been burned away. Never mind, he says. They'll build it up again. They always do.

Now she's afraid of him. You've changed so much, she says.

The situation was critical. We had to fight fire with fire.

You won, though. I know you won!

Nobody won.

Has she made a mistake? Surely there was news of victory. There was a parade, she says. I heard about it. There was a brass band.

Look at me, he says.

But she can't. She can't focus on him, he won't stay steady. He's indeterminate, he wavers, like a candle flame but devoid of light. She can't see his eyes.

He's dead, of course. Of course he's dead, because didn't she get the telegram? But it's only an invention, all of this. It's only another dimension of space. Why then is there such desolation?

He's moving away now, and she can't call after him, her throat won't make a sound. Now he's gone.

She feels a choking pressure around the heart. *No, no, no, no*, says a voice inside her head. Tears are running down her face.

This is when she wakes up really.

XIII

Gloves

Today it's raining, the thin, abstemious rain of early April. Already the blue scilla are beginning to flower, the daffodils have their snouts above ground, the self-seeded forget-me-nots are creeping up, getting ready to hog the light. Here it comes – another year of vegetative hustling and jostling. They never seem to get tired of it: plants have no memories, that's why. They can't remember how many times they've done all this before.

I must admit it's a surprise to find myself still here, still talking to you. I prefer to think of it as talking, although of course it isn't: I'm saying nothing, you're hearing nothing. The only thing between us is this black line: a thread thrown onto the empty page, into the empty air.

The winter's ice in the Louveteau Gorge is almost gone, even in the shaded crevasses of the cliffs. The water, black and then white, hurtles down through the limestone chasms and over the boulders, effortlessly as ever. A violent sound, but soothing; alluring, almost. You can see how people are drawn to it. To waterfalls, to high places, to deserts and deep lakes – places of no return.

Only one corpse in the river so far this year, a drug-ridden young woman from Toronto. Another girl in a hurry. Another waste of time, her own. She had relatives here, an aunt, an uncle. Already they're the objects of narrow sideways looks, as if they had something to do with it; already they've assumed the cornered, angry air of the consciously innocent. I'm sure they're blameless, but they're alive, and whoever's left alive gets blamed. That's the rule in things like this. Unfair, but there it is.

★

Yesterday morning Walter came round, to see about the spring tune-up. That's what he calls the household fix-it routine he goes through, on my behalf, every year. He brought his toolbox, his hand-held electric saw, his electric screwdriver: he likes nothing better than to be whirring away like part of a motor.

He parked all these tools on the back porch, then stomped around outside the house. When he came back in he had a gratified expression. "Garden gate missing a slat," he said. "I can whack her in today, paint her when it's dry."

"Oh, don't bother," I say, as I do every year. "Everything's falling apart, but it will last me out."

Walter ignores this, as always. "Front steps too," he says. "Need paint. One of them should come right off – put a new one on her. You let it go too long, the water gets in and then you get the rot. Maybe a stain though, for the porch, better for the wood. We could put another colour strip along the edges of the steps, so people could see better. The way it is they could miss their footing, hurt themselves." He uses *we* out of courtesy, and by *people* he means me. "I can have that new step in later today."

"You'll get all wet," I said. "The weather channel says more of the same."

"Nope, it'll clear up." He didn't even look at the sky.

Walter went off to get the necessities – some planks, I suppose – and I spent the interval reclining on the parlour sofa, like some vaporous novelistic heroine who's been forgotten in the pages of her own book and left to yellow and mildew and crumble away like the book itself.

A morbid image, Myra would say.

What else would you suggest? I would reply.

The fact is that my heart has been acting up again. *Acting up,* a peculiar phrase. It's what people say to minimize the gravity of their condition. It implies that the offending part (heart, stomach, liver, whatever) is a fractious, bratty child, which can be brought into line with a slap or a sharp word. At the same time, that these symptoms – these tremors and pains, these palpitations – are mere theatrics, and that the organ in question will soon stop capering about and making a spectacle of itself, and resume its placid, off-stage existence.

The doctor isn't pleased. He's been muttering about tests and scans, and trips into Toronto where the specialists lurk, those few who have not fled for greener pastures. He's changed my pills, added another one to the arsenal. He's even suggested the possibility of an operation. What would be involved, I asked, and what would be accomplished? Too much of one, as it turns out, and not enough of the other. He suspects that nothing short of a whole new unit – his term, as if it's a dishwasher we're talking about – will do. Also I would have to stand in line, waiting for someone else's unit, one that's no longer needed. Not to put too fine a gloss on it, someone else's heart, ripped out of some youngster: you wouldn't want to install an old rickety wizened-up one like the one you intend to throw away. What you want is something fresh and juicy.

But who knows where they get those things? Street children in Latin America is my guess; or so goes the most paranoid rumour. Stolen hearts, black-market hearts, wrenched from between broken ribs, warm and bleeding, offered up to the false god. What is the false god? We are. Us and our money. That's what Laura would say. *Don't touch that money*, Reenie would say. *You don't know where it's been.*

Could I live with myself, knowing I was carrying the heart of a dead child?

But if not, then what?

Please don't mistake this rambling angst for stoicism. I take my pills, I take my halting walks, but there's nothing I can do for dread.

After lunch – a piece of hard cheese, a glass of dubious milk, a flabby carrot, Myra having fallen down this week on her self-appointed task of stocking my refrigerator – Walter returned. He measured, sawed, hammered, then knocked on the back door to say he was sorry for the noise but everything was ship-shape now.

"I made you some coffee," I said. This is a ritual on these April occasions. Had I burned it this time? No matter. He was used to Myra's.

"Don't mind if I do." He removed his rubber boots carefully and left them on the back porch – Myra has him well trained, he's not allowed to track what she calls *his dirt* onto what she calls *her carpets* – then tiptoed in his mammoth socks across my kitchen floor; which, thanks to the energetic scourings and polishings of Myra's woman, is now as slick and treacherous as a glacier. It used to have a useful adhesive skin on it, an accumulation of dust and grime like a thin coating of glue, but no longer. I really should strew it with grit, or I'll slip on it and do myself an injury.

Watching Walter tiptoe was a treat in itself – an elephant walking on eggs. He reached the kitchen table, setting his yellow leather work gloves down on it, where they lay like giant, extra paws.

"New gloves," I said. They were so new they almost glowed. Not a scratch on them either.

"Myra got those. Guy three streets over, took the ends of his fingers off with a fretsaw and she's all steamed up about it, worried I'll do the same or worse. But that guy's a numbnuts, moved here from Toronto, pardon my French but he shouldn't be allowed to fool with saws, could of took his head off while he was at it, no loss to the world either. I told her, have to be ten bricks short of a load to pull a stunt like that, and anyways I don't own a fretsaw. But she makes me cart the darn things around anyways. Every time I go out the door, it's Yoo-hoo, here's your gloves."

"You could lose them," I said.

"She'd buy others," he said gloomily.

"Leave them here. Say you forgot them and you'll pick them up later. Then just don't pick them up." I had an image of myself, during lonely nights, holding one of Walter's vacated, leathery hands: it would be a companion of sorts. Pathetic. Maybe I should buy a cat, or a small dog. Something warm and uncritical and furry – a fellow creature, helping me to keep watch by night. We need the mammalian huddle: too much solitude is bad for the eyesight. But if I got something like that I'd most likely trip over it and break my neck.

Walter's mouth twitched, the tips of his upper teeth showed: it was a grin. "Great minds think alike, eh?" he said. "Then maybe you could dump the suckers in the trash, accidentally on purpose."

"Walter, you are a rascal," I said. Walter grinned more, added five spoons of sugar to the coffee, downed it, then placed both hands on the table and levered himself into the air, like an obelisk raised by ropes. In that motion I suddenly foresaw what his last action would be, in relation to me: he'll hoist one end of my coffin.

He knows it too. He's standing by. He's not a handyman for nothing. He won't make a fuss, he won't drop me, he'll make sure I travel in level, horizontal safely on this last, short voyage of mine. "Up she goes," he'll say. And up I will go.

Lugubrious. I know it; and sentimental as well. But please bear with me. The dying are allowed a certain latitude, like children on their birthdays.

Home fires

Last night I watched the television news. I shouldn't do that, it's bad for the digestion. There's another war somewhere, what they call a minor one, though of course it isn't minor for anyone who happens to get caught up in it. They have a generic look to them, these wars – the men in camouflage gear with scarves over their mouths and noses, the drifts of smoke, the gutted buildings, the broken, weeping civilians. Endless mothers, carrying endless limp children, their faces splotched with blood; endless bewildered old men. They cart the young men off and murder them, intending to forestall revenge, as the Greeks did at Troy. Hitler's excuse too for killing Jewish babies, as I recall.

The wars break out and die down, but then there's a flareup elsewhere. Houses cracked open like eggs, their contents torched or stolen or stomped vindictively underfoot; refugees strafed from airplanes. In a million cellars the bewildered royal family faces the firing squad; the gems sewn into their corsets will not save them. Herod's troops patrol a thousand streets; just next door, Napoleon makes off with the silverware. In the wake of the invasion, any invasion, the ditches fill up with raped women. To be fair, raped men as well. Raped children, raped dogs and cats. Things can get out of control.

But not here; not in this gentle, tedious backwater; not in Port Ticonderoga, despite a druggie or two in the parks, despite the occasional break-in, despite the occasional body found floating around in the eddies. We hunker down here, drinking our bedtime drinks, nibbling our bedtime snacks, peering at the world as if through a secret window, and when we've had enough of it we turn it off. *So much for the twentieth century*, we say, as we make our way upstairs. But there's a far-off roaring, like a tidal wave racing inshore. Here comes the twenty-first century, sweeping overhead like a spaceship filled with ruthless lizard-eyed aliens or a metal pterodactyl. Sooner or later it will sniff us out, it will tear the roofs off our flimsy little burrows with its iron claws, and then we will be just as naked and shivering and starving and diseased and hopeless as the rest.

Excuse this digression. At my age you indulge in these apoc-alyptic visions. You say, *The end of the world is at hand.* You lie to yourself – *I'm glad I won't be around to see it* – when in fact you'd like nothing better, as long as you can watch it through the little secret window, as long as you won't be involved.

But why bother about the end of the world? It's the end of the world every day, for someone. Time rises and rises, and when it reaches the level of your eyes you drown.

What happened next? For a moment I've lost the thread, it's hard for me to remember, but then I do. It was the war, of course. We weren't prepared for it, but at the same time we knew we'd been there before. It was the same chill, the chill that rolled in like a fog, the chill into which I was born. As then, everything took on a shivering anxiety – the chairs, the tables, the streets and the street lights, the sky, the air. Overnight, whole portions of what had been acknowledged as reality simply vanished. This is what happens when there's a war.

But you are too young to remember which war that might have been. Every war is *the war* for whoever's lived through it. The one to which I'm referring began in early September of 1939, and went on until . . . Well, it's in the history books. You can look it up.

Keep the home fires burning, was one of the old war slogans.

Whenever I heard that, I used to picture a horde of women with flowing hair and glittering eyes, making their way furtively, in ones or twos, by moonlight, setting fire to their own homes.

In the months before the war began, my marriage to Richard was already foundering, though it might be said to have foundered from the beginning. I'd had one miscarriage and then another. Richard on his part had had one mistress and then another, or so I suspected – inevitable (Winifred would later say) considering my frail state of health, and Richard's urges. Men had urges, in those days; they were numerous, these urges; they lived underground in the dark nooks and crannies of a man's being, and once in a while they would gather strength and sally forth, like a plague of rats. They were so cunning and strong, how could any real man be expected to prevail against them? This was the doctrine according to Winifred, and – to be fair – to lots of other people as well.

These mistresses of Richard's were (I assumed) his secretaries – always very young, always pretty, always decent girls. He'd hire them fresh from whatever academy produced them. For a while they would patronize me nervously, over the telephone, when I'd call him at the office. They would also be dispatched to purchase gifts for me, and order flowers. He liked them to keep their priorities straight: I was the official wife, and he had no intention of divorcing me. Divorced men did not become leaders of their countries, not in those days. This situation gave me a certain amount of power, but it was power only if I did not exercise it. In fact it was power only if I pretended to know nothing. The threat hanging over him was that I might find out; that I might open what was already an open secret, and set free all kinds of evils.

Did I care? Yes, in a way. But half a loaf is better than none,

I would tell myself, and Richard was just a kind of loaf. He was the bread on the table, for Aimee as well as for myself. Rise above it, as Reenie used to say, and I did try. I tried to rise above it, up into the sky, like a runaway balloon, and some of the time I succeeded.

I occupied my time, I'd learned how to do that. I had taken up gardening in earnest now, I was getting some results. Not everything died. I had plans for a perennial shade garden.

Richard kept up appearances. So did I. We attended cocktail parties and dinners, we made entrances and exits together, his hand on my elbow. We made a point of a drink or two before dinner, or three; I was becoming a little too fond of gin, in this combination or that, but I wasn't too close to the edge as long as I could feel my toes and hold my tongue. We were still skating on the surface of things – on the thin ice of good manners, which hides the dark tarn beneath: once it melts, you're sunk.

Half a life is better than none.

I've failed to convey Richard, in any rounded sense. He remains a cardboard cutout. I know that. I can't truly describe him, I can't get a precise focus: he's blurred, like the face in some wet, discarded newspaper. Even at the time he appeared to me smaller than life, although larger than life as well. It came from his having too much money, too much presence in the world – you were tempted to expect more from him than was there, and so what was average in him seemed like deficiency. He was ruthless, but not like a lion; more like a sort of large rodent. He tunnelled underground; he killed things by chewing off their roots.

He had the wherewithal for grand gestures, for acts of significant generosity, but he made none. He had become like a statue of himself: huge, public, imposing, hollow.

It wasn't that he was too big for his boots: he wasn't big enough for them. That's it in a nutshell.

At the outbreak of the war, Richard was in a tight spot. He'd been too cozy with the Germans in his business dealings, too admiring of them in his speeches. Like many of his peers, he'd turned too blind an eye to their brutal violations of democracy; a democracy that many of our leaders had been decrying as unworkable, but that they were now keen to defend.

Richard also stood to lose a lot of money, since he could no longer trade with those who had overnight become the enemy. He had to do some scrambling, some kowtowing; it didn't sit well with him, but he did it. He managed to salvage his position, and to scramble back into favour – well, he wasn't the only one with dirty hands, so it was best for the others not to point their own tainted fingers at him – and soon his factories were blasting away, full steam ahead for the war effort, and no one was more patriotic than he. Thus it wasn't counted against him when Russia came in on the side of the Allies, and Joseph Stalin was suddenly everybody's loveable uncle. True, Richard had said much against the Communists, but that was once upon a time. It was all swept under the carpet now, because weren't your enemy's enemies your friends?

Meanwhile I trudged through the days, not as usual – the usual had altered – but as best I could. *Dogged* is the word I'd use now, to describe myself then. Or *stupefied*, that would do as well. There were no more garden parties to contend with, no more silk stockings except through the black market. Meat was rationed, and butter, and sugar: if you wanted more of those things, more than other people got, it became important to establish certain contacts. No more transatlantic voyages on luxury liners – the *Queen Mary* became a troop ship. The radio stopped being a portable bandshell and became a frenetic oracle; every evening I turned it on to hear the news, which at first was always bad.

The war went on and on, a relentless motor. It wore people down – the constant, dreary tension. It was like listening to someone grinding his teeth, in the dusk before dawn, while you lie sleepless night after night after night.

There were some benefits to be had, however. Mr. Murgatroyd left us, to join the army. It was then I learned to drive. I took over one of the cars, the Bentley I think it was, and Richard had it registered to me – that gave us more gasoline. (Gasoline was rationed, of course, though less so for people like Richard.) It also gave me more freedom, although it was not a freedom that had much use for me any more.

I caught a cold, which turned to bronchitis – everyone had a cold that winter. It took me months to get rid of it. I spent a lot of time in bed, feeling sad. I coughed and coughed. I no longer went to the newsreels – the speeches, the battles, the bombings and the devastation, the victories, even the invasions. Stirring times, or so we were told, but I'd lost interest.

The end of the war approached. It got nearer and nearer. Then it occurred. I remembered the silence after the last war had ended, and then the ringing of the bells. It had been November, then, with ice on the puddles, and now it was spring. There were parades. There were proclamations. Trumpets were blown.

It wasn't so easy, though, ending the war. A war is a huge fire; the ashes from it drift far, and settle slowly.

Diana Sweets

Today I walked as far as the Jubilee Bridge, then along to the doughnut shop, where I ate almost a third of an orange cruller. A great wodge of flour and fat, spreading out through my arteries like silt.

Then I went off to the washroom. Someone was in the middle cubicle, so I waited, avoiding the mirror. Age thins your skin; you can see the veins, the tendons. Also it thickens you. It's hard to get back to what you were before, when you were skinless.

At last the door opened and a girl came out – a darkish girl, in sullen clothing, her eyes ringed with soot. She gave a little shriek, then a laugh. "Sorry," she said, "I didn't see you there, you creeped me out." Her accent was foreign, but she belonged here: she was of the nationality of the young. It's I who am the stranger now.

The newest message was in gold marker: *You can't get to Heaven without Jesus*. Already the annotators had been at work: *Jesus* had been crossed out, and *Death* written above it, in black.

And below that, in green: *Heaven is in a grain of sand. Blake.*

And below that, in orange: *Heaven is on the Planet Xenor. Laura Chase.*

Another misquote.

The war ended officially in the first week of May – the war in Europe, that is. Which was the only part of it that would have concerned Laura.

A week later she telephoned. She placed the call in the morning, an hour after breakfast, when she must have known Richard would not be at home. I didn't recognize her voice, I'd given up expecting her. I thought at first that she was the woman from my dressmaker's.

"It's me," she said.

"Where are you?" I said carefully. You must recall that she was by this time an unknown quantity to me – perhaps of questionable stability.

"I'm here," she said. "In the city." She wouldn't tell me where she was staying, but she named a street corner where I could pick her up, later that afternoon. In that case we could have tea, I said. Diana Sweets was where I intended to take her. It was safe, it was secluded, it catered mostly to women; they knew me there. I said I would bring my car.

"Oh, do you have a car now?"

"More or less." I described it.

"It sounds like quite a chariot," she said lightly.

Laura was standing on the corner of King and Spadina, right where she said she'd be. It wasn't the most savoury district, but she didn't seem perturbed by that. I honked, and she waved and then came over and climbed in. I leaned over and kissed her on the cheek. Immediately I felt treacherous.

"I can't believe you're really here," I said to her.

"But here I am."

I was close to tears all of a sudden; she seemed unconcerned. Her cheek had been very cool, though. Cool and thin.

"I hope you didn't mention anything to Richard, though," she said. "About me being here. Or Winifred," she added, "because it's the same thing."

"I wouldn't do that," I said. She said nothing.

Because I was driving, I could not look at her directly. For that I had to wait until I'd parked the car, then until we'd walked to Diana Sweets, and then until we were seated across from each other. At last I could see all of her, full on.

She was and was not the Laura I remembered. Older, of course – we both were – but more than that. She was neatly, even austerely dressed, in a dull-blue shirtwaist dress with a pleated bodice and small buttons down the front; her hair was pulled back into a severe chignon. She appeared shrunken, fallen in on herself, leached of colour, but at the same time translucent – as if little spikes of light were being nailed out through her skin from the inside, as if thorns of light were shooting out from her in a prickly haze, like a thistle held up to the sun. It's a hard effect to describe. (Nor should you set much store by it: my eyes were already warping, I already needed glasses, though I didn't yet know it. The fuzzy light around Laura may have been simply an optical flaw.)

We ordered. She wanted coffee rather than tea. It would be bad coffee, I warned her – you couldn't get good coffee in a place like this, because of the war. But she said, "I'm used to bad coffee."

There was a silence. I hardly knew where to begin. I wasn't yet ready to ask her what she was doing back in Toronto. Where had she been all this time? I asked. What had she been doing?

"I was in Avilion, at first," she said.

"But it was all closed up!" It had been, all through the war. We hadn't been back for years. "How did you get in?"

"Oh, you know," she said. "We could always get in when we wanted to."

I remembered the coal chute, the dubious lock on one of the cellar doors. But that had been repaired, long ago. "Did you break a window?"

"I didn't have to. Reenie kept a key," she said. "But don't tell."

"The furnace can't have been on. There couldn't have been any heat," I said.

"There wasn't," she said. "But there were a lot of mice."

Our coffee arrived. It tasted of burned toast crumbs and roasted chicory, not surprising since that's what they put into it. "Do you want some cake or something?" I said. "It's not bad cake here." She was so thin, I felt she could use some cake.

"No, thanks."

"Then what did you do?"

"Then I turned twenty-one, so I had a little money, from Father. So I went to Halifax."

"Halifax? Why Halifax?"

"It was where the ships came in."

I didn't pursue this. There was a reason behind it, there always was with Laura; it was a reason I shied away from hearing. "But what were you *doing*?"

"This and that," she said. "I made myself useful." Which was all she would say on that score. I supposed it would have been a soup kitchen of some kind, or the equivalent. Cleaning toilets in a hospital, that sort of thing. "Didn't you get my letters? From BellaVista? Reenie said you didn't."

"No," I said. "I never got any letters."

"I expect they stole them. And they wouldn't let you call, or come to see me?"

"They said it would be bad for you."

She laughed a little. "It would have been bad for *you*," she said. "You really shouldn't stay there, in that house. You shouldn't stay with *him*. He's very evil."

"I know you've always felt that, but what else can I do?" I said. "He'd never give me a divorce. And I don't have any money."

"That's no excuse."

"Maybe not for you. You've got your trust fund, from Father, but I have no such thing. And what about Aimee?"

"You could take her with you."

"Easier said than done. She might not want to come. She's pretty stuck on Richard, at the moment, if you must know."

"Why would she be?" said Laura.

"He butters her up. He gives her things."

"I wrote you from Halifax," said Laura, changing the subject.

"I never got those letters either."

"I expect Richard reads your mail," said Laura.

"I expect he does," I said. The conversation was taking a turn I hadn't expected. I'd assumed I'd be consoling Laura, commiserating with her, hearing a sad tale, but instead she was lecturing me. How easily we slid back into our old roles.

"What did he tell you about me?" she said now. "About putting me into that place?"

There it was, then, right out on the table. This was the crossroads: either Laura had been mad, or Richard had been lying. I couldn't believe both. "He told me a story," I said evasively.

"What sort of a story? Don't worry, I won't get upset. I just want to know."

"He said you were – well, mentally disturbed."

"Naturally. He would say that. What else did he say?"

"He said you thought you were pregnant, but it was just a delusion."

"I *was* pregnant," said Laura. "That was the whole point – that was why they whisked me out of sight in such a hurry. Him and Winifred – they were scared stiff. The disgrace, the scandal – you can imagine what they'd think it would do to his big fat chances."

"Yes. I can see that." I could see it, too – the hush-hush call from the doctor, the panic, the hasty conference between the two of them, the spur-of-the-moment plan. Then the other version of events, the false one, concocted just for me. I was docile enough as a rule, but they must have known there was a line somewhere. They must have been afraid of what I might do, once they'd crossed it.

"Anyway, I didn't have the baby. That's one of the things they do, at BellaVista."

"One of the things?" I was feeling quite stupid.

"Besides the mumbo-jumbo, I mean, and the pills and machines. They do extractions," she said. "They conk you out with ether, like the dentist. Then they take out the babies. Then they tell you you've made the whole thing up. Then when you accuse them of it, they say you're a danger to yourself and others."

She was so calm, so plausible. "Laura," I said, "are you sure? About the baby, I mean. Are you sure there really was one?"

"Of course I'm sure," she said. "Why would I make such a thing up?"

There was still room for doubt, but this time I believed Laura. "How did it happen?" I whispered. "Who was the father?" Such a thing called for whispering.

"If you don't already know, I don't think I can tell you," said Laura.

I supposed it must have been Alex Thomas. Alex was the only man Laura had ever shown any interest in – besides Father, that is, and God. I hated to acknowledge such a possibility, but really there was no other choice. They must have met during those days when she'd been playing hookey, from her first school in Toronto, and then later, when she was no longer going to school at all; when she was supposed to be cheering up decrepit old paupers in the hospital, dressed in her prissy, sanctimonious little pinafore, and lying her head off the whole time. No doubt he'd got a cheap thrill out of the pinafore, it was the sort of outré touch that would have appealed to him. Perhaps that was why she'd dropped out – to meet Alex. She'd been how old – fifteen, sixteen? How could he have done such a thing?

"Were you in love with him?" I said.

"In love?" said Laura. "Who with?"

"With – you know," I couldn't say it.

"Oh no," said Laura, "not at all. It was horrible, but I had to do it. I had to make the sacrifice. I had to take the pain and suffering onto myself. That's what I promised God. I knew if I did that, it would save Alex."

"What on earth do you mean?" My newfound reliance on Laura's sanity was crumbling: we were back in the realm of her loony metaphysics. "Save Alex from what?"

"From being caught. They would have shot him. Callie Fitzsimmons knew where he was, and she told. She told Richard."

"I can't believe that."

"Callie was a snitch," said Laura. "That's what Richard said – he said Callie kept him *informed*. Remember when she was in jail, and Richard got her out? That's why he did it. He owed it to her."

I found this construction of events quite breathtaking. Also monstrous, though there was a slight, a very slight possibility, that it might be true. But if so, Callie must have been lying. How would she have known where Alex was? He'd moved so often.

He might have kept in touch with Callie, though. He might have done. She was one of the people he might have trusted.

"I kept my end of the bargain," said Laura, "and it worked. God doesn't cheat. But then Alex went off to the war. After he got back from Spain, I mean. That's what Callie said – she told me."

I couldn't make sense of this. I was feeling quite dizzy. "Laura," I said, "why did you come here?"

"Because the war's over," said Laura patiently, "and Alex will be back soon. If I wasn't here, he wouldn't know where to find me. He wouldn't know about BellaVista, he wouldn't know I went to Halifax. The only address he'll have for me is yours. He'll get a message through to me somehow." She had the infuriating iron-clad confidence of the true believer.

I wanted to shake her. I closed my eyes for a moment. I saw the pool at Avilion, the stone nymph dipping her toes; I saw the too-hot sun glinting on the rubbery green leaves, that day after Mother's funeral. I felt sick to my stomach, from too much cake and sugar. Laura was sitting on the ledge beside me, humming to herself complacently, secure in the conviction that everything was all right really and the angels were on her side, because she'd made some secret, dotty pact with God.

My fingers itched with spite. I knew what had happened next. I'd pushed her off.

Now I'm coming to the part that still haunts me. Now I should have bitten my tongue, now I should have kept my mouth shut. Out of love, I should have lied, or said anything else: anything but the truth. *Never interrupt a sleepwalker*, Reenie used to say. *The shock can kill them.*

"Laura, I hate to tell you this," I said, "but whatever it was you did, it didn't save Alex. Alex is dead. He was killed in the war, six months ago. In Holland."

The light around her faded. She went very white. It was like watching wax cool.

"How do you know?"

"I got the telegram," I said. "They sent it to me. He listed me as next of kin." Even then I could have changed course; I could have said, *There must have been a mistake, it must have been meant for you.* But I didn't say that. Instead I said, "It was very indiscreet of him. He shouldn't have done that, considering

Richard. But he didn't have any family, and we'd been lovers, you see – in secret, for quite a long time – and who else did he have?"

Laura said nothing. She only looked at me. She looked right through me. Lord knows what she saw. A sinking ship, a city in flames, a knife in the back. I recognized the look, however: it was the look she'd had that day she'd almost drowned in the Louveteau River, just as she was going under – terrified, cold, rapturous. Gleaming like steel.

After a moment she stood up, reached across the table, and picked up my purse, quickly and almost delicately, as if it contained something fragile. Then she turned and walked out of the restaurant. I didn't move to stop her. I was taken by surprise, and by the time I myself was out of my chair, Laura was gone.

There was some confusion about paying the bill – I had no money other than what had been in the purse, which my sister – I explained – had taken by mistake. I promised reimbursement the next day. After I'd got that settled, I almost ran to where I'd parked the car. It was gone. The car keys too had been in my purse. I hadn't been aware that Laura had learned how to drive.

I walked for several blocks, concocting stories. I couldn't tell Richard and Winifred what had really happened to my car: it would be used as one more piece of evidence against Laura. I'd say instead that I'd had a breakdown and the car had been towed to a garage, and they'd called a taxi for me, and I'd got into it and been driven all the way home before I'd realized I'd left my purse in the car by mistake. Nothing to worry about, I'd say. It would all be set straight in the morning.

Then I really did call a taxi. Mrs. Murgatroyd would be at the house to let me in, and to pay the taxi for me.

Richard wasn't home for dinner. He was at some club or other, eating a foul dinner, making a speech. He was running hard by now, he had the goal in sight. This goal – I now know – was not just wealth or power. What he wanted was respect – respect, despite his new money. He longed for it, he thirsted for it; he wished to wield respect, not only like a hammer but like a sceptre. Such desires are not in themselves despicable.

This particular club was for men only; otherwise I would have been there, sitting in the background, smiling, applauding at the end. On such occasions I would give Aimee's nanny the night off and undertake bedtime myself. I supervised Aimee's bath, read to her, then tucked her in. On that particular night she was unusually slow in going to sleep: she must have known I was worried about something. I sat beside her, holding her hand and stroking her forehead and looking out the window, until she dozed off.

Where had Laura gone, where was she staying, what had she done with my car? How could I reach her, what could I say to put things right?

A June bug was blundering against the window, drawn by the light. It bumped over the glass like a blind thumb. It sounded angry, and thwarted, and also helpless.

Escarpment

Today my brain dealt me a sudden blank; a whiteout, as if by snow. It wasn't someone's name that disappeared – in any case that's usual – but a word, which turned itself upside down and emptied itself of meaning like a cardboard cup blown over.

This word was *escarpment*. Why had it presented itself? *Escarpment, escarpment*, I repeated, possibly out loud, but no image appeared to me. Was it an object, an activity, a state of mind, a bodily defect?

Nothing. Vertigo. I tottered on the brink, grabbed at air. In the end I resorted to the dictionary. *Escarpment*, a vertical fortification, or else a steep cliff-face.

In the beginning was the word, we once believed. Did God know what a flimsy thing the word might be? How tenuous, how casually erased?

Perhaps this is what happened to Laura – pushed her quite literally over the edge. The words she had relied on, building her house of cards on them, believing them solid, had flipped over and shown her their hollow centres, and then skittered away from her like so much waste paper.

God. Trust. Sacrifice. Justice.
Faith. Hope. Love.

Not to mention *sister*. Well, yes. There's always that.

The morning after my tea with Laura at Diana Sweets, I hovered near the telephone. The hours passed: no word. I had a luncheon date, with Winifred and two of her committee members, at the Arcadian Court. It was always better with Winifred to stick to agreed plans – otherwise she got curious – and so I went.

We were told about Winifred's latest venture, a cabaret in aid of wounded servicemen. There would be singing and dancing, and some of the girls were putting on a can-can routine, so we must all roll up our sleeves and pitch in, and sell tickets. Would Winifred herself be kicking up her heels in a ruffled petticoat and black stockings? I sincerely hoped not. By now she was on the wrong side of scraggy.

"You're looking a bit wan, Iris," said Winifred, her head on one side.

"Am I?" I said pleasantly. She'd been telling me lately I wasn't up to par. What she meant was that I was not doing all I could to prop up Richard, to propel him forward along his path to glory.

"Yes, a bit faded. Richard wearing you out? That man has energy to burn!" She was in high good spirits. Her plans – her plans for Richard – must have been going well, despite my laxness.

But I could not pay much attention to her; I was too anxious about Laura. What would I do if she didn't turn up soon? I could scarcely report that my car had been stolen: I didn't want her to be arrested. Richard wouldn't have wanted that either. It was in nobody's interests.

I returned home, to be told by Mrs. Murgatroyd that Laura had been there during my absence. She hadn't even rung the doorbell – Mrs. Murgatroyd had just happened to run across her in the front hall. It was a jolt, to see Miss Laura in the flesh after all these years, it was like seeing a ghost. No, she hadn't left any address. She'd said something, though. *Tell Iris I'll talk to her later.* Something like that. She'd left the house keys on the letter tray; said she'd taken them by mistake. A funny thing to take by mistake, said Mrs. Murgatroyd, whose pug nose smelled a fish. She no longer believed my story about the garage.

I was relieved: all might yet be well. Laura was still in town. She would talk to me later.

She has, too, though she tends to repeat herself, as the dead have a habit of doing. They say all the things they said to you in life; but they rarely say anything new.

I was changing out of my luncheon outfit when the policeman arrived, with news of the accident. Laura had gone through a Danger barrier, then right off the St. Clair Avenue bridge into the ravine far below. It was a terrible smash-up, said the policeman, shaking his head sadly. She'd been driving my car: they'd traced the licence. At first they'd thought – naturally – that I myself must be the burned woman found in the wreck.

Now that would have been news.

After the policeman had left I tried to stop shaking. I needed to keep calm, I needed to pull myself together. *You'll have to face the music,* Reenie used to say, but what kind of music did she have in mind? It wasn't dance music. A harsh brass band, a parade of some kind, with crowds of people on both sides, pointing and jeering. An executioner at the end of the road, with energy to burn.

There would of course be a cross-examination from Richard. My story about the car and the garage would still hold if I added that I'd seen Laura for tea that day, but hadn't told him because I hadn't wanted to upset him unnecessarily just before a crucial speech. (All his speeches were crucial, now; he was approaching the brass ring.)

Laura had been in the car when it had broken down, I'd say; she'd accompanied me to the garage. When I'd left my purse behind, she must have picked it up, and then it would have been child's play for her to go the next morning and reclaim the car, paying for it with a forged cheque from my chequebook. I'd tear out a cheque, for verisimilitude; if pressed for the name of the garage, I'd say I'd forgotten. If pressed further, I'd cry. How could I be expected to remember a trivial detail like that, I'd say, at a time like this?

I went upstairs to change. To visit the morgue I would need a pair of gloves, and a hat with a veil. There might be reporters, photographers, already. I'd drive down, I thought, and then remembered that my car was now scrap. I would have to call a taxi.

Also I ought to warn Richard, at his office: As soon as the word got out, the corpse flies would besiege him. He was too prominent for things to be otherwise. He would wish to have a statement of grief prepared.

I made the phone call. Richard's latest young secretary answered. I told her the matter was urgent, and that no, it could not be communicated through her. I would have to speak with Richard in person.

There was a pause while Richard was located. "What is it?" he said. He never appreciated being phoned at the office.

"There's been a terrible accident," I said. "It's Laura. The car she was driving went off a bridge."

He said nothing.

"It was my car."

He said nothing.

"I'm afraid she's dead," I said.

"My God." A pause. "Where has she been all this time? When did she get back? What was she doing in your car?"

"I thought you needed to know at once, before the papers get hold of it," I said.

"Yes," he said. "That was wise."

"Now I have to go down to the morgue."

"The morgue?" he said. "The city morgue? What the hell for?"

"It's where they've put her."

"Well, get her out of there," he said. "Take her somewhere decent. Somewhere more . . ."

"Private," I said. "Yes, I'll do that. I should tell you there's been some implication – from the police, one of them was just here – some suggestion . . ."

"What? What did you tell them? What suggestion?" He sounded quite alarmed.

"Only that she did it on purpose."

"Nonsense," he said. "It must have been an accident. I hope you said that."

"Of course. But there were witnesses. They saw . . ."

"Was there a note? If there was, burn it."

"Two of them, a lawyer and something in a bank. She had white gloves on. They saw her turn the wheel."

"Trick of the light," he said. "Or else they were drunk. I'll call the lawyer. I'll handle it."

I set down the telephone. I went into my dressing room: I would need black, and a handkerchief. I'll have to tell Aimee, I thought. I'll say it was the bridge. I'll say the bridge broke.

I opened the drawer where I kept my stockings, and there were the notebooks – five of them, cheap school exercise books from our time with Mr. Erskine, tied together with kitchen string. Laura's name was printed on the top cover, in pencil – her childish lettering. Underneath that: *Mathematics*. Laura hated mathematics.

Old schoolwork, I thought. No: old homework. Why had she left me these?

I could have stopped there. I could have chosen ignorance, but I did what you would have done – what you've already done, if you've read this far. I chose knowledge instead.

Most of us will. We'll choose knowledge no matter what, we'll maim ourselves in the process, we'll stick our hands into the flames for it if necessary. Curiosity is not our only motive: love or grief or despair or hatred is what drives us on. We'll spy relentlessly on the dead: we'll open their letters, we'll read their journals, we'll go through their trash, hoping for a hint, a final word, an explanation, from those who have deserted us – who've left us holding the bag, which is often a good deal emptier than we'd supposed.

But what about those who plant such clues, for us to stumble on? Why do they bother? Egotism? Pity? Revenge? A simple claim to existence, like scribbling your initials on a washroom wall? The combination of presence and anonymity – confession without penance, truth without consequences – it has its attractions. Getting the blood off your hands, one way or another.

Those who leave such evidence can scarcely complain if strangers come along afterwards and poke their noses into every single thing that would once have been none of their business. And not only strangers: lovers, friends, relations. We're voyeurs, all of us. Why should we assume that anything in the past is ours for the taking, simply because we've found it? We're all grave robbers, once we open the doors locked by others.

But only locked. The rooms and their contents have been left intact. If those leaving them had wanted oblivion, there was always fire.

XIV

The golden lock

I have to hurry now. I can see the end, glimmering far up ahead of me, as if it's a roadside motel, on a dark night, in the rain. A last-chance postwar motel, where no questions are asked and none of the names in the front-desk register are real and it's cash in advance. The office is strung with old Christmas-tree lights; behind it a clump of murky cabins, the pillows fragrant with mildew. A moon-faced gas pump out front. No gas though, it's run out many decades ago. Here's where you stop.

The end, a warm safe haven. A place to rest. But I haven't reached it yet, and I'm old and tired, and on foot, and limping. Lost in the woods, and no white stones to mark the way, and treacherous ground to cover.

Wolves, I invoke you! Dead women with azure hair and eyes like snake-filled pits, I summon you! Stand by me now, as we near the end! Guide my shaking arthritic fingers, my tacky black ballpoint pen; keep my leaking heart afloat for just a few more days, until I can set things in order. Be my companions, my helpers and my friends; *once more,* I add, for haven't we been well-acquainted in the past?

All things have their place, as Reenie used to say; or, in a fouler mood, to Mrs. Hillcoate, *No flowers without shit.* Mr. Erskine did teach me a few useful tricks. A well-wrought invocation to the Furies can come in handy, in case of need. When it's primarily a question of revenge.

I did believe, at first, that I wanted only justice. I thought my heart was pure. We do like to have such good opinions of our own motives when we're about to do something harmful, to someone else. But as Mr. Erskine also pointed out, Eros with his bow and arrows is not the only blind god. Justitia is the other one. Clumsy blind gods with edged weapons: Justitia totes a sword, which, coupled with her blindfold, is a pretty good recipe for cutting yourself.

You'll want of course to know what was in Laura's notebooks. They're as she herself left them, tied up with their grubby brown string, left for you in my steamer trunk along with everything else. I haven't changed anything. You can see for yourself. The pages torn out of them were not torn out by me.

What was I expecting, on that dread-filled May day in 1945? Confessions, reproaches? Or else a diary, detailing the lovers' meetings between Laura and Alex Thomas? No doubt, no doubt. I was prepared for laceration. And I received it, though not in the way I'd imagined.

I cut the string, fanned out the notebooks. There were five of them: *Mathematics*, *Geography*, *French*, *History*, and *Latin*. The books of knowledge.

She writes like an angel, it says of Laura, on the back of one of the editions of *The Blind Assassin*. An American edition, as I recall, with gold scrollwork on the cover: they set a lot of store by angels in those parts. In point of fact, angels don't write much. They record sins and the names of the damned and the saved, or they appear as disembodied hands and scribble warnings on walls. Or they deliver messages, few of which are good news: *God be with you* is not an unmixed blessing.

Keeping all this in mind, yes: Laura wrote like an angel. In other words, not very much. But to the point.

Latin was the notebook I opened first. Most of the remaining pages in it were blank; there were jagged edges where Laura must have ripped out her old homework. She left one passage, a translation she'd made – with my help, and also with the help of the library at Avilion – of the concluding lines of Book IV of Virgil's *Aeneid*. Dido has stabbed herself on the burning pyre or altar she's made of all the objects connected to her vanished lover, Aeneas, who has sailed away to fulfill his destiny through warfare. Although bleeding like a stuck pig, Dido is having a hard time dying. She was doing a lot of writhing. Mr. Erskine, as I recall, enjoyed that part.

I remembered the day she wrote it. The late sunlight was coming in through my bedroom window. Laura was lying on the floor, kicking her sock feet in the air, laboriously transcribing our scribbled-over collaboration into her book. She smelled of Ivory soap, and of pencil shavings.

Then powerful Juno felt sorry for her long-time sufferings and uneasy journey, and sent Iris from Olympus to cut the agonizing soul from the body that still held onto it. This had to be done because Dido was not dying a natural death or one caused by other people, but in despair, driven to it by a crazy impulse. Anyway Proserpine hadn't yet cut off the golden lock from her head or sent her down to the Underworld.

So now, all misty, her wings yellow as a crocus, trailing a thousand rainbow colours that sparkled in the sunlight, Iris flew down, and hovering over Dido, she said:

As I was told to do, I take this sacred thing which belongs to the God of Death; and I release you from your body.

Then all warmth stopped at once, and her life vanished into the air.

"Why did she have to cut off a piece of the hair?" said Laura. "That Iris?"

I had no idea. "It was just a thing she had to do," I said. "Sort of like an offering." I'd been pleased to discover that I had the same name as a person in a story, and wasn't just named after some flower, as I'd always thought. The botanical motif, for girls, had been strong in my mother's family.

"It helped Dido get out of her body," said Laura. "She didn't want to be alive any more. It put her out of her misery, so it was the right thing to do. Wasn't it?"

"I guess so," I said. I wasn't much interested in such fine ethical points. Peculiar things happened in poems. There was no point in trying to make sense of them. I did wonder though whether Dido had been a blonde; she'd seemed more like a brunette to me, in the rest of the story.

"Who is the God of Death? Why does he want the hair?"

"That's enough about hair," I said. "We've done the Latin. Now let's finish the French. Mr. Erskine gave us too much, as usual. Now: *Il ne faut pas toucher aux idoles: la dorure en reste aux mains.*"

"How about, don't interfere with false gods, you'll get the gold paint all over your hands?"

"There's nothing about paint."

"But that's what it really means."

"You know Mr. Erskine. He doesn't care what it means."

"I hate Mr. Erskine. I wish we had Miss Violence back."

"So do I. I wish we had Mother back."

"So do I."

Mr. Erskine hadn't thought much of this Latin translation of Laura's. It had his red pencil slashes all over it.

How can I describe the pool of grief into which I was now falling? I can't describe it, and so I won't try.

I riffled through the other notebooks. *History* was blank, except for the photograph Laura had glued into it – herself and Alex Thomas at the button factory picnic, both of them now coloured light yellow, with my detached blue hand crawling towards them across the lawn. *Geography* contained nothing but a short description of Port Ticonderoga that Mr. Erskine had assigned. "This middle-sized town is situated at the junction of the Louveteau River and the Jogues River and is noted for stones and other things," was Laura's first sentence. *French* had had all the French removed from it. Instead it held the list of odd words Alex Thomas had left behind him in our attic, and that – I now discovered – Laura had not burned, after all. *Anchoryne, berel, carchineal, diamite, ebonort* . . . A foreign language, true, but one I'd learned to understand, better than I ever understood French.

Mathematics had a long column of numbers, with words opposite some of them. It took me a few minutes to realize what kinds of numbers they were. They were dates. The first date coincided with my return from Europe, the last was three months or so before Laura's departure for BellaVista. The words were these:

Avilion, no. No. No. Sunnyside. No. Xanadu, no. No.
Queen Mary, no no. New York, no. Avilion. No at first.
Water Nixie, X. "Besotted."
Toronto again. X.
X. X. X. X.
O.

That was the whole story. Everything was known. It had been there all along, right before my very eyes. How could I have been so blind?

Not Alex Thomas, then. Not ever Alex. Alex belonged, for Laura, in another dimension of space.

Victory comes and goes

After looking through Laura's notebooks, I put them back into my stocking drawer. Everything was known, but nothing could be proven. That much was clear.

But there's always more than one way to skin a cat, as Reenie used to say. If you can't go through, go around.

I waited until after the funeral, and then I waited another week. I didn't want to act too precipitously. Better to be safe than sorry, Reenie also used to say. A questionable axiom: so often it's both.

Richard went off on a trip to Ottawa, an important trip to Ottawa. Men in high places might pop the question, he hinted; or if not now, then soon. I told him, and Winifred as well, that I would take this opportunity to go to Port Ticonderoga with Laura's ashes in their silver-coloured box. I needed to sprinkle these ashes, I said, and to see to the inscription on the monumental Chase family cube. All right and proper.

"Don't blame yourself," said Winifred, hoping I'd do just that – if I blamed myself enough, I wouldn't get around to blaming anyone else. "Some things don't bear dwelling on." We dwell on them anyway, though. We can't help ourselves.

Having seen Richard off on his travels, I gave the help a free evening. I would hold down the fort, I said. I'd been doing more of this lately – I liked being alone in the house, with just Aimee, when she was asleep – so even Mrs. Murgatroyd was not suspicious. When the coast was clear I acted quickly. I'd already done some preliminary, surreptitious packing – my jewel box, my photographs, *Perennials for the Rock Garden* – and now I did the rest. My clothes, though by no means all of them;

some things for Aimee, though by no means all of those either. I got what I could into the steamer trunk, the same one that had once held my trousseau, and into the matching suitcase. The men from the railway arrived to collect the luggage, as I'd arranged. Then, the next day, it was easy for me to go off to Union Station in a taxi with Aimee, each of us with only an overnight case, and none the wiser.

I left a letter for Richard. I said that in view of what he'd done – what I now knew he'd done – I never wanted to see him again. In consideration of his political ambitions I would not request a divorce, although I had ample proof of his scurrilous behaviour in the form of Laura's notebooks, which – I said untruthfully – were locked away in a safe-deposit box. If he had any ideas about getting his filthy hands on Aimee, I added, he should discard them, because I would then create a very, very large scandal, as I would also do should he fail to meet my financial requests. These were not large: all I wanted was enough money to buy a small house in Port Ticonderoga, and to assure maintenance for Aimee. My own needs I could supply in other ways.

I signed this letter *Yours sincerely*, and, while licking the envelope flap, wondered whether I'd spelled *scurrilous* correctly.

Several days before leaving Toronto, I'd sought out Callista Fitzsimmons. She'd given up sculpture, and was now a mural painter. I found her at an insurance company – the head office – where she'd landed a commission. Women's contributions to the war effort, was the theme – outdated, now that the war was over (and, though neither of us knew it yet, soon to be painted over in a reassuringly bland shade of taupe).

They'd given her the length of one wall. Three women factory workers, in overalls and brave smiles, turning out the bombs; a girl driving an ambulance; two farm helpers with hoes and a basket of tomatoes; a woman in uniform, wielding a typewriter; down in the corner, shoved to one side, a mother in an apron removing a loaf of bread from the oven, with two approving children looking on.

Callie was surprised to see me. I hadn't given her any warning of my visit: I had no wish to be evaded. She was supervising the painters, with her hair up in a bandanna, wearing khaki slacks and tennis shoes, and striding around with her hands in her pockets and a cigarette stuck to her lower lip.

She'd heard of Laura's death, she'd read about it in the papers – such a lovely girl, so unusual as a child, such a shame. After these preliminaries, I explained what Laura had told me, and asked if it were true.

Callie was indignant. She used the word *bullshit*, quite a lot. True, Richard had been helpful to her when she'd been nabbed by the Red Squad for agitating, but she'd thought that was just old-times'-sake family stuff on his part. She denied she'd ever told Richard anything, about Alex or any other pinko or fellow-traveller. What bullshit! These were her friends! As for Alex, yes, she'd helped him out at first, when he'd been in such a jam, but then he'd disappeared, owing her some money as a matter of fact, and next thing she'd heard he was in Spain. How could she have snitched about where he was when she didn't even know it herself?

Nothing gained. Perhaps Richard had lied about this to Laura, as he had lied to me about much else. On the other hand, perhaps it was Callie who was lying. But then, what else had I expected her to say?

Aimee didn't like it in Port Ticonderoga. She wanted her father. She wanted what was familiar to her, as children do. She wanted her own room back. Oh, don't we all.

I explained that we had to stay here for a little while. I shouldn't say *explained*, because no explanation was involved.

What could I have said that would have made any sense at all, to a child of eight?

Port Ticonderoga was different now; the war had made inroads. Several of the factories had been reopened, during the conflict – women in overalls had turned out fuses – but now they were closing again. Perhaps they'd be converted to peace-time production, once it was determined what exactly the returning servicemen would want to buy, for the homes and families they would now doubtless acquire. Meanwhile there were many out of work, and it was wait and see.

There were vacancies. Elwood Murray was no longer running the newspaper: he was soon to be a new, shiny name on the War Memorial, having joined the navy and got himself blown up. Interesting, which of the town's men were said to have been killed and which were said to have got themselves killed, as if it was a piece of clumsiness or even a deliberate though somewhat minor act – almost a purchase, like getting yourself a haircut. *Bought the biscuit* was a recent local term for this, used as a rule by men. You had to wonder whose baking they had in mind.

Reenie's husband Ron Hincks was not classed among these casual shoppers for death. He was solemnly said to have been killed in Sicily, along with a bunch of other fellows from Port Ticonderoga who'd joined the Royal Canadian Regiment. Reenie had the pension, but not much else, and she was letting out a room in her tiny house; also she was still working at Betty's Luncheonette, although she said her back was killing her.

It wasn't her back that was killing her, as I would soon dis-cover. It was her kidneys, and they finished the job six months after I moved back. If you're reading this, Myra, I would like you to know what a severe blow this was. I'd been counting on her to be there – hadn't she always been? – and now, all of a sudden, she wasn't.

And then increasingly she was, for whose voice did I hear when I wanted a running commentary?

I went to Avilion, of course. It was a difficult visit. The grounds were derelict, the gardens overgrown; the conservatory was a wreck, with broken panes of glass and desiccated plants, still in their pots. Well, there'd been some of those, even in our time. The guardian sphinxes had several inscriptions of the *John Loves Mary* variety on them; one had been overturned. The pond of the stone nymph was choked with dead grass and weeds. The nymph herself was still standing, though missing some fingers. Her smile was the same, though: remote, secret, unconcerned.

I didn't have to break into the house itself: Reenie was still alive then, she still had her clandestine key. The house was in a sad state: dust and mouse doings everywhere, stains on the now-dull parquet floors where something had leaked. Tristan and Iseult were still there, presiding over the empty dining room, though Iseult had suffered an injury to her harp, and a barn swallow or two had built over the middle window. No vandalism inside the place, however: the wind of the Chase name blew round the house, however faintly, and there must have been a fading aura of power and money lingering in the air.

I walked all over the house. The smell of mildew was pervasive. I looked through the library, where Medusa's head still held sway over the fireplace. Grandmother Adelia too was still in place, though she'd begun to sag: her face now wore an expression of repressed but joyful cunning. I bet you were all-eyecatting around, after all, I thought at her. I bet you had a secret life. I bet it kept you going.

I poked around among the books, I opened the desk drawers. In one of them there was a box of sample buttons from the days of Grandfather Benjamin: the circles of white bone that had turned to gold in his hands, and that had stayed gold for so many years, but had now turned back into bone again.

In the attic I found the nest Laura must have made for herself up there, after she'd left BellaVista: the quilts from the storage trunks, the blankets from her bed downstairs – a dead giveaway if anyone had been searching the house for her. There were a few dried orange peels, an apple core. As usual she hadn't thought to tidy anything away. Hidden in the wainscot cupboard was the bag of odds and ends she'd stashed there, that summer of the *Water Nixie*: the silver teapot, the china cups and saucers, the monogrammed spoons. The nutcracker shaped like an alligator, a lone mother-of pearl cuff link, the broken lighter, the cruet stand minus the vinegar.

I'd come back later, I told myself, and get more.

Richard did not appear in person, which was a sign (to me) of his guilt. Instead, he sent Winifred. "Are you out of your mind?" was her opening salvo. (This, in a booth at Betty's Luncheonette: I didn't want her in my little rented house, I didn't want her anywhere near Aimee.)

"No," I said, "and neither was Laura. Or not so far out of it as you both pretended. I know what Richard did."

"I don't know what you're talking about," said Winifred. She had on a mink stole composed of lustrous tails, and was extricating herself from her gloves.

"I suppose when he married me he figured he'd got a bargain – two for the price of one. He picked us up for a song."

"Don't be ridiculous," said Winifred, though she looked shaken. "Richard's hands are absolutely clean, whatever Laura said. He is pure as the driven. You've made a serious error in judgment. He wants me to say he's prepared to overlook this – this aberration of yours. If you'll come back, he's fully willing to forgive and forget."

"But I'm not," I said. "He may be pure as the driven, but it's not the driven snow. It's another substance entirely."

"Keep your voice down," she hissed. "People are looking."

"They'll look anyway," I said, "with you dressed up like Lady Astor's horse. You know, that colour of green doesn't suit you one bit, especially at your present age. It never has, really. It makes you look bilious."

This hit home. Winifred was finding it hard going: she wasn't used to this new, viperish aspect of me. "What do you want, *exactly*?" she said. "Not that Richard did anything at all. But he doesn't want an uproar."

"I told him, *exactly*," I said. "I spelled it out. And now I'd like the cheque."

"He wants to see Aimee."

"There is no way in Hell," I said, "that I will permit such a thing. He has a yen for young girls. You knew that, you've always known it. Even at eighteen I was pushing the upper limit. Having Laura in the same house was just too much temptation for him, I see that now. He couldn't keep his hands off her. But he's not getting his mitts on Aimee."

"Don't be disgusting," Winifred said. She was very angry by now: she'd gone blotchy under her makeup. "Aimee is his own daughter."

I was on the verge of saying, "No, she's not," but I knew that would be a tactical mistake. Legally, she was his daughter; I had no way of proving otherwise, they hadn't invented all those genes and so forth, not yet. If Richard knew the truth, he'd be even more eager to snatch Aimee away from me. He'd hold her hostage, and I'd lose all the advantage I'd gained so far. It was a game of nasty chess. "He'd stop at nothing," I said, "not even at Aimee. Then he'd pack her off to some under-the-counter abortion farm, the way he did with Laura."

"I can see there's no point in continuing this discussion

further," said Winifred, gathering up her gloves and her stole and her reptilian purse.

After the war, things changed. They changed the way we looked. After a time the grainy muted greys and half-tones were gone. Instead there was the full glare of noon – gaudy, primary, shadowless. Hot pinks, violent blues, red and white beach balls, the fluorescent green of plastic, the sun blazing down like a spotlight.

Around the outskirts of towns and cities, bulldozers rampaged and trees were toppled; great holes were scooped in the ground as if bombs had been dropped there. The streets were gravel and mud. Lawns of bare earth appeared, with spindly saplings planted on them: weeping birches were popular. There was far too much sky.

There was meat, great hunks and slabs and chunks of it glistening in the butchers' windows. There were oranges and lemons bright as a sunrise, and mounds of sugar and mountains of yellow butter. Everyone ate and ate. They stuffed themselves full of technicolour meat and all the technicolour food they could get, as if there was no tomorrow.

But there was a tomorrow, there was nothing but a tomorrow. It was yesterday that had vanished.

I had enough money now, from Richard and also from Laura's estate. I'd bought my little house. Aimee was still resentful of me for having dragged her away from her former and considerably more affluent life, but she appeared to have settled down, though once in a while I'd catch a cold look from her: she was already deciding that I was unsatisfactory as a mother. Richard on the other hand had reaped the benefits of long distance, and had much more of a gleam to him, in her eyes, now that he was no longer present. However, the flow of gifts from him had slowed to a trickle, so she didn't have many options. I'm afraid I expected her to be more stoical than she was.

Meanwhile, Richard was readying himself for the mantle of command, which was – according to the newspapers – as good as within his grasp. True, I was an impediment, but rumours of a separation had been squashed. I was said to be "in the country," and that was marginally all right, as long as I was prepared to stay there.

Unbeknownst to myself, other rumours had been floated: that I was mentally unstable; that Richard was maintaining me financially, despite my wackiness; that Richard was a saint. No harm in a mad wife, if properly handled: it does make the spouses of the powerful so much more sympathetic to one's cause.

In Port Ticonderoga I lived quietly enough. Whenever I went out, I moved through a sea of respectful whispers, the voices hushing when I came within earshot, then starting up again. It was agreed that whatever had happened with Richard, I must be the wronged party. I'd got the short end of the straw, but as there was no justice and precious little mercy, nothing could be done for me. This was before the book appeared, of course.

Time passed. I gardened, I read, and so on. I had already begun – in a modest way, and beginning with a few pieces of animal jewellery from Richard – the trade in second-hand artifacts that, as it turned out, would stand me in good stead in the coming decades. A semblance of normality had been installed.

But unshed tears can turn you rancid. So can memory. So can biting your tongue. My bad nights were beginning. I couldn't sleep.

Officially, Laura had been papered over. A few years more and it would be almost as if she'd never existed. I shouldn't have taken a vow of silence, I told myself. What did I want? Nothing much. Just a memorial of some kind. But what is a memorial, when you come right down to it, but a commemoration of wounds endured? Endured, and resented. Without memory, there can be no revenge.

Lest we forget. Remember me. To you from failing hands we throw. Cries of the thirsty ghosts.

Nothing is more difficult than to understand the dead, I've found; but nothing is more dangerous than to ignore them.

The heap of rubble

I sent the book off. In due time, I received a letter back. I answered it. Events took their course.

The author's copies arrived, in advance of publication. On the inside jacket flap was a touching biographical note:

> Laura Chase wrote *The Blind Assassin* before the age of twenty-five. It was her first novel; sadly, it will also be her last, as she died in a tragic automobile accident in 1945. We are proud to present the work of this young and gifted writer in its first astonishing flowering.

Above this was Laura's photo, a bad reproduction: it made her look flyspecked. Nevertheless, it was something.

When the book came out, there was at first a silence. It was quite a small book, after all, and hardly best-seller material; and although well received in critical circles in New York and London, it didn't make much of a splash up here, not initially. Then the moralists grabbed hold of it, and the pulpit-thumpers and local biddies got into the act, and the uproar began. Once the corpse flies had made the connection – Laura was Richard Griffen's dead sister-in-law – they were all over the story like a rash. Richard had, by that time, his store of political enemies. Innuendo began to flow.

The story that Laura had committed suicide, so efficiently quashed at the time, rose to the surface again. People were talking, not just in Port Ticonderoga but in the circles that mattered. If she'd done it, why? Someone made an anonymous phone call – now who could that have been? – and the

BellaVista Clinic entered the picture. Testimony by a former employee (well paid, it was said, by one of the newspapers) led to a full investigation of the seedier practices carried on there, as a result of which the backyard was dug up and the whole place was closed down. I studied the pictures of it with interest: it had been the mansion of one of the lumber barons before it became a clinic, and was said to have some rather fine stained-glass windows in the dining room, though not so fine as Avilion's.

There was some correspondence between Richard and the director that was particularly damaging.

Once in a while Richard appears to me, in the mind's eye or in a dream. He's grey, but with an iridescent sheen to him, like oil on a puddle. He gives me a fishy look. Another reproachful ghost.

Shortly before the newspapers announced his retirement from official politics, I received a telephone call from him, the first since my departure. He was enraged, and also frantic. He'd been told that due to the scandal he could no longer be considered as a leadership candidate, and now the men that mattered were not returning his calls. He'd been cold-shouldered. He'd been stiffed. I'd done this on purpose, he said, to ruin him.

"Done what?" I said. "You're not ruined. You're still very rich."

"That book!" he said. "You sabotaged me! How much did you have to pay them, to get it published? I can't believe Laura wrote that filthy – that piece of garbage!"

"You don't want to believe it," I said, "because you were besotted with her. You can't face the possibility that all the time you were having your squalid little fling with her, she must have been in and out of bed with another man – one she loved, unlike you. Or I assume that's what the book means – doesn't it?"

"It was that pinko, wasn't it? That fucking bastard – at the picnic!" Richard must have been very upset: as a rule, he seldom swore.

"How would I know?" I said. "I didn't spy on her. But I agree with you, it would have started at the picnic." I didn't tell him there had been two picnics involving Alex: one with Laura, and a second one, a year later, without her, after I'd run into Alex that day on Queen Street. The one with the hard-boiled eggs.

"She was doing it out of spite," said Richard. "She was just getting back at me."

"That wouldn't surprise me," I said. "She must have hated you. Why wouldn't she? You as good as raped her."

"That's untrue! I did nothing without her consent!"

"Consent? Is that what you'd call it? I'd call it blackmail."

He hung up on me. It was a family trait. When she'd called earlier to rail at me, Winifred had done that too.

Then Richard went missing, and then he was found in the *Water Nixie* – well, you know all that. He must have crept into the town, crept onto the grounds of Avilion, crept onto the boat, which was in the boathouse, by the way, not tied up at the jetty as it erroneously said in the papers. That was a cover-up: a corpse in a boat on the water is normal enough, but one in a boathouse is peculiar. Winifred wouldn't have wanted it thought that Richard had gone round the bend.

What really happened then? I'm not sure. Once he was located, Winifred took charge of events, and put the best face on things. *A stroke* was her story. He was found with the book at his elbow, however. That much I know, because Winifred phoned in a state of hysteria and told me so. "How could you have done this to him?" she said. "You destroyed his political career, and then you destroyed his memories of Laura. He loved her! He adored her! He couldn't bear it when she died!"

"I'm glad to hear he felt some remorse," I said coldly. "I can't say I noticed any at the time."

Winifred blamed me, of course. After that, it was open war. She did the worst thing to me that she could think of. She took Aimee.

I suppose you were taught the gospel according to Winifred. In her version, I would have been a lush, a tramp, a slut, a bad mother. As time went by I no doubt became, in her mouth, a slovenly harridan, a crazy old bat, a peddler of ratty old junk. I doubt she ever said to you that I murdered Richard, however. If she'd told you that, she would also have had to say where she got the idea.

Junk would have been a slur. It's true I bought cheap and sold dear – who doesn't, in the antiques racket? – but I had a good eye and I never twisted anyone's arm. There was a period of excessive drinking – I admit it – though not until after Aimee was gone. As for the men, there were some of those as well. It was never a question of love, it was more like a sort of periodic bandaging. I was cut off from everything around me, unable to reach, to touch; at the same time I felt scraped raw. I needed the comfort of another body.

I avoided any man from my own former social circles, though some of these appeared, like fruit flies, as soon as they got wind of my solitary and possibly rotten state. Men like that could have been egged on by Winifred, and no doubt were. I stuck to strangers, picked up on my forays to nearby towns and cities in search of what they now call *collectibles*. I never gave my real name. But Winifred was too persistent for me, in the end. All she'd needed was one man, and that's what she'd got. The pictures of the motel room door, going in, coming out; the fake signatures in the register; the testimony of the owner, who'd welcomed the cash. *You could fight it in court*, said my lawyer, *but I'd advise against it. We'll try for visiting rights, that's all you can expect. You handed them the ammunition and they've used it.* Even he took a dim view of me, not for my moral turpitude but for my clumsiness.

Richard had appointed Winifred as Aimee's guardian in his will, and also as sole trustee of Aimee's not inconsiderable trust fund. So she had that in her favour, as well.

As for the book, Laura didn't write a word of it. But you must have known that for some time. I wrote it myself, during my long evenings alone, when I was waiting for Alex to come back, and then afterwards, once I knew he wouldn't. I didn't think of what I was doing as writing – just writing down. What I remembered, and also what I imagined, which is also the truth. I thought of myself as recording. A bodiless hand, scrawling across a wall.

I wanted a memorial. That was how it began. For Alex, but also for myself.

It was no great leap from that to naming Laura as the author. You might decide it was cowardice that inspired me, or a failure of nerve – I've never been fond of spotlights. Or simple prudence: my own name would have guaranteed the loss of Aimee, whom I lost in any case. But on second thought it was merely doing justice, because I can't say Laura didn't write a word. Technically that's accurate, but in another sense – what Laura would have called the spiritual sense – you could say she was my collaborator. The real author was neither one of us: a fist is more than the sum of its fingers.

I remember Laura, when she was ten or eleven, sitting at Grandfather's desk, in the library at Avilion. She had a sheet of paper in front of her, and was busying herself with the seating arrangements in Heaven. "Jesus sits at the right hand of God," she said, "so who sits at God's left hand?"

"Maybe God doesn't have a left hand," I said, to tease her. "Left hands are supposed to be bad, so maybe he wouldn't have one. Or maybe he got his left hand cut off in a war."

"We're made in God's image," Laura said, "and we have left hands, so God must have one as well." She consulted her diagram, chewing on the end of her pencil. "I know!" she said. "The table must be circular! So everyone sits at everyone else's right hand, all the way round."

"And vice versa," I said.

Laura was my left hand, and I was hers. We wrote the book together. It's a left-handed book. That's why one of us is always out of sight, whichever way you look at it.

When I began this account of Laura's life – of my own life – I had no idea why I was writing it, or who I expected might read it once I'd done. But it's clear to me now. I was writing it for you, dearest Sabrina, because you're the one – the only one – who needs it now.

Since Laura is no longer who you thought she was, you're no longer who you think you are, either. That can be a shock, but it can also be a relief. For instance, you're no relation at all to Winifred, and none to Richard. There's not a speck of Griffen in you at all: your hands are clean on that score. Your real grand-father was Alex Thomas, and as to who his own father was, well, the sky's the limit. Rich man, poor man, beggarman, saint, a score of countries of origin, a dozen cancelled maps, a hundred levelled villages – take your pick. Your legacy from him is the realm of infinite speculation. You're free to reinvent yourself at will.

XV

She has a single photograph of him, a black-and-white print. She preserves it carefully, because it's almost all she has left of him. The photo is of the two of them together, her and this man, on a picnic. *Picnic* is written on the back – not his name or hers, just *picnic*. She knows the names, she doesn't need to write them down.

They're sitting under a tree; it must have been an apple tree. She has a wide skirt tucked around her knees. It was a hot day. Holding her hand over the picture, she can still feel the heat coming up from it.

He's wearing a light-coloured hat, partially shading his face. She's turned half towards him, smiling in a way she can't remember smiling at anyone since. She seems very young in the picture. He's smiling too, but he's holding up his hand between himself and the camera, as if to fend it off. As if to fend her off, in the future, looking back at them. As if to protect her. Between his fingers is the stub of a cigarette.

She retrieves the photograph when she's alone, and lies it flat on the table and stares down into it. She examines every detail: his smoky fingers, the bleached folds of their clothing, the unripe apples hanging in the tree, the dying grass in the fore-ground. Her smiling face.

The photo has been cut; a third of it has been cut off. In the lower left corner there's a hand, scissored off at the wrist, resting on the grass. It's the hand of the other one, the one who is always in the picture whether seen or not. The hand that will set things down.

How could I have been so ignorant? she thinks. So stupid, so unseeing, so given over to carelessness. But without such ignorance, such carelessness, how could we live? If you knew what was going to happen, if you knew everything that was going to happen next – if you knew in advance the consequences of your own actions – you'd be doomed. You'd be as ruined as God. You'd be a stone. You'd never eat or drink or laugh or get out of bed in the morning. You'd never love anyone, ever again. You'd never dare to.

Drowned now – the tree as well, the sky, the wind, the clouds. All she has left is the picture. Also the story of it.

The picture is of happiness, the story not. Happiness is a garden walled with glass: there's no way in or out. In Paradise there are no stories, because there are no journeys. It's loss and regret and misery and yearning that drive the story forward, along its twisted road.

The Port Ticonderoga Herald and Banner, May 29, 1999

IRIS CHASE GRIFFEN,
A MEMORABLE LADY
BY MYRA STURGESS

Mrs. Iris Chase Griffen passed away suddenly last Wednesday at the age of 83, at her home here in Port Ticonderoga. "She left us very peacefully, while sitting in her back garden," stated long-time family friend Mrs. Myra Sturgess. "It was not unexpected as she was suffering from a heart condition. She was quite the personality and a landmark of history, and wonderful for her age. We will all miss her and she will certainly be long remembered."

Mrs. Griffen was the sister of noted local authoress Laura Chase. In addition she was the daughter of Captain Norval Chase who will be long remembered by this town, and grand-daughter of Benjamin Chase, founder of Chase Industries which put up the Button Factory and others. As well, she was the wife of the late Richard E. Griffen, the prominent industrialist and political figure, and the sister-in-law of Winifred Griffen Prior, the Toronto philanthropist who died last year leaving a generous legacy to our high school. She is survived by her granddaughter Sabrina Griffen, who has just returned from abroad and is expected to visit this town shortly to see to her grandmother's affairs. I am sure she will be given a warm greeting and any help or aid we all can proffer.

By Mrs. Griffen's wish the funeral service will be private, with interment of the ashes at the Chase family monument in Mount Hope Cemetery. However a Memorial Service will be held in the chapel of the Jordan Funeral Home this coming Tuesday at 3.00 p.m., in acknowledgment of the many contributions made by the Chase family over the years, with refreshments served afterwards at the home of Myra and Walter Sturgess, all welcome.

The threshold

Today it's raining, a warm spring rain. The air is opalescent with it. The sound of the rapids pours up and over the cliff – pours like a wind, but unmoving, like wave marks left on sand.

I'm sitting at the wooden table on my back porch, in the shelter of the overhang, gazing out over the long straggling garden. It's almost dusk. The wild phlox is in bloom, or I believe it must be phlox; I can't see it clearly. Something blue, that glimmers down there at the end of the garden, the phosphorescence of snow in shadow. In the flower beds the shoots jostle upwards, crayon-shaped, purple, aqua, red. The scent of moist dirt and fresh growth washes in over me, watery, slippery, with an acid taste to it like the bark of a tree. It smells like youth; it smells like heartbreak.

I've swathed myself in a shawl: the evening is warm for the season, but I don't feel it as warmth, only as an absence of cold. I view the world clearly from here – *here* being the landscape glimpsed from the top of a wave, just before the next one drives you under: how blue the sky, how green the sea, how final the prospect.

Beside my elbow is the stack of paper I've been adding to so laboriously, month after month. When I'm done – when I've written the final page – I'll pull myself up out of this chair and make my way to the kitchen, and scrabble around for an elastic band or a piece of string or an old ribbon. I'll tie the papers up, then lift the lid of my steamer trunk and slide this bundle in on top of everything else. There it will stay until you come back from your travels, if you ever do come back. The lawyer has the key, and his orders.

I must admit I have a daydream about you.

One evening there will be a knock at the door and it will be you. You'll be dressed in black, you'll be toting one of those little rucksacks they all have now instead of handbags. It will be raining, as it is this evening, but you won't have an umbrella, you'd scorn umbrellas; the young like their heads to be whipped about by the elements, they find it bracing. You'll stand on the porch, in a haze of damp light; your glossy dark hair will be sodden, your black outfit will be soaked, the drops of rain will glitter on your face and clothes like sequins.

You'll knock. I'll hear you, I'll shuffle down the hallway, I'll open the door. My heart will jump and flutter; I'll peer at you, then recognize you: my cherished, my last remaining wish. I'll think to myself that I've never seen anyone so beautiful, but I won't say so; I wouldn't want you to think I've gone scatty. Then I'll welcome you, I'll hold out my arms to you, I'll kiss you on the cheek, sparsely, because it would be unseemly to let myself go. I'll cry a few tears, but only a few, because the eyes of the elderly are arid.

I'll invite you in. You'll enter. I wouldn't recommend it to a young girl, crossing the threshold of a place like mine, with a person like me inside it – an old woman, an older woman, living alone in a fossilized cottage, with hair like burning spiderwebs and a weedy garden full of God knows what. There's a whiff of brimstone about such creatures: you may even be a little frightened of me. But you'll also be a little reckless, like all the women in our family, and so you will come in anyway. *Grandmother*, you will say; and through that one word I will no longer be disowned.

I'll sit you down at my table, among the wooden spoons and the twig wreaths, and the candle which is never lit. You'll be shivering, I'll give you a towel, I'll wrap you in a blanket, I'll make you some cocoa.

Then I'll tell you a story. I'll tell you this story: the story of how you came to be here, sitting in my kitchen, listening to the story I've been telling you. If by some miracle that were to happen, there would be no need for this jumbled mound of paper.

What is it that I'll want from you? Not love: that would be too much to ask. Not forgiveness, which isn't yours to bestow. Only a listener, perhaps; only someone who will see me. Don't prettify me though, whatever else you do: I have no wish to be a decorated skull.

But I leave myself in your hands. What choice do I have? By the time you read this last page, that – if anywhere – is the only place I will be.

Acknowledgments

I would like to express my gratitude to the following: my invaluable assistant, Sarah Cooper; my other researchers, A. S. Hall and Sarah Webster; Professor Tim Stanley; Sharon Maxwell, archivist, Cunard Line Ltd., St. James Library, London; Dorothy Duncan, executive director, Ontario Historical Society; Hudson's Bay/Simpsons Archives, Winnipeg; Fiona Lucas, Spadina House, Heritage Toronto; Fred Kerner; Terrance Cox; Katherine Ashenburg; Jonathan F. Vance; Mary Sims; Joan Gale; Don Hutchison; Ron Bernstein; Lorna Toolis and her staff at the Toronto Public Library's Merril Collection of Science Fiction, Speculation and Fantasy, and to Janet Inksetter of Annex Books. Also to early readers Eleanor Cook, Ramsay Cook, Xandra Bingley, Jess A. Gibson, and Rosalie Abella. Also to my agents, Phoebe Larmore, Vivienne Schuster, and Diana Mackay; and to my editors, Ellen Seligman, Heather Sangster, Nan A. Talese, and Liz Calder. Also to Arthur Gelgoot, Michael Bradley, Bob Clark, Gene Goldberg, and Rose Tornato. And to Graeme Gibson and my family, as always.

<u>ALIAS GRACE</u>

'Sometimes I whisper it over to myself: Murderess.
Murderess. It rustles, like a taffeta skirt along the floor.'

Grace Marks. Female fiend? Femme fatale? Or weak
and unwilling victim? Around the true story of one of
the most enigmatic and notorious women of the 1840s,
Margaret Atwood has created an extraordinarily potent
tale of sexuality, cruelty and mystery.

'Atwood's prose is searching. So intimate that it
seems to be written on the skin'
Literary Review

'A gift!'
The Times

'A sensuous, perplexing book, teasingly
difficult to pin down: at once sinister and dignified,
grubby and gorgeous, panoramic yet specific . . . I don't
think I have ever been so thrilled . . . Atwood has
pushed art to its extremes . . . This, surely,
is as far as a novel can go'
Independent on Sunday

SURFACING

'They must have missed something, I feel it will be different if I look myself. Probably when we get there my father will have returned from wherever he has been, he will be sitting in the cabin waiting for us.'

A young divorcée returns to the remote island of her childhood in Northern Canada to investigate the mysterious disappearance of her father. Flooded with memories, she is gradually drawn back into her past as the wild island exerts its elemental hold . . .

THE EDIBLE WOMAN

'"Clara," she said, "do you think I'm normal?"
"I'd say you're almost abnormally normal if you know
what I mean. Why?" Marian was reassured. That was
what she herself would have said. But if she was so
normal, why had this thing chosen to attack her?'

Marian is determinedly ordinary. She likes her
work, her broody flat-mate and sober fiancé Peter. But
she reckons without an inner self that wants something
more, that calmly sabotages her careful places, stable
routine – and her digestion. Marriage à la mode,
Marian discovers, is something she
literally can't stomach . . .

'Margaret Atwood not only has a sense of humour, she
has wit and style in abundance . . . a real joy to read'
Good Housekeeping

'Funny, sharp; witty, clever'
The Times

CAT'S EYE

'If I were to meet Cordelia again, what would I tell her about myself? The truth, or whatever would make me look good? Probably the latter, I still have that need.'

Elaine Risley, a painter, returns to Toronto to find herself overwhelmed by her past. Memories of childhood – unbearable betrayals and cruelties – surface relentlessly, forcing her to confront the spectre of Cordelia, once her best friend and tormentor, who has haunted her for forty years . . .

'Not since Graham Greene or William Golding has a novelist captured so forcefully the relationship between school bully and victim . . . Atwood's power games are played, exquisitely, by little girls'
Listener

'Irresistible . . . This book is about life for all of us. She is one of our finest novelists. Read it'
The Times

Now you can order superb titles directly from Virago

☐ Alias Grace	Margaret Atwood	£7.99
☐ The Robber Bride	Margaret Atwood	£7.99
☐ Surfacing	Margaret Atwood	£6.99
☐ The Edible Woman	Margaret Atwood	£7.99
☐ Cat's Eye	Margaret Atwood	£7.99
☐ Wilderness Tips	Margaret Atwood	£7.99
☐ Murder in the Dark	Margaret Atwood	£6.99
☐ Good Bones	Margaret Atwood	£6.99
☐ Eating Fire	Margaret Atwood	£9.99

Please allow for postage and packing: **Free UK delivery.**
Europe: add 25% of retail price; Rest of World: 45% of retail price.

To order any of the above or any other Virago titles, please call our credit card orderline or fill in this coupon and send/fax it to:

Virago, 250 Western Avenue, London, W3 6XZ, UK.
Fax 020 8324 5678   Telephone 020 8324 5516

☐ I enclose a UK bank cheque made payable to Virago for £ . . . .
☐ Please charge £ . . . . . . to my Access, Visa, Delta, Switch Card No.

Expiry Date ☐☐☐☐   Switch Issue No. ☐☐

NAME (Block letters please) . . . .

ADDRESS . . . .

Postcode . . . . Telephone . . . .

Signature . . . .

Please allow 28 days for delivery within the UK. Offer subject to price and availability.

Please do not send any further mailings from companies carefully selected by Virago ☐